to be her girl

9/2021

to be her girl

Emily Cradduck

**toys of
the sun**

toysofthesun.com

Copyright © 2020 Emily Cradduck

This is a work of fiction. Names, characters, places, and events are either the products of the author's imagination or used in a fictitious manner.

All rights reserved. This book or any portion thereof may not be reproduced or used in any manner whatsoever without the express written permission of the publisher except for the use of brief quotations in a book review.

ISBN: 978-1-7356529-0-0

for my dad

Bradley Jay Cradduck

who believed in love

PART I

*Maybe I recognized you because
there's some version of you out there
that's with some version of me,
and that's the life where
my heart beats the loudest.*

It all started the day after my grandma died. Or at least that was when I saw her for the first time. That was when Iris Humphrey came into my life like she'd been there all along, nestled under my skin like the most beautiful seed; cruel and fair and ready to grow wild like a flower through the mud.

Only we weren't actually ready.

1

I woke to the usual sound of Los Angeles traffic. It fought its way down Sunset Boulevard, around the corner, and through my closed bedroom window, jolting me into consciousness. I reached for my earplugs on my nightstand and put them in. It was my only defense against the noise of city life. I rolled over and rested my arm across the side of my face, trying to hide my eyes from the sunlight breaking through. I let out a heavy sigh, feeling my breath skim the side of my arm. I didn't want to be conscious. Whatever was outside could wait.

I kept my eyes shut and tuned out the noise. "Grandma," I whispered and let out a soft whimper. I replayed the last time I saw her over and over again in my head, like hitting rewind would bring her back to life, if only for that moment.

It had been Christmas night, five and a half months earlier. I'd taken a moment of solitude at the edge of the heart-shaped pond beside her house. It was frozen over and illuminated with red and green spotlights coming from my dad's house on the other side.

"Callahan! Callahan!" she exclaimed with a voice much stronger than it'd been all day.

I turned around and saw her shuffling my way, wearing no more than her pale pink nightgown and wool slippers. The New York air felt like pins on my face, and seeing her bare arms only made me colder. I adjusted my scarf and headed toward her. "Grandma, what are you doing? It's freezing out here," I said.

She planted her feet firmly on the ground in front of me. "You didn't say goodbye."

"Yes, I did." I took off my jacket and wrapped it around her frail frame. "You just didn't hear me because you were asleep."

She smiled and gently stroked my cheeks with her hands. "I love you, sweet girl."

"I love you more."

The smile remained on her face, gentle like a petal on a flower. She lifted it to the sky that was dark and grey with clouds. "Remember what I told you," she said, looking back into my eyes. "Always pay attention to the moon."

"I know," I said. "Especially when it's new."

"That's right. That's when the magic begins." She stroked my cheeks again.

I smiled, but I never understood her insistence. I couldn't see a new moon.

June 8, 2013 was the first day without my grandma, but not much else had changed. The world continued to spin, and I continued to wonder why.

Why? What a heavy question for a three-letter word.

I stayed in bed for another hour and contemplated my mundane existence. I opened my eyes and took out the earplugs, letting the outside in. A crow cawed and I felt she was mocking me. I had nothing to say and nothing to do. I was a writer without a story.

I got out of bed and peeked through the curtains, searching for my tormentor.

Caw-caw-caw, the crow exclaimed.

"Where are you?" I asked.

She cawed again, but I still couldn't find her. I sighed and turned around, giving into defeat.

I headed into the living room where my roommate, Signey Miller, practiced yoga in the middle of the room. It was her daily ritual that I always planned to partake in, but never did.

"Hey," she said, withdrawing from her upward facing dog.

"Morning," I muttered.

"Get any sleep last night?" she asked, standing up.

"Not much."

She sighed as she pulled her long blonde hair out of its bun. "That's rough," she said, running her fingers through it.

I shrugged.

"You okay?"

I shrugged again and headed into the kitchen.

Signey worked as a bartender at Jem's, the bar I'd been frequenting since I moved to Los Angeles three years earlier. I knew she'd be up to her elbows in gossip and alcohol when I found out about my grandma, so I didn't bother to send her a message. She heard all the tired tales of our Echo Park neighborhood's romantic ventures, which was beneficial to my scrounged-up words I reluctantly passed off as poetry.

"I was thinking we could go out to dinner before the show tonight," she said, following me. "Annie was talking about this new Mexican place last night and my mouth is still watering."

I sighed in remembrance. In the hour I had lain awake staring at the inside of my eyelids, I decided to spend my weekend watching movies and stewing in despair. I'd forgotten all about the art show I had planned to attend that night. It was a collection of who's who in the Los Angeles indie art scene, and my friend, Ryder Massey, was one of them.

"Oh, yeah," I mumbled, filling the tea kettle with water from the sink.

"What?" Signey asked.

I turned off the water. "I forgot about the show," I said, putting the tea kettle on the stove and igniting the fire below it.

"Are you still going?"

I shrugged again while getting my favorite mug out of the cupboard—the one with the Buffalo Bills logo on it. Their four Super Bowl losses in the early nineties taught me a lot about disappointment at a young age. Persistence too.

I put the mug on the counter, grabbed a tea bag from the cupboard, and dropped it in.

"What's wrong?" Signey paused for a few seconds. "Did your—"

"Yeah, my grandma died."

"I'm sorry," she said. "I know how much she meant to you."

"Means," I said. "At least she's with my grandpa again."

She sighed. "That's a good way to look at it."

"Yeah, I guess."

"Are you going to New York?"

I shook my head no.

"Why not?"

I shrugged.

Signey sighed again and opened the refrigerator. She stared inside for a few seconds and then shut it. "If you don't want to go tonight, I understand. And I don't have to go either. I can stay with you if you want."

"Thanks," I said, "but I don't know what I want."

We stood in silence before the tea kettle started to whistle. I was considering her offer, but when I caught a glimpse of the calendar hanging on the wall behind her, I knew I had to go. It was a new moon.

I spent the day in a daze. I was lying on the couch, mindlessly scrolling through social media on my phone when Signey asked if I was ready. I wasn't sure; it felt like a loaded question. But I nodded my head and followed her out the door anyway.

"I feel like my grandma wants me to go," I said as we walked through the courtyard.

TO BE HER GIRL

"I'm sure she does," she said. "She wouldn't want you to be miserable."

I shook my head no in agreement.

We got into Signey's Jeep and as soon as we pulled out of the garage, I could feel regret build up in my chest. I felt like I needed to go, but that didn't mean that I actually wanted to. The closer we got to the Arts District, the more conflicted I felt.

Signey's phone vibrated in the cup holder between us.

"Can you check that?" she asked.

I grabbed it, entered her passcode that I knew by heart, and read the text message. "It's Annie," I said. "She doesn't feel good and wants to know if you can cover her shift. Duane won't let her leave without coverage…How's she doing, by the way? I mean, besides not feeling well tonight."

"She's better. It's probably not the miscarriage. She gets bad headaches. And Duane knows that."

"Well, that's good. I mean, not the headaches."

"Yeah, just tell her that I'm sorry, but remind her about the show. Oh, and tell her that the new girl was looking to pick up more shifts. Duane knows that too. God, he's such an ass sometimes."

"I love Duane."

She rolled her eyes. "He's not your boss."

"Right," I said. "Okay."

"Oh, and tell her that I hope she feels better."

"Okay."

I texted Annie and put the phone back in the cup holder. I looked out the window and stared at the Los Angeles skyline, wondering if there was more to life. More than getting up and going to work every day. More than bosses and headaches. And more than death, whether it's an eight-week-old fetus or an eighty-six-year-old grandma.

"I think an art show is the best place for you to be tonight," Signey said, reminding me that there was more to life than work and death. There was art.

I sighed. "Yeah."

"And maybe being around Ryder too. He's always so happy. Maybe he can lift your spirits."

"You're really into him, aren't you?"

She smiled, reminding me that there was love too.

So there was art and love. I just wasn't exactly excelling in either of those categories.

We reached the Arts District and parked a few blocks away from the art show. We walked down the graffiti-lined streets and by the time we got to the warehouse, I was fully wishing I wasn't there. I just wanted to curl up in bed and go to sleep, but instead, I was about to surround myself with art that I was too tired to understand.

We waited in line for a few agonizing minutes before we reached the entrance. White lights on a string framed the wide-open door, and beside it was an easel with a sign that looked like a giant tarot card. It read: *Ace of Cups Art Show 2013*. A man with a handlebar mustache checked our IDs, and the girl beside him with pigtail buns on top of her head waited patiently for our cash.

I pulled a five-dollar bill from my wallet, but Signey took a ten from hers. She waved at me to put my cash away and handed the ten to the girl. "The two of us," she said.

"You know I don't like it when you pay for me," I said.

"You should let people do things for you every once in a while."

She let the man with the handlebar mustache stamp her hand and went inside without waiting for my response. I shoved the five back into my purse, got my hand stamped, and followed her in.

We stood beside a fortune teller machine and soaked in the chaos. The warehouse was crowded with art and people who looked like art and indie rock music bounced off every painting and fedora. I saw Ryder, who was about twenty feet to the right of the entrance, smiling and waving us over.

We walked over to his display, which was a table covered with rigid pieces of metal. Scraps of various sizes were welded together like a discombobulated puzzle. Ryder was the product of fine art connoisseurs, but he saw art in everything. Put a dent in a metal trash can and it was art. His family owned art galleries in both Los Angeles and New York City, but he had a love affair with warehouse art shows and admittedly preferred them. He hid his silver spoon so well under his tongue, you'd never know it was there.

"Hey, I'm glad you guys could make it," he said. The smile disappeared from his face, which was rare. "And I'm sorry about your grandma."

I bit my lower lip and nodded my head. "Thanks."

"Thanks for coming still," he said. "Signey wasn't sure if you would, but maybe a little distraction will help."

I hoped so, but it was like a picture of my grandma's face was taped to the wall of my brain, front and center.

I looked at Ryder's display, trying to decipher the pieces of metal he fused together. I assumed it meant something, but in that moment, all I could see was metal. "Yeah, and your art is…ya know, it's…it's great," I said.

"Thanks, I really appreciate…" I heard Ryder say before falling into a memory.

One of Ryder's pieces looked like a couch, and all I could think about was the couch that my grandma sat on all day, every day. It was ugly and brown and I'd sink into it after she pulled my arm to sit beside her. She would shift back and forth between squeezing my hand and stroking my cheek with her finger. And as I stood there staring at Ryder's twisted metal, I realized that she would never pull me onto that couch and ask about my life again. That reality sank into me deeper than I ever sank into that couch.

"…like life," Ryder said as I shook away my daze.

"Are you alright, Cal?" Signey asked.

"Yeah, yeah, I'm sorry," I said. "What'd you say?"

"I just kind of throw everything together and see it later," Ryder said.

"Your art or life?" I asked.

"Both." The smile had returned to his face. "I think life would be a hell of a lot easier if we stopped trying to figure it out. So that's how I approach my art. I don't ask questions."

"You don't have a vision?" Signey asked.

"Sometimes I do, but if it doesn't work out, I just put the pieces where they fit."

"Was that supposed to look like a couch?" I asked, pointing at the metal sculpture. "What's it mean?"

"It means whatever you want it to mean."

I nodded. "Okay, on that note, I think I'll go see if I can find meaning in anything."

I left Signey and Ryder to explore the downtown warehouse that had been turned into an exhibit of sorted imaginations. I wandered aimlessly, not paying much attention to anything. The walls were covered from floor to ceiling with paintings. There were sculptures and handmade jewelry, a large man reading tarot cards and a naked woman being painted. Art was scattered and stationed everywhere I looked.

I walked into the far back corner of the far back room and began to study a display of photography. My eyes tried to soak it all in, as if I'd never seen photographs before. Striking portraits of tired eyes hung beside the innocence of children smiling through dirty faces. Life's contrast was laid out before me. Each photograph had its own story to tell—human nature and its diversity captured and displayed at its most vulnerable. It was the only display to shift my focus and grant me a few moments to forget my own grief.

I became mesmerized by the smallest photograph that hung dead center. It was a black and white print of powerful waves crashing onto jagged rocks along the shore—with the photograph snapped, I presumed, just before swallowing them whole. It looked like the painting that hung above my grandma's couch, and for the first time since she died, I smiled. I had received countless pieces of advice under that painting.

While admiring the photograph, I felt a sudden rush of life inside me. My smile faded into confusion and I held my breath. I turned to find a woman in a long white dress standing at my side.

"Home," she said. She touched her fingers to her long strawberry blonde hair as a welcomed breeze crept in through the open door beside us, blowing it ever so slightly.

I let out the air I had been holding captive, causing a sound much lighter than whatever was going on inside me.

"Home," she said again. She directed her face toward the photograph, and I found myself fixated on her profile as she stared at it. Her little button nose scrunched as if she felt my eyes on her. She must have because it wasn't long before her hazel eyes returned to meet mine. "You were looking at the waves, right?" she asked as her eyes wandered away.

"Yeah," I said, barely above a whisper.

"I took it when I was three," she said, giving me a faint smile. "It was my mom's camera. I don't actually remember taking it, but that's what she always said."

I nodded slightly, curious and oddly overwhelmed.

"It was down the road from my house growing up…The beach," she said. "It was my favorite place…At least when I was three." She laughed lightly under her breath, like a smile with a heavy exhale.

"It's a great shot," I said. "You had more talent when you were three than most people ever will."

"I'm not so sure about that…But thank you."

She didn't explain why she displayed such an old photograph, but she didn't have to. The comfort in her voice said it all. It sounded like the voice in my head as I remembered the painting above my grandma's couch. The waves carried a feeling that she couldn't replicate. But there was also a pain in her words, something between the cracks that she hid under her tongue. I sensed there was so much more to the story, but I didn't dare ask.

Her attention drifted to her display—a dozen photographs hanging on a white panel in a dimly lit room. I couldn't help but study her face as she studied her work. There was something in every line and every curve that struck me. Every impression on her fair skin felt familiar, though I couldn't gather why. As far as I knew, I'd never seen her before. Part of me wanted to share why I had been so drawn to the photograph; part of me wanted to run away.

"Are you an artist?" she asked, redirecting her attention back to me, though I noticed her eyes were looking anywhere but mine.

"A writer," I said.

"My mom always said that writing is a lot like photography. It's taking a moment of time and making it timeless."

"Hmm," I said behind sealed lips. I tried to smile but failed miserably.

"That's the hope anyway," she said with a laugh.

"Ya know, it really is though," I said, doing my best to collect myself. "That's what it means. Photography. It means 'writing with light'…or drawing, maybe…It's from Greek words." I looked at the floor, feeling paralyzed. My entire being was overcome with memories that I couldn't seem to remember.

"Yeah. She told me that too," she said. Her tone had changed ever so slightly, softening as if I'd said something hurtful or confusing.

I looked up, slowly, hoping I'd have something to say by the time my head made it back up all the way. But I didn't, and a man in a t-shirt three sizes too small seemingly fell from the sky. He had hair to his shoulders and stood about my height, a few inches taller than her. He placed his hand on her back, and with that minuscule motion, he also knocked my heart to the floor. She glanced at him and gave a slight smile.

"Thank you," I said. It was an illogical response, but it was all I could muster up in that bewildering moment. I walked away before she could find any more words of her own.

I made it about ten feet before I stopped at another display. The paintings had questionable morals, and I wouldn't have given it a second glance had I not felt compelled to stop. I faked my interest for a few moments before my eyes returned to the woman in the long white dress, only to find that she had the same idea as our eyes met again. Whatever strange sensation had been flowing through my veins must have been flowing through hers too.

TO BE HER GIRL

"Iris Humphrey," I whispered to myself, clutching the business card I had swiped from her table.
Iris. Never had a word sounded so beautiful.

2

"Earth to Callahan. Are you there?" Signey asked, interrupting my daze from the other side of our secondhand table. "Cal."

"What?" I asked, redirecting my attention to her and away from the window.

"I don't know what's worse: your selective hearing or your selective denial."

"Thanks for paying last night," I said, selectively ignoring that comment. "But I'm not *not* going to New York because of the cost."

"I know."

"My dad, mom, and Cora all offered to pay anyway."

"Yeah, and what about them? Don't you want to be there for your dad and your sister?"

"They have each other, and my mom, and my stepmom, and Rhett, and everybody…Perk of a big family, right?" I took the last sip of my hot tea and looked out the window again.

"You should be there, Cal. Go say goodbye."

I looked back at Signey. "She's already gone."

"Okay." She shook her head with a heavy exhale and picked up her cup of coffee. She took a sip, then looked down as she held it in front of her face.

"She didn't even want a funeral."

Signey looked back up and put her coffee down.

"She always said they were too depressing," I continued. "When my grandpa died, we had a barbecue and went fishing in his honor." I chuckled at the memory. She hated fishing.

"I didn't know you were a fisherman," Signey teased with a light laugh.

"Well, I didn't actually fish that day...And I always threw the fish back into the water when I was a kid, which really just seems like torture. I mean, how would you feel if a giant hook fell from the sky, tore through your flesh, pulled you up, and then threw you back to the ground?"

"Depends what was on the hook," she said. "Like do I get a piece of cake in the process?"

I laughed before returning to my daze. I looked out the window and watched two squirrels run in circles in the courtyard below. How simple a life, I thought; running in circles, just for the hell of it. I was always running in circles, but I didn't feel I had the choice. I could never catch up with myself. When the squirrels darted out of sight, I wanted to go with them.

Instead, I grabbed my phone and lay down on the couch. I opened Fodoary, a social media app for sharing pictures and videos. I typed *Iris Humphrey* into the search bar, clicked on her account, and tapped the follow button. I'd already combed through it the night before, but I didn't want to miss anything. She posted mainly professional work, but personal photographs were sprinkled throughout her page. My heart dropped every time I saw that man in the tiny t-shirt.

It was Brooks Hewitt, a musician who owned a small music shop in Silver Lake called Untangled Music, which was a block away from Rowe's—one of my favorite restaurants. I'd shopped there before, but I didn't remember ever seeing him, or Iris. As far as I could tell, they'd been together for years. I knew I was captivated by her, but I didn't understand why his existence in her life dropped my heart below my feet.

"Do you want to go see *The Great Gatsby*?" Signey asked as I scrolled through his pictures. "Annie wants to go before work tonight. It's in 3D."

"I saw it last week," I said, still scrolling.

"So see it again."

I considered it. It sounded like a solid attempt to escape myself, and I needed that, but I shook my head no and told her that I had some things to do. Weekends were usually dedicated to monotonous errands because my weekdays were spent at a nine to five, and my nights were spent writing, which was usually just me staring at the wall with a joint resting between my fingers.

All I needed to do was go to the grocery store, but instead, I found myself at a Goodwill. It was where I usually ended up when I needed to be distracted. No matter my mood, there was always something so enticing about a thrift store—an enchanted land of other people's hand-me-downs. I'd wonder about the previous owners of whatever I was looking at. I'd wonder who they were and what they were like. Sometimes I'd even give them names and stories. But that day, I just found myself hoping that all their grandmas were still alive.

I wandered down the rows of bric-a-bracs, searching for anything that might make my apartment its new home. I was holding an old jewelry box when "Return of the Grievous Angel" began to pour through the store's speakers. Gram Parsons was my grandma's favorite.

I put down the box and soaked in the sound of his voice harmonizing with Emmylou Harris's. I closed my eyes and imagined myself in my grandma's living room. I could see her standing before me, dusting the bookcase and humming right along with them. I smiled and opened my eyes, and that was when the tears began to fall. First one, then two, and then before I knew it, the cure for California's longstanding drought was sliding down my face. I hadn't cried since I was first told of her passing, and apparently I was making up for it all at once. Right there in front of the small animal figurines and candle holders, every displaced tear decided to make an appearance.

TO BE HER GIRL

I crouched down to explore the lower shelves and avoid awkward eye contact with any passersby. I wasn't ashamed of my tears, but my desire to hide was stronger. I wiped them away while my eyes scanned the shelves, searching for something to distract me.

It was another box, one no bigger than the palm of my hand, that caught my attention. I picked it up and ran my fingers along the scratches in the indigo-colored wood. I felt the prick and saw a tiny splinter poking out of my flesh. It took only the rubbing together of my fingertips for it to fall out. I ran my fingers over the box again, risking another sliver, then opened it. The metal hinges creaked, but it opened and closed just fine. Like most things I picked up at thrift stores, I didn't need it for anything, but I wanted it. I found its depleted condition charming.

After flipping the box to check the price, my eyes were just as surprised as my ears had been moments earlier. Etched into the bottom of the tiny box was *Iris*.

3

I moved to Los Angeles in 2010. I wrote for a new webzine that ended up being a flop, and its run lasted less than a year. I struggled through the tedious nature and inconsistency of background acting to make money, then took whatever steady job I could find, which was a marketing and copywriting gig at a small company that sold vitamin supplements. I had creative writing pieces published from time to time, but a freelance writer in Los Angeles still needs to pay rent every month, not every other.

"How was work?" Ryder asked from behind me.

I was at the grocery store with nothing but avocados in my cart and a bag of kale chips in my hand. I was a Los Angeles cliché—not to mention a millennial. I had also not made it to the store on Sunday as planned. Instead, I'd gone straight home after the floodgates opened at Goodwill and started Sylvia Plath's *The Bell Jar* for the umpteenth time. I'd turn to it whenever depression's beast was clawing at my back, and I was beginning to drip blood after months of scratching.

I turned around and Ryder tossed a package of chocolate chip cookies into my cart. I wasn't surprised to see him. Since we met on a flight from JFK to LAX just after the new year, it became almost comical how identical our food shopping schedule was.

I tossed him the bag of kale chips. "It was fine," I said with a shrug.

"What'd you do today?"

"I was working on a new piece, but I can't get it right."

"Did you ask questions?" I asked with a smile.

"Why mess with the magic?" He flashed a grin twice as big as mine. "What are you up to tonight?"

"Nothing. My grandma's memorial was today, so I figure I'll just go home and cry all night." I laughed, but I meant it.

"I'm sorry. Why didn't you go?"

I shrugged. "I don't know. I had a lot to do at work this week. And…I know I should've, but if I went, she'd actually be gone."

"I'm sorry," he said again.

"Me too," I said. I could feel regret in the pit of my stomach. My entire family was together without me.

"Well, thanks for coming to the show the other night."

I thought of Iris. "Yeah, thanks for inviting me. It was a really cool show…And there was a great display of photography. Did you see it?"

"Yeah. Iris Humphrey," he said, smiling like she was the greatest person on earth. My heart spun at the sound of her name. "I think she was the only photographer there."

"Yeah, her."

"Man, she's good with a camera. She sucks life right through the lens."

"You make it sound like witchcraft," I said with a light laugh.

He laughed. "Anything but. She's one of the nicest people I know."

My heart kicked up a notch, knowing I had a mutual friend with Iris, the woman whose existence had been hovering over me like a ghost I couldn't put a face to. "She's a music photographer though, right?" I asked, acting like I hadn't immediately looked her up on the internet. "Like concerts? Because that sounds amazing. To get paid to go to concerts and take pictures. I mean, that's what it said on her business card anyway. Music."

"Yeah, I don't know that she does a lot of concerts anymore though, like random anyway. She's pretty specific to certain bands, both his obligation and personal choice to engage with everyone who was there. "Have you talked to Iris? She's around here somewhere," he said, handing both Signey and me another glass of wine. An open bar was both what I did, and did not, need that night. I accepted either way, ignoring his question if I had spoken to Iris.

Throughout the night, I spotted her a few times and I couldn't help but wonder if she remembered me. It had only been a week since we met, but she gave no indication if she did. I thought maybe she hadn't seen me, or maybe she just didn't care. My mind was running rampant. Who was this woman and why did she have this effect on me? There was a sense of nostalgia that I couldn't comprehend. I just wanted to be around her, that was all I knew.

Eventually I polished off what was surely an entire bottle of Cabernet. I took a deep breath and headed right to her. Not only was I considerably drunk, but Brooks had finally left her side. His presence stung me.

She studied a painting of a hypnotic sunset and her wavy hair matched the bright hues, outshining every stroke of orange and yellow. With my liquid courage, I slid my hand across the upper of her back, as if I'd done it a million times before, as if she wasn't a stranger. I felt my stomach drop, and I wasn't sure if it was the physical contact or the alcohol. Iris turned to me and there was a breath of stillness before I saw recognition fall upon her face. I caught her hazel eyes and noticed their little flecks of green, brought out by her green dress. Smiling, she brushed her bangs to the side of her forehead, delicately, using only the tip of her pinky.

"Hi," I said, almost in a whisper. Like every other part of me, my voice didn't how to handle the moment. My heart and my stomach seemed to be competing for who could do the most flips.

"Hi." She paused and pointed her finger at me. "Last week's art show," she said, as if affirming to herself how she knew me.

"Yeah. We talked about the ocean picture. My friend's family owns this gallery and I just thought I'd say hi. I checked out your work online and I really dug it…I loved the concert shots too…I…

TO BE HER GIRL

Uh…You're…" I could see the words spinning circles in my brain, but I had lost all control. I really dug it? What was I saying? I hadn't a clue. I hadn't even the mind to think about it as I stood before her, slipping further into the abyss. I walked away mid-sentence without even giving her my name.

I headed directly to the bar and requested another glass of wine. I grabbed a small flyer from the stack in front of me, looked over the schedule of upcoming exhibits, and then nervously and drunkenly shredded it to pieces. When the bartender approached me with the wine that he shouldn't have been serving me, I awkwardly shoved the pieces of paper into the pocket of my blazer. I took the glass and chugged.

"Are you sure?" I heard Signey ask as the wine poured down my throat.

I couldn't see her, but I knew the look she was giving me. It was the "you don't need another" look. I turned around with the glass still on my mouth.

"Where've you been?" she asked.

I lowered the glass. "Around."

"Come see this painting. It reminds me of you."

I followed Signey as she led me to a painting of a woman who looked like Iris. I nearly choked on my wine. The woman wore a white suit, and the background was a rainbow swirl. Since the painter was her friend, I wondered if it was actually meant to be her.

"It's nice," I said, looking for Iris. I saw her out of the corner of my eye but looked away quickly. I glanced back at her and then away again. It seemed she was doing the same. I spent the rest of the night dodging her every glance. I couldn't tell if she was seeking me out, or if my mind was just playing tricks on me. But even with the underlying fear of our eyes meeting, I couldn't seem to keep mine off her.

By the end of the night, I had consumed more wine than any art gallery should have provided. I carefully made my way outside to a cement ledge. I sat down with my hands gripping the edge. It was the only way to keep the earth from spinning below me. Signey sat with me while we waited for Ryder to bring his station wagon around. We both stood and I wobbled slightly when he pulled up.

Signey reached for me, but I waved her away. "I'm fine," I said, trying to find any ounce of sobriety inside me. But before I could find it, Iris and Brooks walked through the door that I had just been sitting beside.

I tried to act casual, as if I hadn't seen her, as if I hadn't made a fool of myself. Signey opened the door of Ryder's old Mercedes, and I reached my hand into my pocket. I felt the shredded pieces of paper and, forgetting what they were, pulled them out. A cruelly timed gust of wind caused them to fly all around me. Trying to catch them, I could feel Iris's eyes on me. I could feel her smiling at my silly misfortune. I didn't need to look, so I didn't.

I gave up on the flying papers and got into the station wagon where Signey and Ryder were waiting. I was too drunk to be embarrassed. I was too overwhelmed to care. I was too confused to be anything.

Ryder dropped us off at our apartment, and Signey tried to hide her disappointment as he drove away without her. I staggered up the steep stairs to the second story, half wishing she'd left with him, half wishing she'd stroke my hair and tell me that everything was going to be okay.

She unlocked the door and I followed her inside. I staggered to the couch a few feet to my right and fell face-first onto it. I was being willingly suffocated by the pillows when she sat down beside me.

"Are you okay?" she asked. She held out a glass of water.

"That...that woman," I whimpered, sitting up and taking the glass.

"What woman?"

"I don't know." I sipped my water. My hands gripped the glass as if somebody would snatch it away. "I don't know," I whined again.

"So this isn't because of your grandma?"

"Graaandmaaaa," I moaned. "Whooo is sheeeee?" I carried out those four words as long as I could, whimpering with each breath.

TO BE HER GIRL

"Who is who?" she asked, firmly enunciating each word.
"Iris."
In my drunken state, I tried my best to explain. It was a bit like teaching a foreign language when I didn't even speak it myself. How could I describe what I was feeling if I didn't understand it? Iris felt like a distant memory—one that I couldn't make clear of—but one that was unmistakably there. I was attracted to her in ways that I never had been to anyone, let alone a woman. In a matter of a week, Iris stirred up something inside me. But like those pieces of paper in the wind, I couldn't quite catch whatever it was.

"I'm good," I said, pleasant enough not to aggravate him, but without reciprocating the question so he'd know that I wasn't in the mood for a twisted game of catch up. I just wanted my Rice Krispies. I took a step forward, but he took a step back.

"That's good, we should get together this weekend or something."

He could never pick up on subtlety.

"Seriously?" I rolled my eyes so hard, it hurt. "So you didn't believe me when I said I didn't want to do this anymore?"

"Oh, come on."

"I gotta go," I said as I took another step forward.

"It's always the same with you," he said.

I halted my escape. "What's that supposed to mean?"

"It's all about you. It doesn't matter what anyone else wants."

"What? Are you fucking kidding me right now?"

"Yeah, I don't know why I even bothered. I just thought we could chill."

"I'm sure you have plenty of other girls to chill with. You sure as hell did while we were dating."

"Like you even cared. You only wanted to be around me when it was good for you."

I stared blankly, knowing it was true. I never even called him my boyfriend until I called him my ex. He was just that guy I kept around to curb my loneliness and fulfill my occasional desire for attention. But had I known he was sleeping around, I would have severed our ties sooner.

"Exactly," he said. "I don't need this shit anymore. Like you said, I have other girls."

His arrogance burned through my skin like the cigarette I once watched him put out on his own arm. He rambled on and I tuned him out, focusing instead on the song he was shouting over. It was "Rolling in the Deep" by Adele. I shook my head and laughed, which only aggravated him more. I was never even in the deep with him, and finally I just didn't care. I walked away without saying

another word. I grabbed my cereal, went to the checkout, and drove home.
 As I was putting my groceries away, Signey walked into the kitchen. "Guess who I ran into?" I teased while she opened the refrigerator.
 "Iris?" she asked, who was now occupying space in every conversation we had.
 "I wish. Travis." I slammed the cupboard door shut, unintentionally.
 She froze with the pitcher of water in her hand. "Oh, no. How'd that go?" she muttered. I started seeing him around the time that we moved in together, and she despised him from day one.
 "Oh, ya know, the usual," I said, handing her a glass. "He tried to play nice until his pride was hurt." It was always a pattern with Travis—one that I kept returning to.
 "What'd you do?" she asked, pouring water into the glass. She put the pitcher back into the refrigerator and then stared at me with her eyebrows raised.
 "I laughed and then I walked away."
 "Good job, Cal," she said before leaving the kitchen with her glass of water.
 "A girl's gotta learn someday!"
 I went into my bedroom and fell onto my bed, wondering if everything that happened with Travis was actually for a reason. One day he'd speak to me with nothing but love and respect, and the next he'd treat me like the scum under his shoe. Maybe I didn't think I deserved any better. Or maybe I just wanted to see the good in him so badly that I went blind to everything else. At that point, I was just glad it was over.
 Bored with my thoughts of Travis, I grabbed my phone and scrolled through Fodoary. Surely somebody else's life could distract me from my own. But the first post I saw was a picture of the ocean with the caption: *rolling in the deep. venice beach. july 2013.* It was Iris who posted it.

5

Before I lived with Signey, I lived with Grant Auden, my best friend from college. We had to go all the way to California to meet, even though we'd lived our entire lives in neighboring towns. The problem had been the national border between us. I grew up in Niagara Falls, New York; and he grew up in Niagara Falls, Ontario. He already had dual citizenship because of his American father, but I still promised to marry him if Canada ever wanted him back.

Throughout college and our early days in Los Angeles, we'd often hit the road for no reason and with no destination. We'd sit quietly with our thoughts, listening to the radio or the silence of a back road, resting in the comfort of each other's company. Being alone and being lonely are two separate entities, he'd always say. We often felt lonely, but together, never alone. He was always there to loosen the knot when depression's rope tightened around my neck, and together we found inspiration to get through the day. We were Niagara Falls runaways who found an ally in a California college town. We didn't know what we were running away from, or what we running toward. At times, we didn't even know we were running.

At the same time I received the offer from the webzine, Grant accepted a job as a music teacher at a mid-city elementary school. We packed our cars and moved to Los Angeles a few months after

TO BE HER GIRL

graduation. Pressed for time, we settled into a tiny one-bedroom apartment that sat on the edge of Koreatown. It was infested with cockroaches and the building always reeked of vinegar. We slept on air mattresses and drank a lot of cheap beer in that apartment. We called ourselves humbled and moved out six months later.

Our second apartment sat at the bottom of the hill in Los Feliz. It was a quaint two-bedroom with an exposed brick wall and hardwood floors. It was completely out of our price range and bled us dry, but we were grateful while it lasted. Framed portraits of Patti Smith, Bob Dylan, and Neil Young lined the wall above our living room couch. It was dark green and decorated with oversized purple pillows. We'd sit on that couch and play our guitars, writing songs incomparable to the minds that rested above it. On our last night in that apartment, we converted the couch to its pull-out bed and slept beside each other. He had fallen in love with his girlfriend, Daniella Alves, and they wanted to live together. So he got a new roommate, and I got the couch.

If my road trips with Grant had a destination, it was usually to a concert. But since he had settled into a responsible adult life with a teacher-job and a chef-girlfriend, we usually just went to shows around town, occasionally at The Wiltern, a venue not far from our first Los Angeles apartment.

Despite Grant's six-foot-two-tall frame, which was an inconvenience to those behind us, we always had to be up front. We wanted to see the sweat sliding down the musicians' faces and feel the bass thumping below our feet. Maybe it sounded better from above, but we wanted to be a part of the show.

"Well, here come the photographers," I said as they entered the space between the crowd and the stage. It was an hour after we claimed our unobstructed views, and two since we'd gotten to The Wiltern. "I didn't leave work early and eat my dinner on the

"Well, why don't you ask her out then…"

I wasn't sure if he was asking me or telling me. Grant was always giving me permission that I couldn't give myself.

"She probably doesn't even remember me," I said. "Plus she has a boyfriend."

"You have the same eyes."

"No, hers are lighter than mine…And they've got these green flecks in them."

"I didn't mean their color."

I fell silent and kept walking. Grant always said the heaviest words with the lightest tongue.

He drove me home, and I gave him a tired smile before I got out of the car. I thanked him for the ride and then went into my quiet apartment alone. I tossed my keys onto the coffee table and headed directly into the bathroom. I splashed water onto my face, hoping to rinse the night off. I still didn't understand how Iris made me feel. The first time I saw her wasn't the first time I knew her, that much I did know. But the knowledge of her existence was a gift I wasn't prepared for.

I grabbed the towel that hung next to the sink and dried my face. I froze when I caught a glimpse of my reflection in the mirror. "Oh…that's who," I whispered to myself, in complete awe. Iris's familiar face with the familiar freckles reminded me of my own. The pattern gracing her right cheek decorated my left. Her striking cheekbones, the shape of her chin, and the curves around her mouth—they reflected mine. I thought Iris was the most beautiful woman I had ever seen, and suddenly I was realizing how similar we looked. I couldn't believe it, but there it was, staring right back at me. With the same eyes.

I threw the towel into the sink and shut off the lights. It was the only time in my life that my own face took my breath away.

6

I waited for Grant at our usual table at Rowe's, and our usual waitress brought our usual drinks. For runaways, we had become creatures of habit. Like our frequent concerts, my dinners with Grant were my constant. Whether once a week or once a month, I relied on them. Except for occasional nights at Jem's and Ryder's invitations to art shows, my social life was lacking. I didn't put much effort into changing it.

"You're late," I joked as Grant sat down across from me, putting a bag at his feet.

"Sorry. I think it was your turn too, wasn't it?" He laughed. One of us always was.

"Did you walk?" He lived only a few blocks away and usually did.

"What'd you get?" I peeked under the table at his bag.

He reached his hand under the table and then placed the bag on top of it.

I pulled out a box of guitar strings before tossing them back, exchanging them for the bag's other occupant, a used vinyl copy of the Grateful Dead's *Shakedown Street*. "Nice," I said, running my fingers over the jagged edges of its cardboard cover. After a few moments of admiration, I noticed the name on the price tag. "Untangled Music," I whispered to myself. "Do you know who owns this store?" I asked, raising my voice only slightly.

"Uh, yeah, Brooks something...Brooks..."
"Hewitt," I said.
"Yeah, that's it. Daniella's brother took guitar lessons from him."
"Seriously?"
"Yeah. How do you know him?"
"I don't." I took a sip of my Stella Artois. "He's her boyfriend."
"Iris's?" He raised his dark brows.
"Yep. Small world, right?"

And it only seemed to get smaller and smaller. I wasn't sure if I was looking for things or if the Universe was pelting them at me, but in the three months since I met her, I noticed everything in my world continued to point to Iris. Her name was suddenly everywhere and everything under the sun reminded me of her. The Law of Attraction felt like a gross understatement.

Modern technology was both a blessing and a curse. It allowed me to be a part of her life without actually being a part of it. Maybe I couldn't talk to her, but on social media, I could see what she posted and what she liked. It was as close as I could get to exploring her mind, and that was fast becoming my favorite place to be—inside her mind. It was the most beautiful mystery I had ever met.

Thanks to Fodoary, I couldn't help but notice how often we were doing, speaking of, thinking about, and liking the same things at the same time. She would do things like: post a picture of Stevie Nicks shortly after I wondered if she liked Fleetwood Mac, as if answering me; and follow accounts and like posts in the same minute that I did. She even posted a picture of a frog while I was dreaming about a frog, and the picture was almost identical to what had been hopping through my subconscious. Things were getting weird. It was becoming a daily occurrence, and the word "coincidence" was burning a hole in my tongue.

Was this the Universe's grand sense of humor? Or was it telling me something?

I knew Iris spent time at Untangled, and I often considered stopping in. But my feelings for her were only growing, and I knew if I went to her boyfriend's shop to see her, it would have crossed a line. I couldn't control how I felt, but staying away from the shop was one of the few things I could. Every time I went to Rowe's, my heart beat a little faster, wondering if she was just down the street.

After I got home from my dinner date with Grant, I cracked open another beer, put on some tunes, and sank into the couch. The comfort of my living room was typically how I chose to spend my Friday nights.

Instead of doing anything productive, like write, I sat with my phone and my fingers took me to Iris's Fodoary. A few minutes before I checked, she had posted a picture of Colin Dumont, an indie rock musician I was a fan of. The caption read: *currently catching up with this dude*. I felt dizzy as I scanned the background of the picture with the familiar brick walls and the stained glass windows. She was at Rowe's. We must have just missed each other. My mind raced in seventeen different directions.

What exactly was the Universe trying to tell me?

7

"Okay, I'm ready," I said, walking into the living room. Signey sat at the table, shuffling through her school work from Los Angeles City College. She looked at me with what felt like a mixture of concern and pity. "Are you sure you're okay?" she asked.

"Yeah, I'm fine." I lied.

Her phone buzzed. She picked it up and read a text message. "Well, I hope so because Ryder's on his way."

"I'll be fine." I hoped.

She nodded and shut her textbook.

"Child Development and Growth?" I asked, reading the cover. "What about your art classes?"

"It's only one class. I don't know. I'm just trying it out." She shrugged. "There's no money in art and you can't bartend forever," she said in a low mocking tone. "According to my brother anyway." She paused. "And my sister."

"Don't they both hate their jobs?"

Signey rolled her eyes.

"And you enjoy bartending." I ran my finger along the beads around my neck. "But I still think you should make jewelry again."

She sighed and shook her head slightly. She motioned her hand toward her textbook. "It's not that bad…And hey, it can't be harder

than taking care of drunk people."
"Or me."
We laughed and Signey stood up. "Exactly. Now go put your coat on and let's wait outside."
I grabbed my coat and followed her outside. We were going to an art show, and it was only the night before that I learned Iris would have a display. Four months since I first laid eyes on her and she occupied every crevice of my thoughts. We had spoken only twice, but she lived so deeply under my skin that I often forgot.

It had been two months since Iris and I last breathed the same air at The Wiltern, and my stomach spun with anticipation.
"Is there wine?" I asked Ryder while we waited in the lobby for Grant and Daniella.
"I don't think so," he said.
"Probably for the best," I muttered under my breath.
Ryder slid his arm around Signey's waist, and I felt like a fifth wheel.
By the time that Grant and Daniella arrived, I was wishing I'd invited Michael Jefferson, a personal trainer who I met hiking at Runyon Canyon. He wanted to take me out, but Travis had left such a bad taste in my mouth that I swore off dating, which I was never really into anyway. I figured doting over Iris from a distance was a safer bet.
I followed the others as they admired the paintings. It was hard to focus knowing Iris was somewhere in the sea of art. My desire to be a part of their coupled coupledom with Michael was short-lived. Iris was the only one I could think of. I wanted to keep moving, but I tried to respect their desire to actually enjoy themselves. Every time we stopped, Signey and Grant would glance at me. They couldn't avoid the nervous tension that seeped out through my skin.
"Does Ryder need to talk to every single artist?" I discretely asked

Signey. It was like if he didn't talk to everybody, his head would fall off or something.

"Just go," she said. "You're not gonna have any fingernails left by the time we make it that way."

I dropped my hand from my mouth.

I wandered into the crowd and away from my friends. My rushed pace slowed the closer I got to the photography wing. The last time I had spoken to Iris, I was a drunken mess. I wondered if I should even attempt to, even though I wanted nothing more. I wondered if my brain would function or if I'd just slur some words and run away again. I thought of Brooks and wondered if he was by her side. I selfishly hoped he wasn't.

Iris was nowhere to be found when I saw that familiar photograph from about ten feet away. "One, two, three…" I whispered to myself, counting the steps toward it, hoping it'd calm me.

Her display differed from the one four months earlier. The aesthetics were the same, the heart remained, but the photographs were new. A feeling of pride overwhelmed me, as if I had known Iris and her work all my life.

I stood in front of that photograph of the waves, placed in the center just as it had been the last time, when she appeared at my side. I took a moment to soak her in. She smelled like lavender. Not the artificially sweet kind, but a natural herbal scent, like a garden at the edge of the woods. I imagined that was what heaven smelled like.

My eyes wandered, exploring her body like they had a mind of their own. Down to her hands, up to her lips, back down to her chest. She wore a low-cut blouse that revealed her light freckles, like sun kisses on her silky skin, trickling down into her cleavage. I wondered if she caught me looking.

"Home," I finally said.

She laughed, causing every hair on my arm to stand upright.

"Home," she said.

"Hi." My voice trembled. "I'm Callahan." My brain was

functioning so far, albeit barely.

"It's nice to see you again, Callahan. I'm Iris."

My heart jumped at the sound of her voice saying my name. She remembered me, but I wondered if she remembered what I had said at the gallery—that I looked her up, that I was a fan of her work. She needed no introduction, though I loved every second. I pushed that night to the back of my mind.

"I was drawn to that photo before because it reminds me of the painting above my grandma's couch. It's almost identical," I said.

She smiled and I couldn't help but do the same.

"She died the night before so it…" I paused. "It was just really nice to see."

She placed her hand on her bare chest, and I wondered if she caught me looking again.

"I'm so sorry to hear that," she said.

"I think it was the first time I smiled after she died."

"Were you close?" Empathy saturated her voice.

"We were. She lived in New York, where I'm from, but she was a big fan of the telephone so…" My gaze got lost in the photograph. I was desperate for eye contact, but we couldn't keep it. Staring into each other's eyes was like staring directly at the sun.

"What was she like?"

I looked back into Iris's eyes. In the four months since my grandma had died, nobody asked that. I received condolences but nobody, not even Signey, had asked what she was like. My California comfort rested mostly with Grant because he had met her.

"She would grab my face with both hands and kiss me right on the mouth." I laughed under my breath. "I didn't enjoy it much, but after her passing, I longed for it.

"I'm glad you had her," she said.

"Me too."

We held our words for a few moments and stared at those waves as if they were moving. We were surrounded by noise, but I swore I could hear our hearts beating.

"My mom died when I was sixteen." Her soft voice sharply cut our silence. "That's why the photo is so important to me. It was our place."

My curiosity of her life was at an all-time high, but my heart sank with the knowledge of her heartbreak. Her eyes glistened when I asked if her mom was a photographer too—a spark of joy in the sorrow. She nodded and gave me a slight smile. Even her tragic was beautiful.

She told me how she watched sunset after sunrise after sunset after sunrise on that beach with her mom, and how she sat there for hours after she died, but hadn't been back since. I remembered the feeling I had that first night—how I felt there was so much more to the photograph's story. I wished I hadn't been right.

"Where's the beach?" I eventually asked. "Maybe I'll go there for you."

"Wren, California. It's a small town up north that nobody's ever heard of."

My jaw dropped in a wide smile, and she smiled back in confusion. "I went to Wren College," I said. I couldn't believe it. Iris's hometown was just on the other side of the hill from Wren Valley, where I went to college. I spent four years of my life living twenty minutes away from where that photograph had been taken. The internet never told me that.

"Wow. Small world," she said, echoing what I already knew. "What brought you there from New York?"

"My grandma did." I laughed lightly under my breath. "She asked me to look up something about the bird, but I found the college instead…It just felt right."

We both smiled and as my mind searched for something else to say, twins who resembled the ghost of Gram Parsons joined us. "That's a beautiful shot," the slightly shorter one said. He pointed at a photograph of a Joshua Tree sunset, which was my favorite from that night.

Iris smiled and thanked him.

TO BE HER GIRL

As the other twin inquired further about the photograph, I pulled the lip balm from my pocket and applied it to my lips. After putting the cap back on, I dropped it. Iris and I both bent over to pick it up. She got to it first and after we stood upright, she handed it to me. Our fingers touched and my body relaxed. I bit my lower lip, trying to soften the sigh that was falling from my mouth. Her lips were pressed tightly together, as if she was trying to do the same.

I looked at the twins, realizing that Iris had yet to respond. I didn't want to share her, but I knew I had to. She was there for her photography, not me. "Well, I should probably go find my friends," I said, looking back at Iris. "And I'll probably see you later because I'm sure they'll want to stop by here. I'm with Ryder Massey. I think you know him."

"Yeah, I do. I'll see you around then," she said.

We gave each other a faint smile and I walked away, but slowly so I could still hear her voice as she spoke to the twins. It was soft and pure and a slightly higher pitch than mine. It was the most beautiful voice I had ever heard.

I wandered around the show, searching for my friends and trying to shake the daze that Iris always put me in. By the time I found them, they had already seen her, so I never did see her again that night. I wasn't sure if I was disappointed or relieved. For as much as I wanted to be around her, I feared the fire growing inside me.

8

"Twenty-five," I said, staring into the mirror. My face looked tired and insecure. "Write any novels lately?" I asked myself. "Didn't think so. Just a book of nothing by Callahan Thomas." I scoffed at my reflection. "Happy freakin' birthday."

Still scowling, I walked into the living room where I found two dozen balloons drifting across the hardwood floor. "Ohhh myyy God," I said.

A pink balloon bumped into my leg and I picked it up. *Happiness* was written across it in black marker. I looked around and saw that every balloon had a different word on it. *Success. Wealth. Love.* Et cetera. I couldn't fight the smile growing on my face.

I heard Signey's bedroom door open and turned around.

"Happy Birthday," she said. She smiled and kicked a balloon my way.

That evening, Ryder picked up Signey and me, and we headed over to Grant and Daniella's place in Silver Lake. Daniella cooked my favorite meal, which was a grilled cheese sandwich and tomato soup, and then after dinner, we smoked weed and watched funny videos on the internet. I laughed so hard that I cried. It distracted me enough to forget about my self-appointed failures, but not enough to forget about Iris. I couldn't seem to get her off my mind, no matter what I was doing. Her face swirled around my mind like a gumball in a never-ending machine.

I grew quiet watching my friends. Signey with Ryder. Grant with Daniella. I sat with Daniella's cat, stroking his long ginger mane, until he bit my hand and ran off. I felt like an outsider, even though I was the reason we were all together.

As they debated which video to watch next, I slipped out onto the balcony. I inhaled the cool November air and blew it back out. Iris is out there somewhere, I thought. She was so close, yet completely out of reach. "Be happy," I whispered, hoping she'd feel my words.

"Talking to yourself?" Grant asked after sneaking up beside me.

"Something like that." I smiled lightly.

"All the best minds talk to themselves."

"Or the crazy ones."

"Maybe they're one and the same," he said with a smile.

My laugh faded into a sigh. "Weren't we just eighteen?" I asked, falling back into my hole of self-pity.

"Oh, about seven years ago," he said, grinning. "Remember your nineteenth birthday?"

"San Francisco," I recalled.

"Yeah, that year." He laughed under his breath.

"The infamous 'too many pot brownies' birthday." I laughed.

"I think it was licking the bowl free of batter that got us. Whose idea was it to leave the house in the first place?"

"Mason's." I smiled.

Mason Riley was my college boyfriend. After indulging in the pot brownies, we wandered around the neighborhood, and then, still stoned, we sat in the living room with our bloodshot eyes watching *Saturday Night Live* with his parents. His dad threw popcorn at us as we stared into the abyss.

"We had some good times up there, didn't we?" Grant said. "Remember the next morning when we sat at the kitchen table in complete silence while Mason's mom made us pancakes?"

"That was mortifying. I think I was still stoned." I laughed lightly and shook my head.

We took a few moments of silence until my loud, deep breath interrupted it.

"You're alright, Cal. You know that," Grant said with a gentle smile. "Time is two things: irrelevant and unstoppable. It's always happening. Everything is always happening."

"I guess…" I sighed. "It's all an illusion, right? This world." I said, pondering every second of my life. "So does anything even matter?"

"Sure it does," he said. "The book you're supposed to write will come to you when you're supposed to write it. Don't beat yourself up." I hadn't said anything about my ever-present doubts, but I didn't need to with him. "Don't worry about a bad today when it could make a better tomorrow."

"It feels like an awfully long night."

"More time to dream. And sometimes we need that."

"Yeah, and building strength and all that jazz, right?" I laughed. "It's just a matter of getting through the mud, I guess."

"Somebody once told me that depression and optimism are free to coexist," he said.

I smiled and looked to the sky. It was me who told him that on a dark night in college. I was never without the thread of my tenacious loneliness, but I always managed to wear a thin layer of optimism.

"Oh," he said, gently nudging my arm with his elbow, "and I expect to be listed on the dedication page whenever you do write that book." He gave me an assuring smile.

"For Grant…" I said, placing my hand over my heart, "who ponders life's biggest questions with me…when he already knows the answers."

Grant laughed as he let out a fit of air. "If I had the answers, I'd be dead."

I laughed as the others joined us on the balcony. Ryder held my birthday cake, which was my favorite—red velvet with vanilla frosting. It had a two and a five-shaped candle ablaze on top. I pressed my lips together tightly, trying to hide my smile as they sang to me.

"Make a wish," Ryder said.

I blew out the candles and wished for Iris's happiness.

"What'd you wish for?" he asked. But before I could respond, he jumped to the side and gasped. His sudden jolt caused the cake to fly out of his hands and into the bushes below. "Fuuuck," he said.

The rest of us burst into laughter as the cat ran back inside.

"He scared the crap out of me! I'm so sorry!"

Nobody could even get a word out, we were laughing so hard.

"Thank God you blew the candles out," Ryder said and joined us in our laughter.

Signey lay down on the floor inside, laughing too hard to stand. I wiped the tears from my eyes and stepped over her. I fell onto the couch, holding my stomach as it shook with laughter. I was laughing so hard, my face hurt. And for a few minutes, I forgot the depths of my loneliness.

Later that night, I went into my bedroom and saw that a red balloon covered with hearts had made its way in. I picked it up and batted it to the ceiling. I watched as it floated back down to my face. *Iris*, in bold letters, was headed right between my eyes. "Figures," I said, laughing and shaking my head. "Of all balloons."

I fell onto my bed and scrolled through Fodoary on my phone. Iris's latest post was a picture of her and Brooks, and any joy I felt popped like a pin to that balloon. "Maybe I should've wished for my happiness too," I said to myself. I smoked a joint and then cried myself to sleep.

I dreamt I was riding on a train with Iris. She was watching the ocean through the window. I was watching her. She turned and gave me a smile. "I wished for your happiness," I told her. "I should've wished for ours."

"So make another wish," she said. Her eyes sparkled like the sun bouncing off the water. I could have drowned in those eyes, no matter my level of consciousness.

"Us...happy...together," I said, getting my redo.

She smiled again and we slipped into silence. I wasn't sure where we were going, but we were headed north along the Pacific. We were passing through Santa Barbara when I woke.

Another beautiful dream interrupted by the drumming of my alarm clock and my mundane reality. I hit snooze and fell back into my fantasy. It had been so vivid; it felt more like a memory. I didn't want to let go.

I was eating my lunch in the break room at work when I allowed myself to look at Iris's Fodoary for the first time that day. It was usually the first thing I did in the morning, but I didn't want that picture of her and Brooks to crash the high of my dream. But with her latest post, coming mere seconds before I checked, that dream took on a whole new meaning that Brooks could never touch. It was a video of the ocean taken from the window seat of a train.

solitary traveler. somewhere along the pacific. right now.

"Ho-ly-shit." I nervously played with my hands, cracking my knuckles and biting my fingers. I got up and paced the room. I sat back down. I scrunched my face and gently tapped my forehead repeatedly. "What? What? What?" I kept refreshing the page, thinking I was seeing things, but it was still there.

I thought of Grant's comment from the night before—how time was irrelevant. Was I remembering something Iris had yet to tell me, something she had yet to do, and inserting myself into the memory? Was it just a coincidence or was my subconscious bending time? Perhaps my dream was actually an alternate universe where I was on the train with her. My brain hurt with the possibilities.

I didn't have a novel published yet, but my life was turning into a story that even I couldn't make up.

9

I sat at my desk and tossed a small rubber basketball into an equally small hoop. It hung on my closet door, and I only got up when the ball didn't bounce back. I was working on a short story, but the words were coming to me at the pace of a turtle triathlon. With the finish line nowhere in sight, I decided to walk the three blocks to Jem's. A change of scenery usually stirred up something.

I still felt on edge when I got to Jem's. I made my way through the dimly lit bar and restaurant. The only lighting was from the wooden candlestick chandeliers and the small lights on the wall. They hung below picture frames full of dried-up flowers and moss. The dim atmosphere was comforting, but the crowd was off-putting. It had been one of Echo Park's hidden gems, but word was spreading and now the dining area was always packed at eight o'clock on a Saturday night. It was good for Signey's income, but bad for my love of its seclusive nature. I bypassed the host stand and snagged the last open bar stool.

"The coffee shop is down the street," Signey blurted from behind the bar.

"I've got nothing," I said, pointing at my head.

She put a Stella in front of me before I even finished taking off my coat.

"Onion rings, please," I said, unwrapping my scarf. But she ignored me. "Sig?"

"Cal." Her eyes widened as she tilted her head slightly, pressing me to turn toward the door behind me.

With Brooks at her side, Iris stood before the hostess with four fingers raised. I spun my stool back around only to find Signey's eyes wider than they were before.

"What are they doing here?" My face fell into my hands.

My heart beat louder with every step Iris took toward me until finally, with my face still buried in my hands, I felt her at my side, squeezed between stools. I lifted my head, turning it to have our eyes meet for just a second. I assumed they'd rather fall out of our heads than succumb to the intensity.

"Hi," Iris said with a smile. "Small world again."

"Hey…Do you want a seat?" I pointed at my stool and she politely declined.

I smiled and reciprocated her politeness as she introduced Brooks and me. He wore a leather jacket above the same Bob Dylan t-shirt that I owned.

"Nice shirt," I said. "I've got the same one."

All he did was nod his head and give half a weak smile. He ordered drinks and I sat in an awkward silence. Signey made them and then he walked away.

"Sorry," Iris said, then sipped her rum and Coke. "What's your favorite Dylan tune?"

"That's the worst question," I said. "I'd say 'Tangled Up In Blue,' but wouldn't everybody?"

"Tonight I'll Be—" she said.

"Staying Here With You," we said together.

She laughed and sipped her drink again.

"Yeah," I said, smiling. "That one takes the cake, doesn't it?"

"*Nashville Skyline* was my mom's favorite album, so I heard it all the time growing up. She never made me go to church, but we'd listen to Bob Dylan every Sunday morning."

"That's not a bad way to spend 'em."

"No, it wasn't."

"Do you ever miss Wren?" I asked, then took a sip from my bottle of Stella.

"Not really. Unless I'm stuck in traffic." She laughed. "I guess I do miss the simplicity of a small town sometimes. But a room will always feel more crowded when everybody knows you. It's hard to hide in a small town." She took another sip of her drink. Her lips looked so soft around the skinny red straw.

"Are you hiding?" I asked.

She laughed lightly. "I was born here actually, but when my dad died, my mom moved us back to her hometown because everything here reminded her of him."

My heart felt like it was pushed off a cliff. I already knew that her mom had died, and now I knew that both her parents were gone. I wanted to ask about her dad, but I lost my chance when Brooks shouted for her over the noisy bar. He stood with another couple, waving Iris their way.

"I guess my table is ready," she said. "It was nice seeing you." She smiled like she was being forced to.

I wanted to smile back, but my mouth wouldn't budge. A slight nod of my head was all I could manage. I watched her walk through the dim bar to her table, wishing I was going with her. I want pictures with her, I thought as she passed the photo booth. Someday, I thought, someday. I spun my stool back to the bar.

"Are you okay?" Signey asked, putting my onion rings in front of me.

I nodded, moving my head only the slightest bit.

She stared at me for a few moments with a look I would come to know like the back of my hand. It was like I was falling to pieces right in front of her, but there was nothing she could do to stop it. After I asked for another drink, she gave me a brokenhearted smile and got back to work.

I sat at the bar and nursed my beer for almost an hour before Signey asked how long I was going to stay. Iris was still there and I couldn't bring myself to leave. It was like we were magnets. My brain would say, "go," but my body wouldn't move.

"Go home," Signey said, echoing my brain.

"Yeah, I think I will." I drank my last drop of alcohol. I put on my layers and headed toward the back exit, one slow step at a time.

Just as I started down the hallway, Iris came inside through the door I had planned to walk out of. We both stopped. There was ten feet of air between us, but it didn't feel like it. We just stood there staring into each other's eyes like we were trying to say something, but couldn't figure out what. "I know you. I remember you," it must have been.

That hallway I had walked so many times before felt like a portal to my own personal cosmos. I couldn't say if it felt like the blink of an eye or a long, hot summer. Time? What was time? I couldn't think. I couldn't move. But it was then that I knew what I had known for six months. Suddenly I believed everything that my soul had been trying to tell me.

It was the disruption of another trekking down that long hallway that reintroduced the concept of time. I turned without saying a word and left through the front door.

I staggered the three blocks home in a complete daze. I was drunk on a confusing clarity. I couldn't be bothered to adjust my scarf, even though December's Santa Ana winds were slapping my face. My tears felt like ice as they streamed down my cheeks. "I'm in love with her. I'm in love with her. Oh my God, I'm in love with Iris," I whimpered. Every time I said it felt more liberating than the last.

"I'm in love with her," I told Signey the next morning over breakfast.

She didn't say it, but I could see the word "duh" written all over her face.

"It just doesn't make any sense. Nothing makes any sense," I said.

"Life would be awfully boring if it always made sense."

"True."

"So what's it feel like…to fall in love?"

TO BE HER GIRL

"With a person you hardly know? Terrifying." I let out a half laugh, half whimper. "But honestly, how it feels...I think I was born in love with her. I just entered a realm of awareness."

10

Spending New Year's in the city again? read the text message from Mason.

You know it, I messaged back before tossing a long sleeve shirt into my suitcase.

Hit me up if you have the time. I'd love to see you

My fingers paused as I caught a glimpse of the small indigo box with *Iris* etched into its wood, still sitting empty on my dresser. *Will do. Happy Holidays!* I eventually replied.

A huge perk of my job was that it was closed over the holidays every year, so I'd spend the post-Christmas stretch in New York City with Cora and her husband, Rhett Hayes, an architect from Long Island. Mason had lived there for three years, but we saw each other only once during that time. I wondered if he'd provide some relief from my heart that was burning a hole through my flesh. The thought of seeing him both soothed and clawed at it.

Mason was my first love. He was my first real relationship, my first everything. We met through mutual friends our first semester at Wren. He was teaching me how to skateboard when I fell and sprained my ankle. He gave me a piggyback ride to his car parked several blocks away. We dated until the end of our junior year, though I always kept him at a comfortable distance. I loved him, but I was bored and depressed. I had nothing for him, so I let him go.

TO BE HER GIRL

We remained friendly senior year but spoke rarely after graduation. I moved to Los Angeles. He moved to New York City. That was that.

    I thought of him a lot after I acknowledged my love for Iris. My feelings for her blew everything I had ever felt for him out of the water. I knew I was in deep when I realized I loved her flaws more than I ever even loved his beauty. There was really no comparison. She was the sun and everyone else was merely floating space particles. She reached me like no one else ever could, without even lifting a finger.

I got off the plane and walked into the Buffalo Niagara International Airport, greeted by Buffalo's own Goo Goo Dolls blasting on the sound system. In the seven years I had been flying back from California, it seemed like they were playing every time that I did. I wasn't surprised to hear their song "Iris" on my way to baggage claim, but it didn't make it any easier.

    A couple of days later, I listened as Cora sang along to that same song as we rode up the long paved driveway to my grandparents' house. My grandma had been gone for six months, and my grandpa for over four years, but I couldn't think of it any other way. My heart felt heavier with each spin of the tires.

    My aunt and uncle moved into the house after my grandma passed away. In turn, they inherited the responsibility of the Christmas gathering. I was afraid to see what they had changed. I paced myself as I walked through the house, but it wasn't much. Most of the furniture was still there and the same artwork covered the walls. All that was missing since my last visit, exactly one year earlier, was Grandma.

    I sat in the wooden rocking chair in the living room and rubbed my grandma's old ring between my fingers. My dad had just given it to me. My mom and stepmom, Rebecca, chatted across from me on that ugly brown couch. I couldn't bear to sit on it.

"Anything? Cal?" Rebecca asked me. I could hear her, but I wasn't listening. I was lost in the painting of the waves, still hanging above the couch, wondering how Iris was spending her Christmas.

"Sorry…What?"

"Anything new for me to read?" she asked.

"No," I said, disgruntled. I had only bits and pieces of stories floating around on my computer, and I hadn't had a thing published since August. All I could write was lovesick poems. Though for the first time in ages, my inspiration came from my own heart, rather than the shattered pieces that Signey peeled off bar stools. Either way, I didn't want to share with her because I didn't want any questions about my imaginary love life.

"I'm sure you'll have something soon," my mom said.

"I hope so," I said before busting out a fake smile, then looking at the waves again.

"Why do you keep staring at that painting?" Nathan asked as he shook the rocking chair from behind me. He was still the same little twerp who dared me to cross the frozen pond when I was nine.

"Because I miss Grandma," I said, which was a perfectly valid excuse, "and I like it."

This caught my uncle's ears and he stopped in his tracks. "Oh dear, Callahan, we're putting a new painting there. It's bound to live in the garage," he said in his Irish accent. "Do you want it?"

"Yes," I replied without hesitation or any clue how I'd get it back to Los Angeles, as it was too large for my suitcase.

I slipped the ring on my finger, and then with my glass of wine in my other hand, I stood up and smiled at my uncle before I left the room. I hadn't needed to fake my smiles earlier. I'd been having fun with my family and happy to see them for the first time in a year, but I was slipping. My mind was chasing my heart, and my heart was on the other side of the country.

I went into the sunroom and sank into the soft cushion on the wicker chair. There were at least two dozen people in the house. I needed a moment of peace and quiet. I let out a heavy breath of air followed by, "Dammit."

"Dammit."

I turned my head and looked at the large cage on the other side of the room. I hadn't noticed my grandma's cockatoo, Billy, had woken up. She'd always insist she put him on the phone whenever I called. "Grandma. Grandma. Grandma," I'd say while she held the phone to his beak.

"Dammit," he echoed again.

"Billy!" I jumped up and the wine splashed in my glass. I crossed the room and put my finger between the slim bars of his cage. I wiggled and stretched my finger, but he was too far to reach.

"Silly Billy!" he squawked, bobbing his head. "Silly Billy!"

"Hey, buddy! How's life?" I pulled my finger from the cage and remembered the sound of my grandma's voice. It had always been so full of love whenever she spoke of her beloved Billy. "Do you miss Grandma? Because I do," I said somberly.

"I do. I do," he echoed in the same somberness, fluffing his feathers.

"And do you know who else I miss? I miss Iris. A lot. I really miss Iris. I don't know how or why, but I do." I chugged the rest of my wine. "And I love her. I really, really love her." The words still sounded foreign falling from my mouth, even though I was saying them every day. "I'm in love with Iris."

"Iris!" he mimicked. I wasn't sure if he picked up her name just then, or if he knew it from the flowers that lined the pond in the spring, but I realized the risk I had taken confiding in a talking bird. "Iris!"

"Dammit," I said again.

"Iris!"

I shushed him.

"Dammit! Dammit! Dammit!" he repeated, dancing on the perch in his cage.

"Are you teaching sweet, innocent Billy bad words?" Cora asked, having snuck into the room without me noticing.

I walked back to the other side of the room and placed my empty glass on the table. I shrugged and sank back into the chair.

Cora sat down across from me and ran her fingers through her long brown hair. It always looked fuller and healthier than my dirty blonde. "Damn, what?" she asked.

Damn, why do I feel like this? *That's what*, I thought. I was with my family! I was having fun! It was Christmas! Dammit!

I sat in silence and looked out the window. I didn't know what to say because I still didn't understand. All I knew was that my world had changed forever the moment I saw Iris. I knew that a world with her was the only world I ever wanted to live in. Nothing seemed to matter without her anymore. Any distractions were short-lived. She was all I could think about. And as far as Signey and Grant were concerned, she was all I could talk about. *Iris this* and *Iris that*.

"Iris! Iris!" Billy was on the verge of spilling my secret.

"Iris?" Cora asked.

"Dammit," I said.

As a kid, I admired Cora because she was the smartest, coolest, prettiest girl in school. And then as a teenager, I hated her for those same reasons. I steered far from her footsteps because I was sick of being "Cora's little sister." I outgrew those feelings by the time I left for California at seventeen—mostly. But while I doubted my college education, Cora didn't doubt hers. She found a good, well-paying job as an environmental consultant for a nonprofit right after graduation. I was still tossing pennies in the dark.

I tried not to compare myself to my sister, but it wasn't easy, especially when I was sitting in her refined Manhattan apartment. I lounged on her oversized couch, staring at the wooden plaque that read *Hayes* above her fireplace, wondering what my life would be like had I stayed with Mason. Would I be sitting in my own New York apartment with *Riley* scrawled above my fireplace?

I held my phone in one hand, while the other rested on the bare skin of Jerry-Garcia, Cora and Rhett's Chinese Crested dog, who lay sprawled out beside me on the couch.

"Should I see if he's free?" I asked. With his white hair poofing around his bald face, he almost looked like the human Jerry Garcia, only without the beard. He jumped off the couch and scurried into the kitchen. I took that as a "no" and tossed my phone onto the coffee table. I was taking dating advice from my sister's dog.

I never did reach out to Mason. I barely left the couch. I rang in 2014 with Jerry-Garcia and Netflix after I lied to Cora and Rhett about a nonexistent headache. Cora stared at me with her sympathetic eyes before they left for their friend's annual party. I had been looking forward to it, but I just wasn't in the mood for cheerful faces and small talk.

After Billy outed me on Christmas, I told Cora all about Iris. She neither doubted nor questioned anything. Not my love. Not my sexuality. Nothing.

"How do I love her though?" I asked. "I barely know her."

"If you needed a reason, it wouldn't be love," was all she said.

11

My descent into a crippling depression began when I was twelve. I skipped classes at school and stole pot from my mom's not-so-secret stash. I took little to no interest in anything that wasn't my bed.

By fourteen, I had become so numb that I woke up one morning and swallowed half a bottle of acetaminophen instead of going to school. I immediately regretted my reckless cry for help and stuck my fingers down my throat. I threw up in the toilet and then walked to the top of the stairs. I stood in a daze and threw the empty bottle at my mom down below. Telling her in so many words was just too difficult. "I took them all," was all I could manage.

I spent the day in the hospital, but all they did was prescribe me more pills and make me drink charcoal, which I threw up all over their white tile floor. The physical discomfort was all I could feel. The rest of me was still numb. I went home that night feeling just as empty as I had when I swallowed the pills. They hadn't filled me with anything. I stood in the hallway beside my bedroom door and pressed my body against the wall. It was cold and hard—concrete in a New York winter. I just needed to feel something solid, something real. I needed to know I was alive.

Aside from drinking charcoal and taking antidepressants, I was required to start therapy. It was either that or get locked away. I spent most of the mandatory sessions staring at the framed puzzle behind my therapist. She never did let me finish counting the pieces. Her nosy questions always interrupted my concentration. She wore cat-eye glasses and sweater vests that she knitted herself. Good for you, I thought, they're hideous. Her shrill voice made me angry. I'd whisper a few words every now and then, but mostly I'd just grunt and groan at everything she said.

"You're allowed to be happy, Callahan," she said at the end of my last session, six weeks after my overdose. "Give yourself permission to be happy. Only you can do that."

"Then what the hell am I doing here?" I asked.

She sighed and I walked out.

On the drive home, my mom asked if it helped.

"Did what help?" I asked. "Talking to a shrink?"

She stopped at a stop sign and looked at me in the passenger's seat.

"No," I said.

She looked forward and drove again. "I thought you were depressed when you were five," she said. She waited for a response, but I didn't give one. "You were sitting on the couch one day, staring blankly at the wall in front of you. I asked what was wrong and you looked at me so calmly, it was eerie. You just shrugged and went into your bedroom...It became a pattern. You'd mope around like you had the weight of the world on your shoulders, and then you'd go play like you forgot. We didn't know what to do. We still don't."

"Neither do I," I mumbled.

She sighed heavily and I feared she would cry.

"Are you happy?" I asked. "She said only I could make myself happy, but apparently I couldn't even do that when I was five."

She sighed again and stopped at another stop sign. "I think it would've helped if you actually talked to her," she said, looking at me.

"That's not what I asked. Did Dad make you happy?"

She looked forward and drove. "He did."

"Then why'd you get divorced?"

"Callahan," she said, glancing at me quickly before focusing again on the road.

"I'm just trying to understand."

"Understand what?" she asked, glancing at me again.

I looked forward and leaned my head against the side window. "Anything."

My depression was a nagging and persistent affair that felt like a free fall without a parachute. And without Iris, it felt amplified. It also robbed me of sleep. That's how I knew there were eighty-eight full squares on my bedroom ceiling. The others were cut off at the wall. Insomnia had accompanied me from childhood, just as depression had. I should have been writing, but I wasn't. Instead, I was counting ceiling tiles by the glow of my nightstand lamp.

I rolled out of bed and moved to the couch at eight a.m. Signey walked through the front door just as I lay down. "You're home late," I said as she tossed her coat onto the rack.

"You're up early for a Saturday," she said. "Still on east coast time?"

"Nope, just never slept. Been awake since eight a.m. New York time yesterday...How's Ryder?"

"We didn't really sleep either," she said as she strolled into her bedroom.

I was counting ceiling tiles and she was having sex. I almost texted Michael right then and there. He was still asking me out, slick as ever. I was still finding excuses. It wasn't even the sex I longed for; it was the intimacy.

I pulled up my favorite picture of Iris that was saved on my phone. It was a self-portrait she had posted on Fodoary, and her smile beamed through the screen. It usually gave me one of my own, but instead, I was overwhelmed with a surge of grief that left me utterly lost. Love hurts, I thought. But that wasn't it. I didn't know what it was. It didn't even feel like my own pain. It felt like I was wearing somebody else's shoes. My feet slipped right in, but something wasn't quite right.

I stewed half the day, then hopped into my car and went wherever the tires took me. The road was always my antidote for emptiness. I drove through Hollywood and up Laurel Canyon. I drove through the Valley and ended up at a Goodwill in Tujunga. I bought a wooden cat that I didn't need and completed my circle back to Echo Park.

I put the cat on top of the bookcase and poured a bowl of cereal for dinner, unable to shake whatever I was feeling. I curled up in bed and fell asleep by seven p.m.

I dreamt I was with my grandma at the beach—the one from Iris's photograph. We sat in the sand with an old camera beside us. We didn't speak or touch or even look at each other much. We just watched the waves and listened as they rushed to shore.

I woke in a daze shortly before midnight. There was a release of sadness, but I felt even stranger. A peculiar sense of death had overwhelmed the dream in a way I couldn't fully comprehend. It was merely a fact of life, a peaceful one at that.

I turned on my lamp and sat up. I could feel something, or someone, hovering. I swung my legs over the side of my bed and looked at my closed bedroom door. It opened, just a crack, but considering it had been shut completely, chills ran down my spine. I froze in fear and stared.

After a minute or two, I stood up and walked to the door. I slowly pulled it open all the way. I shut it, jiggled the door knob, and then opened it again, reassuring myself that nothing was broken. I looked back at my shut bedroom window, and then walked through the open door, slowly. Chills ran down my spine again. I checked every window in the apartment. All closed. I looked for Signey. Not home. I went into her bedroom and took the sage from atop her dresser. I lit it and walked through the apartment. "I'm sorry," I whispered. "You're not bad, I know. I just don't know who you are." I finished the unnecessary cleansing ritual and went back to bed.

I lay in the dark for an hour, feeling too odd to sleep. I grabbed my phone and opened Fodoary. My phone's glow blinded me in the darkness and I had to squint. I scrolled through the posts, unable to distract myself until I came across a photograph that Iris had posted while I was asleep. It was of a woman whose wavy red hair flowed halfway down her back. She sat in the sand with her arm around a little girl. The smiles on their faces should have been contagious, but I could feel my already tired heart drop. "It's her," I whispered. Then I read the caption.
mom and me. the beach. september 1984.
Tears slid down my face and I clicked on her account. She had posted another photograph while I slept. It was of a cotton candy sunset, painted with soft pinks and soft blues, falling into a sandy desert. The middle of nowhere, it seemed.
"be sure to live in the blending horizon. keep one foot on the earth, but the other on the sun." - sara lovell, my beautiful mother, who flew beyond the horizon twenty years ago today.
I mumbled to myself, trying to decipher what I'd been feeling. I was soaking up Iris's pain like an already heavy sponge without even knowing it. "Twenty years…Her mom died when I was five," I whispered, remembering what my mom had told me. If I felt Iris's pain that day, could I have felt it when I was five? I wiped the tears from my eyes and fell back asleep. It wasn't until the next morning that I realized who had opened my door.

12

Michael had an overly anxious pug named Penny. He claimed his water bottle was bone dry when we met hiking in the fall and asked if I could spare a drop from mine for Penny, who was already nudging at my feet. After a few minutes, he admitted it was a lie and used his smooth talk to drag my phone number right out of me. I didn't cave in to his incessant invitations until January, but by the end of the month, I was seeing him regularly.

We went to Rowe's on our first date, but parking in that neighborhood was like a losing game of Tetris. The only parking spot was in front of Untangled. I looked inside and walked past the window so slowly that Michael asked if I wanted to go in. Yes, I thought. "No," I said. I didn't see Iris. I always wondered if I would. Everywhere I went, and every time I went. I couldn't drive down the street without wishing I'd pull up at a red light next to her. My eyes were always peeled.

As much as I tried, I couldn't force my attraction to Michael, which was a shame because he was undeniably gorgeous. He was crisp and clean and his physique rivaled that of a stone statue. His smile was so bright that I could see his pearly white teeth from a mile away. It just didn't matter. Iris was the only one I wanted. I dated Michael because he wanted me.

I tried to hide my reluctance, but he provided me with bottomless whiskey like he could tell. He had a handle at his apartment one night, and I drank straight out of it. My mind wanted a break from Iris and my body wanted sex, so I kept drinking.

I removed my top and then lay on his bed, drunk enough to want it, but sober enough so that he wasn't taking advantage. He unzipped my jeans and slid them off with my underwear. He positioned his head between my legs without wasting any time. I arched my neck as he reached his hands up my side. His tongue felt like a knife, but I expressed pleasure anyway.

"Iris," I whispered.

He didn't even flinch. He must not have heard me, I thought in utter horror. We carried on. It was brief and uninspiring. I sobered up and drove home.

A few nights later, we went to The High Street Theatre, which was on Hyperion Avenue. It catered primarily to local and obscure bands, and one of my favorites, Jewel's, was playing. I knew Iris was a fan, but I didn't know for sure that she'd be there, even though I did. I didn't know, but I knew. Either way, I wasn't going to let it stop me from going, nor was it the only reason I went. I was a fan too, and I had been before I met her.

I sat at the bar with Michael and a glass of whiskey-ginger ale. I turned to the door every minute or so, looking for Iris. She skipped the opening band but showed up between sets. The bar was shaped like an oval and separated the dance floor from the front room, though the place was small enough to see the stage from every corner. She and Brooks landed directly behind us on the other side. The only thing between us was time-stopping air and alcohol. I gave her a smile and a nod, pretending I hadn't a clue she'd be there. She did the same. I clung to Michael, leaning my body against his and stroking his neck. I wasn't thinking much, but a part of me wanted to make Iris jealous, to make her realize that it was her body she wanted mine leaning against.

A DJ took over the small stage after the show, and I found the courage to approach her. I was drunk, but not sloppy drunk like I had been at the gallery the previous summer. She was chatting with Brooks and some friends. It seemed like she had a million of them, which was something I could never say about myself. I placed my hand on her back, not really caring if I was interrupting anything. She turned around, not looking surprised in the slightest, as if she'd been expecting me.

"Here we are again," I said.

She smiled and I felt weak in the knees. Her smile could guide every ship to shore.

She always looked more beautiful than the last time I saw her, like a flower that could never wilt. She wore white flared pants and a beige jacket with flowers sewn up the sleeves. She looked like an absolute dream, like a Gram Parsons song. I wanted to whisk her away, out of that bar and into the desert. I wanted to kiss her under the stars. I wanted to feel her heart beat against mine with the sandy earth below us and the desert sky above us.

All in time, I thought, all in time.

"How are you?" she asked with a dulled enthusiasm. Her smile had been so genuine, but there was a fear in her eyes that drowned it almost immediately.

My stomach dropped. "I'm doing alright. How about you?"

Our eyes shifted. We couldn't keep contact again.

She nodded. "Good."

I introduced her and Michael, who stood at my side. Brooks eyed me like he knew, and then he walked away.

"Did you get the new album yet?" I asked Iris.

"Yeah, it's so good. They didn't play my favorite song from it though," she said.

"Which one?"

"'Let Me Know.'"

"Oh, I love that one," I said. "Let me know when eternity comes knockin', knockin'," I sang softly.

"If it says hello, I'll stop blockin', blockin'," she sang just as soft.

"Hey, I'm Paige," the woman standing on the other side of Iris said to me. She had been talking with someone else, but apparently thought interrupting my precious time with Iris was more important. It was Paige Lancaster, Iris's best friend since childhood. She had a vintage-inspired clothing line, and Iris took photographs for it. I already knew who she was because of Fodoary.

I introduced myself and Michael, who just put his hand up in a wave.

"So how do y'all know each other?" the woman beside Paige asked. I knew who she was too. It was Leah John. Iris loved to post photographs of her friends. But I knew who she was because of her music. Iris didn't have friends with normal jobs. Leah pointed her finger from Iris to me and back again.

I looked at Iris. Iris looked at me and then at Paige. "Art," Iris said to Leah.

I thought the answer was either way more complex or way simpler than that.

"Are you an artist?" Leah asked me.

"I sell vitamins," I said.

"Oh," she said. "That's nice."

I smiled and looked at Iris, who smiled back.

Brooks walked up and put his hand on Iris's lower back. I thought he must have been trying to kill me.

"It was nice to meet you," I said to Paige and Leah. "And I'm sure I'll see you around again," I said to Iris.

"Good seeing you," she said. "Let me know when eternity comes knockin'."

I smiled lightly and darted to the restroom. I stared at myself in the mirror and shook my head. "You idiot," I said. I was mad at myself for walking away, but I was drunk and Brooks made me queasy.

I staggered back out and stood at the edge of the dance floor, unsure where Michael had disappeared to. I spotted Iris through the break in the crowd just as the DJ turned up Patti Smith Group's "Because the Night." I watched her dance under the glow of the lights with her friends. She whipped her hips around, and my stomach felt like it was housing the entire butterfly kingdom. There was just nothing I could do about it. The woman I loved more than anything was dancing to my favorite song, and all I could do was stand there and feel those butterflies. Watching her was like watching my heart dance around outside my chest. I needed another drink. I turned around and Michael already had it.

I sat with him at the bar and drank my whiskey like my life depended on it, like Iris's life depended on it. I finished it within minutes and Michael ordered me another. I only let him touch me when I was drunk, so he was rather generous with purchasing alcoholic beverages.

Iris and her friends left the dance floor and stood on the other side of the bar. Every time I looked at her, she'd look away quickly. I grabbed my glass of whiskey and decided to dance. Michael followed me onto the floor, but I kept my distance. He returned to the bar.

"So what's your deal?" the woman who danced beside me asked.

"What deal?" I laughed and kept dancing. Her energy was too bright to be annoyed by an invasive question. That and I was too drunk to care.

"Why are you with that guy if you so clearly don't want to be?"

I stopped and took a sip of my drink. "Because I want to be with her, but I can't be." I pointed discretely in Iris's direction.

She stopped dancing and stood close. "Which one?"

"The short one with the long strawberry blonde hair."

"You have a lot more restraint than me."

"How's that?" I asked and drank some more.

"If I wanted her, I'd go get her. I wouldn't let anything stop me."

I drank again. I was getting sloppy and the room was starting to spin.

EMILY CRADDUCK

    I left the dance floor and fell into the lounge chair near the front door. Michael followed and I asked him for a cup of water. Iris and Brooks crossed in front of me and then through the door. She didn't even look my way. I didn't know if she didn't see me or if she just didn't want to. Michael returned with my water and I took one sip of it, then pounded the plastic cup onto the table at my side. I got up and walked out so quickly that I must have left smoke in my wake. Michael followed without a word and drove me home in silence.

―――――

Michael asked me to be his girlfriend in mid-March. We were on our way to a concert and he had me trapped. I wanted to jump out of his car and run away. Instead, I told him I wasn't into labels and liked things the way they were, which was code for: "I like you…I'm just not that into you. Thanks for keeping me company…for now." I was too depressed to care about the guilt that was eating me alive.
    At the concert, we stood in the center toward the front, with just two rows of fans in front of us. It was even more important for me to be up close now, given the chance that Iris might be working. But except for that one night in August, she never was. I always held out hope and went home disappointed. Her absence always ruined everything.
    I watched the photographers take their place. First a short bald guy, then a woman with face piercings, a preppy guy who looked out of place, a man way too tall to be in front of me, someone who appeared androgynous with an afro, and then her—there she was. Once again, more beautiful than the last time I saw her. Her wavy hair was in a ponytail, which it rarely was. I obsessed in my mind how beautiful her ears were. Attached earlobes, just like mine. I watched her adjust her camera, too afraid to get her attention, and then I watched her make her rounds during the opening band. I didn't see her look my way even once. I was convinced she saw me while I wasn't looking and avoided my direction on purpose.

I didn't know who the band was, but I liked them. I discovered that only after Iris left the photographers' pit and I could focus on something other than her. I took my phone from my pocket to take a picture, but Michael grabbed it out of my hands before I could.

"What the hell?" I turned to find a smile on his face. I laughed and reached for my phone, but he put it into his pocket. "Give me my phone," I said.

"It's a distraction," he replied.

"I was gonna take a picture."

"Why?" he asked. "They're right there, right now."

"Exactly. Now give me my phone," I said, getting annoyed.

He gave it back and I snapped a blurry picture.

"I just think—"

"Shh!" I interrupted.

The band finished their set. I raised my eyebrows at Michael and tilted my head. "You were saying?"

"I just think that taking pictures is saving half-assed memories instead of living them as they happen," he said. "Wouldn't you rather have the memory?"

"Well, I wanted to take a picture to savor the memory in case I forgot because I liked that band, but instead, the memory is now of you stealing my phone when all I wanted was to take a picture," I rambled. "Photography is art, Michael. Look it up." I smiled sarcastically.

"I'm not saying photography is worthless," he said, "but society has gone mad. It's like if it's not posted on the internet, did it even happen?"

"What's wrong with sharing?"

"Nothing. Just because I don't have social media doesn't mean I'm against it. But does it matter?"

"Does what matter?"

"Exactly," he said with a smirk.

"Pictures capture experiences," I said. His smirk bothered me.

"But are you actually experiencing it or just taking pictures?" He spoke in riddles. He did that often and it annoyed me more times than not.

I didn't need the picture, but maybe I needed the moment, I thought, ignoring Michael. Maybe I needed the moment of Michael ruining the moment. I was overthinking everything, like usual.

I never did hear from that band again. Their existence in my world became nothing but a vague memory and a blurry picture. And Michael was right; it didn't matter. But I posted it online anyway, just to spite him. I captioned it: *Like two bodies passing in the dark night, if we don't see each other, were we both really there? Does it matter?*

Sometimes the consequence of the moment is all we need to remember.

Iris and I finally locked eyes when she came back out for the headliner. She nodded her head in acknowledgment, but looked at me as if she'd seen a ghost. Her entire body shivered as we stared from about ten feet away, prompting her to look away. We didn't say a word to each other, and I never caught her looking my way again that night.

I didn't see Michael for almost two weeks after the concert. And I only did then because he teased me with my favorite wine right after Iris posted an old picture of Brooks on Fodoary. Drowning in a red blend sounded like a good idea.

I went to his place after dinner and immediately asked for the wine. I laughed but I wasn't kidding. It was why I was there. He got two bottles out of the refrigerator, then poured us each a glass and we went into his bedroom. He carried the glasses. I carried the bottles.

"I should've known wine would get your attention," he said later that night. He smiled but I didn't bother to fake one back. He held me tight as we stood in the center of his bedroom. I could feel his heart beating through his sculpted chest. I could barely stand and grimaced at the two empty wine bottles sitting on his desk. He had only one glass. I had drowned, alright.

He kept trying to kiss me, but I turned my head every time. Sleeping with him was one thing, kissing him was another. Iris's lips were the only lips I ever wanted to taste. I had longed for intimacy, but as it turned out, I didn't want it with anyone if I couldn't have it with her. Sex with Michael was only ever a result of alcohol, but no matter how drunk I was, I could never bring myself to kiss him.

"Come on," he said meekly. He tried to hide his frustration, but his voice was dripping with defeat.

I freed myself from his arms. Pity seeped out of my eyes just as the wine had poured down my throat. "I'm sorry. I'm in love with someone else," I whispered as I crawled onto his bed behind me.

"Iris. I know. I heard you say her name, and I saw the way you looked at her. I'm not blind."

I buried my face in my hands.

"But I'm the one who's here," he said. He sat down beside me and took my hands in his.

"It doesn't matter," I said, looking back up. The alcohol had removed any filter from my mouth. "She's the love of my life. She's my soulmate."

"But she's with that guy," he argued.

"I don't think they're together anymore."

I didn't know why I said that.

We lay beside each other after a failed attempt at sex. Desperate pity sex. We didn't utter another word and before I knew it, it was four a.m. I had fallen in and out of consciousness thanks to the wine. Until then, Mason was the only guy I had ever slept beside. Like kissing, I felt it far too intimate. And just as I had with Travis, I always left Michael's in the dead of night.

With Penny in tow, he walked me to my car in the early morning drizzle. The street lights beat against the wet sidewalk like the weight of my conscience. Loud and heavy.

I gently kissed his cheek, and he asked me to stay.

Sighing, I looked to the sky and let the rain sprinkle my face. There was no point in pretending anymore. Iris was my heart and I wouldn't survive a transplant.

I knelt beside Penny and squeezed her smushed face, knowing I'd never see her again.

13

Ryder moved to New York City the first week of April. He and Signey had already fizzled, and we were both single again. We joked about getting a couple of cats.

"We can't though," I said and took a sip of my Cabernet. "Iris is allergic."

She had recently posted a photograph of a stray with the caption: *allergy cat blues. highland park. march 2014.* So I just assumed.

"We can't get a cat because Iris is allergic?" Signey sounded concerned, even though we were joking about the cats. She sat down across from me at our table after pouring herself another glass of wine.

"Exactly." I laughed.

"You've been wanting to adopt a cat for years," she said.

"Yeah, and maybe there's a reason I haven't."

"Because of Iris?" She took a sip of her wine.

"Maybe," I said. "Our desires change. But yeah, no matter how crazy it sounds, if Iris is allergic, I can't have one. I really believe we're going to be together…And that's what matters to me. She's my dream."

Signey and I simultaneously drank our wine like we were both sick of the conversation already.

"Maybe we can get a bird." I laughed again.

Signey didn't laugh though. I could tell she was growing tired. I was tired too.

One night in March, shortly before I stopped seeing Michael, I lay sprawled across the kitchen floor, high as a kite and drunk as a skunk. I checked Fodoary and saw that Iris had posted a photograph of the Echo Park Lake fountain. The caption read: *GET UP! echo park. march 2014.*

I got up.

I stumbled into the living room where Signey was reading. She'd let me soak on the floor in tears when I needed to, but would always help me up when it was time. She never went too far.

"Look what Iris posted," I said. "Do you think she knew I was on the floor?"

There had been many times when I sensed that Iris was feeling low or flying high, and her social media would always reflect that I was right. If I could feel her emotions, I didn't figure there was any reason that she couldn't feel mine. Either way, it got me up. Iris got me up.

Signey noted its possibility and got back to her book. I thought "Iris" was the prettiest word there ever was, but I imagined it was becoming nails on a chalkboard for Signey. I couldn't blame her; I was annoying even myself.

Iris's heartbreak had been coming to me in waves for months, and the hammer finally hit the nail right around that time. I was toppling over, carrying both hers and my own. It felt a lot like the grief that I carried on the anniversary of her mom's passing. It was planted deep inside me, but I knew it wasn't of my own life. Sometimes I'd wake to it in the middle of the night and then carry it all day. It'd rush through me when I least expected it.

In my heart of hearts and every nook of my soul, I knew what it was. I shared my suspicions with Signey, but I didn't know what to make of it. My instincts were always right when it came to Iris, but to know something that I couldn't possibly know was overwhelming.

It was mid-April when it seemed that Signey no longer heard screeching when she heard the word "Iris." I staggered into the living room one morning while she sat on the couch. "Finally! I thought you'd never get up," she said. It was ten a.m.
"What?" I mumbled.
"You were right," she said. She smiled and shook her head with a look of overwhelming belief across her face.
"About what?" I was too tired to be curious, but her enthusiasm halted my progress to the kitchen anyway. I had only slept an hour or so, and no more than a few hours a night in weeks.
"You might want to sit down." Her face lit up with a wide grin. "I almost woke you up when I got home from work."
"I was awake," I said, starting to walk away, too grumpy to care.
"Iris and Brooks broke up."
I froze. I definitely wasn't getting a cat.
"I heard Jamie Lear talking about it at the bar," she said. "They broke up last month. And he said it was for the best."
I stared out the window, allowing a slight smile across my sad face.
"You're a nosy bartender," I said, returning my gaze to Signey. "But I'm glad you are. Thanks for telling me."
"Of course." She smirked. "Are you okay?…This is good, Cal."
"Yeah…" I said as a twisted form of relief, hope, and pain surged through my body. I turned around and went back into my bedroom. I crawled into bed, trying to sort out my feelings and decipher them from Iris's. Sometimes I could feel her broken heart more than I could feel my own, and I could only hope she knew that she wasn't alone.

14

Happy Birthday! was written across a white cake in pink frosting. I smashed my fist into it, filled my hand full, and shoved a giant piece into my mouth. I could almost taste it.

Red and yellow balloons floated across the patio and onto the green grass. The foil balloons tied to the patio furniture danced with the incoming breeze. And the light from the sun sparkled across the pool, and its heat beat on my bare skin.

I dove head-first into the water. That was when I woke up.

Part of me felt fresh and rejuvenated; the other part felt dull and lonely. I didn't see Iris anywhere in the dream, but I could sense her. She always hovered over the dreams that she wasn't even in. She was embedded so deeply into my subconscious. She was everywhere, all the time.

I stayed in bed for almost an hour before Signey started knocking on my door. One knock at first, two knocks a minute later, and then eventually a steady tap dance by her fingers all over my white wood door. "Stop fantasizing about Iris and get up. There's a whole world out there. Let's go," she said. She didn't like to waste daylight, and we had plans to go to the flea market, where we'd go at least every other month. We'd scout out the furniture we wanted when we could afford it, and would usually leave with no more than a bag of incense because we never could. She liked to get there early because parking was the bane of her existence, and the earlier we got there, the easier it was.

She usually abandoned me when we reached it, but I always loved the booth full of hundreds upon hundreds of old photographs. Family pictures from the nineties, eighties, and beyond. Times when people developed film instead of keeping memories on smartphones. Who were these people and how did their personal pictures end up in my hands on a Sunday morning in Los Angeles? I wondered, but never asked where the pictures came from.

"This looks like something Iris would wear," I said to Signey as we shuffled through a rack of dresses. It was a strapless white dress with red roses embroidered around the waist. It flowed to the ground and would have been much too long for Iris's short frame. But I no longer searched for things that I'd like, but rather what Iris might. I wanted to see the world through her eyes so badly that my own were going blind.

"That's gorgeous," Signey said. "You could buy it for her if you were dating…if you ever asked her out."

It was May 18, a month since I learned that Iris was single.

"Yeah," I said, disgruntled, "I know."

Signey apologized and moved to the next rack.

I could feel Iris so much that day that I thought she might come walking right toward me. I looked for her around every corner, even more so than usual.

She probably loves flea markets, I thought; God, I wish you were here with me, Iris.

Sometimes the voice in my head talked to her more than it did to me, and when it combined with my gut, I knew I had to listen. And in that moment, I was being told to check social media, so I did. Only she hadn't posted. Damn, I thought, I was so sure. I put my phone back into my pocket and kept walking. I looked for Signey, who disappeared after I looked through the old family pictures, like usual.

I stopped again and pulled my phone from my pocket, feeling a draw to Paige. I pulled up her Fodoary and sure enough, she had just posted a picture of Iris. She sat cross-legged in the grass, wearing a long floral sundress and a smile that caused me to gasp from pure joy. The caption read: *Happy Birthday, Iris Renée Humphrey! I Love You!*

I stared at my phone with the biggest grin, giddy to know her middle name, giddy to know her birthday. I didn't even remember my dream until I got into bed that night.

I wandered around the flea market with a hushed enthusiasm, imagining what I'd get for her, had we been together. I looked over a table of jewelry before forking over my only twenty-dollar bill and walking away with a silver necklace. Dangling from its chain was a small silver wire that wound tightly around the top of a deep green emerald. I walked only a few feet before I stopped to put it on. I looked down at my chest and held the small emerald between my fingers. I let it go and placed my hand over it. I could feel my heart beating against my hand, and Iris's birthstone beat right along with it.

15

I had started sharing my poetry about Iris on social media shortly after the new year. I didn't have much confidence in poetry and seldom shared it, but I desperately posted in hopes that she'd read it. I didn't know if she ever peeked in on me, like I did her, but I figured it was worth a shot. I had tried to interact with her a few times before, but it was never acknowledged. I didn't know if it was due to deaf ears or chosen blinders. Her following was much larger than mine, but I didn't figure there were many Callahans. She had to have known it was me. But I was left to wonder and it was all I seemed to do. Wondering if she knew how I felt, if she felt the same way, wondering if she recognized our connection—it all drove me mad. How could she not know?

I hid hints in plain sight that I was talking about her, to her. It felt like I was screaming with my mouth sewn shut. Selfishly, I wanted her to know. I wanted her to know everything. I had always worn my heart on my sleeve, and I wanted her to see it.

On the anniversary of my grandma's passing, I went hiking at Griffith Park. A small area of rare seclusion had become the place I'd go to talk to her. A large rock embedded into the dry dirt on the edge of the hillside became my tombstone for her. I would talk to her a lot, about anything and everything. Sometimes I just couldn't bear to burden the living, so I burdened the dead.

I felt the tears caress my face as I spoke aloud about Iris. "Does she feel it too?" I begged, prayed, and cried for a sign. "Please… Please…" My voice grew weaker with every plea. As I wiped the tears from my eyes, a white feather, the size of my pinky finger, floated before me and landed on the holy rock. It felt like a sign, but I was too tired to believe it. "It's just a feather," I muttered to myself.

Still, I immediately checked to see if Iris had posted anything on Fodoary that related to a feather. I was growing accustomed to things like that happening, but this time there was nothing. I was also beginning to stretch and see whatever I wanted to see. I headed home with tears sliding down my face the entire drive. I checked again when I got home. Still nothing.

I cooked a frozen pizza and watched *When Harry Met Sally*. I wasn't sure if I loved romantic comedies because I was a hopeless romantic, or if I was a hopeless romantic because I loved romantic comedies. Either way, I cried at the movie's end, no matter that I'd seen it at least a dozen times before. "Why'd it take them so long?" I asked the air. "Life is too short."

I checked again to see if Iris had posted. She had, and it was a photograph of a bird flying high in the sky. The caption read: *i feel it. the valley. june 2014.*

"Patience, dear child," my grandma always said. I could almost hear her whisper it into my ear that night.

The next weekend was the second annual Ace of Cups Art Show. It was Friday the thirteenth and a cool June night, just as it had been a year earlier. Only this year, the moon was full. Signey was at work, and Grant and Daniella were in Sacramento visiting his grandparents, so I went alone and didn't get there until it was almost over. I had spent the hours after work and the weeks leading up to it debating whether I should even bother. But I knew I had to. It didn't even feel like a conscious decision, but one that was made for me, for *us*, over my head.

I dressed in my favorite outfit, a tank top and jeans that I thought made me look most attractive. I wore my new favorite jacket, a faded denim that I scored at an Out of the Closet, and Iris's birthstone hung around my neck. It came off only when I showered.

I made my way through the familiar warehouse. Both returning artists and new filled the vast space. There was little circulation, and the air was hot and muggy. My denim jacket suddenly felt suffocating. I paced myself as I followed my previous footsteps to that back room.

It was much more crowded than the year before, but I spotted Iris immediately. I stopped at a high top table. It was covered with empty plastic cups that'd been abandoned by their drunken suitors. I needed booze too, but I fought the urge. Iris stood casually with her hands on her hips and talked to Paige. She wore a long black dress with embroidered roses down the side that looked nearly identical to those on the dress at the flea market. I nervously tapped my fingers on the table until a couple at the next one over started to stare. I realized my nervous taps had turned into a hectic pound and stopped.

Every doubt I ever had about Iris circled my brain like bees around a hive. I knew I loved her. I knew we were soulmates. But I couldn't deny how crazy it all sounded. My fingers began to bounce off the table's surface again as rapidly as the words raced around in my head. Why am I here? What am I doing? My thoughts consumed me as I watched Iris from the shadows and questioned my sanity.

Her smile calmed me from across the room, though she looked a bit weary. I couldn't even imagine my face, standing there like a deer in headlights, feeling stoned, even though I wasn't. I always felt a certain level of highness around her, a natural high that I could never replicate. It was crippling that night and I couldn't shake the fog.

EMILY CRADDUCK

Paige headed my way and I quickly turned toward the wall. I kept my back to her as she walked by, unsure if she'd seen me. I took off my jacket and tied it around my waist. It was getting hard to breathe.

I looked back at Iris just as she walked out the open door that offered the only airflow into the jam-packed room. I approached her display and my eyes desperately tried to capture all of her work. With the exception of the ever-present waves, the look of her collection had changed. Many of the photographs had harsh lighting, and a few were intentionally out of focus, or rather the focus was where it was least expected. She always tried something new, which was something I admired most about her. She was ever-evolving, just like the world around her. As numb to my surroundings as I was, a smile crept onto my face as pride clawed its way through.

I heard Iris's voice from outside and something came over me. I dashed through the doorway as if I had no control over my body. I didn't think about going outside; I just went. I felt weightless. Whatever force had brought me to the show in the first place was in control.

I found her with her back to me, staring into the small, dimly lit courtyard. If someone had been outside with her, they were gone. Our heartbeats were the only sign of life. I placed my hand on her shoulder, getting my fingers tangled in her soft strawberry blonde hair. She turned around and I gently pulled away my hand.

"Hi," she said softly.

We were swallowed by stillness, but I felt chaos creep up my spine. Words had been beating against the inside of my skull all night, but now I couldn't find any. My mouth felt numb and my tongue felt like it was the size of my brain. I just stood there silently, dripping with sweat and vulnerability, like a naked statue on display. My eyes wandered, darting all over her body. I admired her messy bangs, escaping from the black beret resting upon her head, curling up above the rim. I noticed the scar on her shoulder and her crooked tooth. Her imperfections were perfectly imperfect. I wanted to soak her in, every drop of her.

She put her hand on my arm and moved it up and down, caressing my skin with hers. She pulled it away for a second or two, but put it right back. Her eyes shifted repeatedly to my left, and I felt there was somebody behind me, but my mind was empty, like a dry paintbrush with unknown intentions. I didn't know what was happening any more than she did. There was an undeniable force that carried me that night, something otherworldly that put my foot in front of the other, and eventually pulled the words from my mouth.

"It's me. It's me. Don't you see, Iris? It's me," I said softly. I could feel the words slipping out the corner of my mouth. My heart was no longer on my sleeve, but in the air between us, falling through the cracks of space. I was waiting for her to catch it. "It's me," I repeated. "It's me."

"Callahan," she finally whispered. Her lips stretched repeatedly across her face, as if she wanted to say more, but hadn't a clue what. She just stood there rubbing my arm as if it could heal the brokenness inside me. I must have looked like a giant broken heart with limbs.

Our eyes stopped shifting, and we stared into each other's deeper than I ever thought possible. I could see her soul stirring inside her. I could feel mine jumping out of my skin. She continued to rub my arm, and it was only our touching skin that soothed the intensity of the moment.

It was the longest minute of my life, and yet it happened all too fast. I placed my hand on her shoulder again with the same mindless compulsion that carried me outside. I leaned in close and my face met her hair. It smelled like lavender. She always smelled like lavender. I felt my lips move, but I didn't know what I was going to say until after I said it.

"Let me in," I whispered into her ear, without a clue where the words came from. If we are not of this earth, neither was that night.

I didn't even catch a glimpse of her reaction. I turned around without hesitation and saw that it was Paige standing behind me. She stared and held my jacket. I hadn't even noticed it had fallen from my waist. I took it without uttering a word. I stormed through the decorated warehouse as swiftly as the storm I had created in the courtyard. I didn't stop until I was at my car a few blocks away. I sat down on a cement ledge in front of a nearby building, unsure of what I had just done, unsure of what to do next.

I remembered that I had a notebook in my car. It was an empty pink journal that I found abandoned on a picnic table at Griffith Park the week before. I grabbed it, a pen, and then returned to my spot on the ledge. I didn't think; I just wrote. I scribbled words onto those pages quicker than they could appear in my mind.

June 13, 2014

Iris,

 I wish I could explain to you what I've experienced since we met last June, but I fear I don't often understand it, myself. I could write a novel right now, telling you everything that has happened, everything I've known and felt, but I'll spare you. It seems you are the one person in this world who I am undeniably connected to, in a way that only two humans can be. The ties that bind us are unwavering and ours alone. I remember the feeling of familiarity that invaded my bones the moment I saw you. I remember the longing I felt, almost immediately, like I knew you ages ago and we were finally reuniting.

 I'm sorry that I caught you off guard. For whatever it's worth, I thought you knew. But you seemed so far away and I can't gather why. But still, I know there is something about me that stirs you inside. I know there is something you are trying to hide, and something you are trying to run from—that I could see. Eyes don't lie, Iris. You know me, just as I know you. Because if our hearts aren't connected, then how do I feel every crack in yours?

 I came here tonight, not for the art around us, but to look into your eyes. I'd go anywhere for that. I'd go anywhere to reach you.

 And I will reach you.

 I promise.

Callahan

My shaky hands tore the pages out and folded them into a

crumpled mess. Urgency rushed through my veins and I raced back to the warehouse with those pieces of paper, the heaviest I had ever carried. By that time, the show was over and the crowd had barreled into the street. I wasn't looking for Iris as much as I was just floating through the chaos. But I saw her standing at Paige's SUV and my mind spun into a frenzy. I couldn't let her leave without the letter. I looked down at the crumpled mess of paper, bleeding with my heart's ink, and when I looked back up, she was gone.

Once again, my feet moved without the assistance of my brain. I walked directly to the SUV and found Iris sitting in the passenger's seat with the door still open. I stopped beside it and stared inside. Iris looked at my face and then immediately away. My eyes wandered from her face and down her body, rapidly darting from limb to limb, flesh to fabric. Her long black dress had a slit all the way up her leg, and she wore ankle boots below it. They were black and shiny, but slightly scuffed. I made my way back up to her eyes. Her face dripped with an empathy that I could only see in my own reflection. She looked at me like she never wanted to look away. But she did.

"Just take it," I finally said, handing her the letter, after what felt like a lifetime of silence.

She took it.

I turned around and walked away. And again, I didn't stop until I was at my car. I got inside and sat in a daze. I clutched the pink journal, filled ever so briefly, now empty again. After a few minutes, I started my car and drove home, feeling simultaneously defeated and empowered. I said too much. I said too little. But I said it. I finally said it. And I didn't regret it. Not a single tear fell that night. Still, I wondered which was worse: to create chaos, or to deny magic. But I knew I did what I had to.

PART II

*Maybe we're just two stars
shooting next to each other,
following the same path.
Or perhaps,
we are the same star.*

16

My grandma once told me, "The further you run from your destiny, the closer you get to it. Like the train to the tracks, it will always find you. Derailments are merely an obstacle you were built to overcome." The problem was, my patience was about as thin as a penny flattened on those tracks.

It was hard to get out of bed the morning after the art show, so I didn't. By late afternoon, still in awe that I finally told Iris how I felt, I wrote another letter in the notes of my phone.

June 14, 2014
Iris,

I'm sorry. I'm sorry that I came on so strong. I'm sorry that I made you uncomfortable. I'm sorry that I blindsided you and then walked away. But I'm not sorry that I told you, as selfish as that sounds. I have been carrying this around for a year now, and I'm tired. I am so tired, Iris.

I don't remember much of what I wrote on those crumpled pages last night, whether those words ever met your eyes or not, but I promise there was truth in every one.

I'm sorry that I didn't go about things normally, but nothing about this has been normal. I didn't know what else to do. And to be honest, I didn't even know what I was doing. I still don't.

How do you escape someone when everything around you and everything inside you is screaming their name? How do you escape your own reflection? Even my skin reminds me of you.

It's been hard to wrap my mind around, so I can't even imagine how you felt as I stood before you last night. Again, I'm sorry. I've come to realize that the strangeness of life's realities far exceeds the strangeness of our imaginations. And it seems that I read your pages before you even write them.

I don't know what to expect of this, but please say something, anything. I'm only human, and my heart beats so completely differently since I found you. I'm just trying to catch my breath.
Callahan

    I rolled out of bed and took her business card from the bulletin board above my desk. I had pinned it there the night we met. Her professional email address was all I had. I could only hope that nobody else had access to the account, though I didn't much care. I sent her the letter and got back into bed.

    I curled up in a fetal position, but my nerves ate away at me and I couldn't stay still. I tossed and turned until I finally lay flat on my back. I took a deep breath and stared at the ceiling. But I couldn't concentrate enough to count the tiles. It felt like my heart was beating to the ceiling, thumping out of my chest. I sat up on the edge of my bed, but my knees bounced just as high. I couldn't stop the shaking. I could feel uncertainty consume my body, just as it had everything else. My heart, my mind, my soul—they couldn't all be lying, could they? Could this world truly have no meaning? If my connection with Iris didn't, surely nothing did. I couldn't fathom that she didn't feel it, but she seemed so distant. It was like she knew; she just didn't want to.

    The days passed in a slow blur as I waited for a response.
    I didn't sleep for four days. Not a wink.
    She didn't respond. She didn't acknowledge me.

TO BE HER GIRL

In the year since we met, every song on the radio, and every gust of wind seemed to be a message from Iris. But there I was, asking for words, and she wouldn't say a thing. I feared that everything was in my head, of my own warped creation. I had read that coincidences are the humor of the Universe, but I was growing tired of the joke.

Signey asked why I didn't just ask her out to dinner, but I didn't have an answer. Cora said I probably scared her, probably overwhelmed her, but I was scared and overwhelmed too. Grant told me to give her time to process, to have patience, but I couldn't find any. I couldn't soothe the ache in my soul.

The intensity of the love was matched only by the intensity of the pain. I couldn't understand how Iris could deny us, why she wouldn't respond. I began to doubt everything I had ever believed about her, everything I had felt and experienced, which caused me to doubt everything else, because doubting her and doubting love was doubting existence. During one of those sleepless nights, I screamed, "no," so harshly that I didn't even make a sound, like a broken whisper barely reaching the air. My heart felt like a balloon in my chest that wouldn't stop inflating. I thought it would burst. I wasn't sure what to believe, so I didn't believe anything. And that was perhaps the scariest moment of my life—the moment I didn't believe.

It felt like death.

The weekend after the art show, I went to my grandma's California tombstone for the sole purpose of yelling at her. I thought of the last time I had been there two weeks earlier—how I asked for a sign if Iris felt it, and how I seemingly got an affirmative answer. But maybe I didn't. Timing was everything, or perhaps, it was nothing. It just felt so cruel, so unfair. The only thing I knew to be true in this world was the one thing I couldn't touch.

With my muddy sneakers, I kicked it repeatedly, leaving my

prints on the rock. "Why?" I asked over and over. "Why?" I half expected an immediate answer, but didn't get one. "I don't understand," I whimpered with tears streaming down my face. I had never felt more broken in my life, and I couldn't understand why. Feeling rejected by Iris was the greatest pain I had ever known. It was like being rejected by myself.

Later that night, I absentmindedly filled the bathtub with lukewarm water, stripped my clothes, and slipped in without fatal intention. *Drip. Drip. Drip.* The water fell from the faucet slow and steady, one drop at a time. I stared at the drain below it, wishing I could fill the tub higher. I wanted to drown. I wanted to die. If I couldn't be with Iris, I didn't want to be alive at all. Nothing mattered. Nothing was worth it.

I put my head under the water, for mere seconds at first, but I did it again and again, longer each time. It was only reflex that brought me above the surface.

Until it didn't. My body felt limp with no desire to escape my tomb of water.

I eventually felt myself pulled to the surface. And when I rose, gasping for air, there she was. Iris sat before me at the foot of the tub. She wore a purple blouse that I'd never seen before. Her hair was still long and wavy, but she looked slightly older; and even more beautiful, if possible. At first she seemed concerned, but the moment a smile lit up her face, two children appeared. They both looked about five and leapt toward me with bright eyes and wide smiles across their faces. The little boy, clinging to my left arm, looked just like my dad. And the little girl, with her small arms wrapped around my neck, had her long hair in braids with freckles across her nose. I sat in awe, in bliss. The pain had faded from my chest. No words were spoken, but they, and Iris, were telling me to stay. I had never felt more love in my entire life. I had never felt more needed. I didn't know if it was a foretelling vision, or a hauntingly beautiful hallucination. But it saved me. They saved me.

17

The week before I told Iris, I had one of the most surreal, bizarre, and memorable dreams of my life. Snippets of her life flashed before my eyes, from infancy to adulthood. I was narrating the visions to my mom as if introducing her. In reality, I had yet to mention Iris to her at all.

Suddenly I was skateboarding through an unfamiliar park. It felt freeing at first, but then someone, or something, grabbed me. I watched as my skateboard rolled away in the opposite direction. The next thing I knew, I was falling down a rabbit hole, swirling through the darkness. Flash to standing before a group of men in what appeared to be an underground cave. They all had long dark hair and beards, and their clothes screamed anything but modern. I assumed the 1800s at the latest. A man, in a long and white flowy top, held one of my shoes. It was one I'd been wearing the last time I saw Iris. "We need to knock you down to your core," he said, waving his free hand over the purple high top. It disappeared as he lowered his hand, leaving only the white platform intact. As he waved his hand back up, he continued, "in order for you to build each other back up," and the shoe reappeared.

I woke in a state of complete surrender. The dream had been so vivid and intense that I was emphatically confused to be lying in my own warm bed. I analyzed it in my mind, combing over every detail and writing it down as to not forget a thing. I didn't figure I could be knocked down any further. My core already felt raw and exposed. But while that man may have been born only in my mind, I couldn't shake the feeling that the message hadn't been.

By the end of June, I was bitter and withdrawn. I didn't drown myself, but my core was still shaky. I was sleeping again, but barely. My depression was crippling and I didn't care to loosen the knot around my neck. I wore my broken heart on my sleeve like a scarlet letter. We all face heartbreak and I didn't see any point in trying to hide it.

One night, I slunk like a sloth across the floor, dragging my feet and pulling with my hands. I was crawling to my phone I had thrown onto the couch across the room. It didn't matter how drunk I was, the missed call that appeared on my phone was clear as glass. My grandma's phone number had long since been disconnected, but there it was, listed under recent contacts. Once again, I had been pleading for answers and whining about Iris.

Shortly after I reached my phone, I called Grant. It was approaching midnight and Signey was at work.

"What's going on? Are you okay?" he asked.

"Uh, yeah. My grandma called," I said casually.

"Just now? Is everything okay?" He sounded confused, worried, and like he'd been asleep when I called.

"No, not my mom's mom. My dad's. The dead one." I was concentrating on not slurring my words. "And not like when she called you, no, nope, not like that. She called my phone."

Grant was not only highly intuitive, but he also had a knack for communicating with the other side. I had been feeling spirits at an increasing level, as if meeting Iris opened up a channel I didn't know I had. But it was a gift he was always aware of, whether he wanted it or not.

TO BE HER GIRL

A few months earlier, my grandma reached through him as loud and vibrant as she had been in life. I didn't doubt a word he said, not only because I felt her presence, myself, but because he was saying things that he couldn't possibly know. It was frightfully comforting. Just before he felt her slip away, he grabbed my hand and gave it a gentle squeeze. "Don't worry about Iris," he said. His eyes widened, as the words surprised even him. I made him swear up and down, left to right, inside and out, that she was the one saying it and not him. But he didn't have to convince me of anything; I knew he wasn't making it up. It was just one of many times that I felt reassurance from her that Iris was in fact completely a part of me, just one of a million messages and signs that I felt her name stamped upon.

"She called your phone? What do you mean?" Grant carefully asked after a yawn.

"I was in a drunken fantasy about Iris and then I got mad and then when I checked my phone it said that she called." I sent him a screenshot. "That phone number isn't even in the family anymore ...I don't understand."

"Don't even try to. Get some sleep, Cal," he said, knowing my mind was going a million miles a minute.

"I can't sleep."

"I know. But try."

I knew I loved Iris, but I was questioning my sanity again. What was real? What wasn't? I couldn't decipher it anymore. I never really could, and maybe that was my problem. Or maybe it wasn't. I didn't know anything, or I knew everything. And I didn't know what I needed more: to see her, or for her to see me.

Grant picked me up the next afternoon without telling me where we were headed. I rarely liked surprises, but I was too tired to fight him. He took me to a roller rink, and I was surprised mainly to be excited.

EMILY CRADDUCK

It was a foreign feeling.

We stuttered at first, having been at least fifteen years since either of us had four wheels attached to our feet, but slid into the swing of it after a minute or two. Colorful spotlights and laser beams bounced off the shiny wood floor and chased us around and around. It felt like we did one hundred loops around that oval rink, and probably did. The nineties tunes bounced off the muraled walls like shadows in the direct sun. When Chumbawamba's "Tubthumping" played, we fell to the floor and stood back up, over and over. My heart was shattered, but for that afternoon, I was a kid again, engaging in life's simple pleasures, pain-free. I wasn't afraid of anything, not even falling flat on my face.

Later that night, in such a good mood, I checked Iris's Fodoary. I'd been trying not to and was being advised against it. It was self-inflicted pain. I had un-followed her account to prevent her posts from appearing on my screen without warning. But pain wasn't what it caused that night. It was anger.

Iris had posted a video of her and her friends roller skating, and I was beside myself. I had done something I loved, something I hadn't done in ages, and she was doing it too, at the same time. But she wouldn't acknowledge it or simply wasn't paying attention. My frustration was boiling over and I just wanted to yell, "Open your eyes, Iris! Open your goddamn eyes!"

It was a few days before I could accept that it was just another fit of reassurance, another episode to kill any lingering doubts. Jokes of the Universe aside, there was no such thing as coincidence with us. Everything was just another brightly lit arrow pointing in each other's direction. Denying it was like knowing the sky was blue, but looking for reasons it wasn't.

Iris and I, we were born to collide. I knew that. It was her who I feared still didn't. I told the Universe it was time to play with her.

The following weekend, Grant and I did something else we hadn't done in ages. We road tripped it up the coast to Wren Valley, just for the hell of it. Work was closed for the Fourth of July and I was aching to get away. Daniella packed us a cooler full of food and reminded us not to be reckless. Before we even got out of Los Angeles, I vowed not to mention Iris at all.

Somewhere in central California, we sat at a rest stop and ate Daniella's oversized sandwiches. I took a sip of my water and a cute guy caught my eye, which caught Grant's. He was tall and slender with dark curly hair and a Lou Reed t-shirt. He skated around the parking lot with his friend, occasionally returning to his car to take a swig of Mountain Dew. He reminded me of Mason. "I'd kiss him," I said to Grant, who just smiled. I wasn't sure if the guy caught me watching, but his skateboard ended up running into the curb a few feet away from our picnic table.

"Nice board," Grant said, no doubt striking up a conversation for my benefit. He didn't skate, but he was able to bluff his way through the conversation as if he did. He stretched, waiting for me to chime in, but I said nothing.

After a minute or two, the cute guy's friend hollered from the car, "Humphrey! Let's go!"

Humphrey gave us a nod and skated away.

I looked to the sky. "Seriously?"

Grant laughed.

"Do you see what I have to deal with? It's not funny!"

But it was funny. And I laughed too.

"Iris probably just met somebody named Thomas," Grant said.

"She probably did," I said, wondering if she could escape me any more than I could escape her.

We finished our lunch and hit the road again, taking our time up the 5. It was half the point of the trip, if not all of it. We screamed along with Patti Smith and crooned with the Eagles. We listened to indie rock in silence and talked about our old college days. After weeks in a pit of darkness, I felt okay. I felt like me, even if I didn't know who that was.

We drove into Wren Valley around six p.m., stoked for a weekend on our old stomping grounds. We crashed with Jared Stein, Grant's roommate in college. He was overly sarcastic and obnoxious, but he had a big heart and two couches. We lit fireworks in his backyard, and then drank beer and played music in his garage until three a.m.

After breakfast, Grant and I headed over to Wren College. We wandered around campus without interruption or distraction, and for a second it felt like we never left. We both struggled in college. I dealt with depression, and Grant always had questions that he could never answer. We both felt everything so deeply and stumbled around like battered but beating hearts with legs. Tracing our old footsteps made me realize how good we had it those days. I longed for the simpler times, even the times that didn't feel so simple. We hiked our old trail through the woods and relished in its silence. The only sound was the rushing creek and the snap of the twigs below our feet. But all I could think about was the beach and how I wanted to find the spot from Iris's photograph. My attempt to escape reality was only bringing me closer to its source.

We planned to avoid Wren, despite one of our favorite restaurants sitting right in the center of town, but before hitting the road on Sunday, we caved. I said I wouldn't fall into despair, and Grant said he'd catch me if I did. Driving around those streets was like driving into her past. I knew them well, but it felt like I was seeing them for the first time. We ate an early lunch and then wandered aimlessly on foot. We weren't ready to head back to Los Angeles, even though I had to work the next morning.

As we wandered, I felt more anxious with each step. "She's here," I whispered.

I knew the direction we were headed was leading me to Iris. A sense of all-knowing overcame me, which usually came without knowing. My body was out of my hands, just as it had been the night of the art show. Grant matched my pace, which had slowed, but I couldn't bring my feet to a stop. I was in a trance, wanting to turn around, but being unable to.

I eventually stopped near a clothing boutique owned by Paige's sister, Kate. I stood with my feet glued to the ground, while Grant stood beside me in silence. Iris's smile lit up the windowfront, and my heart exploded into a million little pieces, splattering all over the sidewalk.

It was only a matter of seconds before my feet were freed and I rushed past the shop, racing to a nearby park. Grant, once again, matched my pace. I collapsed onto a bench, trying not to fall into a frenzied mess, but Grant sat beside me and I fell into his arms and wept.

The trip back home felt like the longest drive of my life. Grant offered to drive it all, but I wouldn't let him. I was wired and nauseous and out of my mind. I needed something to concentrate on, so I concentrated on the road.

"We're magnets," I eventually said, barely above a whisper.

Grant leaned forward to turn down the volume of the stereo. "Rhiannon" was playing. Iris reminded me of a Fleetwood Mac song, light but strong.

"I knew that was her friend's store," I said. "I remembered it…but I didn't remember where it was. My feet just took me there…to her." Tears slowly slid down my face. I didn't bother to wipe them away. "How'd I know?"

"You already know how," he answered.

"But why were we both there? At the same time. Why? Nothing happened…So what was the point?"

"I don't know," he said. "But maybe someday you will."

His eyes surveyed the surrounding scenery. I couldn't tell if it was passing us, or if we were passing it.

18

July 7, 2014
Iris,

    It doesn't seem there is a road I can take in this world that won't lead me to you. You are everywhere because you are everything—the good, the bad, every extreme, and everything in between. You are the air I breathe and the beat of my heart. Was I just supposed to pretend I didn't find you? Was I just supposed to forget? Denying my love for you would be like denying the flesh on my bones. It's always been there.

    My friend, Grant, and I drove up to Wren Valley for the weekend. It was his idea and an impromptu trip, just to get away. I've been completely withering of late. A few days earlier, I dreamt you and I were at the beach—the one from your photo. "Will you be there?" you asked. Only I didn't know what you meant. It was just this morning I learned that you were part of a photography exhibit in town. I wish I could explain how insanely proud of you I am. Maybe that doesn't make sense—how proud of you I am—but not much of this does.

    Anyway, no, I wasn't there. But as we wandered around Wren, I became overpowered. My feet were no longer my own. I just kept moving and moving. They led me to your friend's store—one I used to shop in—and I saw you through the window. I felt frozen at first, but then I ran away. I don't know if I did that for your sake or mine.

    Why won't you respond? Haven't you read anything? This is killing me. I feel like you're staring at me like I have two heads while I scream nonsense *at you. Only it's not nonsense.*

I don't need your assurance to know who we are. One. Your denial won't change that, nothing can. But God, how it'd be nice to know what you thought, how you felt. I may know your soul, but your mind is a beautiful mystery. So please, from one beating heart to another, say something.

I didn't ask for any of this, Iris; I just chose not to fight it. The switch has always been on; it was only a matter of seeing the light. And after we met, it wasn't long before I realized you were that light—the one I've always known. And so I miss you. That's all. I just wish you'd believe me.

You can't outrun what's eternal, Iris. Why would you want to?
Callahan

I sent her the email on Monday night. I hadn't done much at work that day, other than stare at my computer and play with my fingers. It was clear that Iris didn't want to talk to me, but I had long since thrown any self-respect and dignity out the window.

But again, she didn't respond. Her silence stung worse than hearing something that I didn't want to hear, mainly because I was still left to wonder. I was a shattered soul and a questioning fool. I could only hope that she didn't think I was crazy. But if loving her was crazy, then I had gone completely mental. I was losing my mind trying to find hers.

I hid the indigo box in my sock drawer and took my grandma's painting off my living room wall. The box was still empty, and my uncle had the painting shipped to me back in January. It had been hanging above my own couch. Signey just watched while I shoved it in the closet, high up on the shelf, hiding it behind shoe boxes and old magazines. "Whoever invented love should've installed an on/off switch," I said. She simply sighed. There was nothing she could do to help me. There was nothing anybody could do. I feared the only one who could save me from Iris was Iris.

———

Traffic was at a standstill, even more so than usual—a crawl at best—and all I wanted was to get home. It was Friday and I had only a few more blocks to go before I didn't have to leave my apartment for two whole days. Leah John came on the radio and I looked at the control panel to change the station. Then I felt the jolt, causing my stomach to drop. I looked up and realized I had rear-ended the pickup in front of me. I saw no serious damage, which gave a pinch of relief, but I still had to deal with it. I followed the red truck as it turned onto a side street and pulled over.

A man, who appeared to be in his sixties, got out of the truck. His short grey hair matched the scruff on his face, and he wore a plain white t-shirt and blue jeans. He looked eerily familiar. I wondered for a second or two if I had seen him in some movie. Whenever someone looked familiar in Los Angeles, that was always my first thought.

"I am so sorry," I said as we met between our vehicles. "It looks like just a few scratches." I traced them with my fingers, inspecting my havoc.

"Oh, I think those are old," he said with his hands on his hips. "Your car looks fine."

My little black car had so many scratches that I couldn't keep track of where they came from.

"Are you sure?" I asked. "Do you want my info?"

"Nah, don't sweat it, kid." He smiled and patted my back. "Just keep those eyes open." His were piercing blue and carried a kindness that soothed my shakiness.

"I will."

He headed back to his still open door, but turned around to give me another smile. He lifted his hand in a wave, and then he hopped back in and drove off.

I was unusually calm on the last stretch home, but I couldn't shake the feeling that I knew that man. I searched my mind for how and it hit me as I pulled into the garage. "Oh my God." I parked and grabbed my phone. I scrolled through Iris's pictures on Fodoary as fast as my fingers and phone would go. "Holy shit, it's him." There wasn't a doubt in my mind. Even the red pickup was in a shot.

I stormed into the apartment, frustrated with just a hint of shock. I shouldn't have been surprised in the slightest. Signey lounged on the couch, flipping through a magazine.

"I hit him! I hit his truck!" I stomped my feet repeatedly and flailed my arms like a child having a temper tantrum. "I hit him!"

"Hit who?" Signey shouted over my stomping.

"Iris's stepdad!"

She shot up and tossed the magazine onto the coffee table. "What?" she asked, pressing her fists hard into the cushions.

"I just rear-ended Iris's stepdad," I said, finally stopping my tantrum. "And he couldn't have been nicer. And he couldn't have felt more familiar. What is this life?"

"Are you gonna tell her?"

I looked away from Signey and sighed heavily.

"No?" she asked.

I looked back at Signey. "She'd probably think I did it on purpose." I shook my head in disbelief and went into my bedroom.

19

One night, I had a dream so crystal clear that, had it not been so unusual, I could have mistaken it for a memory. I stood alone, high on a platform built of plywood. The room was small and wooden steps met the platform with the concrete floor below, where a group of men—including Michael and Travis—had gathered. One by one, a man would join me on my pedestal, and together, we'd all decide that he wasn't the one for me. Then he'd return down the steep steps.

I felt discouraged and turned away from the men. But just as I was losing all hope, I felt a hand on my shoulder. I turned to find Iris. She wore all white, like she often did in my dreams. She smiled, like an angel who knew the secrets of the Universe, and held out her hand. I placed mine in hers, and she led me down the stairs and out the door.

Hand in hand, we strolled into a world more vivid than anything my waking eyes had ever seen. Rolling hills were covered with the greenest grass and the greenest trees. The sky and a pond were the bluest of blue. It was bright and bold and flawless. After soaking it in, I looked at Iris. Our eyes remained locked, though I could sense our now naked bodies. She gently laid me down and I could almost feel her hands on my sleeping body. We made love over and over, and over and over again. I could feel our love across all realms.

TO BE HER GIRL

I woke in a state of pure bliss, keeping my eyes closed and reliving it in my mind until reality simply couldn't be fought any longer.

On the surface, Iris's gender didn't bother me. Romantic love between a man and a woman is no different than romantic love between any two others—no matter their gender, or lack of gender identity. But deep down, despite how I tried to deny it, I felt the nagging fit of difference—another piece of me standing on the outside of societal expectations. I truly never wanted anything other than to be with her; I just thought something had to give. My love was already outside the box.

But it wasn't long until I realized that the only thing that had to give—was me into myself. Because love *is* love. And, if anything, something finally made sense. There had always a part of me that knew that Iris—the one, the love of my life, my ultimate soulmate—was a woman. I figured that out after combing over past thoughts and feelings. It wasn't that I hadn't been listening; I just hadn't met her yet.

And so I was happy to love her. I was proud to love her. And I loved that she was a woman.

I didn't feel the need to address my sexuality publicly, to formally come out of the closet. I didn't think so anyway. The love I had for Iris was ours, but with my overwhelming desire to express it, the words continued to spill.

I often wondered if my parents had figured it out. They didn't have social media, and I never mentioned the gender-specific poems I'd been posting. If they knew, they never let on, and the nagging feeling of secrecy was constantly hovering over me. I wasn't trying to hide anything, but I wasn't openly sharing with those who loved me most. And suddenly I was aching to be open. I wrote them a lengthy story in a third-person narrative, detailing the love a girl had for another, and the connection that bound them. A brief postscript revealed that it was about Iris and me. They responded with love and were full of gratitude that I shared.

Labels are man-made. Love is not, I wrote. I had also penned an essay about sexuality, published by the webzine that held me as a freelance writer. They published me often after the one I worked for fell through the cracks of the internet, but it was the first piece they accepted in almost a year. The essay made no specific mention of Iris, but of everything I had written for them, it was the most personal.

And so my family read my truth. I knew it wouldn't make a lick of difference to them, but I shook uncontrollably as the acknowledgments poured in. I smoked a joint, went for a run, did some yoga, and even made an attempt at meditation. Nervousness rattled my bones, but I smiled the entire time.

20

I could see the reflection of the stars in her eyes, swirling and twinkling like a kaleidoscope. It was the only way I knew it was nighttime. I focused on nothing else. I could see nothing else. We just stared into each other's eyes forever.

Or at least until my alarm went off.

If it was only in my sleep that I could be with Iris, then I wanted to sleep forever. Except that morning, my alarm was warmly welcomed. I was New York bound.

My mom picked me up later that evening. I closed my eyes as we drove away from the airport, hoping to fall back into my dream.

"You missed a double rainbow yesterday," she said.

I opened my eyes. "I know. You sent me a picture."

"Did you know the Greek Goddess of the rainbow is called Iris?"

I closed my eyes again and rested my head against the window. "Yeah...I'm tired."

My mom fell silent and changed the radio station until what she heard satisfied her. It was Patti Smith Group's "Because the Night."

"Oh, here ya go," she said, bobbing her head along.

My heart soared as I remembered Iris dancing to the song at High Street.

Later that night, we opened a bottle of wine and my mom tried again. "So...what's she like?...Iris," she said.

"The Greek Goddess of the rainbow? You're the one into Greek mythology. Shouldn't you know?" I took a sip of my wine.

"Okay. You don't have to tell me." She sipped her wine.

"I don't know, it's just…" I shook my head with a smile. I didn't know what to say. She may have been a part of me, but technically, I barely knew her. "I wrote something on the plane," I said. "Do you want to hear it?"

She gave an affirmative nod.

"She was the kind of girl Bob Dylan wrote songs about. Down to earth, but bold in the most beautiful ways. She had an edge, but only the kind you felt when you weren't looking. If you paid close enough attention, you'd see that she was the purest of stardust, gliding through the air without cutting it."

"That's really good," she assured me. "Were you listening to Bob Dylan?"

"Yeah."

"Why's it in the past tense?"

"It's just a story," I said. "We're infinite." I pulled up a picture of Iris on my phone to show her. "It's still hard to believe how beautiful she is." And it was. I would think: Wow…That's her…That's the one…That's what she looks like…I never expected her…But what a beautiful surprise.

"Whoa, I thought that was you. I was about to ask when you had bangs," my mom said, taking my phone from my hand. "Yeah, she's gorgeous. You look alike. Same smile."

"I know, it's weird, but I can't compare to her. I swear she gets more beautiful every day."

"She looks a bit older than you though."

"Not really," I said. Iris looked much younger than her age, but then so did I. "She turned thirty-seven in May." I had figured out her age on the anniversary of her mom's passing. "So eleven and a half years."

"Oh."

"Oh, what?"

"That's a big difference."
"So," I said. I didn't care.
"Well, I hope you get your happy ending."
"There is no ending."
"Then a happily ever after." She smiled and sipped her wine.
"I'm going to marry her." I smiled and sipped my wine.

I stopped at the cemetery the next day. I stood at my grandparents' grave, unsure of what to say. I apologized for kicking the rock at Griffith Park and for nearly offing myself. "I just don't understand," I said, wondering if it even mattered. The only thing I knew for sure in life was that I loved Iris, and some days, that was enough.

I headed to The Pond afterward. "I thought it was very courageous of you," my aunt said, sitting on that old couch. "To be yourself in a world that tells you not to be—it's inspiring. You know we love you, and we're glad you are who you are."

"Thanks," I said with a faint smile. I was still hesitant to talk about Iris with my family. The circumstances were too perplexing to get into. To them, Iris was a photographer who I met at an art show, who I was madly in love with, but wasn't with for reasons beyond my control. Details of our irrefutable connection, the premonitions, the synchronicity, and our intertwined emotions were lacking. I shared with my parents through the email, but I didn't see the point in delving into it when Iris still wouldn't talk to me. I was afraid of sounding like a lunatic. "It's why I love Grandma's painting so much," I said. "Is that Ireland?" I pointed at the new one above the couch.

My uncle looked up at the painting above him and smiled. "Sure is."

"When was the last time you went back? I feel like it's been a while."

"Oh, a few years too many," he said, looking back at me.

"I remember when I asked you why you didn't live there anymore and you told me it was because I wasn't there."

"I remember that too," my aunt said. "You made me and the boys thank you for not having to live in Ireland."

I laughed. "I was like seven."

"It was never a lie," my uncle said, smiling.

He looked away from me and at my aunt, who had turned to him in the same breath. Suddenly I understood that it was because he loved her more than he loved Ireland, and that she was his home.

He returned his attention to me. "There are sacrifices and there are compromises, and love is worth a great deal of them," he said, as if he knew where my mind had gone.

I nodded and sighed.

"You need a minute?" my aunt asked.

I nodded again and went outside. I climbed into the rowboat and was drifting across the heart-shaped pond when I got a text message from Signey. *Have you checked Iris's Fodoary lately?*

No...trying not to. Why? I replied.

Check it

Iris had posted a photograph of two women sitting on a park bench. I didn't recognize either of them, but I recognized the park right away. It was Tompkins Square Park, just a few blocks from where Cora and Rhett lived, and from where I would be in just a matter of days. The caption read: *reunited. new york, new york. july 2014.*

Omg are you kidding me?? How is this even possible? I texted Signey.

So ridiculous! But so you two

I guess I can't be surprised anymore...but come on

Wonder how long she'll be there. Are you going to reach out to her?

I don't know...she doesn't seem to care

I wanted to scream, but my dad and Rebecca were sitting on their patio within earshot. I'd end up telling them after I stormed into the house anyway.

"Do you believe it's meant to be? That the two of you are meant to be together?" Rebecca asked.

"With every ounce of my being," I said.

"Then you just need a little patience."

My dad whistled "Patience" by Guns N' Roses and I glared at him with the fire of a thousand suns. He stopped.

"I know. I just miss her," I said.

My dad grabbed my head and kissed the top of it. "It'll be when it's supposed to be," he said before leaving the room.

"It's hard for him to see you hurting when there's nothing he can do," Rebecca said. "Are you planning on seeing Mason? Maybe you need a breather from her. Go have some fun."

I paused for a second, wondering if my stepmom was encouraging me to have sex with my ex-boyfriend. "Yeah, I think so. My friend, Ryder, lives there now too."

"That's good. Keep that heart and mind open."

I was madly in love with a woman I hardly knew, believed we were of one soul, and convinced we would spend the rest of our lives together based on a few meetings and chance happenings. I didn't think my heart or mind could open much further.

I went to the Falls on my last morning in town, which was something I rarely did and hadn't done in years. When something is in your backyard, it's easy to take for granted. But the surge of my emotions since learning that Iris was in New York City felt like the rush of the water, and it was calling my name. I felt one with the complexity of nature, the complexity of its simplicity. It had been almost two months since I told Iris, and I was still drowning in her silence.

My grandpa loved the Falls tirelessly and took Cora, my cousins, and me often when we were kids. As teenagers, it became a bore. When I was fourteen, I told him I didn't want to go, and I carried the sadness in his eyes for years.

The last time I had gone was with my grandparents and Grant five years earlier. Grant and I saw each other occasionally over summer break, but he had never visited the American side of the Falls. When he mentioned it at my grandparents' house, my grandpa jumped at the opportunity to show him. "What do you think, Miss Callahan?" he asked.

"Let's go," I said.

The memory of his smile would overtake the memory of his sad eyes from years before. He died just two days later.

Unlike my grandma's expected passing, his death caught us off guard. He wasn't exactly the picture of health, but we didn't anticipate his heart attack either. It was only my grandma who didn't seem to be crippled by shock. Standing before the Falls five years later, I wondered if she had known, in the way I knew Iris, if they felt each other rushing through their bloodstream, as I felt her.

I watched an elderly couple, who stood about ten feet to my right, and remembered something that my grandpa had said to me that day five years earlier. I remembered it so suddenly that it felt like he was telling me again. "Chances are it'll feel like the wrong time, but don't worry, the right love will find you at the right time." I had been telling him about my recent split from Mason.

"I found Mason at the right time," I told him.

"Was he the right love?" he asked, already knowing my answer.

"He was at the time."

"Well, timing is funny. It has the power to either keep you sane or drive you mad."

"Or both at the same time." I laughed, unaware of the ripple that Iris's timing would create four years later. Finding her was both. She was the cement block around my feet and my life jacket, simultaneously.

"That's true," he agreed. "You go through life thinking it's one thing, and then one day, it's just not anymore. But that doesn't mean it's not what it's supposed to be."

As we left the Falls that day, I knelt down to pick a flower, but my grandma stopped me, insisting I needed to let it grow. I had forgotten how finicky she always was about it. She loved to garden and its analogies always crept into her advice. Whenever I complained about growing up, as I thought it was taking much too long, she'd say, "Flowers don't bloom before they're ready. They won't last if they do." One time I made a snarky remark about flowers only being seasonal anyway, so she said, "Oh, but the seeds." I could never outwit her.

    I tried to focus on my grandparents' advice, but my heart felt like a ticking time bomb. If time is a line, then life is a maze, I thought; a twisted, complicated, jumbled up maze.

21

When I arrived in New York City, I considered telling Iris that I was in town. Instead, I just posted a picture on Fodoary and hoped she'd see it.

Cora and Rhett were still at work when I got to their place, but Jerry-Garcia greeted me at the door on his hind legs. He'd skipped doggy daycare that day just for me. He followed me into the guest room where we both passed out on the bed. I woke a few hours later to Cora rummaging through my backpack and Jerry-Garcia nowhere to be found. "Umm, hi," I said, sitting up. "What are you doing?"

"Oh, hey, sorry," she said. "Do you have a lighter?"

"No, I don't. And it's nice to see you too." For the amount of detail they paid attention to, she and Rhett somehow lost lighters like a needle in a haystack. "Oh, wait." I reached over and pulled open the nightstand drawer, taking out the lighter that I hid in January. "Here you go," I said, handing it to her.

We made our way into the living room. Jerry-Garcia was curled up on the couch with his favorite stuffed animal, a blue squirrel I'd gotten him for Christmas. Cora scooched him off, and we took his place on the couch. I hoped to spend less time on it than I had on my last visit.

"Rough day?" I asked, watching Cora roll a joint on her coffee table.

"Nope, just a long one," she said. I thought both she and Rhett worked too much, but it afforded them a nice lifestyle that I could dip my toes into from time to time. "I'm glad you're here now though," she said, passing me the joint.

"Iris is in town," I said after I took a hit.

"What? Why?" she asked, taking the joint from my fingers.

"I don't know. I guess because I'm here. That's how it seems to work."

"Did you tell her?" she asked before she took a hit.

"No. I'm tired of talking to a ghost. I'm trying to get through to somebody who can't even get through to herself."

"That's the way you see it," she said, holding out the joint.

"Whose side are you on?"

Cora rolled her eyes just as Rhett came bolting through the door. He closed it behind him while Jerry-Garcia howled and spun in circles. Rhett gripped me from the side, momentarily lifting me off the couch. "Alright, let's get Cal off this couch," he said.

"I think you just did," I said, adjusting myself back into my cross-legged position. I took the joint and inhaled.

Rhett kissed Cora on the top of her head and rubbed the top of Jerry-Garcia's. "How's L.A.?" he asked, walking into the kitchen.

"It's good," I said. "How's the architecture?"

I passed the joint back to Cora. Jerry-Garcia watched like he wanted in on the action. She took another hit and exhaled. Jerry-Garcia bit at the smoke.

Rhett leaned on the counter that separated the kitchen from the living room. He nodded his head and said, "It's good," in the same tone I had used. He always said that I didn't converse enough, which was only true half of the time. I talked too much or not at all.

"Well, that's good," I said. "Looking forward to all the buildings."

The first time I met Rhett, I was nineteen, and he gave me a bear hug so tight that I thought my insides might explode. And I swore he knew every detailed fact about every New York building. I'd just smile and say, "Oh, wow," whenever he told me about the arch of a doorway or the history of a bridge. I considered introducing him and Ryder, just to see who could out-talk the other.

Cora passed the joint to me and I took another hit. I tried to pass it back, but she waved her hand and shook her head no. I finished it while she and Rhett shared the details of their day. Afterward, they took me to a nice little Chinese restaurant and all I could think about was how Iris had once mentioned on social media that Chinese food was her favorite. Ugh, I'm so annoying, I thought to myself. I couldn't even remember what I thought about before her.

I woke the next morning to the smell of fresh blueberry pancakes. I may have been a failure in the kitchen, but Cora was anything but. She could whip up a delicious meal from scratch and make it seem effortless, even enjoyable. I hated cooking.

"I don't understand how you get by," she said. "You need to learn."

"Cora, I burn soup," I said while smothering my pancakes with maple syrup. "I'm a lost cause."

"Do you want some eggs?" she asked.

I cringed and shook my head no. I wondered if Iris liked eggs.

"What do you even eat? Anything of substance?" Rhett asked.

"I eat kale," I said.

"So you're a cannibal," he said before shoving a forkful of pancake into his mouth.

"Hey, don't take that away from her," Cora said. "She once survived an entire summer on cereal alone."

"I think the key word there is survived," I said.

Rhett laughed, and then sipped his coffee. I wondered if Iris liked coffee, or if she was a tea drinker like me.

I let out a sigh and took a bite of my pancake, exhausted by my constant thoughts of Iris. Sometimes she didn't even feel like a person, but this lingering presence that controlled my life. No matter how hard I tried to stay present, she was always lurking.

TO BE HER GIRL

Mason lived in the Williamsburg neighborhood of Brooklyn, just across the East River from Cora and Rhett's East Village apartment. After dodging him over the holidays, I figured I should give him a call. He offered to come into Manhattan, but I wanted to take the ferry.

He took me to a pizza joint a few blocks away from his place. I sat across from him in a small corner booth, feeling both comforted and sad. I was filled with nostalgia, but my mind was still with Iris. She overwhelmed my memories of him like she'd been there all along.

"How's the museum?" I asked, trying to distract myself.

"It's good," he said before devouring half a breadstick in one bite.

"So history is still the same?" I joked.

"There's always something new to learn." He grinned and devoured the other half of the breadstick. "How's the writing? Any new articles?"

He handed me the opportunity to bring up my love for Iris on a silver platter, had I wanted to discuss the same-sex love essay. "Not in a while," I said. It was an easily proved lie, but I wasn't ready to talk about it with him. Like my parents and Michael, he didn't have social media, so I didn't figure he read any of my poems about Iris.

"Blocked?" he asked.

"Mummified."

"Dead?"

"I'd like to think I'm preserving what I've got for later. I'm just trying to speak your language," I said with a laugh. "I'm glad you're doing so well. A good job and all. How about a wife and kids? You got a wife and kids somewhere I don't know about? How about a house in the Hamptons?"

Mason laughed and wiped the marinara sauce from the corner of his mouth. "Not that I'm aware of," he said. "How about you? A wife and kids somewhere?"

"Not that I'm aware of."

After dinner, we went back to his apartment, and I was suddenly craving his attention. His shaggy light brown hair was teasing me as it dangled in front of his green eyes. In college, I'd brush it to the side and then he'd shake his head with a smile, causing it to fall back into place. I was admiring it and thinking about those days as we lounged on his couch watching some horrible movie and drinking cheap beer.

"What?" he asked through his crooked smile.

He caught me watching him instead of the movie.

"Nothing," I said, then took a sip of my beer. "It's just good to see you."

A few minutes later, he was on top of me with my subtle invitation. Nothing seemed to change. His lips were just as soft and his tongue still mingled perfectly with mine, yet I felt something was missing in our kiss. The chemistry we once shared was either dead and gone, or we just couldn't find it. I thought it must have been mutual until he pulled back and looked into my eyes like he did when we were eighteen. My necklace with Iris's birthstone rested upon my chest, and he dragged his fingers along the chain. Iris and I had never been together, but suddenly it felt like I was cheating on her. I realized then that it always had. I felt an absurd sense of guilt.

"I've missed you," he whispered.

I gripped his wandering hands to hinder their southbound journey. No matter how drawn to him I still was, I knew I had to pull back. I couldn't use him as a distraction, and I couldn't pretend to focus—not with him. My body craved him, but my heart was still elsewhere.

After more kissing, I tilted my head to the side and gave him a slight smile. He lay beside me and rested his head on my chest, signaling his surrender. We'd been together enough for him to recognize I was done. He was always so patient with me in college, and it'd make me want to kiss him again. Except it didn't that night. It wasn't his head I wanted riding my heartbeat.

We lay in silence as the flickering light of the television bounced off the walls of his living room. I watched the ceiling fan spin ferociously above us as Mason lay still beside me. I wanted to want him, but I wanted Iris more. I imagined what it'd be like to have her rest her head on my chest, for her hair to tickle my skin, and I couldn't help but smile.

I could even smell her. It was a sensation that had been coming to me for months. It wasn't the smell of lavender alone, but a deeper scent, like lavender mixed with sandalwood and a pinch of vanilla. I could never pull it from air; it came like the wind, but I knew it was her. I'd freeze and soak it in, stopping time until it faded. Sometimes I was so overwhelmed by her scent that it'd line the walls of my mouth and fill it full, allowing me to taste her from a world away. Her taste swirled with Mason's that night, leaving me dizzy.

"You're still a mystery, Callahan Thomas," he said, apparently catching my momentary bliss.

"I'm an open book," I said, sitting up.

He laughed as he sat up.

"Okay, I'm an open book with fine print," I said.

"That you are."

"It was good to see you, Mason, but I think I'm gonna head out."

"That you are," he repeated, smiling and shaking his head.

He got me an Uber and I snuck back into Cora's by midnight. I went into the guest room where Jerry-Garcia was asleep on the bed. I fit my body around his and stared blankly into the dark room.

I felt empty.

The next night, I met Ryder in Midtown for dinner. He asked about Signey but seemed happy with his move. He worked at his family's gallery, where we would attend a show afterward. I wondered if Iris would be there, and I couldn't deny that I hoped she would be. I considered asking Ryder, but instead, my thoughts just echoed what my grandma always said: "What will be, will be."

After dinner, we walked to the gallery before breezing by the crowd in front of it. It had the same look as the one on Melrose, only it was much smaller. Ryder promised not to leave my side, as I didn't know anybody else there, but he did. I felt shaky and scanned the room for a bar. I didn't see one.

Alone in the crowded space, I wandered the gallery. I surveyed the bright and bold paintings, unaware of their meanings. I figured they all must have one. Strokes and splashes of colors decorated the once blank canvasses. Some were tight and inside the lines; others were boundless and followed no structure. I followed them around the corner and into a room I hadn't known was there. It was full of abstract sculptures. They reminded me of Ryder's metal pieces, though they were much larger and vaster in material and design.

I studied a piece with two thick silver beams. They were bound to the base below them, encased within a thin ring connecting the base to the top. The beams each had a wavy edge, facing each other and curved in opposite places, as if it were one piece split in two. Between them was one golden block, attached at the center, and two smaller silver ones, each fastened toward the top of their respective beams. Two minds, one heart, I thought. It was called *One Flame*. I looked to my left and saw Iris standing in the corner.

Every fiber of my being had felt her presence before my eyes confirmed it. I walked to the opposite corner, unsure of what to do. My knees nearly gave out, and suddenly I was grateful for Ryder's abandonment.

She was with the two girls from her photograph—including Felicity Ross, who was not only one of the featured artists, but the creator of the piece I was admiring.

I wanted to approach Iris. I wanted to scream and shake her and knock some sense into her. I wanted her to see that the Universe would keep putting us in the same place at the same time, no matter what we did or where we went.

Instead, I just watched her as she kept her back to me. She wore tight navy blue pants and a form-fitting white top. Her hair was straight, which it rarely was. With every catch of her face, I was transported back to the night we met when I studied it so carefully, unaware of what the woman behind it would come to mean to me. Everything.

I admired her hand as it held a glass of wine. I wanted to be that glass, held by her so tightly, and I wanted to be that wine as it touched her lips and her tongue. I just wanted her to want me back. She took a sip as she jokingly raised her pinky. She still gave me butterflies, with just the lift of her finger. When I saw her laugh, I knew I had to leave. As I walked away, I felt like a fish out of water, gasping for one last breath. She was my air supply. She was my everything. And I didn't even know if I was her anything.

I wasn't sure if she saw me, and as I searched for Ryder, I didn't know if I even wanted her to. I thanked Ryder for having me, but told him I had a headache and needed some sleep.

I stood outside the gallery, unfazed by my lack of umbrella in the downpour. I paced from puddle to puddle, feeling the water seep through my shoes. It dripped down my face and soaked my hair and my clothes. Still, I couldn't leave. I rounded the block again and again for an hour. I couldn't even be anywhere near Iris without the gravitational pull yanking my heart out of my chest.

In a numbed daze, I eventually walked the two miles back to the apartment. The raindrops were a substitute for the tears that wouldn't fall. I figured she had already stolen them all.

I strolled into the apartment like a sopping wet dog. Even Jerry-Garcia seemed to cringe. Rhett took him into the bedroom and left Cora to deal with me while I stood dripping in the kitchen. I stuck my head under the faucet and chugged the filtered water that poured out of it. Cora looked at me like the time I had stumbled into the house drenched and drunk when I was fourteen.

I changed into dry clothes and sat with Cora on the couch. I explained what happened and her immediate response was, "Maybe it's for the best that you left her alone."

"I just don't understand," I said like a broken record. I was afraid it'd be my epitaph. I could see it so clearly: *She didn't understand* engraved into my tombstone.

"What don't you understand?" Cora asked.

"Nothing happened. We keep winding up in the same place… and nothing."

"If you could say anything to her right now, what would it be?"

I shook my head in contempt at her stupid question. I wasn't in the mood for a therapy session.

"Well, maybe that's it," she said after my silence.

"I just want her to believe," I whispered.

"Maybe she's just not ready to."

22

I might not have told Iris that I was at the gallery while we were at the gallery, but as soon as I got back to Los Angeles, I sent her another email.

July 26, 2014
Iris,

 For years, my dad and a few other relatives have lived on the same property in New York. Gracing the center, between the houses, is a pond in the shape of a heart. My grandpa had it crafted as a gift for my grandma. Decades later, I'd ask him the occasion. He simply smiled and said, "It was Tuesday." He never needed a reason to shower her with love. The pond was something of beauty that he wanted for her.

 I was floating across that heart-shaped pond when I found out you were in New York City. It was only a few days before my own planned visit, and Ryder had already invited me to the show at the gallery. I didn't know your friend would be a part of it, or that you'd be there.

 Her piece called 'One Flame' struck me. I was admiring it when I turned to find you, not far from where I stood. Eventually I left and roamed the Manhattan streets back to my sister's apartment in the rain. I knew I needed to leave you alone, but honestly, I stood outside for a while, hoping you'd come out and find me. Of course you never did.

 In a matter of weeks, I've twice agonized over you falling before my eyes, far from our homes here in Los Angeles. But maybe it wasn't nothing. I don't believe in coincidences; I believe in the cosmos. What do you believe in?

It'll be a while before I can drift across that pond again, but its sentiment reaches me every day. The earth is ever-evolving, and both my grandpa and grandma have passed on, but their love will live forever.

I don't know where fate and free will meet, but shall I ever figure it out, I hope you'll meet me there.
Callahan

    I hoped that would be it. She might respond this time, I thought. But after almost a week of waiting, I left comments for her on old Fodoary posts because she hadn't—inconsiderate words about how much pain I was in and how she was the only one who could help. I was drunk and bitter. I was hurt and angry and afraid. I deleted them the next morning, but I could feel the ache in my bones. She read them.

    "Oh! I forgot to tell you," Signey said as we sat at the table later that day. "Annie's pregnant again...On purpose this time."

    "Aw, good for her," I said. "Is she gonna keep working there?"

    "Well, yeah. Why not?"

    "I don't know. I guess that was kind of sexist." I cringed at myself. "I just think it'd be funny to see a pregnant woman behind a bar ...serving you alcohol."

    "Well, life is funny." Signey smiled and stood up.

    "I guess so. And hey, maybe she'll get better tips."

    Signey laughed and walked into her bedroom. She came back out with rolling papers and a grinder filled with weed. She sat back down and rolled a joint while I stared at my grandma's painting. I had rescued it from the closet only a few days after I shunned it.

    "I sent Iris another letter," I said, admitting only to the heartfelt words I thought over and not the hurtful ones I didn't.

    "Did she say anything?" Signey asked. She tried to coat her voice with hope, but we both knew she had lost it. Her defeated optimism made me feel like a failure, like I had let her down. If a connection as strong as mine and Iris's couldn't prevail, what could?

"No." I turned to find her handing me the freshly rolled joint.

"I'm sorry...But what more can you do?"

"I don't know. Sometimes I still don't know what I'm supposed to feel, let alone do." I picked up a lighter and lit the joint. I took a hit and passed it back. "Did I ever tell you my yearbook senior quote?"

She shook her head no as she inhaled.

"Either my heart is on my sleeve or it's all an illusion."

"Who said that?" she asked after blowing smoke into the air.

"I did."

"You wear it well."

"Do I? What's it gotten me? I think it's just shattered pieces taped to my arm at this point."

"You put yourself out there. You did what you thought you had to do, and that's more than a lot of people can say. So like I said, what more can you do?" She sighed and passed the joint back.

"I guess I can try harder." I took a hit as my eyes returned to the painting.

"How?"

I exhaled slowly, fearing the words that were following the smoke through my lips. "By letting go."

After we finished the joint, I went into my bedroom and stared at my reflection in the mirror. It was getting hard to recognize who was looking back at me. I picked up my guitar, sat on my bed, and with the capo on the fourth fret, I strummed and picked and plucked those strings until my fingers were raw and strained. Slowly at first, but eventually at a pace that was matched only by my swirling thoughts. The words raced through my mind, but I couldn't stop strumming. The tears streamed down my face, so I shut my eyes even tighter. Playing music was supposed to be when I didn't have to think. Why wouldn't the words leave me alone? I just wanted to strum the pain out of me.

When my fingers couldn't strum anymore, I set aside my guitar and sat at my desk. I took out the pink journal from the drawer. The letter I tore from those pages was the only time it had been used.

August 2, 2014

Dear Iris,

The thing is, I'm just a fucked up girl in a fucked up world who doesn't know how to handle what was placed before me. You. I am so sorry for the words I spewed at you recently, whether you saw them or not. It was like I touched the fire and then blamed you for getting burned. It wasn't fair. But beyond that, everything I have ever said to you has been true, but often sad and desperate.

Honestly, I don't understand what I'm becoming. Your happiness is my greatest wish, but I think I often forget that your happiness is of your own choosing. And right now, your life has nothing to do with me, no matter who I believe us to be.

I just want to move on. I've accepted that I will always hurt. But I want to move on. It's a process, but I am trying. There's just been this nagging feeling that something has been left unsaid, but maybe it's supposed to be. There could never be enough words anyway. Or maybe we just don't need any.

Sometimes it feels as though the earth is spinning without me. That's how the world feels knowing you're out there, but being unable to reach you. I guess I'll just tread the best I can. I don't know what will happen in this life, but I know that you are a part of me, and this story is far from over.

I love you, Iris. I always have, and I always will.

Love,
Callahan

I tore the letter from the journal and grabbed my lighter. I went into the bathroom and stood in the tub, where Iris had once appeared with our envisioned children. I held my lighter to the crisp white paper, but the flame wouldn't keep. I went back into my bedroom and with singed edges, I let the letter cool and tucked it away in the back of my desk drawer.

I got higher and listened to The Civil Wars' *Barton Hollow* album on repeat for four hours. "To Whom It May Concern" reminded

TO BE HER GIRL

me of Iris. Everything reminded me of Iris. It felt like a good antidote, but around hour two of my binge, I dug out the letter, took its picture, and emailed it to Iris. I wanted to leave her alone, but I wanted to apologize. I just couldn't stop. I wanted her to live her life, but selfishly, I wanted her to know it would lead to me. Trying to let her go was like ripping my heart out of my chest, but only being able to hold it as far away as my arm was long.

It wasn't until hour four that I realized I had said, "I love you." It was a given, but I had danced around those three words so delicately. I didn't regret it, but I knew she wouldn't respond. I couldn't fool myself anymore. Perhaps letting go was impossible, but moving on wasn't, I thought—I hoped.

23

Signey's and my favorite thing to do together was to blast the stereo in the living room, take turns on the song choice, and move until we couldn't move anymore. We'd drag out my mini trampoline and had four hula hoops between the two of us. We'd drink beer and sweat out our emotions. They were our own personal dance parties. One night had been especially memorable because Paige had posted a video of Iris hula hooping. I just rolled my eyes and got back to spinning my hips.

The next day was the second Saturday of August, and I was incredibly restless. I had gotten a sound night of sleep after an evening of dancing with Signey, but the morning air felt heavy. The summer seemed to drag on, and I just wanted it to be whenever I saw Iris next.

I walked into the living room, which was still occupied by the trampoline and hula hoops. Signey sat on the floor with art supplies sprawled out around her. Her time with Ryder had relit a spark that had been dimming inside her. She made jewelry again and was always crafting something. That morning, it was a large canvas painting. The problem was, her easel was broken and my small one wasn't large enough. I painted only occasionally and always on a small canvas. Typically, I'd just splashed color on the canvas and swirl it around. Signey had patience that I couldn't muster, and frustration would always kill my vision.

I loved to witness her rediscover her talents, but that morning, I found myself annoyed with the newspapers protecting our living room floor from her artistic vision. She apologized but virtually ignored me after I grunted when tripping on an empty plastic bag. She knew when to let my grumpiness be, especially when it came out of nowhere. She had once muttered, "Somebody woke up on the wrong side of the bed," under her breath, and it escalated into a bitter argument that left us both distraught.

That morning, I couldn't gather if it was Iris's anguish or my own. Sometimes the line was so incredibly blurred. But other times it was dramatic, swinging to either side of our shared spectrum. I was still learning to decipher the difference.

I made breakfast, even though eating felt insignificant, and sat at the table. My grandma's painting stared at me, drowning me with those pivotal waves, as I slowly sipped my cup of hot tea. Even the sound of my own breath was annoying me, but Signey had Joni Mitchell spinning on the record player, and her pure voice singing about life's illusions comforted me.

After I finished my tea, and without much thought, I packed my backpack with a bottle of water, the pink journal, a few joints, and some snacks.

"Where are you going?" Signey asked.

"I don't know yet," I said.

She nodded and carried on with her abstract painting. But I knew exactly where I was going. I was going to Wren. I was going to that beach. It was noon and I could reach it before dark. I was so determined that I didn't even consider I didn't know where along the coast it was, or that it'd be nearly impossible to uncover after the sun went down.

"Meet me there, Iris," I said under my breath.

"What?" Signey asked.

I shook my head and then grabbed a pillow and blanket from my bedroom.

"Don't be stupid," she said when I came back out. The casualness in her voice irritated me more than the words.

"Don't get paint on the floor," I said.

She shook her head then returned to her painting.

I said, "Bye," like I was being forced to and stormed out.

I drove and I drove and I drove. Then I realized how ridiculous it was and called myself an idiot, shouting over the stereo in my car. Iris would not be at that beach, no matter how hard I tried to tell her, telepathically, to be. I made it through the Angeles National Forest before I turned around. I hightailed it east to Lancaster and eventually landed somewhere near Joshua Tree.

I stopped at a small restaurant called Outskirts to grab a bite to eat for dinner. It was rustic and in the middle of nowhere—the only place to eat for miles, I presumed. I couldn't figure out what it was on the outskirts of. I stepped out of my car to discover the air was hot and dry. It must have been at least one hundred degrees, yet it still felt lighter than the air I woke to. It was dusty, but I could breathe. The restaurant's wooden exterior matched the interior, which matched the tables and the bar. The stools were aged and worn and likely hadn't been replaced in decades. I loved its authenticity and felt like I stepped back in time as I entered through the batwing doors.

There was a lone customer sitting at the bar—a man who must have been in his forties, dressed in a bedazzled fringe tank top and white high water pants. He had slicked-back black hair, like a Jheri curl matted down with layers of gel, and multiple earrings in each ear. A long white feather rested behind his right. His dark skin appeared to be covered with sweat, but the closer I got, the more I realized it was glitter. It was just enough to make him sparkle. "Wooo, it's hot outside, isn't it?" he exclaimed as I sat down a couple of bar stools over.

"Yeah, sure is," I said. I gave him a faint smile and picked up the menu, which was only one laminated page.

"You just passing through?" he asked, swirling a handful of french fries in a bowl of ketchup.

"Something like that." I nodded, then traced the words on the menu with my finger. There was less than a handful of things to choose from.

"What can I get you?" the waitress behind the bar asked. She had a kind face and wore a pale blue blouse that matched her eyes. The name *Gloria* was sewn over her left breast with a red thread. She had disheveled blonde hair and her bangs stuck to the sweat on her forehead. I guessed that she was in her thirties, but her eyes looked like they had seen so much more than her years. There was a stirring sadness in the air that surrounded her.

"Just a cheeseburger and some fries," I said.

"Anything to drink?"

Her simple question brought me to a pause. Yeah, whiskey, please, I thought. But I asked only for water. I figured it best since I had smoked a joint before I came inside. She nodded and disappeared into the kitchen, leaving just me and the exuberant man sitting to my left.

"Dalfour Hickey," he said.

"I'm sorry, what?" I said.

"That's my name!" He laughed. "In case you were wondering."

I wasn't. I thought it to be an odd name, even made up maybe.

"Oh…Hi…I'm Callahan," I said, reluctantly.

"Well, it is so nice to meet you, Callahan. Can I call you Cali?"

"Please don't," I said with a light but forced smile.

He laughed again. He had a loud laugh, a cackle really, one I'd never forget. "Do you travel often?"

"Not really…You?" I figured he would force me into a conversation, so I might as well cooperate.

"Oh, heavens yes! I've been everywhere. Up. Down. Left. Right. You name it, I've been there."

He got into a long narrative about backpacking across Europe, horseback riding in Australia, and hitchhiking to New York City. I thought he was either batshit crazy and believed his own lies, or the most interesting man I had ever met. But the more he spoke, the more I believed it was the latter, and that every single word jumping from his mouth was true. Either way, I was drawn into his orbit, captivated by his stories and with the enthusiasm in which he told them.

"So you go everywhere alone?" I asked.

"Oh, I'm never alone. I make friends everywhere I go," he said. I could believe that. He sucked me in, after all. "It was a promise I made to someone, to see the world."

"And they couldn't see it with you, I take it?" I asked cautiously and caught a glimmer of sadness in his bright brown eyes.

"His name was Henry. He was the love of my life." Dalfour Hickey stared forward. He was silent for the first time since I sat down beside him. And for the first time since our conversation began, I thought of Iris. "It was cancer," he continued, looking back at me. "It came on fast and it came on strong. We made plans to travel the world, but he was gone within a month. I've seen a lot, but there's still so much more world out there." His voice had grown somber, yet still enthusiastic. "Wooo," he said, pushing on through. "Do you hear that, Henry? Much, much more."

Gloria refilled my water glass and gave Dalfour Hickey a sorrowful look. I could feel the comradery in the air between us. Three tattered souls wearing the same spirit, differently.

"I'm sorry about Henry," I said.

And then he told me all about him. They met in art school. San Francisco, 1988. Henry had been ostracized by his family after confessing that he was in love with another man. Dalfour Hickey was from a well-off, supportive family and vowed that Henry would never be without. They spent six years together, living and breathing art and love, but never traveled outside California together. After the diagnosis, they dreamed up vacations. And after Henry's untimely death, Dalfour Hickey spent the next two decades going on them. And much, much more.

"You still seem so happy," I said.

"That's because I am happy!" He cackled.

"But don't you wish he was with you?"

"Oh, he's always with me," he said, placing his hand over his heart. "Even death couldn't do us part."

The tears welled up in my eyes and I told him all about Iris. The love of Dalfour Hickey's life was dead, but he still loved it. The love of mine was very much alive, but I felt deader than a doornail without her.

Much like Iris's arrival into my life, Henry had appeared during a trying time in his, like the sun peeking through the clouds. I echoed the words about love's timing that my grandpa had left me with and said, "Life happens when you least expect it to, I guess."

"Look around, child," he insisted. "Life is always happening."

I allowed a brief smile to flash across my face. "I guess."

"You have to shift your perspective, sweet Callahan. Do you think I was this jubilant after Henry died? No! I didn't get out of bed for two long months. But I loved Henry and Henry wanted me to see the world, so I got up one day, took a cab to the airport, and boarded the first plane they'd let me on. My heart was beating a little slower, but it was still beating."

I sighed. "Did you…ever find anybody else?"

"Of course, Callahan." He cackled. "Oh, of course." He smiled and appeared lost in his thoughts for a moment. "I loved another, but some people are only meant for a little while. I'll find it again though. Love is a cycle. It'll always come back around."

I remained silent, doubting I could ever love another.

"Not that I need to," he continued. "I have me. And I have Henry. His love still surges inside me. Twenty years without his physical presence hasn't changed that. It's just evolved into something different. I still feel him."

"I understand that." I reached for the bill that Gloria had left for me long before.

Dalfour Hickey placed his hand over it and cackled loudly.

I laughed and allowed him to pull the bill his way. "Thank you, Dalfour Hickey."

He took the feather from behind his ear and handed it to me. "Love is meant to be freeing."

―――――

Instead of pulling up to the beach at sundown, I pulled into my garage. A day trek across Southern California left me feeling refreshed and at ease, albeit tired. After showering and resting for a bit, I sent Grant a lengthy text message, detailing my day, even joking about my absurd thought of meeting Iris at the beach. *I knew she wasn't there*, I wrote. *I just wanted to believe I could will us into the same place. Don't worry…I'm over that. How was the concert?* He and Daniella had gone to a show at The Wiltern that night. They'd invited me to come along, but it sold out before I got a ticket.

It was phenomenal. She just gets better and better, Grant replied. *And it's a good thing you didn't drive all the way up there. Iris was working at the Wiltern tonight…*

Of course, I texted back, *of fucking course*

I lay in bed, swirling Dalfour Hickey's feather between the tips of my fingers and wondering what would have happened had I gone to the show that night. But I knew my night had gone as it was meant to. Perhaps our free will is already our fate, I thought, merged like the sea meeting the sky.

24

Sometimes I would watch myself cry. I would watch the water well up in my eyes and then watch it fall. The slower the tear slid down my face, the more satisfaction I got. I was still alive. I was pushing on, slowly, but still fighting. Sometimes I just needed to feel it, to feel it all—everything that came along with Iris—love, pain, and the whole wild ride. Staring into the mirror was staring down my despair. I was nothing, but I was everything. It was pathetically satisfying.

Dalfour Hickey had been a light in my dim summer, and I did my best to abide by his advice—to shift my perspective. I was trying to find a little peace of mind, piece by piece. But without closure, I couldn't seem to sew the pieces together.

I didn't post much anymore, but Iris made a few references to my letters on Fodoary. Or so it seemed. I couldn't even be certain she had read them. We were always riding the same wavelength, so it could have been nothing, though that would contradict one of our similar notions. Not only had she captioned a photograph of the sky with: *meet me there*, after I wrote those three words to her, but she captioned another with: *maybe it wasn't nothing*, which I wrote after our corresponding trips. But whenever I saw oasis approaching, I was thrust into a mirage. She still eluded me. I couldn't even wonder anymore. It hurt to. It felt like a million little pins poking at my brain.

I watched my tears in the mirror a few nights after my drive. Iris had captioned a photograph of the open road with: *move on*, and it absolutely gutted me. Had it been my blood she was out for, we would have been drowning in it.

I couldn't be sure of anything, but I was cracking. I was torn between wanting to forget her, and the fact that I never could. My blood, sweat, and tears were flowing through the cracks as I tried to reach her.

I sat down at my desk and tried to write, something I hadn't been doing at all, but couldn't even string two words together. *Help* was all I wrote. The blinking line after it tortured me. "That's all I've got," I said to it. It kept blinking like a bully taunting me on the playground.

Later that night, I lay still in bed and opened my eyes suddenly from a fantasy about Iris. It was 1:08 a.m. I couldn't sleep and hadn't at all. I stared into the darkness for a few moments before there was a bright flash of light in the center of my bedroom. Had I blinked, I would have missed it. It was diamond-shaped with long and lean points and radiated a warmth that I felt deep in my bones. I stared, unsure what I had just seen, but felt no need to question it. I felt safe and comfortable, as if the arms of an angel were wrapped around me. I had no thoughts and felt only contentment. It was pure love, untouched by the harshness of the world. After a while of uninterrupted bliss, I drifted to sleep with a smile decorating my face, like the Universe, itself, had painted it. It didn't feel surreal in the slightest. In fact, nothing had ever felt more real.

That evening, I went to Grant's after work. Daniella was out of town, but she left him an assortment of pre-cooked meals, and I had every intention of taking advantage of them.

"It felt like she was glowing inside me," I said while we waited for our pesto-crusted chicken strips to heat up.

"Like the night I was singing?" Grant asked.
"No. There was a healing comfort to it. It wasn't intense like that night. It just was. It was beautiful."

It had been back in early April when it felt like Iris was restlessly turning inside my body. We were writing a song while Grant strummed his guitar. Like usual, I started talking about Iris, and so he sang a song to her from my perspective. That was when I started to feel it—to feel her in a way I never had before. "I feel weird," I said softly.

"Should I stop?" he asked.

"No. You're actually comforting it. It's just that same feeling I've been having lately...like she's in distress...and I'm just trying to ...like she's upset about something."

"I'm not much of a thief, but I'd do anything to steal your pain," he sang. It was shortly after her split from Brooks, though I hadn't yet known it. He kept singing and he kept strumming. I felt weirder and weirder.

As his voice stuttered, I softly insisted, "Keep going. She feels it."

"*She* feels it?" he asked, before beginning to sing again. "Maybe I can't see who you are to me, and maybe I don't know what my eyes do show, or maybe it's that I'm afraid of you, my earth angel, my sky of blue," he sang, more vibrant and louder than he had all night. The lyrics poured out of him like he had known them his entire life, though they were born only as he sang.

He stopped strumming and held this hand firmly over the strings. "This is weird," he said. "It's like I'm writing from Iris. And I'm not saying that I am. It just feels like I'm writing from someone, which is a strange sensation." He said it so casually. "Are you okay?"

"Keep going," I whispered. My body was hunched over as if I couldn't carry the weight inside me.

He carried on for another minute before singing, "I'm just taken aback..." as I felt whatever was going on inside me cease. "Oh, I think I lost it," he said after the words slipped away. "You okay?" he calmly asked again. "I don't want you to ride on whatever I channel ...because I don't know what it is." My silence concerned him. "Talk to me, Cal."

It would be another minute before I said, "I'm just waiting for the words." My body was still top-heavy as I rested my elbows on my knees, unable to move or even lift my head. The sound of my heavy breathing interrupted the gaps of silence. We had been audio recording it all, and I'd listen to it occasionally, whenever I needed a reminder. "She's struggling with so much," I said. I spoke without thought that night. I had no way of knowing what was going on with Iris. I just felt it.

Much like the nonchalance that he thought he was channeling Iris, the flash of light didn't perplex Grant. I'd insist on explaining the lack of an earthly light source and my sobriety anyway. As he flipped back and forth through his books, and combed through his own thoughts and feelings, he kept coming to the same conclusion.

"A Guardian Angel," he said. "But that doesn't necessarily mean it was someone who has passed. Our consciousness is layered, and the soul is both the simplest and most complicated thing there is. The energy, the light, the source...I think it's all beyond human comprehension."

"It was Iris," I said.

He nodded his head.

"I feel selfish," I said.

"Why?"

"You know...for telling her everything when maybe she's just not ready to know...Maybe I'm not even ready. I probably just made her think I'm crazy."

"Probably." He laughed lightly, but I was afraid that he meant it.

TO BE HER GIRL

I sighed and shook my head.

"Don't worry about it so much," he said.

"It's just…I want us to be together, ya know, but something keeps reminding me that we're never actually apart."

"Loneliness is an exhausting illusion, isn't it?"

I sighed softly under my breath. "I just want to be with her so bad, for real, ya know."

"I know…Just let it be, Cal…Let it be."

―――

Drifting to sleep that night, I thought of all the ways she had come to me throughout my life, since the birth of my mind and the birth of my body. The faces she wore in dreams and the signs that floated before my eyes. I hadn't yet known Iris Humphrey, but it was her. It was unmistakably her. I got every message that she didn't even know she was sending.

The only part of her I could reach was the part I held inside me, and it had to be enough. It just had to be. And I had to listen to her silence. It was only that I didn't believe it. So I clung to my patience like my fingers gripping the edge of a cliff. "Don't worry about Iris," I said, reminding myself of my grandma's words. "What will be, will be, and it'll be when it's meant to be." It felt like I had already waited a billion years, so what was a billion more? "Please don't make me wait a billion years," I whispered.

PART III

*Our love came before our first birth,
and will live beyond our last death.*

25

I dreamt Signey and I were sitting in an elegant theater. The seats were red and cushioned with wooden armrests, and a sleek painted mural covered the walls. It was the kind of theater built for plays, but the kind that came screaming to life with rock n roll.

Without uttering a word, Signey stood up and walked away. As she crept down the aisle, excusing herself while hitting the knees of those she was passing by, I noticed Iris. She sat in the seat on the other side of where Signey had been. I wasn't surprised, though I hadn't known. The look on her face reflected mine. She hadn't known I was there either, but nor was she surprised.

I looked for Signey and found her sitting a few rows behind us with Grant. They watched with cautious smiles. I turned back to Iris and with one empty seat between us, I nodded my head for her to scooch toward me. She did without hesitation, but as our faces got closer and closer, I could see the fear in her eyes. But she kissed me anyway. I could almost feel her tongue in my mouth. I could almost taste her. As she pulled back, ever so gently, I saw something in her eyes that I hadn't yet seen. Relief.

My dreams of her were contradictory. They made me want to sleep forever, but they also had me looking forward to a future that I truly believed we'd have, awake.

I was unusually peppy at work that day. My co-workers had

grown accustomed to my sour mood, but I was back in my boss's good graces after some ideas proved beneficial. "T.G.I.F.," I kept saying. "T.G.I.F."

It was August 22 and over two months had passed since I told Iris how I felt. She was never far from my mind, and I accepted that she never would be, but I was trying to force one foot in front of the other, rather than crawling through life.

It was a chilly seventy degrees at nine p.m. as Grant, Daniella, and I walked from my place to Jem's that night. The sky was grey and the air was light. I wore my denim jacket and a plain white tee that hid the emerald dangling from the chain around my neck. I pulled it out and rubbed it between my fingers while Grant and Daniella held hands beside me. My mind echoed: She's always with me. She's always with me. She's always with me.

Jem's was packed, but Signey had reserved us a booth. I waved to her as she catered to drunks at the bar. She nodded her head, unable to free her hands from the mixed drinks she was crafting. I spotted Annie on the way to our table and said, "Congratulations," even though I wasn't sure she couldn't hear me. She was starting to show, and I could read her lips as she thanked me. She looked like hope.

We ordered some appetizers and I drank my usual bottle of Stella. My nerves suddenly ate away at me and I danced my fingers all over the table, not quite moving them as quickly as my brain wanted them to go. I was on the edge of something; I just wasn't sure what. All I knew was that I craved ice cream. "If you could only have one flavor for the rest of your life, what would it be?" I asked Grant and Daniella. Iris had been wearing a shirt with an ice cream cone on it in my dream.

"Easy. Chocolate Chip Cookie Dough," Daniella said.

"Mint Chocolate Chip?" I asked Grant, already knowing.

"Yeah, and let me guess…strawberry," he said, smirking, like I wanted to eat Iris's hair or something.

"Actually I was going to say Neapolitan."

Grant threw his hands in the air. "That's three flavors!"

"It comes in one carton."

"You would." He laughed.

We breezed through the night, simply enjoying our Friday. I felt a buzz that was completely unrelated to the alcohol.

Shortly before eleven, Signey slid into the booth beside me. "How are you feeling?" she asked.

"She's being weirder than usual," Grant said.

"I'm fine…" My words were softer and slower than they had been all day. "She's here, isn't she?"

Signey nodded her head.

"Well, that's how it goes. We know that," I said. But I still didn't know what to do. This wasn't Wren or New York City. It was Jem's. It was my neighborhood. It was my turf. She had been there before and was bound to be there again. I'd known it was only a matter of time before we crossed paths right there in Los Angeles, with nowhere to run. "I'm not leaving," I said, shaking my head. "She knows I come here. If she sees me, she sees me. If she wants to talk, we'll talk. I'm not running away this time." I bit my nails with my elbow resting on the dark wood table.

Signey gently pulled my hand away from my mouth. "I gotta get back. Holler if you need anything." Then she wove her way through the crowd and back to the bar.

I looked at Grant and Daniella sitting across from me. They looked back in the way that a neurotic child holds fragile glass.

"So," I said.

Grant stroked his chin, no doubt wondering if there was anything he could say to help. After a few moments of silence, I pushed aside my drink and excused myself.

I stood on the back patio for a few minutes, anxiously waiting for Iris to come out and find me. Despite the cool air, my denim jacket suddenly felt suffocating again. I fanned it out around my stomach, and then my gut led me back inside. I took only one step down that hallway, where Iris and I had gazed into each other's eyes eight months earlier, when I saw her passing its entrance. She froze and looked my way. She wore a cream-colored shirt that looked like the one from my dream, only without the ice cream cone. It was a loose short sleeve, and she wore tight maroon pants that hugged her hips below the oversized shirt.

I saw her gasp for air and I felt it in my own lungs.

Once again, that hallway was frozen in time.

"Hi," I mouthed. I couldn't feel myself breathing anymore. I couldn't feel anything. She stared back, like a statue. My feet felt just as frozen, but somehow I put one foot in front of the other, and one step at a time, I walked down that hallway toward her, calm and with ease, not frantically adrift like the last time I saw her. It was a bit like approaching a wild animal. I thought if I moved too quickly, she'd run.

I could feel the waves in the pit of my stomach as I got closer. I was suddenly aware of myself again and Iris didn't move. I stopped two feet in front of her. It was the longest walk of my life. "I'm sorry," I whispered.

"I'm sorry," she whispered back.

With those two words, I knew she had read everything I wrote to her, and everything I wrote about her.

"Maybe I shouldn't have told you things, Iris, but I did…And if you ever want to talk about it…" I sighed as I searched for words. "I'm sorry."

After a tedious silence, she softly asked, "Do you want to go get some ice cream or something?"

"Yes," I said, letting out a fit of air. "Yes, I do." I laughed under my breath in complete awe.

We stood silently again. I bit my lower lip and she bit hers. We stopped when we noticed our similar mannerism.

"I'll meet you out front," she said.

TO BE HER GIRL

"Okay."

She turned around, seemingly without a second thought, and walked away. I watched her until I couldn't see her anymore, then headed back to the table and told Grant and Daniella. I asked them to tell Signey, and then waited outside for what felt like eons until Iris joined me. "Do you know The Amber Creamery?" she asked.

I nodded. "Yeah."

Amber was one of the lone surviving ice cream shops in a sea of frozen yogurt chains. Iris and I said nothing as we walked the two blocks to it. There was an understanding and awareness in the air that consumed us. We both knew we'd eventually have to use words, but I figured it was her turn to talk. I had said enough. I looked up at the night sky and thanked the stars hiding behind the clouds. Perhaps fate and free will had finally aligned in our favor.

But by the time we got to Amber, it was already closed.

"I'm sorry. I thought they were open until midnight," Iris said.

I knew they weren't. I just had no concept of time whenever I was around her.

We stood in silence for what felt like forever again. In reality, it must have been about ten seconds. "Maybe I should've just asked you to go for some ice cream," I finally said and laughed under my breath. "Ya know, instead of saying everything I said."

I wasn't nervous, but I was. It wasn't awkward, but it was. I couldn't believe what was happening, but I could.

Her smile sailed under her breath into a laugh. "Maybe," she said. "I have ice cream at home. Do you still want some?"

I could tell her words surprised even her.

"Depends," I said, like an idiot but with a smile. "What flavor?"

"Neapolitan. That way you get a little of each."

I laughed and shook my head. "Okay, Iris. Okay."

26

Iris lived in Silver Lake, only a couple of miles away from my Echo Park apartment. Like the walk from Jem's to Amber and back, we kept quiet during the five-minute ride in her old Chevy. I watched her hands on the steering wheel, and she kept her eyes on the road. The air was brimming with soft tension as John Legend's "All of Me" played on the radio. Love songs didn't seem to make sense until I found her.

"It's a nice car," I said after we got out of it. It was a two-door Chevrolet Nova. Burnt orange with a cream-colored roof. "What year is it?"

"Seventy-seven," she said. "My stepdad replaced the engine a few years ago. It was my mom's."

I nodded and admired it. "You were born in seventy-seven, right?" I asked, looking back at her.

"Yeah..." she said slowly, almost like a question.

"I was born in eighty-eight."

She let out a breathy laugh and shook her head.

We walked out of the garage and down a narrow stone path into a courtyard. There were two buildings on either side, each with two apartments. Hers was on the second story, farthest from the garage. I followed her up the stairs, feeling like I was under a spell. Was this really happening or was I about to wake up from another dream?

TO BE HER GIRL

She unlocked the door to her apartment. Number three. I gulped as I followed her inside. Art covered the walls, both photographs and paintings, just as I'd imagined. "Nice place," I said, following her into the kitchen, feeling the need to pinch myself.

"Thanks. I've only been here a little over a month, but I like it," she said, getting the carton of Neapolitan out of the freezer. She pulled two red bowls from the cupboard and two spoons from the drawer.

"Where were you before?" I asked, then regretted it immediately. I feared the elephant in the room.

She told me that she and Brooks had rented a house not far from there, thus bringing up the elephant. She moved out after they split and stayed with Paige in Los Feliz. I just nodded and handed her the ice cream scooper that had been sitting in the dish rack next to the sink.

"So when'd you know?" she asked, scooping ice cream into the two red bowls.

"Know what?"

"That I left him." Her voice stuttered a little.

"Well, technically, I didn't know for sure who left who...until now," I said, trying to make light of her question. "But my roommate overheard some of your friends at Jem's back in April." I was playing with my fingers when she slid a bowl of ice cream across the counter. "But I guess I had known for a while before that."

We walked over to her table up against the wall, occupying the space between the kitchen and the living room. I sat across from her and shoveled ice cream into my mouth.

"I'm sorry I never responded to your emails," she said.

I swallowed my ice cream abruptly, chilling the walls of my throat. "Oh, yeah, about those...I'm sorry."

"I didn't know what to say...So I didn't say anything." She stirred her ice cream around in her bowl. "It broke my heart. I hope you know that. Not saying anything broke my heart."

"I'm sorry. That's not what I wanted."

We both ate a few scoops of our ice cream.

"I don't know," she said. "I guess I just was too afraid to. But I've always known..." Her voice grew softer. She looked down into her bowl and stirred her spoon around. "I don't know what I knew...But I knew something." She looked up at me. "Do you remember that night at Jem's?"

"In December?...Yeah." I ate another scoop of ice cream, giving myself time to process what was happening. "I'll never forget it."

"It was like...I don't know..." She put a spoonful of ice cream in her mouth without finishing her thought. We both knew she didn't need to.

"I know," I said.

"I referenced your letters in some of my Fodoary posts though. I hoped you'd see them and know that I read them and was thinking of you."

"I did." I smiled lightly and scooped more ice cream into my mouth. "I love your pictures and their captions." I paused then said, "Well, most of them," under my breath.

"Most of them?" She laughed lightly.

"Never mind," I said, shaking my head.

She stared at me silently.

"You wrote 'move on' once," I said, "and I was afraid you were talking to me...But then I thought maybe you were talking to yourself."

"I was. I was talking to myself."

I nodded. "Yeah, I'm sorry I brought it up."

"It's okay. I hope you know I love your writing. You're good with words."

"Thanks. That means a lot coming from you."

"I'm not gonna lie though...it did make me feel weird sometimes." She let out a nervous laugh.

"Yeah, sorry," I said.

We ate more ice cream, and had more time to process.

"Did you see me in Wren or New York?" I asked.

TO BE HER GIRL

"No," she said, "but after I got your letters, it made sense, what I was feeling. I remember looking around, but you must've just left. I think maybe it helped me believe...your letters...because I did, I believed everything you wrote. I just couldn't admit to it. But it was everywhere...You were everywhere." She spoke in a near whisper. "I still don't understand it, but here we are."

She picked up her bowl and drank the melted ice cream, and I had never loved her more.

"Do you want a glass of wine?" she asked after putting the bowl back down.

I almost fell out of the olive green chair, but managed to simply nod with a smile.

She went into the kitchen and poured us each a glass of a Northern California red blend, without knowing it was my favorite. She sat back down across from me and we shifted our topic of conversation. We moved beyond the elephant of Brooks and the dinosaur of my letters to the simplicity of life. We talked about photography and writing and travel and books. She mentioned weird movies and bands that I'd never heard of, and at times, I didn't even know what she was talking about, but I hung onto every word. I had gone through so much turmoil since I met Iris, and there I was, sipping wine in her apartment just after midnight, like nothing. Any tension had melted with the ice cream. I had no feelings of animosity because of her silence, nor did I count the days I had waited for that moment. I just lived it as it was happening. I had never been so happy in my entire life.

I told her about the car accident with her stepdad, explaining that I'd seen him in her photographs.

"That was you?" she asked.

"He told you?"

"Well, I noticed the scratches and asked what happened."

"He said those were old."

"He said they might've been."

"Weird you noticed then."

"I guess," she said with her mouth in her wine glass.

"So you're still close with him?"

"Charlie...Yeah...Good ol' Charlie Lovell," she said, looking into her wine glass as she spun it around. She took another sip, then put it back down. "He's the only father I've ever known. He still lives in Wren, but he has to come down for work sometimes, so he visits me when he does."

"That's nice," I said. "How old were you when they got married?"

"I was six and even then I could see how good he was to my mom. He was really patient with her. I look back now completely in awe of him." She raised her shoulders to her ears with her lips pressed together, then she dropped them back down as she exhaled slowly. "He's always been good to me too." She shook her head and briefly looked away. "Neither of us could bear to be in the house after my mom died, so he rented an apartment for us until we went back a few months later. But I think it was even harder then. But we lived there until I moved down here after high school with Paige. He didn't have kids of his own. Just me. So he's always stuck around."

"I'm glad he has."

"Me too."

"Did he ever remarry?" I asked before sipping my wine.

"Married, no, but he's been with his girlfriend for years. She's good for him."

"Does she have kids?"

"No." She sipped her wine. "What about your parents?"

"They broke up when I was eight." I sighed and pressed my lips together, then sighed again. "The stars are still there, and so, so am I."

Iris squinted her eyes with a curious smile, faint but present.

"That's what my dad told me the day he moved out. He went to Florida for a while. I was so mad at him, but I'd..." I shook my head gently, getting lost in the past. "I'd still stand in the backyard every night, begging the stars he'd come home."

"Oh," she said through a tender sigh.

I shrugged and brushed it off. "My dad was an alcoholic and my mom couldn't handle it anymore. But they also just kind of grew apart, I guess."

"*Was?*" She swirled her wine around in her glass.

"He's been sober for a decade now."

"Good for him." She took a sip of her wine.

"Yeah, I always thought I'd be an alcoholic because of him."

"Are you?" she asked without the slightest bit of caution.

I took a sip of my wine. "No." We drank more until the silence grew awkward. "Anyway, my dad remarried when I was thirteen …And it was hard at first, but she's good for him too. I think she's the reason he got sober. She's friends with my mom now too, which is weird." I laughed. "But it works, I guess."

"She didn't remarry?"

"No, and she was single for a long time. But her boyfriend moved in last year."

"Do you like him?"

"Yeah."

"Are you closer to your mom or your dad?"

"My mom, but I'm more like my dad…which is probably why. I spent most of my time with my grandma when I was at his house." I took another big sip of wine. "That night at Jem's, you mentioned you moved to Wren after your dad died…I wanted to ask…but you got called away before I could."

She sighed. "A bus plowed into his motorcycle." She sighed again. "He was only twenty-five, and suddenly my mom was a twenty-three-year-old widow with a baby…I don't think she ever got over it."

"I'm sorry…"

"It's okay. They're both gone now anyway…I'd like to think they're together." She stared into space for a few seconds while sipping her wine. "She loved Charlie a lot, but she always looked so broken when I asked about my dad…So I don't know much about him because I stopped asking. He didn't have any family around either, so pretty much my only connection to him is my blood and my name." She sipped her wine before saying, "And my savings, I guess," under her breath.

I wanted to ask how her mom died, but I figured she'd tell me when she was ready. She spoke a little about her but didn't say much. The way she tip-toed around it terrified me. I excused myself to the restroom, needing to stop my mind from imagining the worst, and to catch my breath as I experienced the best.

Iris directed me through the living room and around the corner. It was the last door at the end of the hallway. I wanted to peek into her bedroom as I walked by, but I was afraid she was watching.

I closed the bathroom door behind me and leaned up against it. "Oh my God," I whispered to myself. I sighed heavily through a smile, then pulled my phone from my back pocket. I had been so enthralled with Iris that I hadn't even noticed I'd been sitting on it for two hours. I had text messages from both Signey and Grant. I sent them the same reply. *I'm in heaven. Pinch me...but leave me alone! I love you I love her omg*

I tried to calm myself down from my thoughts of Iris's mom and focus on the fact that I was with Iris, in her apartment, in the middle of the night. I checked my appearance in her mirror and was pleasantly surprised with my esteem for how I looked. I smiled at my crooked tooth that was the same as Iris's crooked tooth, just on the other side, and ran my fingers through my dirty blonde hair, which was the same length as Iris's, only she embraced her waves while I straightened mine.

I headed back down the hall and caught a glimpse of her bedroom as I walked by again. The walls were white like the rest of the apartment, and it had the same dark hardwood floor. The bed was in the center of the opposing wall with a tall cushion headboard. It was neatly made, unlike mine, with a dark purple blanket and white satin pillows.

When I rounded the corner back into the living room, she was sitting on the couch, sipping her wine. My glass and the bottle sat on the large barnwood coffee table in front of her. Beside the wine was a vase filled with pebbles, a few ceramic coasters being unused by our glasses, various remotes, and a week-old copy of the *Los Angeles Times*. The lower shelf had a stack of large hardcover photography books, including *The Best of LIFE* published in 1973. It was the same special edition that my mom had. I'd grown up looking through it.

    I sat down beside her, over a foot away, which was much too far. The couch was dark blue and large, and as comfortable as it looked. Iris was barefoot and had her legs tucked underneath her. I caught a glimpse of her toes that were decorated with white nail polish. It felt oddly intimate. I slid off my sandals and sat cross-legged. I hoped I wasn't intruding, but it was her who had moved the wine to the couch.

    The soft tension in the air matched our voices as we talked about everything except who we were to each other and how we felt. It hovered around us, but we had already spoken all we could of it that night. It was one thing for me to tell her with letters; it was another to tell it to her face.

    "Do you want another?" she asked after we sipped the last drops of that bottle of wine. Her voice was meek but inviting.

    I smiled with my lips pressed together. There she was, Iris Humphrey, the woman who had evaded me for over a year, enticing me to drink more wine and greet the dawn. I said, "Yeah," and I said it just the way I had the night I met her. The first word I ever spoke to her. It seemed like a lifetime had passed since then, but it also felt like yesterday.

    We both stood up, but I froze as she brushed by me. Our bodies touched for only a moment, but it was just enough. She stopped and looked into my eyes like nobody ever had, or ever could. The longing inside me and the intensity of the moment caused a heavy inhale and a quick exhale. She took her right hand and with the tips of her fingers gently stroked my cheek. The tears welled up in her eyes, just as they did in mine.

    "Are you real?" I whispered.

"As far as I know," she said.

Our lips touched and we kissed for a moment or two. When we came back for more, we opened our touching mouths ever so slightly and rested our lips. We weren't in any rush. We were trying to catch our breath by breathing in each other's. But then she slid her tongue into my mouth, and I could finally taste her for real. She held my face while we kissed, and my hands slid gently down her arms.

I kissed her cheek, and then gently moved my lips down to her neck. And with my face buried in her skin, I could smell it—that scent that had been coming to me for months—lavender and sandalwood and vanilla drowning me in pure love and lust. After soaking it in, I moved my mouth back up to hers.

Passion consumed us and our pace kicked up a notch. We kissed harder and breathed heavier. Her arms were around my neck and she reached her hands down the top of my t-shirt. I could feel her fingers pulling across the skin of my back like she was caressing me to life. It must have been working because I had never felt so alive.

She gently pulled herself back, and we both attempted to catch our breath. She slowly slid her finger down my arm, and then she took my hand in hers and led me into her bedroom.

We stopped next to her bed and I tried to sit down slowly, but gravity found me and I landed quickly on her soft mattress. She laughed and I smiled. I put my hands on her waist and slowly slid them down to her hips and back, caressing her perfect curves. She leaned in and kissed me. I scooched my body backward and she followed. I slowly fell to my back and she landed gently on top of me, still kissing me with her beautiful mouth. My body trembled beneath her as she gently moved hers, crashing into mine softly like soothing waves. It felt like she was finally telling me everything that she could never say.

After a few minutes, she sat up and stared into my eyes.

"I'm sorry I can't stop shaking," I said. "It's just…I'd say I waited a year for this…but it feels like I've waited lifetimes."

She smiled lightly and pulled her shirt over her head. I gasped loudly, unable to conceal the erotic energy rushing through my body. She sat, breathing heavily at my side for a few moments, before leaning into me and kissing my neck. Her hand wandered and found its way up my t-shirt, gently stroking my stomach. My hand met hers and I arched my back and began to pull off my shirt. I sat up and pulled it over my head.

She smiled before leaning in and kissing me again. With our mouths together, our bodies gently fell back onto the bed. She pulled her mouth away from mine and kissed my chin and then my neck and then finally my chest. She moved her lips over to my shoulder while slowly sliding my bra strap off with her finger. Mine were lightly wrapped around her arms. I moved them to her back and massaged my thumb across the clasp of her bra before undoing it. She sat up and let it fall off her and onto me. I stared and gulped, then sat up and took off my own.

I fell back to the bed with her breasts pressed against mine. She kissed my mouth before following her previous pattern down to my chest, this time kissing my bare breasts. I tilted my head back and closed my eyes, soaking in everything that was happening, everything I'd been waiting for.

She pulled back and I opened my eyes to find her staring directly into them. She slid her finger down the center of my stomach before lightly dragging it back and forth across my skin at the top of my jeans. I gasped for air as she slid her hand down over my jeans. She gently massaged between my legs as our mouths met again. After a few moments of kissing and massaging, our lips separated just enough for our eyes to meet. She tugged at the top of my jeans with her thumb. I nodded and she slid them off, along with my underwear. She began to crawl back over me, but I cocked my head to the side with a smirk. I raised my eyebrows and she knew what I meant. She smiled and took off the rest of her clothes.

She lay at my side as we kissed, then she reached her hand between my legs again. I adjusted my body accordingly, and she gently grazed her finger over me before sliding it inside. The others followed suit, and she was able to make me feel a way that no man ever had. I let myself moan as she gradually took me higher and higher until I reached the most incredible climax I ever had.

She cupped her hand between my legs, and I placed mine over it. I lay there, breathing heavily and staring at the ceiling, as if it was the first time I'd been intimate with anyone. My mind couldn't grasp what my body was feeling. I'd never felt so high. After catching my breath, I sat up and stared at her. "I don't know how on earth you just did what you did to me…It didn't even feel earthly at all…But I want you to know that I've never…been with a woman." My voice was shaky, even though I didn't feel nervous.

"Neither have I," she said. "Not like this anyway."

I didn't ask what she meant. But whatever she had just done to me felt like an eleven on a one-to-ten scale of expertise. Instead, I just kissed every inch of her body above her waist, hoping I could please her as she had just pleased me.

With my mouth between her breasts, which were considerably larger than mine and perfect, I reached my hand between her thighs and slowly slid it up. When I finally felt how wet she was with my fingers, I gasped just as loudly as she did. I massaged her lightly before moving my mouth down and tasting that wetness with my tongue. Her gasps for air, sensual moaning, and whispering of my name was the most incredible song I had ever heard. Apparently I was an expert too. After she climaxed, we lay still wrapped around each other for a while before she went down on me, and again did something to me that nobody else could.

After I again returned the favor, though I couldn't tell who was enjoying it more, we kissed and intertwined and moved together in sync. The energy was flowing through our bodies as if we had only one. The sensation I felt from the tips of my fingers to the tips of my toes was unlike anything I had ever experienced. This must be what magic feels like, I thought. I had always believed in it, but I only knew it existed when I first saw her.

Finally we lay still again and she asked if I was comfortable, with her head resting on my chest and her hair tickling my skin. She was rubbing the emerald between her fingers. I said, "Yes," and kissed her head. I had never been more comfortable. To feel her naked body pressed up against mine as I held her in my arms that first time felt like the absolute peak of my existence.

It felt like home.

We were finally able to keep eye contact that night, and hers beamed that same relief as they had in my dream.

27

I was afraid to fall asleep, fearing I'd be in my own bed, alone, when I woke. The sun was already up when we finally closed our eyes.

But I did wake up in her bed that morning, and Iris was still asleep beside me. I didn't move for a while, just stayed beneath her purple blanket, wearing nothing but my emerald necklace. I had never slept naked before that night. When she woke, we both smiled, remembering that the night had been real.

I threw my white t-shirt back on and a pair of her blue cotton shorts. She tossed on another pair, along with the same No Doubt t-shirt that I owned. It was black with neon pink lettering and from their seven-night stand at the Gibson Amphitheatre two years earlier. I was at night one. She was at night two. "We just missed each other," I said with a smile, grateful we had finally caught up.

We sat at the table again, eating breakfast this time. Unlike me, Iris loved eggs and made herself some scrambled. I had a slice of toast and a cup of tea. She drank coffee, and she drank it black. I watched her hold her large white mug as she gripped it tightly. It had a big green eye on it. "For Iris," she said, laughing under her breath. She sipped her coffee slowly, even after it cooled down.

I felt unbelievably at ease. It was like we had breakfast together every morning of our lives, and would for the rest of our days. We didn't say much, but we were comfortable in our silence. We slid into that morning like a hand into its custom-made glove. Finally something with us was easy.

By noon, we were making love on her couch.

I dove into her record collection soon after. She had records that I loved, ones that I wanted, and a bunch I had never heard of. I already knew our taste in music was similar, still I couldn't believe it when I found a Gram Parsons record. I put it on the player as a tribute to my grandma.

"Do you have a big family?" Iris asked after I mentioned her.

"Yeah," I said. I walked back over to the couch and sat next to her. "My mom only has two siblings, but my dad has seven, so I have like a million cousins."

She turned and leaned back against the large pillow resting against the arm of the couch. She rested her legs across my lap. "Mostly older or mostly younger?"

"Both," I said, rubbing her legs. "I'm smack-dab in the middle. What about you?"

"My mom had an older sister, but she died when I was little. And then her husband—my uncle, I guess—moved with my two cousins to Michigan. I haven't seen them since."

"I'm sorry…That's rough," I said quietly. It felt like I had swallowed a brick.

"Charlie has some family in Wren, so I got to know them growing up…But I always felt like an outsider, ya know? I hated being an only child…Do you have only one sister?"

"Yeah. Cora. She's good. I'll share her if you want."

Iris laughed and said, "Okay, thanks."

I rubbed her legs again and took a deep breath that caught me off guard. I smiled and she smiled back.

"I used to think I was a twin," she said. "I was so convinced I had a twin out there somewhere. I remember I even checked my birth certificate when I was little."

"Whoa…I thought that too," I said. I had forgotten all about it until that afternoon.

I excused myself to the restroom, and then on my way back to the couch, I stopped to admire the photographs on her bookcase. I picked up the picture frame that held one of her mom. She was looking to the side, and the photograph appeared to have been taken mid-laugh. Her hair was a darker shade of red, but her face was the same as Iris's. "She was beautiful," I said.

"Inside and out," Iris said, sitting up. "She just hurt too much."

I put the frame down, walked over to the couch, and sat beside her.

"She killed herself," she mumbled.

There it was.

She stared at the photograph from across the room before looking back at me. "It was a Tuesday morning."

We sat silently, staring at each other, until she sighed.

I put my hand on top of hers and rubbed it. "It's okay, Iris...You don't have to tell me if you don't want to."

She took my hand in hers and gently squeezed it. "But I do."

"Okay," I said softly. It felt like firecrackers were exploding in my chest. The brick still sat heavy in my stomach.

"It was January fourth, nineteen ninety-four. She was thirty-nine. I was sixteen. Charlie was out of town and...I went into her bedroom because I...and then into her bathroom...and she was on the floor...and there was..."

She paused. Tears dripped off both our faces. I could tell she hadn't told the story in a long time.

"There was alcohol by the sink and empty pill bottles on her nightstand," she continued. "And I just started shaking her and screaming. I didn't know what to do, so I just sat there with her. I didn't know who to call. Charlie forgot his pager, so I didn't how to reach him. And her parents were both dead, and her sister was dead, and my dad was dead, and now she was dead too. At first I wanted to believe it was an accident, but when Charlie got home that night, we found the letters. One for him. One for me."

We both shook and cried, but still held each other's hand. I didn't know what to say. "I'm so sorry," was all I could find. I took my other hand and gently stroked her cheeks, wiping away her tears.

"She was…she…I always thought she was so strong, ya know. But I always knew there was something wrong too. She just felt everything so much. She would talk about how precious and beautiful life was. She would tell me to listen to the birds and to watch the butterflies. She had the kindest heart, and she'd tell me that I should never take life for granted…But then she took her own."

"Did she say why in her letter?"

"Not really. It was just words of advice and love, drenched with sorrow. I'm not even sure how planned it was when it happened. I mean, it definitely wasn't an accident. She'd overdosed before. She knew what she was doing every time she mixed alcohol and pills that way. And she wrote about it in her journals. She wanted it to happen. The letters didn't even have a date on them, so it was like she knew it eventually would. I think she wrote them to make sure she left us with something when it did. She said she was sorry and that she'd always be with me."

"I believe she is."

Iris took her hand from mine and wiped the tears from my face. "Yeah, I was just so angry with her so for long." She sighed and wiped away her own tears. "I guess sometimes I still am."

I nodded and leaned back against the couch. She did the same and rested her head on my shoulder.

My own battle with depression and history of suicidal thoughts weren't far from my mind, and I couldn't help but feel hypocritical. But I was mad at her mom too. I understood but was still troubled by it. After a few minutes of silence, I told Iris of my struggles and what my mom thought when I was five, and she spoke briefly of hers. It was all too much, and we eventually shook our heads through our tears and changed the subject. I didn't mention the bathtub incident from earlier that summer.

EMILY CRADDUCK

We had a late lunch delivered with no intention of leaving the apartment until we had to. I hadn't a care what was going on outside that door. I hadn't even checked my phone since I texted Signey and Grant around two in the morning.

We ate Chinese food on the floor of her living room while discussing the more sensible subject of animals. Grateful Dead was spinning on the record player, and I told her about Cora and Rhett's dog, which led to my grandma's bird, and eventually the history of every pet I ever had. She told me she was allergic to cats, as I had suspected, but grew up with a dog named Archie, which was the name of my first cat.

We skipped dinner but had another bowl of ice cream. It was like we were running on pure stardust. Our energy was unstoppable.

After finishing the carton of Neapolitan, she showed me her office that housed her photography equipment. There was a Christmas stocking on the wall above her desk, which made me laugh. It had fallen from a box while she was unpacking, so she hung it up rather than putting it away. It was almost Christmas, she figured, though it was only August. Her every quirk made me smile.

High on a shelf sat her mom's old camera, unused for years, and the photograph of the waves that first introduced us hung on the wall.

I sat on the floor, flipping through an album of her mom's work. There were several photographs of Iris and several of the beach. I told her when she was ready to go back, I'd drive. She simply smiled and shuffled through a folder of her own photographs.

I found a picture of her dad leaning against his motorcycle. He was short with golden blond hair and a perfectly chiseled jawline. Iris had his little button nose and the same round eyes. And by the stance of his body and the smirk on his face, I could tell she had inherited his confidence too. She told me the picture had been taken the day before the accident, and I felt my heart ache for her misfortunes again. I wanted to go back to that day when I rear-ended her stepdad and thank him.

She spun around in her chair and set the folder on her desk. She moved the computer mouse, waking up her iMac.

I shut the album and stood, peeking over her shoulder. "You take a lot of the audience," I said.

She was searching through a digital folder of old concert shots. "They're just as much a part of the experience," she said.

I turned around to put the album I had been holding on the bookcase behind us.

"Here it is," she said.

I turned to find a picture of me on her computer. It was from a concert two years before we met. She came across it by chance a few days after the art show in June.

"I couldn't stop crying after I found it," she said quietly, as if she hadn't wanted me to hear.

"Whoa," I said just as quietly.

We breezed over that moment with another reminder stirring in the air. Our lives were like two winding paths with their meetings hidden beneath the snow.

I sat back down on the floor and opened the shoebox sitting at her feet. We were silent for a few minutes while I looked through a stack of old Polaroids.

"Callahan," she said, breaking our silence.

I looked up with a smile and a stomach full of butterflies.

She snapped a shot of me with her 35mm film camera. It was the second photograph she ever took of me, but the first with personal intent. "My sky of blue," she whispered as she turned to put the camera back on the shelf.

My heart skipped a beat, remembering Grant's song, but I said nothing.

We crawled into bed around midnight. We kissed until the muscles around our mouths grew tired and then let our hands do the rest.

"I have an idea," she said, snug in my arms with her head on my chest.

I kissed her head. "You mean something other than this?"

She looked up at me. "I'm hungry."

"Hey, if you wanna eat again…" I smirked with a shrug. "I'm a willing participant."

She laughed, then kissed my lips and walked out.

I covered my face with my hands, hiding my giddy smile from the empty room.

I walked into the kitchen where Iris was raiding her cupboards.

"Making something?" I asked.

She turned around with a bag of sugar in her hands.

"Aw, you're so sweet."

She laughed. "Sugar cookies."

She put the sugar on the counter and poured us both a glass of wine. She drank several sips before I even had one. She took charge of the mixing of ingredients and was quieter than she'd been all day. I mostly stood back and watched.

"Oh, shit," she said after scooping the dough onto the cookie sheet.

"What?"

"I didn't preheat."

I turned around to the oven. "What do I set it to?"

"Umm," she said.

I heard the pouring sound of a massive amount of powdered substance.

"Fuck," Iris said over the crumpled sound of a paper bag.

I turned around and saw her covered hips to toes with sugar. It surrounded her feet like a pile of sand. I pressed my lips together tightly, trying not to laugh, but I couldn't help it and burst into an uproarious sound of glee.

"Oh, this is funny?" she said, smiling. She looked down to her legs and then back up at me.

The bag of sugar sat near the edge of the counter. I walked over and pushed it back toward the wall. "And I thought I was the one who would make a mess. I'm just sorry I didn't see it happen." I knelt onto my knees, then sat on the heels of my feet. I rubbed her legs, then wiped sugar off her thigh with my finger. I looked back up to her face, staring down at me. "I mean, I know I said you were sweet and all, but…" I licked the sugar from my finger.

"Yeah, you're sweet too."

"Yeah?" I said. I looked back at her legs and rubbed them again. Then sugar poured over my head.

My jaw dropped and I looked up at Iris. A mischievous grin spread wide across her face. "You…did not just do that." I stood up and mimicked her smile.

"Oh, I think I did." She placed the now empty bag on the counter.

I wiped sugar from my shoulders and spread it across her cheeks. She rubbed it into my hair and onto my stomach. I scooped it off the floor and then rubbed it on her arms. We wiped and rubbed and scooped and laughed until neither of us could stand. Tears of joy streamed down our cheeks as we sat together on the floor.

I rubbed the sugar around on the black and white checkered tiles. "Hey, it's almost like we're at the beach. Wanna make a sugar castle?"

She laughed, then leaned in and kissed me. "I have a better idea." She pulled her sugar-covered shirt off over her head. She raised her eyebrows, then stood up and walked away without another word.

I followed her into the bathroom. We stripped our clothes and hopped into the shower. The sugar spun down the drain with the water while we got reacquainted with each other's bare bodies. Every mark on her skin was a story I was dying to know.

We cleaned the kitchen, washed our clothes, and finally baked the cookies. Then again, we fall asleep at sunrise.

By eleven a.m., we were eating another breakfast of her eggs and my toast. After we finished, I walked to the record player in the living room. I pulled Bob Dylan's *Nashville Skyline* from her collection and turned around to find her on the couch. I showed her the album and shrugged with a slight smile.

She nodded and smiled back.

I put the record on and walked over to the couch. I sat beside her and she took my hand in hers, resting them on her lap.

"On Sundays we listen to Bob Dylan," she said.

"That's not a bad way to spend 'em."

Blood on the Tracks followed *Nashville Skyline*. Then we watched *Say Anything...* and *Bruce Almighty*. The day was slipping, and we fought the ticking clock by doing as little as possible. We knew it'd fly by quicker if we dove into it, so we caressed it and rested side by side, just enjoying each other's company. We knew the time was coming. I had to be at work Monday morning. I'd have to leave.

When she dropped me off at my apartment shortly after sundown, I finally had the nerve to ask why she invited me over, when she had been so afraid to let me in.

"I don't know," she said. "I guess I was more afraid to let you go."

I pulled a pen from my purse. I grabbed her hand and wrote my phone number on her palm. "There's no other place for me to go."

I put the pen on the dash in front of me and we kissed. I opened the car door, even though getting out of it was the last thing I wanted to do.

"Your pen," she said.

"Keep it." I smiled. "Will you call me?"

She smiled. "Yes."

I learned so much about her that first weekend we spent together. It was as if our entire lives had been leading up to it. They had certainly been leading to each other. Getting to know her was the greatest experience I'd ever have. Every word she spoke was a gift, and every peek into her mind, the most beautiful surprise.

After what felt like floating into my apartment, I dug my stocking out from the back of my closet and hung it on the wall by my desk.

With her, it was always Christmas.

28

I was both excited and apprehensive all day on Monday, checking my phone constantly. I confidently left things in her hands, quite literally, when I gave her my phone number, but for all I knew of Iris, she could have let me slip through the cracks of her fingers, willingly.

My feet nearly burned through my living floor as I paced in circles after dinner. "Maybe I shouldn't have stayed the whole weekend," I said. "Maybe it was too much for her."

"She wanted you to," Signey reminded me.

And she had, but I knew if Iris was anything like me, which she was, too much of a good thing was never a good thing. Suddenly I was afraid of everything that had happened. I tried to shift my focus and helped Signey string some beads, which just resulted in me pricking my fingers and drawing blood. Halfway through a calming joint, around nine o'clock, my phone rang. It was an unfamiliar three-two-three. "It's her," I said. I bolted into my bedroom and shut the door behind me.

"Hello," I answered.

"Callahan?"

"Iris?"

"Hey," she said. "Sorry it took me so long to call you."

"That's okay. I'm used to waiting for you." I laughed while pacing in my bedroom.

She laughed. "Your patience is to be admired."

"You're worth it."

"Are you sure?" she asked. I could hear her smile.

"Yes." I could hear myself smile. My entire body could feel myself smile. I lay down on my bed and we talked for two hours. Just before we hung up, she asked if I wanted to come over after work the next day, which was the easiest question I had ever been asked.

If Monday had felt like a year at work, Tuesday felt a decade. My stomach did somersaults all day. The weekend had been spontaneous; I didn't need to think about anything. But I wasn't sure what to expect that night—if I should eat dinner first, pack a bag, bring some wine. As I agonized shortly before five, she texted me. *you drink stella, right? i picked up a case...how's pizza sound? i've been craving it...but whatever you want is fine with me*

I had been craving pizza too. We were disgustingly in sync.

I packed an overnight bag, just in case, and tossed it into the back of my car. I didn't want her to think I was expecting anything. If I was merely in for a night of beer and pizza, I would have been just fine, as long as I was with her. Just one moment with her was worth enduring a million without. I figured beggars couldn't be choosers.

I picked up a pizza on my way over and then sat in my car with the hot cardboard box in my lap. "It's happening. It's happening. It's happening," I said to myself. I smiled and took a deep breath.

I walked slowly to her apartment. It still felt too good to be true. I stopped at the front gate and took another deep breath. I balanced the pizza box on one hand and pulled my phone from my pocket with the other. I opened our text message thread and scrolled to find the passcode to open the door. I put my phone back into my pocket and entered the numbers into the keypad. Pound. Zero. Six. Two. Five. I heard the buzz and pushed the door open. I was in.

I walked up the stairs to her apartment and balanced the pizza box on my hand again. I knocked once and she opened the door. "Hi," she said. She gave me a cautious smile.

"Hi," I said, smiling back.

"Come in." She stepped back and waved her hand.

I followed her inside and into the kitchen. I put the pizza on the counter while she cracked open two bottles of Stella with a guitar-shaped bottle opener.

"Do you play?" I asked.

She scrunched her face. I smiled because it was adorable, but I could tell she didn't understand.

"The guitar," I said.

"Oh," she said, looking at the bottle opener. "No. This was Brooks'. I'm not sure why I have it." She put it back on the window sill.

"Oh," I said, regretting my question.

"You?" she asked.

"Just a little, for fun."

"Play for me sometime." She smiled and handed me a bottle.

"Maybe," I said, taking the beer. But I didn't want to because her ex was a professional musician, and I sang about as well as a stray cat in heat.

"So how was work?" she asked, grabbing two plates from the cupboard.

"They're making a new supplement, so we had to taste test different samples. They're liquid so basically we were taking shots all day."

She laughed as she grabbed a slice of pizza from the box and put it on a plate. She handed it to me before getting another for herself. "Any good?" she asked, walking over to the table with her plate and bottle of Stella.

"They were all too sweet or too bitter," I said, joining her at the table.

"Do you take the vitamins?"

"Not really. They're for kids. But if I'm sick, my boss usually gives me a bottle of something." I took a sip of my beer. "What'd you do today?"

"Well, mostly, I thought about you." She smiled and sipped her beer.

I smiled back, surprised by her candid response.

A couple of hours later, I was grabbing the bag from the backseat of my car. She had asked me to stay after we made out on her couch. I walked into her bedroom where she was sitting on the edge of her bed with her legs crossed.

"I'm glad to see you came prepared," she said. She laughed under her breath.

"Well, ya know, I didn't think I should show up to work in the same clothes two days in a row," I said, setting my bag on the chair in the corner of the room.

"Clothes are overrated." She uncrossed her legs.

I walked over and sat on the bed next to her. I gently tugged the collar of my loose shirt, looking at my skin beneath it. "Overrated?" I asked, looking back at her.

She slid her hand across my stomach and pulled the shirt up at my hip. "Overrated." She continued to slowly pull it up, just at the side, stroking my skin with her free fingers. I put my hand on hers, and together we pulled my shirt off over my head.

We removed the rest of our clothes before making love atop her purple blanket. It was as if nothing else existed. Clothes? What were clothes? With every touch, it was like she was sharing the secrets of the Universe with me, like we were transcending realms. If I had used words to communicate how I felt, she was using sex, and I felt it in every way possible.

The rest of the week would play out the same. I'd come over after work, stay the night, wish I didn't have to leave, go to work, come back. We had moved painstakingly slow and then incredibly fast. I spent over a year longing for her and then within the matter of a week, my toothbrush had a new home.

We developed a back and forth routine of talking and making love and talking and making love and then talking some more. I listened more intently to her than I had to anyone else in my entire life. I clung to every word she spoke as if I'd never heard it before. I knew that when I took my last breath, all my greatest conversations would have been with her, so I held on to everything. Even the sound of her exhaling between her words made me high.

On Friday night, we went to Amber. I walked close to her after we got out of the car. I wanted to reach for her hand, but was unsure how she'd react. No matter how close we already were, it'd still only been a week. And we were in public.

I opened the heavy glass door.

"Ah, it's open this time," she said with a laugh.

I smiled as she walked inside in front of me. It was eight o'clock and surprisingly slow. Amber was trendy, but not in a way that made you feel pretentious just for being there. It had an old jukebox, a few pinball machines, and board games that were usually missing half of the pieces.

She got the coffee flavor in a dish, smothered with peanuts and chocolate syrup. I got strawberry on a cone.

"Boring," she said after I ordered and handed the cashier a twenty.

"Says the person who drinks her coffee black," I said. "I always have ice cream in a dish at home. I like cones. And I don't like nuts."

"Well, it's a good thing I don't have any then."

We both laughed and the teenager behind the register smirked as he handed me my change.

On the way to a table, I grabbed Iris's arm as we passed the jukebox. "Hold on. Hold this," I said, handing her my nutless ice cream cone. She took it and I stuck my hand into my purse, rummaging for quarters. I pulled out a handful and inserted them into the jukebox. "Pick a song," I said, hitting the button, searching through the albums inside. But before she could say anything, *Nashville Skyline* came up. I stopped and we looked at each other. She nodded and I selected Bob Dylan's "Tonight I'll be Staying Here With You."

I looked around after we sat, hoping there would be somebody I knew—somebody to see me with the most beautiful woman in all of Los Angeles, all of California, and all of the world. But I knew nobody and that was just fine. I knew Iris. I finally knew Iris.

Saturday evening, I lay on her bed and watched her dress for work. She slunk into her tight black pants, and all I could think about was later that night when I could watch her undress. If the body is a temple, I wanted to live in hers.

I finally had the nerve to ask what she meant when she said, "Not like this anyway," on our first night together. I was afraid to hear about her prior sex life.

"I've made out with a couple of women before, but nothing more than that. Pants stayed on," she said while zipping up hers.

"Oh," I said.

"Two. One once. The other for a few weeks."

"Oh," I said again.

"Neither were anywhere near as good as you." She smiled.

"Oh." I smiled.

"Why?"

"You're just really…good."

She laughed. "So are you…But I told you I'd never been with a woman like that. Didn't you believe me?"

"I know. I'm sorry. I guess we're just really good with each other."

She smiled as she grabbed her black beret from a hook on the wall. She turned to her mirror, putting her back to me.

"You were my first, by the way, the first woman I've ever kissed. And you'll be my last, my only," I said, looking at her reflection. I couldn't stop my lips from curving into a smile.

She laughed awkwardly as she adjusted her hat. It was as if I had asked her to marry me or something. I never understood how she could go from, "You're all I want," to, "I'm so afraid to have you," in a matter of seconds.

I met Grant at Jem's shortly after Iris left for work. I hadn't seen him since the week before or Signey since Wednesday. We sat at the bar and they both stared at me like I was out of my mind.

"We're getting to know each other," I insisted.

"You're living together," Signey said from behind the bar. "The weekend was one thing, but Cal, it's only been a week. Take a breather."

"Most couples only go on one date the first week," Grant said.

"We're not most couples." My heart spun at the thought of us being a couple. "And it's been so much more than a week," I reminded them.

"But in the real world, Cal, it's—"

I cut Signey off with a death glare before she could finish that sentence.

"She ignored you all summer. Just don't forget that," she continued.

"Somebody she barely knew told her that they were soulmates and that they loved her," I said. "Of course she didn't say anything. What was she supposed to say?"

I had my own answers to that question, but I was getting defensive. I tried my best to put myself in Iris's shoes. What would I have done? Probably the same thing. We hadn't talked about it since the first night, and I didn't want Signey and Grant to bring it up either. It was a dark cloud we could both sense was coming, but we were enjoying the sun while we had it.

"I'd marry her right now," I said. I sipped my beer and shook my head at their worried faces. "Just be happy for me. You know how long I've waited for this. Don't act like I wasn't in the wrong just because you love me."

"We're just saying that maybe you should sort some things out first. It won't just go away," Grant said. "If you don't approach the beast with caution, it's going to bite you."

"Are you calling Iris a beast?" I asked.

"I'm calling life a beast."

"Since when are you cautious?"

Grant laughed and shook his head.

I refused to admit it, but I knew we had gotten completely carried away. I just didn't see any point in stopping. Not until she wanted to anyway. On the drive back to Iris's, I contemplated going to my apartment instead. It was only for a second, but I gave it a thought. I wouldn't let Signey or Grant under my skin. They didn't understand. Iris wanted me there. She wanted to see me and I wanted to see her. That was what mattered.

I kissed Iris the second I walked inside before even saying a word. "I missed you too," she said, laughing. We kissed again and I could feel her smile against my lips. She's all I need, I thought, she's all I need.

Later that night in bed, something dawned on me as I admired her face. "Your freckles," I said.

She puckered her lips and squinted her eyes, as if trying to read my mind.

"It's Pyxis." I ran the tip of my finger down her cheek, connecting them. "Gamma. Alpha. Beta. It's a constellation, Iris. They're stars." I got up and looked at my matching freckles in the mirror. "Never noticed."

I had taken an astronomy class in college, and it was one of the constellations I remembered. It's a mere line, but I was strangely drawn to it.

"What's it named for?" she asked as I crawled back into bed.

"A compass."

29

Iris already had plans to attend a party at Paige's house on Sunday, and when we woke up that morning, she asked if I wanted to come along. I sat there dumbfounded in her bed. Of course I wanted to. Of course I wanted to get to know her friends. But my stomach started to spin. My friends had their concerns, and I could only imagine that hers did too. I wasn't sure what I'd be walking into.

After listening to Bob Dylan, we swung by my apartment to pick up my bathing suit. She parked in front and started muttering under her breath.

"What's wrong?" I asked.

"Nothing." She flashed a smile.

I was unconvinced, but let it be.

Iris followed me into my apartment, doing her best to hide how bizarre she felt. "Hey," I said to Signey. She sat at the table slaving over a piece of jewelry. Her growing collection was becoming her livelihood. "You remember Iris?" I smiled.

"Never heard of ya," Signey said to Iris.

They laughed and exchanged hellos. Iris gave me an inquiring look and with my affirmative nod, invited Signey to Paige's. I pointed to my grandma's painting above the couch and headed into my bedroom. When I came back out, I found Iris staring at the painting. She looked like she was lost in a memory.

"You okay?" I asked, sliding my hand across the lower of her back.

She turned to me and gave a gentle smile. "Yeah."

I gave her the same smile.

Paige's house was a gorgeous one-story, just up the hill from my old apartment with Grant. With Signey trailing behind us, Iris and I strolled into her backyard with our fingers laced. Our hands were bound together as if they had been born that way. Whatever hesitance we had been feeling on Friday night had vanished.

The back patio was already smothered with people, and the pool was full of them. Signey and I looked at each other like we had just landed on another planet, completely out of our element. They all seemed to have successful careers they actually wanted. Musicians, designers, and actors. Artists all across the board. We figured they must have more money than the two of us put together in their back pocket alone. Our lives felt almost comical. Intimidated, we searched for the kids' table. We wound up in the only empty lounge chairs while Iris floated around like a social butterfly. I couldn't keep up.

"Was it your idea to invite me?" Signey asked.

"No, but I'm glad she did," I said. "I need you to distract me from the fact that the word 'rebound' is practically written across my forehead."

"Is that what you think you are?"

"No, but probably everybody here does."

"Probably." Signey looked around. "But it doesn't matter what they think."

I sighed under my breath. "Oh, shit, Paige is looking right at us," I muttered. "Shit, she's coming over."

"Did she know we, or you, were coming?"

"I don't know."

Paige stopped right in front of me and smiled. "Hi," she said.

"Hi. I'm with Iris," I said.

"I know."

"I wasn't sure if you remembered me. This is my roommate, Signey."

"Hi," she said to Signey, still smiling. "And of course I do." She ran her hands over her long side braid and asked where Iris was.

I pointed to the other side of the pool where Iris was chatting with somebody she hadn't introduced me to yet.

"Make yourself at home," Paige said before heading toward Iris.

Signey and I removed the clothes over our bathing suits and hid them under the chairs. We got into the pool and were splashed about five seconds later. Leah John was relaxing on a lounge float when her boyfriend, Jamie Lear, also a musician, knocked her over from underneath. He was the one who unintentionally told Signey about Brooks and Iris's split. They both laughed and apologized.

"I'm sorry I don't remember your name," Leah said to me, "but I know we've met."

"Callahan. We met at the Jewel's show at High Street."

"That's what I thought," she said. "I'm Leah. This is Jamie. Are you with Iris? Is she here?"

I smiled. "Yeah."

"She was supposed to come to Nashville last weekend to take some photos for me, but she cancelled at the last minute. She said something came up. She's lucky I love her to pieces."

"Oh." It was me, I thought, I came up. Signey and I looked at each other, trying to conceal our smiles.

"What?" Leah asked, noticing.

"She's over there," I said, pointing at Iris, "if you want to give her a piece of your mind."

Leah laughed. "Maybe I will." Jamie splashed her from behind. "See y'all around," she said as they got out of the pool.

I watched as they spoke with Iris. I watched while Iris engaged with everyone. I was both amazed that this incredible person was a part of me, and genuinely grateful just to know her. She was a flame to a world full of admiring moths. But I couldn't shake the feeling that I was out of place. Signey and I hid out in the pool, feeling like two baby ducks wading in a pond of successful swans.

"I'm gonna go catch up with Iris," I told Signey after a while. "Wanna come?"

She shook her head no, pinched her nose with her fingers, and sank under the water.

I snuck up behind Iris and put my hands on her waist. She wore a see-through slip over her bikini and my stomach fluttered with butterflies. Even after all that time, even surrounded by all those people, she still gave me butterflies. Sometimes all it took was just the thought of her. But she was talking to a good-looking guy with a six-pack, and I felt a twinge of jealousy. The way he eyed her made me uneasy. I feared her friendliness could be mistaken for something it wasn't, and I wanted to make sure he knew where she stood. With me. She took my hands in hers, and with my arms wrapped around her, introduced me.

With every introduction that day, I kept waiting for her to say girlfriend, but she never did. I was trying to keep my expectations at a reasonable level, especially considering the long road we had taken before that week, but my heart's hope was out of my hands. It wanted what it wanted.

The guy with the six-pack jumped into the pool, and I asked Iris about Nashville.

"Oh, yeah, Leah said she talked to you," she said.

"And you cancelled because of me?"

"Yeah, but I set her up with a great photographer that I know in the area. I saw the photos. They turned out amazing."

"They would've been better if you took them...But I'm glad you didn't."

Iris smiled and for a second, I thought she was going to kiss me, but she didn't. I hid my disappointment by scanning the crowd for

Signey. I saw her talking with Paige and Kate. "Looks like Signey made some friends," I said.

"I told them about her jewelry. It's good."

"Oh, that's why you invited her."

"Yeah, that and I thought you'd want me to." She smiled.

After dropping off Signey, Iris and I headed back to her place and over a bowl of Neapolitan, spoke of our deep connection for the first time since our first night together.

"So what was the real reason you felt uncomfortable when you saw where I lived?" I asked, then listened intently while she explained.

Two weeks before I handed her that first letter after the art show, Iris sat in her friend's car, right where she had parked that afternoon. Paige's cousin, Tori, a tarot card reader, was visiting and crashing at Paige's house for the week. Iris was still living in the guest room. With Paige out of town for a night, they restlessly hit the road and followed it wherever it took them. Tori was behind the wheel while Iris rode shotgun. Tori wasn't overly familiar with Los Angeles and, as she put it, let the Universe steer. The first place they landed was outside my apartment, stopping only because Tori felt compelled to. From there, she drove by Iris's house with Brooks, old apartments, and places she'd worked. None of which Tori had even been aware of until that night. After a brief trek up the Pacific Coast Highway, they eventually turned around and headed back.

"It was like she was giving me a tour of my life in Los Angeles …backward," Iris said. We could barely look at each other. "I don't know how else to describe it. It felt surreal and supernatural, like time ceased to exist, even though it was like that's what we were being shown. Time…We figured the first place we went was where I was going next."

"Me. I was next." My lips curved up ever so slightly. I told her about the night that Grant sang to me and played the recording, then about the night that my grandma reached through him, telling me not to worry.

Afterward, we crawled into bed together, but it felt like we were a million miles apart.

"I guess the Universe wants us to know how connected we are." I laughed, trying to lighten the mood.

"I guess so," she said somberly.

I wanted to tell her not to sound so depressed about it. But I just said, "Good night," instead.

"Good night."

I leaned in and kissed her lips. I pulled back and she gave me an unconvincing smile.

"It is what it is," she said, tugging the blanket over her chest. "What will be, will be."

My heart raced at those words, but I didn't dare tell her why.

"What will be, will be, will be." I sighed and closed my eyes. Sometimes I saw her best with eyes shut.

Work was closed for Labor Day on Monday, but I left in the morning, just as I had the previous week. I didn't need to give much of an explanation as the air carried our awkwardness from the night before. Talking about the weird things that happened only made it weirder. Signey and Grant were right—I needed a breather.

Signey was doing yoga in the living room when I got home. She opened her eyes from savasana, surprised to see me. We sat at the table and I tried to explain Iris's experience, but like my nights with Grant and so many others, it was near impossible—not without sounding like a fictional piece of nonsense anyway.

"We're fine when we're in the moment," I said, "but the second we try to talk about it, we both shut down." I stared out the window, watching a squirrel in the courtyard. She looked up at me as if she

TO BE HER GIRL

knew I was watching her. She froze, then darted out of sight. I looked back at Signey and sighed.

"What are you thinking?" she asked.

I bit my lower lip and shook my head. I was thinking about nothing and everything at the same time. I didn't know what to do. Like Iris said, it was what it was. "Maybe some things are better left unsaid."

"You threw a lot of words at her," Signey reminded me, as if I could forget.

"Yeah…and she didn't say anything back."

"You can't move this fast and not talk about it. Even the best car has to stop in the pit."

"Okay then you talk about it with her." I widened my eyes and left for my bedroom.

I called Iris a few hours later. She was downtown somewhere with her camera. I hated that I left that morning and wanted to make it up to her, even though my leaving was a mutual, though unspoken, idea.

I drove to her apartment and taped a note to her door, asking her to be at my place at eight. I couldn't bear another minute without her, but I wanted to wait until Signey was at work for the night.

My front door had a note that said: *I'm open*, and straight ahead the record player had one that said: *Spin me*. I had an old 45 of Sonny and Cher's "I Got You Babe" that had just the right amount of static before the opening notes. Once I heard it, I came out of my bedroom and leaned against the archway between the hall and the living room. I held a rainbow-dyed rose against my cheek. Iris turned to me and laughed. With my free hand, I directed her my way, using only my pointer finger. When she reached me, I took her hand and led her into my bedroom.

On the floor lay a blanket, and on the blanket were a dozen red roses, a bottle of wine, and a Neapolitan ice cream cake. "I wasn't sure whether you liked picnics or not, but I figured this was the best kind," I said, handing her the rose.

She took the rose from my hand and smelled it. "It's perfect."

"I Got You Babe" was still spinning in the living room. We sang along with it like an offbeat attempt at karaoke, using the rose as our microphone. When the song ended, she grabbed my guitar and held it toward me. I shook my head no.

"Please. I wanna hear you play," she said.

I sighed and put the rose on my nightstand.

"Please." She stuck out her bottom lip. "I'll get naked for you."

I took my guitar and sat on my bed. How could I say no to that?

I played Van Morrison's "Brown Eyed Girl" because it was one of the few songs that I knew by heart. Iris sat on the blanket and sang along with me.

After I finished, I said, "Okay, I held up my end up the bargain. Now get naked."

She laughed. "Hmm."

"Hmm." I put my guitar on its stand and joined her on the blanket.

She leaned forward and kissed me. "You're my brown-eyed girl," she said so closely that I could feel her breath on my cheek.

I smiled so hard, it hurt. I loved that she called me her girl. It was all I wanted, to be her girl.

After devouring some cake and a glass of wine, we devoured each other right there on my blanket-covered floor.

30

After Iris left the next morning, we took a step back. We spoke on the phone daily, but she had to work every night so we stayed at our own apartments. By the weekend, though, we were ready to dive back in. On Friday, we sat on the patio at Amber eating our ice cream, and I joked that it was the most normal night we'd spent together. We had gone to Rowe's for dinner and were anticipating our first night together since Monday. I missed the feeling of her exploring my body, and I missed hers.

As I grazed my fingertips across the small of her back, just below her flowing crop top, I heard a familiar voice. Please don't see me, please don't see me, please don't see me, I thought. But he did and, "Hey, Michael," slid off my tongue. After leaving Rowe's, I thought we had dodged a bullet, being so close to Untangled, but the Universe always has something up its sleeve.

Michael stopped next to our table. "Hey, how've you been?" he asked in a warm, yet melancholic voice.

"Good," I said. "You remember Iris?"

Of course he did. It was a cruel question.

"Hi," Iris said.

He gave her a disheartened look and nodded his head. "This is my sister, Aaliyah."

I had hoped the girl at his side was a new girlfriend, not his sister.

She said, "Hi," but nothing else. She didn't seem overly thrilled to see me, and I couldn't blame her. I reciprocated her greeting but hoped they'd go away.

"How's the writing?" Michael asked.

"Oh, ya know," I said. But even I didn't. I wasn't writing at all. "So how've you been?"

"Good," he said, nodding his head slowly.

He continued to nod for several moments, and I nodded my head right along with him. The awkward silence consumed us all. Ice cream melted down my hand.

"Well, it was nice seeing you," he finally said. I wasn't sure if he meant it, but he flashed that megawatt smile that I remembered him for.

"You too," I said.

He touched his fingers to the rim of his baseball cap and walked away, down the street, around the corner, and out of my life.

"Well, that was fun," I said to Iris, then ate my ice cream cone.

"How long were you together?" she asked, then casually scooped ice cream into her mouth. I nearly choked on mine. I didn't want to talk about my former flings with her, especially not in public. I thought we had already told each other enough on the phone just the night before. I told her about the few guys I had dated, and she told me about the ones she had. I didn't want to discuss it anymore.

"Not long at all," I said anyway. I wiped my mouth and the ice cream from my hand. "We started talking in September, but we didn't go out on a date until the beginning of January. And then our last was at the end of March."

"Oh, so the same time that Brooks and I——"

"Yeah," I interrupted. "Our timing is ridiculous."

"That's one word for it." She ate the last of her ice cream and then touched her tongue to the corner of her mouth.

"The bad part about the timing was his. He was chasing me while I was chasing you. I still feel awful about it. I wanted to believe that I was just as much a distraction for him as he was for me, like a crush to crush everything else, but then I realized that he actually loved me and I was just a horrible person."

"You're not a horrible person," Iris assured me. "Maybe you were a catalyst for him, like he realized that he could truly love somebody or something. Maybe that's all anybody is."

"But it's best when it works both ways. A catalyst isn't affected, and I think I was. I think I always am."

"That's just science," she said. "A catalyst sparks change."

"So every person we date is just to change us?"

"Maybe change is too strong of a word…Or I don't know. Maybe it's not. How'd he affect you?"

"What?"

"You said he affected you."

I shrugged. "I don't know. He made me feel loved, I guess. Or desired, at least. I couldn't reciprocate it, but I hadn't felt that since Mason. But now there's you, so I'm all set."

"Are you?"

"What kind of question is that?"

She shrugged and wiped her mouth with a napkin, even though she had already licked her lips clean. "What about that other guy?"

I sighed. "Travis? I don't know. He was interesting and he gave me weed. But he was kind of a dick. I guess if anything, he made me realize that I deserved better. But then, ya know, I was kind of a dick too."

"Well, somebody has to be the one to show you that you're a dick." She laughed and I did too. "You're not a dick," she said, shaking her head. She stood to leave. "You ready?"

"What is this, a one-way street?" I asked on reflex. I didn't actually want to go there.

She raised her eyebrows and sat back down. "Brooks gave me a home and a family."

I nodded.

"Everybody else was just sex." She laughed.

"That's not funny."

"I was kidding."

She either wasn't or she just didn't know.

"Well, we have each other now." I forced a smile and stood up.

She stood up and kissed me on my lips. She pulled back and we both smiled. We'd never kissed in public before.

I was sitting on the couch scrolling through Fodoary when Iris hollered for me to come into the bedroom later that night. I walked in, hoping to find her naked, but she was fully clothed and holding a white silk robe. "Will you put this on?" she asked.

"Uh, sure. Why?" I slid my hand down the arm of the robe.

"Because I've been wanting to photograph you since the day I laid eyes on you."

"Whoa, wait a second." I pulled my hand away from the robe and raised both hands in the air. "What?"

"Please."

I dropped my hands to my side.

"You don't really have to do anything," she continued. "Just take everything off and put this on."

"Fine." I stripped off my clothes and stood naked in front of Iris.

She stared with a crooked smile on her face and said, "Mmm," softly under her breath.

"I don't think the photographer's supposed to look at the subject like that." I raised my eyebrows and mirrored her crooked smile.

"It's hard to be professional when you look like that." She handed me the robe. "As much as I'd like to keep staring."

I put on the robe and clutched my emerald necklace. "I'm keeping this on."

She tied the robe's sash around my waist. "I was hoping you would."

"Michael once told me that taking pictures was robbing you of real life experiences. I don't think he meant art, but ya know, just in general."

"Photography is its own experience," she said.

"I know," I said. She didn't have to tell me. I saw the life in her eyes every time she touched her camera.

"It's preserving how things are, truthfully, whether it's staged or not. Life and art are ultimately one and the same. Photography is to remember how things were in that single breath of life, that heartbeat of space and time."

"Like your mom said, it's a lot like writing…Okay, now what?"

"The kitchen."

I nodded my head. "Okay."

We went into the kitchen and I didn't know what to do. I had never been photographed in such a way and felt comfortable only because it was Iris behind the lens. She didn't instruct me as much as she just instructed my surroundings. "Just be you," she said, which seemed bizarre because I was certainly out of my normalcy. "You're too beautiful not to capture."

"Whatever you say, Iris."

I strolled around the kitchen like a curious housewife in search of her lost fantasy, realizing I was living mine, and hoping I would never lose it.

In the week that followed, we fell back into our old pattern. I stayed at her place, and we lived well in each other's company. The hardest part of falling asleep and waking up beside her was keeping myself from saying, "I love you, Iris," as I had grown accustomed to. It was how I had ended every day and started every morning for months, but I had dreamed of sharing her bed for a year, so it was well worth the sacrifice. As much as I wanted to shout it from the rooftop, I still feared she'd run before I finished the sentence. I only mouthed it when she wasn't looking.

On Saturday morning, we hopped into her old Chevy and drove down to Joshua Tree on a whim. It was just to get away, together.

Like me, Iris craved the open road. She constantly surrounded herself with people, and it was only on the road that she allowed herself some much-needed solitude. When she was restless, she often found herself in the deep desert or a busy shopping mall. Two polar opposite environments that create the same isolation. I understood completely because I was just the same and did just the same. Both the hustle and bustle of a crowd, and the silence of nature forced me to look around. Often it's only with solitude that we truly open our eyes to the world around us. The noise dims our chaos and the quiet soothes it. We weren't feeling restless and had no plans to visit a mall, but the desert was something of beauty that we wanted to share. The good in the world should always be appreciated, not just when we're on the edge of forgetting it.

We passed the dive where I met Dalfour Hickey, and I felt a drop of his spirit warm me. I hoped we'd run into him, but I knew our friendship was frozen in time, and I was okay with that. Pointing it out, I only mentioned it was there that I had met an astounding character with an interesting look, who reminded me that everything wasn't always as it appeared, but there was always something to see.

We stopped occasionally to wander, but the sun was scorching and the triple-digit heat was draining. We spent most of the afternoon in the car, driving through Joshua Tree National Park. She kept the stereo low, the speed slow, and her hand on my thigh. We kept to the isolated areas and didn't see another soul for hours.

After we climbed a rocky hill, to where the air was slightly cooler, we sat with our skin melting into each other's. The smell of her skin under the desert sun was enough to drive me wild. It took all I had not to make love to her right there on the rocks. Instead, I settled for her lips and the feel of her breath whispering into my ear. Though we didn't say much. Sometimes the shared air said enough. With her, I felt happy in a way I had thought lived far beyond my wildest dreams. But there she was.

We came across a campground and inquired about staying. Late

Saturday afternoon and it seemed unlikely, but we did eventually stumble across a vacant spot. The problem was, all we had was the two camping chairs that lived in her trunk.

We marked our turf. She paid the fee. And we ventured out to find camping necessities.

She insisted that she'd been wanting to buy a tent anyway, but I cringed as the bill went up and up and up. An air mattress, some blankets, pillows, a cooler, food, ice, lots of water, and a couple of hundred dollars later—we headed back to our spot in the desert where we had left the two chairs.

After pitching the tent and eating our sandwiches, we realized that we didn't have any firewood. It was too hot anyway. Evening time and it was still in the nineties. We sat in the tent, stripped to as little clothes as publicly possible, and ate uncooked marshmallows with the already melted chocolate.

As the daylight began to fade, she insisted on taking some photographs of me. I felt disgusting after a day of unbearable sweating, but she wasn't easy to say no to. "No close ups," I said as we both put our tank tops back on.

"Trust me," she said. "You look beautiful no matter what."

I walked over to the picnic table. "Here?" I asked.

She nodded and I sat on top of it. She took her camera out of her bag and adjusted the settings. I stared wistfully into the horizon and let her work her magic. I trusted her.

She took a few shots and then walked over to the table and set her camera down next to me. I picked it up and got off the table. "My turn," I said.

"What?" Iris asked, laughing.

I looked into the viewfinder and took her picture. I lowered the camera away from my face. "Sit down," I said. "I'm about to take the best photograph ever taken."

She sat down on top of the table. "Oh, and how's that?"

"It's simple. You're in it."

Iris smiled and I smiled back. I nodded my head toward the sunset and there she looked. I brought the camera back up to my face, but lowered it again to see her better. Her hair blew slightly in the wind, but she kept her arms in her lap. She was leaning forward with her hands dangling over her knees. I looked at her fingers and wanted to put a ring on one. She lifted her hand to brush her hair away from her face, then put it back down. I watched her, this beautiful woman who I knew in the way that I knew my own soul, completely and yet not at all, and felt all the love that ever existed, all in that moment. I took a deep breath and soaked it in.

Iris looked at me. "Take a picture, it'll last longer," she joked.

I laughed and she looked back to the horizon. I looked into the viewfinder and took her picture again. I lowered the camera and looked at the screen, switching between the two photographs I had taken.

"Well, was it the best photograph ever taken?" she asked, looking back at me.

I looked up. "The first one was…The one where you're smiling." I walked to the table and sat beside her, setting the camera behind me. "And actually the photographs you take of yourself are the best ever taken."

Iris laughed under her breath and shook her head.

"Too much?" I asked. "I'm always too much."

"The colors are incredible tonight," she said, looking at the sky.

I smiled, but I wasn't watching the sunset. I was watching her. I wanted to see it through her eyes.

"Don't miss seeing this beauty, Cal," she said, looking at me.

"I see all I need to see," I said.

She smiled and looked back at the sun melting into the sand. I closed my eyes.

"Well, now you're not seeing anything," she said.

"Oh, that's not true, Iris," I said, still smiling. "I have the lines of your face memorized. Even a blind man could see you through me." I laughed under my breath and opened my eyes.

She laughed. She had this giggle that both melted and excited me.

"It's true," I said.

She grabbed my face with both her hands, and we laughed through our kiss.

She pulled back and opened her mouth slightly. She closed it and I wondered what she wanted to say, but I didn't ask. She got off the table and grabbed her camera. She put it back into her bag and headed toward the tent. She stopped and turned back to me. "Are you coming?" she asked.

"Of course I am," I said.

I'd follow you anywhere, I thought.

I got off the table and walked over to the tent. Iris crawled inside as I took off the hood. I got into the tent and lay down beside her. "We'll be able to see the stars now," I said, looking at the sky through the mesh roof.

"Perfect," she said before kissing me.

We made out for a while and then went back outside. We sat on the picnic table again and looked at the stars.

"There's the Big Dipper," she said, pointing at the sky. She lowered her arm and put her hand on my thigh. "Or the Little Dipper."

"The Little Dipper. See the one there on the end," I said, pointing. "That's the North Star. The Big Dipper's just below it." I lowered my hand and put it on hers.

"So where's Pyxis?"

"Well." I sighed.

"You don't know?"

I took her hand in mine and pointed her pointer finger at the North Star. "That's the North Star, right, so Pyxis is," I slowly lowered our hands, "waaaaaay down there." I intertwined my fingers with hers and we rested our hands in my lap. "It's below the horizon, but it's still out there somewhere."

"Somewhere," she said, resting her head on my shoulder.

"We can come back in the winter and find it then."

"I can't wait."

Eventually we crawled back into the tent. We made love under the stars, and then stared into each other's eyes as if it were the last night on earth. She opened her mouth slightly, just as she had earlier. She closed it, then opened it again. "I love you," she said as softly as she could.

My heart skipped a beat and without thought, I said, "I know." I smiled and tucked her hair behind her ear. "I love you, Iris."

She smiled. "I know."

"Thank you for telling me."

She kissed my lips and then pulled back slightly. "Thank you for reminding me."

We made love again and just before she slipped into sleep, I whispered, "We are extraordinary," into her ear. I knew she heard me when her mouth curled into a smile. I kissed her cheek with the constellation we shared, then fell asleep beside her.

Despite the heat, I slept soundly that night in the desert. I usually did with Iris by my side. I woke when I heard her whisper, "I love you, Callahan," shortly after sunrise. Seeing her face that morning was like staring into heaven. As far as I was concerned, she was my Eden. I always thought I couldn't love her more if I tried, but somehow I always woke up having done so, effortlessly.

We started back to Los Angeles around eleven a.m. The ride home was long and tiresome. After half an hour, I turned the music up so I wouldn't fall asleep, but she turned it back down.

"Sorry," I said. "Too loud?"

"Sorry," she said, adjusting her hands on the steering wheel.

"For what? It's fine. I just turned it up because I'm tired."

She didn't answer, so I redirected my attention out the passenger's side window and whistled along with the quiet radio.

A few minutes later she said, "You're gonna find things out about me that you don't like."

TO BE HER GIRL

"No, I won't," I said, watching her as she stared at the road in front of her.

"Yes, you will."

"Well, we'll cross those bridges when we find them." I turned my head to look at the same place she was. In front of us.

We both got lost in our thoughts, coaxing us back into silence. I thought a lot about Mason and Travis and Michael, though I wasn't sure why. I only wanted Iris. I watched her balance her thoughts between the road and something else, and I wondered if I was good enough for her. I tried to tell myself that I was, that I deserved her and she deserved me, that I couldn't question why she would love me any more than I could question why I loved her. Because for as many reasons as she gave me to love her, I loved her without reason, and couldn't she feel the same about me? I wanted to believe that, but I had a sinking feeling in my stomach like I didn't.

31

Iris told me she loved me after only three weeks of dating. It would have seemed soon had I not told her before we even started. Normalcy just wasn't our style. All we could do was hold on as we rode the merry-go-round. I didn't shy away from saying, "I love you," again, but she'd just smile and say, "You too."

But if "love" was too heavy of a word for her, the word "money" wasn't. It was a feather on her tongue. It was an anvil on mine.

Iris's parents both left her far too young, but not without a hefty inheritance. The money she made from her photography was merely sprinkles on a three-tier cake. I swallowed my pride as she paid for nearly everything we did together. Amber was always my treat, but that was about it. When she said, "I never thought I wanted to buy a house until I met you," it might have scared me even more than it did her. Her lips were squirming as if she was trying to draw the words back into her mouth. I was in love with the thought of having our own house together, but wary at the prospect of living off her.

We were going out every night. There was always an event or a party, or just a few friends hanging out at Paige's house. Leah and Jamie were about to head back to Nashville, and Iris wanted to see them whenever she could. After our quiet weeks together, she was submerging us into a constant sea of people. Aside from meeting

Grant and Daniella at Rowe's one night, it was her who dragged me around.

I walked into her apartment after work on Thursday. I put my purse on the table by the door, and saw Leah and Jamie on the couch. "Hey," I said, slipping off my shoes.

"Hey," they said in sync.

"How's the vitamin business?" Leah asked.

I laughed while hanging my coat on the rack. "It's a dream come true." I walked into the kitchen where Iris was pouring wine into four glasses. "Hey."

"Hey, how was work?" She finished pouring and placed the bottle on the counter. She leaned in and kissed me.

"I thought we were just gonna relax tonight."

"We are."

"Alone."

"Don't be anti-social."

"I'm not anti-social. I'm just highly selective with when I want to socialize."

She laughed and picked up two of the glasses of wine. "Grab those, would ya?"

I picked up the other two glasses and followed her into the living room. I drank as I walked. I sat down on the loveseat next to Iris and handed her a glass. She'd given hers to Leah and Jamie. "I thought you guys were headed back to Nashville tonight," I said.

"We're taking a red-eye," Jamie said.

"Which was a horrible idea because I have a meeting in the morning," Leah said.

"You wanted more time in L.A.," he replied.

"Yeah, my bad." Leah laughed and took a sip of her wine.

"About the new album?" Iris asked. She held her glass in one hand, while her other was on my thigh.

"Yep." Leah nodded her head.

"To the new album," Iris said, raising her glass in the air.

We all raised our glasses and said, "To the new album," and

drank.

"So when are y'all gonna come visit Nashville?" Leah asked. "You haven't been in a while."

"I don't know." Iris looked at me. "You wanna go sometime soon?"

I shrugged.

We drank our wine while listening to some of Leah's new songs. Her alt-country vibe mingled with folk and I loved everything I heard. I wanted to feel excited. I wanted to soak it all in. But I hadn't eaten since lunch and the wine was getting to my head. "I'm gonna go lie down," I said after a sad ballad came to its end.

"We should get going anyway," Leah said. She took her last sip of wine and stood up.

Jamie agreed and took both their empty glasses into the kitchen. I followed with mine. Iris had poured herself another and still had half a glass left. I rinsed the three glasses while Jamie walked back into the living room. I joined them as Leah and Iris stood hugging by the front door.

"Alright, take it easy," Leah said to me.

"You too," I said.

"Come visit."

"Okay." I nodded and gave her a smile.

We hugged as Jamie opened the front door. We all said goodbye and they left. I walked over to the couch and lay down. Iris sat on the loveseat and sipped her wine.

"What's for dinner?" she asked.

"I don't care," I said.

"You just wanna order Chinese?"

"No."

"I thought you didn't care."

"I don't want that."

"Well, then what do you want?"

"What do you want?"

"Chinese."

"Then why'd you ask?"

"To see what you wanted."

I closed my eyes and rested my arm across my face.

"We should go to Nashville soon," she said a few minutes later.

"Okay," I said. "What's for dinner?"

"I just ordered Chinese. I got you the orange chicken."

"I said I didn't want it."

"Then don't eat it…Do you have plans after work tomorrow?"

"Yeah," I said.

"What?"

"This."

"The couch?"

"Yep."

"Well, there's an art show in San Francisco that I want to go to. It's tomorrow night, but I thought we could fly up and stay for the weekend. Or maybe we could just drive. I'm down for another road trip."

I removed my arm from my face and opened my eyes. "I can't," I said, sitting up. "I have work tomorrow. You just said that."

"I thought you could take the day off."

I looked at her empty glass sitting next to the coaster. "I'm behind on my student loans," I said, looking back at her.

She stared at me with her curious eyes.

"That's why I can't go," I continued. "I can't afford to."

"Don't worry about it. I'll cover it," she said.

"Iris, no, you don't understand what I'm saying. I have bills to pay and not enough money to pay them. And yeah, I know it's my fault because I spend money that I shouldn't, but…"

"Okay, but—"

"But the point is I can't afford to miss a day of work," I interrupted, frustrated that she hadn't considered my finances. Or lack thereof.

"How behind are you?"

"What?"

"On your student loans? What do you owe?"

"A lot. But you wouldn't understand that. You don't understand what it's like to pay for something that was supposed to help, when in reality, I'm at a job that does nothing for me."

"You're right," she said. "I guess I don't."

"That's right because you didn't even go to college," I said without thinking. "You just knew people. That's how you got your career. People asked you to take pictures and they liked them, so they asked you to take more."

"Yeah, you're right. I didn't go to college. I learned about photography from my mom before she killed herself."

Silence interrupted sharply. It felt like I'd been stabbed in the gut.

"I'm sorry," I said. "I didn't mean it like that. I just mean that you didn't have to struggle when pursuing your passion in the way that most people do…in the way that I do. Your path was different. It's fine. Just don't forget that mine was different too…And I'm not even close to being there yet. But I'm still paying for it."

"I'm sorry…And I shouldn't have used my mom like that."

"It's okay. I know you've struggled. It's just been in different ways…worse ways. I wouldn't want you to have to struggle any more than you have. And I'm sorry because I know you've worked hard to get to where you are…I'm just…I don't know…"

"Was that our first argument?" she asked with a smirk.

"Well, my heart may be on my sleeve, but my foot is often in my mouth," I said, giving her the same smirk. "Is dinner being delivered?"

"Yeah, and it's already paid for."

We went to Paige's house after dinner on Friday. I didn't want to go, but there was no point in fighting it. Kate was in town from Wren, and Iris was going with or without me. And I preferred it was with.

We pulled into the driveway behind Signey and walked to the front door. Iris opened it without knocking, and Signey and I followed her inside. We walked through the foyer and into the living room. Kate was on the couch and Paige was on the floor, rolling a joint on the glass coffee table. "Hey," they said simultaneously. They were born less than a year apart and could easily pass for twins. The only difference was Paige's long dark hair was always in a side braid, and Kate styled hers into a short wavy bob.

"Oh, let me see them," Kate said, noticing Signey's bag.

Signey put her bag on the coffee table and sat on the couch beside Kate. She pulled out sketches and several pieces of jewelry, placing them onto the coffee table. Paige finished rolling the joint just in time to look. Iris and I were sitting on the loveseat. I closed my eyes and rested my head on her shoulder.

"These are beautiful," Kate said.

"They're a perfect fit for the store," Iris said.

"They really are, and they'd be a great start to launch the jewelry division at the line," Paige said.

I opened my eyes and watched as they all oohed and aahed over Signey's jewelry. I rolled my eyes in my mind. It was all too storybook. Signey had just gotten back into making jewelry, and it was already about to pay off. My jealousy caused knots in my stomach. I was happy for her, but I'd been writing for years. When was it my turn?

I closed my eyes again while they discussed business for a few minutes. "Never mind, we'll talk about it later," Paige eventually said. I opened my eyes and watched her light up the joint. She took a hit and passed it to Kate. I lifted my head from Iris's shoulder. My neck ached. It felt like my head had been glued there.

"You alright?" Iris asked me.

"Yeah, I'm fine."

She kissed my forehead.

We smoked the joint, but I remained quiet while they all laughed and talked. I felt like an outsider in my own body. I left to use the restroom and when I returned, it didn't seem that anyone other than Iris had noticed I was gone. I sat back down beside her and rested

my head on her shoulder again. I closed my eyes.
"Hey, wait, is that from the store?" Kate asked.
"Cal," Iris said after a few moments of silence.
I opened my eyes to them all looking at me. I lifted my head from Iris's shoulder. I looked down and realized that the cardigan I was wearing was in fact from Kate's store. "Oh, yeah," I said. "I think I did get it there."
"Such a small world," Kate said.
"When was the last time you were in Wren?" Paige asked. She had moved into the chair she'd been sitting in front of.
"July," I said.
"Ohhh, yeah. That's right." Paige nodded her head slowly and pressed her lips together.
I hadn't told her before that, but I knew how she knew. It was in a letter, and Iris already told me that Paige had read them. I was more afraid of her opinion of them than of Iris's. No matter how Iris felt now, I knew that Paige hadn't forgotten about the weight they had burdened her with. At least that was where my mind went. And so the floors of her house felt like egg shells. But maybe I was just walking too heavy.

Later that night, Iris and I were in her kitchen when I let my feelings about Paige slip. She had asked why I'd been so quiet at her house.
"I just don't think she likes me very much." I shrugged.
"What? Why on earth would you think that? You have no reason to think that," Iris said. She finished scooping ice cream into our bowls and tossed the scooper into the sink.
"I don't know. Never mind. I just wish she hadn't read the letters."
"Well, I'm sorry," she said, putting her hands on her hips, "but I needed somebody to talk to."
"I know and I don't blame you for that. I'm sorry."

"Just don't put it on Paige because you feel guilty for writing them." She removed her hands from her hips, and I watched them fall to her side.

"Guilty? You think that's all I felt?" I asked, returning my gaze to her face. "You think I didn't feel terrible? Like an idiot? Because I still do."

"Okay. I know. I'm sorry. You shouldn't feel that way." She took two spoons from the drawer and put them in the bowls.

"Well, I do and I'm still sorry for forcing that all on you. I should've accepted that you weren't ready from day one, letter one, but here we are."

"Cal," she said after putting the ice cream back into the freezer. She picked up the two bowls and walked over to the table, setting them down. She turned back to me and said, "It's fine."

"No," I said. "I knew what I was doing. I knew we hardly knew each other. But I was desperate and needy and just didn't care. I wanted you to see me."

We were both silent, staring at each other with as much intensity as my letters. Then I took a loud, deep breath.

"Your silence felt like a knife stabbing my already bleeding heart, and I couldn't stop the life from draining out of me," I said, speaking firmer with each word. It was like her casual mention of my guilt flipped a switch inside me that I didn't even know was there.

She just stood there and listened as the words poured out of me, and the tears out of my eyes.

"I scared you. I know that," I continued. "But you hurt me in a way that nobody ever had, like nobody ever could. It felt like I was pouring my heart and soul into a bottomless vase. Where were you? Where were you to catch me? I'm aware that it was my choice and I own that, but it took every ounce of courage I had to tell you how I felt. I had to get it off my chest. I couldn't breathe. And I wanted to share it with you, to share what I had experienced, to share who we are. I wanted you to believe. Because I knew you felt it, and I wanted you to know that I felt it too. I hated what I was doing to you, but I almost died because of what you did to me."

My words came to a severe stop, but the tears continued to roll down my face, just as they did down hers. I felt relief for telling her that she hurt me, but by bringing up the night in the bathtub, I knew I had opened up something that I didn't want to. Iris was not to blame for my stay beneath the water's surface. Just thinking that she had been left me rattled with remorse, and vocalizing it left me gutted.

We stared at each other through our watery eyes, and I knew I'd have to explain. I had to tell her about wanting to die that night in the bathtub, and I had to tell her about the vision that saved me.

I walked over to the table and sat in the same chair that I always sat in—the olive green one closest to the living room—while she sat in the light purple chair on the kitchen side. I told her as calmly as I could while we sat in complete stillness.

"I don't know what to say. I never know what to say," she said, crying harder with each word. "I knew I was hurting you, Callahan. I knew it and I felt it, but I didn't know how to stop it. I couldn't bring myself to give into you. I couldn't bring myself to give into how much I loved you because I didn't understand it. I still don't. I couldn't confront it like you could. I am so sorry that I hurt you, more than you will ever know. That's the last thing I ever want to do. It tore me up inside, but I didn't know what to say. So yeah, I said nothing. I was afraid, Cal. I am not perfect, so take me off this pedestal."

"I don't have you on a pedestal, that's the thing. I see you and your imperfections. And I still love you more than anything. I see you, Iris. I see you."

And we did see each other. We were just having difficulties seeing ourselves.

Iris was right when she suspected my guilty conscience, but my feelings of Paige's cautious demeanor toward me weren't without merit. Like Signey and Grant held my ankles as I dove into Iris, Paige was holding hers. We felt the water differently, but we were both drowning. Like Iris, I never claimed to be perfect, but diving into her was diving into my imperfections. My flaws were amplified, and I was being thrust into insecurities that I didn't even know I had.

With the door open, we walked right into everything we'd been avoiding. "You let me think I was crazy," I said. "How could you let me think I was crazy?" I rubbed my hands over my face and groaned. I moved my hands to the air around my face and clenched my fists. "I thought I was losing my mind." I dropped my hands to the table and put my face in them.

"How did I do that?" she asked.

I lifted my head. "Because I told you who we were to each other and you knew it, but you ignored me."

She rubbed her face in the same way that I had and then put her hands in her lap. "I just told you, I was scared. I didn't know what to do. I felt crazy too."

"Well, then I guess we're just crazy together," I said.

"You were overwhelming me. You were being so compulsive. What you were saying…It was just too much."

"Well, if I say too much, it's only because you don't say enough. You say things and then you don't."

"What do you want?" she shouted, throwing her hands in the air. "Do you want me to say 'I love you' again?" she asked, holding her hands to her chest. "I love you! I love you!"

"Don't do that," I said as calmly as I could. It was exactly what I wanted, just not like that. I cried while she spun her spoon around her bowl of melted Cookies and Cream. Eating ice cream at the table had been our defense against tension. It just wasn't working that night. "It's because it's not Neapolitan," I muttered.

"What?"

"That's why we're fighting. This isn't our ice cream." I pouted like a child who didn't get her way.

She shook her head and let out a breathy laugh. "God, I love you," she said firmly, as if she needed to acknowledge it for herself.

"You too," I said through my pout.

EMILY CRADDUCK

We survived our first fight, and I had my first taste of make-up sex. Still, I was restless. Iris's bed had quickly become my own, but after tossing and turning for an hour, I went into the office so at least one of us could get some sleep. Half awake, she mumbled for me to stay, but I needed to write. Before Iris, it had been my lifeline.

People often don't see the error of their ways until much later, myself included, I wrote. *Humans are nothing, if not a work in progress—growing from birth till death.*

And Iris was catapulting me into my deepest transformation. I had felt it since the day we met, but now I could feel it more than ever. My bones were stretching in her presence.

I hammered away at my computer until dawn with a sinking feeling in my stomach. I knew I had written an essay that was good enough to be published, but I had to fight with Iris to get it.

I felt both weak and confident as I slipped back into the bedroom. My mind was still crowded, so I grabbed my weed and went back into the office to smoke. Halfway through my joint, I returned to the bedroom and sat in the corner chair to finish it. I wanted to see Iris. I wanted to remember why life was worth it. I sat there and watched her sleep, loving her more with every rise and fall of her chest. I knew she was all I wanted, but I was still trying to figure out who I was. And sometimes I wasn't sure if she was helping or hurting. She made me forget and remember all at the same time.

32

The weather was dim and overcast when I woke up just before noon. As much as I loved a blue sky, a grey one was fitting. Iris and I made up after our fight, but the atmosphere was still bleak, though she wasn't even home. She left a note on the kitchen counter saying that she was meeting a friend for brunch, which seemed weird because she hadn't mentioned it. I let it slip under my skin and left.

She called around half past one to ask where I was. When I told her I'd gone home, all she said was, "Oh." It was still weird to consider Iris's apartment my home, even though it was where I had slept nearly every night for almost a month. I wanted space, even if only for the afternoon. Signey asked what was wrong, but I just shrugged and hid out in my bedroom.

Iris picked me up around six for dinner at Rowe's. I didn't really feel like talking to her. She said I was overwhelming, after all. But I didn't want to talk to her, with her. We could sit in silence for all I cared. I still wanted to play footsie with her under the table as we ate.

We were talking about dreams when Brooks walked in. I figured at the rate the weekend was going, I might as well tell her about my premonitions. I had been biting my tongue on those. When I asked why she had been on the train back in November, she said it was because she felt like it. That's why she did things. Because she felt like it. She and Brooks had been fighting and she was antsy, so she rode the train to Santa Barbara, took some photographs, felt better, and hopped on a train back.

His ears must have been burning because he looked right at us. We both knew it was only a matter of time before we ran into Brooks, we just didn't talk about it. Iris parked an extra two blocks away to avoid parking in front of Untangled that night.

"I guess we didn't need to park so far away," I said.

She turned around and I shoved the rest of my pizza into my mouth. Brooks had to walk past us to get to the only open table. Iris looked back at me and said, "Well."

Brooks and his date stopped beside our table. She appeared to be Iris's polar opposite. She was tall and shy with a purse so large that I assumed her entire kitchen was inside it. She pulled out a piece of gum and chewed it rapidly, blowing bubbles as they awkwardly stood beside us. He introduced her, but she didn't say a word. It was a cordial but uncomfortable two minutes.

After they left us to sit at their table, I said, "Well."

Iris wiped her mouth with her napkin. "You ready?"

I could tell on the drive back to my place that she wanted to be alone, which was rare. If there was one thing that Iris Humphrey hated, it was being alone. I asked her to stay, and she did.

I followed her into my bedroom and closed the door behind us. She sat on my bed and played with her fingers as her hands rested in her lap. I sat down beside her and slowly pulled the white bandana from around her neck. I kissed her and gently grazed my fingers up and down her arms. If she was weary of my words, I wanted to distract her in other ways. She just let me take her as her body trembled with my every touch.

"You are loved beyond your wildest dreams," I reminded her.

Her gentle smile told me that she believed me.

Iris's insecurities were buried deep beneath the surface, and you had to dig to find them, but I knew they were there. I wanted nothing more than to hug her so tightly that I squeezed them right out of her. Sometimes she'd stumble over her words if something was slipping out, or she'd try to hide behind a smile. "You can't hide your eyes," I'd tell her, which would only make her try harder. It was like she painted over her scars, unaware that I had already accepted them as my own. I wasn't sure if she needed me to save her, or if I just wanted her to save me.

After listening to Bob Dylan over breakfast on Sunday morning, we went to the flea market with Signey. She laughed when we neared the booth with the old pictures because it was Iris who mentioned that she loved it. "You two are meant for each other," Signey said before she strolled away.

"I know," I whispered, smiling at Iris.

We spent some time sorting through the pictures—giving the people in them names and stories—and then before catching up with Signey, we stopped at a table of sunglasses. The *buy one, get one half off* sign lured me in. "Hey, you want a pair?" I asked.

We walked under the small white canopy, and she tried on all the ugliest pairs of sunglasses. I found it cute until she settled on a pair that swallowed her face.

"Are you serious? They're huge," I said, laughing.

"Yeah, I like these ones," she said, looking in the mirror.

"Seriously?"

She looked back at me. "Yeah."

"Iris...you look like a fly. A cute fly, but a fly."

"And your point?"

"My point is you look like a fly," I said with a light laugh.

She smiled and adjusted the pair on my face. A much smaller pair.

I walked over to the older man standing in the corner of the booth. I pulled some cash from my pocket and tried to hand it to him. "Just the two," I said.

He tilted his head and pointed at Iris, who was already sorting through a rack of t-shirts in the next booth. "The little lady over there already paid," he said.

"Oh, okay. Thanks," I said, putting the cash back into my pocket.

I walked over to Iris, who held a Neil Young t-shirt. "I love that shirt," I said.

"You want it?" she asked.

"No. Grant has it."

"Oh," she said, putting it back. She walked over to the next rack. I followed her. "Why did you do that?"

She stopped rummaging and gave me a confused look. "Do what?"

"Pay for the sunglasses. I was the one who asked if you wanted a pair."

She shrugged. "I don't know. I just gave him the money while you were trying them on."

"Yes, you do, Iris. You did it because you have more than me."

"What's the big deal? It was only fifteen bucks."

"It's not a big deal, but if I offer to buy, just let me buy."

"Okay." She gave me a faint smile and adjusted the giant sunglasses on her beautiful face.

"Thank you," I said, pulling the cash out of my pocket and handing it to her.

She hesitated, but she took it and shoved it into the back pocket of her tight blue jeans.

―――――

Monday was our one-month anniversary, and despite our insecurities, Iris and I seemed to be back to where we were before our fight. We slid through it, no matter how slippery it had been, and made it to the other side. I knew there'd be more rough moments ahead, but with each other, we'd always have a soft place to land, no matter how far the fall.

TO BE HER GIRL

We still hadn't solidified our relationship status, but I called her my girlfriend when she wasn't listening. We already shared a bed, so I didn't see any reason not to. It was only her who still feared the word. She joked over breakfast that to celebrate one month made her feel like she was in junior high again. I didn't care. I had plans. I wanted to celebrate us, especially after our trying weekend.

The night I told Iris about Pyxis, I mentioned how the ceiling in my childhood bedroom had been covered with glow-in-the-dark stars. She never had any, but said she wished she did. And when we made love under the stars in Joshua Tree, we wished we could every night. The stars were mostly dimmed against the city lights of Los Angeles, so artificial stars would have to do. After work, I headed back to my place and covered those eighty-eight and odd ceiling tiles in my bedroom. Three larger blue ones mapped out Pyxis.

When Iris got to my place, I met her out front instead of inviting her up, which prompted her to give me a curious look. "What are you up to, Callahan Thomas?" she asked.

"I'm hungry," I said. "Let's go."

I smiled and she did too.

The last time I had walked from my apartment to Jem's was the night she asked me to get ice cream. I was well aware of that as we strolled hand in hand down Sunset Boulevard. About halfway there, I stopped for a moment to admire her. Her skin was glowing, and the waves of her hair were loose and perfectly messy, just as I loved them most. She wore the same long white dress that she'd been wearing when we first met. "Was this outfit intentional?" I asked, beaming.

Her answer was a smile, which was enough for me.

"God, you're so beautiful," I said.

She smiled again and squeezed my hand.

It was something I still couldn't grasp, how beautiful she was, and sometimes I found myself looking at her as if it were the first time. She had this light that radiated from the inside out. It only made her drop dead gorgeous looks even more alluring. She was attractive in every sense of the word. And I got to hold her hand. I got to love her. I had never felt more blessed than I did in that moment.

Jem's was slow that night, but Signey reserved my favorite booth for us anyway. The tables were always decorated with a candle in a mason jar, and when Iris and I walked in, we saw that every candle was on our table. The host nodded his head toward our booth and winked.

I assured Iris that I didn't have anything to do with the candles, while the host took them back to their rightful homes, but the look on her face when she saw them made me wish that I did.

As she looked over the menu, which I never had to do because I always ordered a grilled cheese sandwich and tomato soup, I noticed the dried-up flower framed on the wall above our table. "Is this the one that's always been here?" I asked the waiter.

"I don't know," he said, "but I don't think anything has been moved."

"Signey!" I shouted across the room. "Come here!"

"What's up?" she asked with a smile after she landed beside us.

"A: Thanks for the candles. And B: Has this always been the one here?" I asked, pointing at the frame.

"Yeah, why?"

"It's an Iris."

"Wow, no wonder it's always been your favorite booth."

"No wonder."

Iris smiled. "How long have you been sitting at this table?"

"Ever since I moved to Los Angeles."

We ate our dinner and before we left, we visited the photo booth.

I pushed back the black curtain, and Iris stepped inside. I followed and sat beside her on the small bench. I closed the curtain and pulled three one-dollar bills from the front pocket of my jeans. I'd stuffed them in there for the occasion.

"How should we start?" I asked as I inserted the bills into the machine.

"We'll just wing it," Iris said, pressing the buttons on the touch screen in front of us.

3...2...1... The numbers flashed on the screen. I looked at Iris and she looked at me. We both smiled and the camera flashed. We looked back at the screen. 3...2... Iris gave the peace sign with her right hand and I widened my mouth into the biggest grin I could give. 1... The camera flashed. 3... Iris stuck her middle finger in the air. 2... "Iris, no," I said, laughing. I covered her hand with mine and she laughed too. 1... The camera flashed. 3...2...1... We kissed and the camera flashed.

"Sorry, it was a reflex," Iris said as I stepped out of the booth.

"What, kissing me or giving the middle finger?" I asked as she followed me out.

"Both, I guess."

"Weird reflex."

"Old habits die hard."

We laughed and waited for our strip of black and white photos. I pulled it from the slot after it printed.

"That actually turned out great," I said, laughing and pointing at the picture where I had covered her middle finger.

"Aw, see, it always works out," Iris said. She smiled and I kissed her perfect lips.

We said goodbye to Signey and walked over to Echo Park Lake. We didn't talk, just held hands and put one foot in front of the other, together. The sky was clear and the stars were abnormally visible that September night. "Look," I said, as we stopped just before the water, "the stars came out for you."

She looked up and then into my eyes. "They came out for us."

It was the corniest thing she ever said to me, but it truly felt like they had.

Walking around the lake with Iris that night was easily the happiest moment of my life. She was everything I ever wanted, and everything I didn't know I did. It was the simplicity of our time together that solidified what I had felt from the moment I laid eyes on her. She wasn't just the love of my life; she was the very root of my existence.

We headed back to my apartment and lounged on the couch, downing half a bottle of wine. I didn't even notice until we finished that I never put on the music I had picked out. The sound of her voice was all I needed. We could get lost in a conversation about anything and everything for hours.

"Wait here," I said before going into my bedroom. When I came back out, she joked that she thought maybe I'd be returning in some sexy lingerie. "Maybe for our two-month," I said, sitting back down beside her. I held the small indigo box with her name etched into it.

"What's that?" she asked.

"I'm always finding things that remind me of you," I said, flipping it over. "I found it the day after we met." I turned it right side up and opened it. "And I found this yesterday." I took out a small mariner's compass, about the size of a quarter. "Don't lose it," I said, placing it into her hand. I could see the tears well up in her eyes.

"I don't have anything for you," she said.

"Iris…You're here…That's all I need."

And I meant it.

She closed her hand around the compass and put both her hands on my cheeks. She kissed me, then said, "I love you."

"And I love you. And I've got one more thing."

"Oh God, Cal," she said, smiling.

"It's not much," I said, standing up.

I held out my hand and she took it. She stood and we walked into my bedroom.

"Oh my God," she said, laughing through her tears. "Glow-in-the-dark stars."

"And," I said, smiling and pointing to the ceiling.

"Pyxis," she said.

"Pyxis," I echoed.

"I love it. I love you."

And so we made love beneath the stars.

33

After Monday night, I hoped we'd spend the rest of the week simply. Iris was always moving and I was getting worn out. I loved spending time with her friends, but after long days at work, I just wanted to stay in sometimes. I wanted to put my feet up with Iris at my side, as we debated what to eat for dinner and fought over the TV remote, like normal couples. It was a nice vision; it just didn't really happen.

On Tuesday, we attended Colin Dumont's album release party. When he sang a song called, "The Moment I Came Alive," Iris gave me a gentle smile and squeezed my hand. "This reminds me of you," she said. The night was mostly simple, but Brooks and his bubble gum chewing date were there, and the air was undeniably awkward.

Wednesday, Paige hosted a dinner party for people who worked on her line, even Signey. I didn't see any reason for Iris and me to be there, but we were.

Come Thursday, I finally asked if we could stay home and relax. But her friends were going bowling, and she wanted to go too. Eventually I told her to go without me, and she did. I figured a night apart would be beneficial, even though I missed her. She was the blood rushing through me, but she was not my veins. I was only beginning to realize that.

I took advantage of the alone time and got some writing done. I was scribbling ideas into my notebook when my pen ran out of ink. I grabbed another from the top of Iris's desk, but it didn't work either.

I opened a desk drawer to look for another. I didn't see a pen, but my letter—the one I had given to her after the art show three and a half months earlier. I took it out and unfolded it. I held it in my hands as they shook. I read my words and felt just as shaky as my hands. I had been so out of my mind that night and couldn't remember most of them. "Oh Jesus, Callahan," I said to myself.

I folded the letter and set it on the desk. I pulled up the emails I'd sent her on my computer and read those too. I had always tried to imagine her reading them, but I never really could. It felt like I was standing at the edge of a cliff shouting, "I love you!" without knowing where the words were landing.

"She must've thought you were fucking crazy," I said to myself. I rested my elbows on the desk and covered my eyes with my hands. They got wet as I cried. "It's fine. It's fine. It's fine," I repeated. I pulled my hands from my face and wiped away my tears. "It all worked out. You're here. You're together. Different steps, same path."

I was afraid my letters had hurt us, but the chick is not born without the crack of the egg, and my words were the crack. That was how I had to see it. I thought we needed to be together, and that was how it happened. Because without my blood, what would be the point of my veins?

I went to put my letter back where Iris kept it and noticed it had been resting on a stack of journals. They were aged and worn, and because of their condition, I couldn't deny my curiosity. I picked up the one on top, a red pocketbook with a gold ribbon marker. I felt a familiar sensation rush through me as I held it. It was the same feeling I had on the anniversary of Iris's mom's passing. I froze for a moment, then opened the small book. In blue ink, the first page said only: *Love is the most divine sickness.* It was signed *Sara Lovell.*

After closing it slowly, I placed the journal belonging to Iris's mom back into the drawer where I found it, carefully. But her words still echoed through me. I couldn't consider loving Iris to be a sickness, but at times, it certainly resulted in something severely unhealthy.

I heard the front door open, put away my letter, and shut the drawer. I stood up and walked into the kitchen. Iris had her head in the sink, drinking water straight out of the faucet. "Thirsty?" I asked.

She lifted her head and shut off the water. She turned around to face me. "You're still up."

"Appears that way. How'd you do?"

"What?" she asked.

"Bowling. Did you get any strikes?"

"I bowled a sixty-nine." She raised her eyebrows.

I laughed and shook my head. "You didn't drive, right?"

"Why?"

"Because you're drunk."

"Paige drove." She walked over to me and put her hands on my hips, pulling my body into hers. "And so what if I am? You love me no matter what, right?"

"Yes," I said. "No matter what."

"Because we're soulmates, right?"

"Yes, Iris."

"That's what you like to say."

"Yes, Iris." I smiled and shook my head again. "Don't you think so?"

"Shut up," she said and kissed me.

I was in the kitchen after work the next day—leaning against the counter, scrolling through Fodoary on my phone, and whistling—when Iris walked in from the other room. I didn't know she was home. "Hey," I said.

"Hey."

I kissed her, but she seemed reluctant to kiss back.

"How was work?" she asked.

"The same as always. How was the shoot?"

"It was good, but I'm exhausted. I just got home a little bit ago." She opened the refrigerator and pulled out a beer. "You want one?"

"Maybe later," I said. "I was thinking we could go to Jem's tonight with Grant and Daniella."

She shut the refrigerator and placed her beer on the counter. "Oh, so I should go out with your friends, but you wouldn't go out with mine?" She raised her eyebrows and smirked. She grabbed Brooks' bottle opener and opened her beer.

"Please tell me you're kidding, Iris. The ratio of us hanging out with your friends compared to mine is about ten-to-one."

"I'm kidding," she said. But she still rolled her eyes like I was throwing myself a pity party or something.

"Okay, so do you want to go?"

She sighed and put the bottle opener back. "It's been a long day." She sighed again. She opened the refrigerator and took out the peanut butter. She unscrewed the jar and scooped some out with her finger. She stuck it in her mouth, sucked it clean, and then put away the jar.

I sighed and shook my head with a smirk. "Iris, come on."

"You can go without me tonight." She grabbed her beer and walked over to the couch.

"I don't want to go without you. I missed you last night."

"We don't have to do everything together all the time." She sat down and sipped her beer.

I clenched my jaw before saying, "No, I guess not."

"Okay, so go," she said.

I walked over to the coffee table and stood across from her. "Is that what you want? You want me to leave?"

She shrugged before taking another sip of her beer.

"Well, whatever," I said, walking away.

"It's just too much sometimes. You're obsessed with me."

I stopped and turned around. "Of course I'm obsessed with you. I'm in love with you. Where the hell is this coming from?"

She shrugged and chugged her beer. She placed it on the coffee table. I shook my head and walked away.

"You're too loud in the morning," she said.

I turned around and walked back over to her. "What?"

"You whistle too much."

"Yeah, and you leave your dishes lying around and don't refill the water pitcher. Why are you acting like this?"

"I don't know," she said. She bit her lip harshly and cracked her knuckles.

I groaned. Sometimes I woke to the sound of her cracking her knuckles in the middle of the night, and it was starting to haunt me in my dreams. It was one of the things I had gleefully anticipated—her annoying little habits that I wanted to live with. But at times, they were the things I was beginning to think that I could live without.

"And use the fucking coaster," I said, pointing at her beer that she had placed right beside it. "I know you like your art, but it's not just for decoration."

"It's my beer. It's my table. It's my apartment. Not yours," she said.

We stared at each other silently. It was the final straw and we both knew it.

"I'm sorry," she said lightly. "I didn't mean it like that."

"It doesn't matter, Iris. I'm going home," I said as calmly as I could. Tears fell from my eyes.

"Callahan, just…" She let out a sigh and never finished that sentence.

I looked around her apartment, trying to keep my tears from turning into a full-on sob. We both knew what was happening. The world was catching up to us.

"I'll see you later," I said. I stared at her, but she couldn't bring herself to say anything. I took a deep breath. I thought if I inhaled enough it would soothe my burning heart. But all it did was make me choke.

I put on my coat and shoes, and grabbed my phone and purse. I put my hand on the door knob and then turned back around. I looked at Iris sitting on the couch. She looked at me like she was a puppy abandoned under a bridge. I thought maybe I should stay, but then she looked away. I turned around, opened the door, and left.

I walked to the market on the corner and got myself a pint of Neapolitan ice cream. I walked back to my car and then drove to my apartment. Everything I was told when we started dating was bouncing around in my head. "Just don't lose yourself," Cora would say. But somewhere along the way, I let that happen. I lost myself in her, and I lost her in me. We were a blur, and I didn't know where she ended and I began.

I walked into my apartment and put the ice cream in the freezer. I calmly walked over to the couch, but before my body even touched the cushion, I began to cry. I sat down and took my phone from my pocket. I called Cora and she answered with an immediate, "What's wrong?"

I bawled for at least minute before I could even get a word out. "It doesn't matter how well I know her or how much I love her," I finally said.

"What happened?" Cora asked.

"We went from zero to sixty in record time."

"Yeah, you did."

"We're feeling the whiplash."

"Are you at your apartment?"

"Yeah, and she's at hers."

"Maybe that's okay for now."

"I don't know what's happening," I said. "One minute we're fine and then the next, she can't even look at me. She's the most complicated woman on the face of the fucking earth."

"And you're a walk in the park?"

"Thanks, Cora," I said sternly through my tears.

"Callahan, be realistic here. How many times were you together before you moved in? Since you met, how many times had you talked before you were living together? It was only a few times, right? Over the course of a year."

"Yeah," I muttered.

"You barely knew each other and now you're together all the time. That's a lot to handle."

I sighed heavily without opening my mouth, feeling the air escape through my nose. "It's like we were morphed into this untouchable creature, and now it's eating us from the inside out."

"Well, you are whatever you decide to be."

"What am I supposed to do, Cora? Stop talking like a fortune cookie and tell me what to do. You're my sister, that's your job."

"No. No, it's not. I can't tell you what to do and even if I could, you wouldn't listen. You never have. You've always been your own person, and you have to remember that Iris is her own person too."

I bit my lip and stared at nothing.

"Cal?" Cora asked after a long silence.

I sighed loudly.

"Get some sleep," she said. "I'll call you tomorrow."

"Good night," I said.

"Love you."

"Love you too."

Instead of going to Jem's, I sat on my couch and drowned myself in whiskey. The stereo was on full blast, and I swore I heard my neighbors below me pounding on their ceiling, but it could have just been the bass. I didn't care either way. While eating my Neapolitan right out of the carton, I burst into tears and threw it at the wall. Instead of cleaning it, I just scribbled a note for Signey on our chalkboard, apologizing for our new wall color.

Eventually Iris called. I answered but said nothing.

"Are you okay?" she asked.

"No," I muttered.

"Are you drunk?"

"Very."

"Can I come get you?"

I didn't respond.

"Cal."

I still didn't say anything.

"I'm coming over."

"Okay."

Twenty minutes later, there was a knock on my door. I opened it to find Iris with a heart-shaped balloon and a Neapolitan ice cream cake. For a moment, I was less interested in her apology than I was curious where she got a large foil balloon at midnight.

I just wanted to love her and be with her and forget about everything else. Fighting with her was hard, but I knew that nothing would ever be as hard as living without her. But it wasn't just the words that hurt; I could feel her slipping through the cracks of my hands, and I didn't know if I had the strength to catch her. I was still trying to catch myself.

We didn't say much that night. We didn't make love. We didn't even eat that cake.

34

On Sunday afternoon, we met Grant and Daniella at Amber. It was Iris's idea. I figured to make up for Friday. But she couldn't distract herself from whatever was on her mind. She was quiet and somber, and I could tell that something other than me was stirring inside her. When we got back to her apartment, I said, "Tell me...Please...Tell me what is wrong," as gently as I could.

"I'm fine," she said.

But she wasn't fine and I knew it. Her face dripped with a despair that I couldn't quite put my finger on. I stared at her with an empathy that I didn't understand. No matter the distance seeping between us, our emotions were still dramatically tied.

About ten seconds after insisting that she was fine, she sat on the couch and buried her face in her hands. I sat beside her and she fell into my arms, sobbing uncontrollably. Her body shook as I held her.

"Iris, what's wrong?" I asked with a shaky voice.

Iris sat up and looked into my eyes. Tears poured out of them. "She would've turned sixty today."

"Oh, baby, I'm so sorry."

"But she left. She left me. Wasn't I enough? Wasn't I enough to save her?"

I could feel my heart breaking. I could feel hers. I placed my hands on her cheeks and stared into her eyes like her life depended on it.

"You are more than enough, Iris Renée Humphrey. Don't you ever doubt that," I said. I brushed her hair out of her face with my fingers before sliding my hands into hers. "There was nothing you could've done. She loved you so much. She still does. She always will. I can't tell you why she took her own life, and I wish more than anything that she hadn't. I wish it wasn't you who found her. I wish she was still here. I wish I could've met her."

I paused to wipe the tears from Iris's eyes as she stared into mine.

"But this life, it's temporary," I continued. "It's almost like it's a dream. It's an illusion. We are so much more than this world. I don't know where she is now, but I know that she's with you. She's always with you. I promise. I know it hurts. I know it's not the same, not having her here, and there's nothing I can do to change that. But if I can do one good thing in this life, I hope it's that I make you feel that you're enough. I hope it's that I make you feel loved. Because you are worthy of every ounce of good that this world has to offer, and I will do my best to bring it to you. I love you so much, and I am so sorry that she's not here to tell you how much she does too."

She listened intently but, "I love you," was all she could say back.

I kissed her forehead and wiped away our tears. I adjusted my body and leaned against the back of the couch. I lifted my legs and put my feet on the coffee table. She lay down and rested her head on my lap. She closed her eyes and mouthed, "I love you."

I brushed her hair back from her face again and stroked her cheek with the side of my pointer finger. "I love you," I mouthed back.

I eventually leaned my head back and closed my eyes.

Tuesday was Daniella's birthday, and Grant had a group of tables reserved at her favorite restaurant downtown. "I'm almost forty," Iris said while we waited at a red light on the way there. She stared out the window in the passenger's seat, rather than looking at me.

"And?" I asked.

"That's a long way off for you."

"And?" I repeated. "Would you change my age? Because I wouldn't change yours. It just reminds me of how much time we've already wasted apart…And you're only thirty-seven. Don't get ahead of yourself."

She looked at me and said, "The light's green."

There were about a dozen of us at dinner, but Iris seemed reluctant to engage with anyone. It was hard to enjoy myself when she sat in the corner sulking. "Could you not ruin my friend's birthday, please?" I whispered as her moodiness became apparent to the others. She rolled her eyes like I was talking down to her or asking for the impossible.

After dinner, Grant pulled me aside as we waited for the valet to bring our cars around. Iris stood with her arms crossed, like a child whose mom wouldn't stop talking to a friend at the grocery store.

"What's up with Iris?" he asked.

My heart dropped. Even when she was upset around other people, she'd put on a front like she wasn't. But she just couldn't seem to do it that night, or didn't care to. "I don't know," I said. "She's been miserable lately. And really fucking immature."

"How are you guys doing?"

"Again, I don't know." I shrugged. "I don't know where she is, and I don't know what to do. It's like when she said, 'I love you,' she flipped a switch and went back to wherever it was she came from. We're not really talking about it."

I paused to watch Iris. She stared down the street, looking at what, I didn't know. I looked back at Grant and said, "Maybe avoidance is the key to survival."

"Acceptance is the key to survival."

"Maybe," I said after a silent nod. "I just want to be there for her, with her, but sometimes I'm afraid I'm smothering her just by being in the same room."

"It's because your love brings out everything, every bit of beauty and every trace of ugly."

"Why though?" I asked. "Why the ugly? I'm trying to understand it, but she doesn't seem to want to. I'm like the painting that hangs above her couch. It's her favorite; she can just never decide what it means. I catch her studying it sometimes, but she always insists it's better left without interpretation."

"Maybe it is," Grant said.

"I don't know."

The valet drove up in my car.

"Alright, I'll see ya later," I said.

"Later," he said, pulling me in for a hug. "It'll be fine."

I stepped over to Daniella, gave her a hug, and wished her a happy birthday. I walked to my car, tipped the driver, and looked at Iris. "You ready?" I asked. I was careful not to say anything to set her off, half expecting her to fall to the ground in a temper tantrum if I did.

After we got home and ready for bed, we sat at the table with a bowl of Neapolitan. "I'm sorry you've been upset about something," I said after I finished mine. "Grant asked me what was wrong."

"I'm sorry. I shouldn't have gone. I just wasn't in the mood," Iris said.

"Ya know, I thought maybe avoidance was the key to survival, but Grant mentioned that acceptance was. I'm sorry if I'm too much for you."

She shrugged and scooped her last bite of ice cream into her mouth. It felt like she was looking right through me. My patience was slipping.

"What do you want from me?" I asked, unable to hide my annoyance.

"Callahan, don't start." She dropped her spoon into her empty bowl, making a loud clinking sound.

"No, I want to know. Who am I to you? Am I just some kid who became infatuated with you? Who you thought you could take for a ride?"

She stood up and walked away.

I got up to follow her but stopped abruptly. I leaned over the table and reached for the shelf on the wall above it. I grabbed the wine bottle from our first night together. It was filled with petals from wildflowers I'd given her the week after. Her silence infuriated me and out of blinding frustration, I threw it.

She came running back out and found those petals and shards of glass scattered across the kitchen floor. "Callahan! What the fuck?"

I stood there, completely heartbroken I had shattered that bottle. I just wanted to tell her to talk to me, but my temper beat me to the punch. "I can't keep up with you," I said. I covered my face as a loud sob broke out of me. I moved my hands, now wet with tears, to the top of my head. "I don't know what you want from me." I let my arms fall harshly to my side.

"Neither do I," Iris said. Tears slid down her cheeks.

"Don't you want to find out anymore? Why can't you just talk to me?"

"I don't know...I don't know."

"Well, figure it out. Talk to me. Look at me."

"I am looking at you."

I shook my head and walked to the closet. I grabbed the broom and swept up the broken glass and petals. I took a plastic bag from below the sink and put them into it. I tossed it into the trash can and put the broom back into the closet. Iris stood still and watched the entire time. I walked over to her, but she shook her head and said, "I can't...I just can't right now." She started to walk away. We were both still crying.

"What did I do? What the fuck did I do?" I asked.

She stopped and shook her head again. She turned around to face me. "Nothing," she said. "I'm sorry. I love you." She turned back around and went into her office.

I walked over to the couch and lay down. I could hear her crying through her closed office door, but I didn't dare go near her.

EMILY CRADDUCK

I stayed in the living room and cried quietly for hours. I hoped she'd come out to get me, but she never did. Around one a.m., I wrote her a letter and left it on the kitchen counter. I eventually fell asleep on the couch.

That morning was the first time she didn't wake up to see me before I headed out for work.

October 1, 2014

Dear Iris,

Syracuse University conducted a study about falling in love. They concluded that it takes about a fifth of a second…but I don't buy it. There is no way it took me that long to fall in love with you.

I know talking about it still makes you uncomfortable. I'm sorry I tried to pull it out of you last night, and I'm sorry about the bottle. It feels like I'm always sorry about something.

I don't know if I did something wrong or if you've just changed your mind. It seems when we fell into each other, we were forced to fall into ourselves, and maybe it's just become too much. Don't worry, I feel it too. I don't imagine we can unknow anything, but I suppose we can run. I just don't want to. I want to ride out every storm with you, even the ones we've stirred up within each other.

Gamma. Alpha. Beta. We'll always have our compass, remember?

I want to spend my life discovering all that you are. For everything I know, there's that much more that I don't. No matter how well I know you, I will never know you completely, which is beautiful because that means I will never stop learning. My favorite book will always have another chapter, and my favorite song, another verse. There is no end to you, so there is no end to me.

By shutting down, I am only more determined to break through your walls. You will never meet anyone as curious as me. I will always be your greatest admirer.

Again, I'm sorry about last night. I just wish you'd stop hiding away.

Have a great day, Iris. I hope you get some good shots. You always do.

I love you.

Always,
Callahan

TO BE HER GIRL

I had an irrational fear that she had the locks changed while I was at work. Fortunately I was wrong, but my stomach still had a knot the size of my head. My letter was no longer on the counter, but in its place was one for me.

Callahan -
"Someday you will find a love so full that you can only succumb to it after you succumb to yourself. But you mustn't fret, it'll still be there tomorrow, just as it was before you found it. Remember, it is only these bodies that perish, never our soul, never our love."
My mom left me with those words and as I read them again last night, I could only imagine that she was speaking of you.
I love you with everything that I have and everything that I am. Please don't ever doubt that.

- Iris

Iris had a photoshoot for an up-and-coming band in Palm Springs that day. I knew she wouldn't be home until after dinner, so I planned accordingly. I picked up the same bottle of wine from our first night—the one I had smashed—and a Neapolitan ice cream cake. I decorated the table with a bouquet of roses and a dozen white votive candles in amber-colored glass holders. After scattering rose petals across the bed, I covered her bedroom ceiling with glow-in-the-dark stars, including another blue trio to represent Pyxis.

"I hope it's okay that I'm here," I said when Iris came home. "You didn't answer when I called...or any of my messages...I'm sorry."

"Oh, babe," she said, catching a glimpse of the table. "Yeah, it's okay that you're here."

"How was the shoot?" I asked as casually as I could.

"It was good...chaotic, but good. I'm sorry I wasn't really paying much attention to my phone."

I nodded but didn't believe her. She was always checking her phone. She was just awful at communicating. But in that moment, I didn't care.

"They asked if I'd be interested in shooting a music video for them," she continued.

"Iris, that's awesome," I said, beaming.

She smiled then pressed her lips together. "You get any writing done?"

"No, but I'm sure I will soon. I'm just happy more opportunities are coming your way. I really, truly am. I'm happy you're doing so well...I'll catch up." I reached for her hands and held them in mine. "You rise, I rise. I rise, you rise."

She looked down slightly, trying to hide the smile lighting up her face. But she looked back up and gave up the fight, flashing me a smile and kissing mine. "Thank you..." She gently pulled her hands from mine and ran her finger along the edge of the table. "It's beautiful." She pulled a rose from the vase and smelled it before handing it to me. "You're too good to me."

"I don't know about that, Iris...but I'm trying." I smelled the rose and placed it between the burning candles.

She placed her hand on my cheek and then tucked my hair behind my ear. "I love you so much, it scares me."

"I know."

She kissed me softly before pulling back. She gave the cake a side glance and me a smirk. "It's almost like I can have my cake and eat it too."

"We'll make it work," I said.

She nodded but looked a bit unsure.

"I love you, Iris. I love you...you and your big stupid sunglasses." I pulled them from her cleavage and put them on my face.

"They do look like fly eyes."

"But a cute fly."

"A cute fly," she said, laughing. "I love you."

After some cake and wine, we blew out the candles and she told me how cold her bed had been without me.

"Oh, I think we can fix that," I said. I put out my hand and nodded my head toward the bedroom.

She placed her hand in mine and smiled.

We went into the bedroom, and first she gasped at the rose petals decorating the bed, and then she laughed at the stars. I picked up a pile of petals and tossed them into the air. They fluttered all over us and one landed on my face, tickling my skin. She laughed softly and brushed it off.

She unbuttoned my shirt, and I felt my stomach flinch as if it were the first time she touched it. She slipped my shirt over my shoulders and tore hers over her head. The sight of her green bra over her silky skin was orgasmic enough, but she slid it off and willed me backward onto the rose-covered bed.

"Any thorns?" she asked. The corner of her mouth curved upward. The other side followed suit a few moments later, and she laughed with her lips sealed.

I shook my head no, then she kissed me hard on my mouth. She pulled back and suddenly it felt like we were in a bubble full of a billion pieces of passion. It was all we had to breathe. We stood and tore off the rest of our clothes. We stared at each other in silence until she grabbed my hands and pressed me up against the wall. She kissed me again and pressed her body into mine. Our fingers were laced perfectly and I could feel her tighten her grip. I arched my body forward and hers moved right along with it.

Still kissing, we stepped over to the bed, and I landed on top of her as we fell onto it. She scooched herself backward, and I crawled over her until our legs were no longer dangling over the edge. To the rhythm of whatever song that was pulsating through my body, I moved mine into hers. We didn't stop kissing until our breathing became so heavy that we had to. I slid my body down slightly and rested my head on her chest, lying on top of her like we were two puzzle pieces perfectly fit together. We calmed our breathing, and I rubbed a petal between my fingers.

"I fucking love you so fucking much," she said.
"I fucking love you too."
She laughed and her body shook below me. I pressed my hands into the bed, tearing the petal between my fingers, and pushed myself up. I smiled and lay on my side next to her.
She rolled over and stared into my eyes. It was hard to believe so little time had passed since we couldn't keep contact.
"I'm sorry," she said.
"I'm sorry too. I know I'm overwhelming sometimes. I just love you so much. I don't know what to do with all these feelings I have. I don't mean to smother you with them."
"I know. At least you never ran from them."
"Like I do everything else?" I sighed.
"What are you running from?"
"If I knew, maybe I'd stop running."
"If you don't stop long enough to look around, how will you ever know?" She inhaled deeply, which seemed to catch her off guard. Her exhale sailed into a smile and she kissed me.
"Are you happy, Iris?"
"With you? Yeah, I'm happy." Her eyes glistened and she smiled again.
I smiled and wrapped my leg over hers. "But I mean really happy. Deep down happy."
"Why?"
"Because you seem so sad lately...And I don't want you to be sad. I want you to be happy."
"Happiness comes in moments. That's all I can ask for. Those moments." She tucked my hair behind my ear and stroked my cheek. "You give me those moments."
"Good. Because you deserve to be happy."
"Do I?"
I kissed her lips. "Yes," I said in a firm whisper. "Always."
A star fell from the ceiling and landed between us. We laughed and I put it back up. I walked around the bed, picking up the rose

petals.

"What are you doing?"

"I don't want them to leave a stain," I said.

The star fell again.

"Dammit," I said and laughed.

She laughed and put it back up.

I placed the petals on her dresser and lay back down beside her. We kissed and made love and I never wanted to stop. I wanted to hold her until the earth ceased to exist. We talked for hours until her eyelids became too heavy. When she told me she loved me, I believed her. And when I said we could spend every night like that, I wanted to believe myself.

She slept with her arm across my stomach, while I lay awake and still, until my alarm clock sounded. There was something about that night that compelled me to hold on to every second of her in my arms. I clung to the feel of her skin and the smell of her hair, unsure of what the daylight would bring.

She gave me a faint smile when she woke and said, "I love you," as she rolled over to her side of the bed.

"I love you, my beautiful Iris," I whispered.

We shared a kiss before I left, wishing I never had to, knowing I did.

The air was different when I came home after work. Our life felt like a roller coaster and I was getting nauseous. She asked about my day over dinner—she had a grilled cheese sandwich and tomato soup waiting for me—but didn't say much else.

"What's wrong?" I asked as she incessantly stirred her soup without eating it.

She didn't look up from her bowl. She just flared her nostrils slightly. Her nostrils always flared when she was being serious or about to say something she was unsure of. Sometimes if they didn't,

I knew she wasn't paying attention.

"I don't think you should come here after work tomorrow," she said faintly.

Everything inside me exploded into flames. "What?" I asked, hoping I misheard her, but knowing I didn't.

"Maybe we should just…"

"Iris, what are you saying?"

She shook her head while staring at the table.

"No…No," I said, shaking my head too.

"I just think…" She looked up at me with her big beautiful weeping eyes.

"No. No," I repeated as I cried. "No…I need you…Please, please don't leave me…I need you."

"I think it'd be for the best if we focus on ourselves for a while…"

I couldn't believe my ears. Just the night before she never wanted to let me go, and now she wanted me to leave.

"How can you give up on us?" I stuttered, trying not to throw up the sandwich I just ate. "So easily."

"This isn't easy. How could you think this is easy?" she asked as tears rolled down her cheeks. "Please don't put this all on me. You're just as lost as I am."

I stared at her, searching for words. "You're right. This is on me," I finally said. My tears raced hers, streaming like the force of nature that we were together. "I threw myself at you and when you finally took me, I thought it was enough. I thought love was enough."

"I'm sorry," she said. "I just think we could use some time apart."

"Ya know, when I found you, I thought maybe I had found myself, and I never believed in anything more. That's why it was so hard when you wouldn't acknowledge me. It was like everything I ever believed in was wrong. I understand now. I do. Maybe I put too much on you. But after all we've been through, do you really think walking away would help?"

After a minute without words and only the sound of our crying, she said, "Everybody always leaves me anyway."

TO BE HER GIRL

"You can't do that!" I shouted, sobbing. "You can't tell me to leave and then say that. This isn't a game, Iris. This is our life. You can't test me like that. If you want me to go, okay, I'll go. But I will never leave you. Never. It's impossible."

She covered her mouth and shook her head. "It's just too much," she said behind her hand.

I never wanted to kiss her more than I did in that moment, but I was afraid to touch her. I was afraid we'd both turn to dust. We just sat at her table, same as we had that first night, and cried. I told her I'd have Signey come back for my things. I didn't have the strength to collect them that night. My chest felt tighter and tighter with every passing second.

Neither of us could stop crying as we mumbled things back and forth. "I can't be who you want me to be," she said.

"You already are, Iris," I said. "You already are." But it didn't seem to matter.

Eventually I stood up, tossed on my coat and slipped on my shoes. She walked me to my car and when we got to it, we just stood there with tears silently sliding down our faces, unsure what to do. Whatever we had been doing for the last six weeks was ending as quickly as it began.

"Gamma. Alpha. Beta," I finally said, tracing her freckles down her cheek. "We will find our way back to each other. I promise. I love you, Iris Renée Humphrey, more than you will ever know, more than I will ever know."

"I love you, Callahan Anastasia Thomas," she said after tracing my matching freckles.

It was hard to look at her, so I looked to the night sky, with its few visible stars, through my watery eyes. I wanted to see Pyxis, but knew that I couldn't. I looked at the moon instead. Half full, it stared right back at me, grimacing at my misery. I had to look away.

We kissed and I could taste her salty tears on her lips. I had never held anybody as tightly as I did hugging her that night, but eventually I had to pull away from her trembling body. We stood silently, gazing into each other's eyes like we'd find Pyxis in them. Moving at all felt like an option in that moment. I could have lived in her eyes until my body gave out. But as the air brought a gentle breeze, I knew that it wasn't.

I turned away, got into my car, and drove off. I couldn't bear to look in the rear-view mirror, but I knew she was still standing in the street watching me.

It was the hardest thing I ever had to do.

PART IV

*She was the sweetest drug
I ever touched,
and the most beautiful habit
I ever tried to break.*

35

Being with Iris was everything I dreamt of and more. I thought we could handle whatever life threw our way, whatever we threw at each other, but maybe we just couldn't handle ourselves. I drove in a trance, and when I got back to my apartment, I wasn't sure how I made it alive.

I staggered up the steps. It felt like there were a million of them. I hit the door of my apartment slow and steady with my palm. I hit it over and over, harder each time. I was too weak to use my key and too weak to call for Signey. Eventually I had to muster the strength to pound.

Signey opened the door in a state of shock that couldn't compete with my own. "What happened? Why are you home?" she asked as I slowly stepped past her. She shut the door and turned to find me calmly taking my grandma's painting off the wall.

I placed it on the floor and turned back to Signey. "I don't have a home anymore," I said. A tear slid down my face and soaked into my upper lip. I licked it with my tongue that could still taste Iris. "I don't know what happened," I said as more tears fell. "She thinks we need time to ourselves."

"Oh, Callahan…"

"I can't breathe without her," I said, starting to sob and hyperventilate.

Signey reached her arms around me as I fell to the floor. She held me as I rocked back and forth. I planted my elbow onto my knee, while my other knee dug into the floor below me. My hands held my head tight like a vise.

The next morning, the alarm on my phone went off as scheduled. Signey had walked me to my bed after helping me up off the floor, and I somehow slept solidly until it did. I texted my boss to say that I wouldn't be making it into work that day. I never wanted to go back. I never wanted to leave my room. What was outside it for me, if not Iris?

Signey talked to me from the other side of my bedroom door throughout the weekend. I'd whimper a few words every now and then, just so she'd know I was still alive, even though I barely felt I was. I survived that weekend on two cups of chocolate pudding and a few glasses of water. I slept with the pillow Iris used and clung to her white bandana like a baby clutching her blanket.

After Signey left for work on Sunday night, I absentmindedly drove to Iris's. I tapped on her front door, gripping the key tightly in my hand. When she opened it, I could tell she had already seen me through the peephole, standing broken on her doorstep. I couldn't even respond when she asked what I was doing because I didn't know. She took a step back, signaled me to come in, and then closed the door after I did.

"I just thought maybe if you saw me…" I said, staring at the floor and squeezing one hand with the other. "Please…" I looked back up at her face.

"Please, baby, please don't do this," she said.

I thought it might have been easier if she hadn't called me baby.

"Me? Me don't do this?" I whimpered. "What are you doing, Iris? Why?"

"I just can't," she said, barely above a whisper.

TO BE HER GIRL

"Can't what? Be with me?"

"Please, Cal...Please."

We stared at each other, and I tried to communicate everything I was feeling without words. "Okay," I eventually said. "Okay."

"I'm sorry..."

I mouthed, "I love you," before placing the key onto the table beside the door.

She nodded her head slightly. Her lips barely moved, but I could see her tongue press against the back of her upper front teeth, and I knew she was saying it back.

I stayed home from work again on Monday, blaming the flu, which wasn't far from the truth. I was completely physically ill. I told my boss not to expect me on Tuesday either, perhaps not until Thursday at the earliest.

Paige met Signey for lunch and gave her the things I had left at Iris's. Clothes, food, toiletries, three pairs of shoes, my copy of Patti Smith's *Just Kids* that she was reading, *Jane Eyre* that I was, the letter for me that she'd left on her kitchen counter, and two pairs of my sunglasses.

And she gave me her pair of giant fly eyes, which caused my quiet tears to turn into a loud and heavy sob.

Iris kept the photo strip from Jem's photo booth, the vase still filled with roses, the candles in their holders, those stars, and my Grateful Dead t-shirt that she always slept in. I loved when she wore my t-shirts, especially that one because it was so old and faded that I could see her skin right through it.

And she kept the compass.

I called her, but she didn't answer. I resorted to my old method and emailed her. I was weak. I felt as old and faded as that t-shirt.

October 6, 2014
My beautiful Iris,
I miss you so much already, and I'm not sure how to make it through the days without you. I'm not sure how to breathe.

Please, Iris...
Run all you want, just let me run with you. We're in this life together, remember? I want to watch every sunset and every sunrise from every corner of this earth with you. I want every adventure and every misstep of my life to be with you.
You. You. You.
It's always been you. It'll always be you. I didn't expect you, but I choose you. And I'll choose you every time, every chance that I get, again and again and again. I will never give up on you. I will never give up on us.
Please, Iris...
What good is being human, if I can't be one with you?
I love you.
...Me

Unlike my previous pleas for attention, she responded within minutes. It just didn't read as I wanted.

please, callahan, please let things be, just for now. i'm sorry. i love you. don't ever forget that.

It wasn't that I forgot. It was just that, suddenly, I didn't want to remember. I took off my emerald necklace that had become much too heavy. I kissed the emerald and placed it gently into the indigo box. Then along with her bandana, the pillowcase she used, her business card, her sunglasses, the letter for me that she'd left on her kitchen counter, the letter for her with the singed edges, two wine bottles—one filled with rose petals, my Sonny and Cher 45, the shrunken balloon with her name on it, the foil one I had popped, and those glow-in-the-dark stars—I tucked it into a larger one. After I slid the box under my bed, I noticed my stocking hanging on the wall by my desk. I tore it off and threw it into the closet.

I tried to hide everything away, everything that reminded me of her. The problem was, I couldn't put the stars in a box. And again, the artificial ones would have to do. I tried not to wonder if her ceiling was still covered or not.

I didn't look at the sky for eight days after that, intentionally anyway. I didn't willingly listen to music. And I didn't sleep. My boss sent me home from work one afternoon after I hallucinated purple bubbles. I crawled into bed and stayed there for the rest of the day, trying not to think about anything. But it was impossible. Without Iris, life seemed impossible.

When I finally looked at the sky again, it was after I checked Iris's Fodoary. It was her first post since the night before we broke up. I had been sitting beside her when she posted that one, which was a photograph of me from our first weekend together—that shot of me rummaging through her old Polaroids in my white t-shirt and her blue cotton shorts. She didn't caption it, telling me that it said enough. Her new post was a photograph of the sky with the tops of palm trees reaching up to it. Below, it read: *everything is everywhere. don't forget to look around. earth. october 2014.*

And so I looked at the sky, even if I didn't want to.

Against my wishes, Signey reached out to both Cora and Grant. I couldn't blame her; I was deteriorating before her eyes. They gave all the tired advice I knew they'd give, telling me to take care of myself and to have patience. Just to survive took all the patience I had.

Grant came over and sat with me during one of my sleepless nights. We sat on the old couch with a joint I felt too tired to smoke. He took only one hit and left it to sit in the ashtray on the coffee table in front of us.

"How long was she with Brooks?" he asked.

My blank stare turned to him sharply. "Why on earth would you bring him up?"

He remained silent.

"Seven years," I said. "I wasn't a fucking rebound, Grant."

"I didn't say you were. But do you honestly think she could get out of such a long relationship and then jump right into another one forever?"

"Do you honestly think you're helping?" I picked up the joint and relit it. I inhaled as hard as I could. I coughed and felt the fire from my throat to my lungs.

Grant took the joint from my hand and put it back into the ashtray, then gave me the glass of water that sat beside it. I finished it and placed it next to the coaster.

"I could feel her broken heart as if it beat in my own chest," I said. My throat, lungs, and heart continued to burn. "When they broke up."

"And now?"

I stared blankly again.

"Trust the process," he said.

"What process?" I asked stubbornly.

"Life…Love…You and Iris."

I shook my head with a scowl. I thought it all to be an awfully cruel and unusual process. It was as if I had been blind my entire life, and then suddenly I could see. How could I go back to being blind again?

Our sudden split surprised my parents more than anyone. I chalked it up to them only knowing what I was telling them and not being there to see it—to see me as I fell through the cracks of love. To them, Iris and I were like a firework that didn't go off. The fuse sizzled and sparked, but when it came time to shoot into the sky, it stopped suddenly. And that's exactly how I felt, like a dud, like a dead firework.

When I told my dad how broken I felt, he echoed the same words to me that my grandma had spoken to him during my parents' divorce, "Whenever you feel broken, place your hand on your chest. Let yourself feel how you still work."

And I remembered what she told me. At nine, it went over my head, but at twenty-five, it ripped right through me. "A broken heart that still beats is tragically beautiful."

36

Signey found me drunk on the kitchen floor, leaning against the wall with a handle of whiskey in one hand and Iris's bandana in the other. "I was supposed to surprise her with sexy lingerie tonight," I mumbled. She didn't ask what I meant. She just sat down beside me and took the whiskey from my hand. It was the twenty-second of October, three weeks since I'd last seen Iris, and I felt as lonely as my chest without my emerald necklace. I still found myself reaching for it. But it wasn't there.

I wasn't drinking much, with that night's exception, but I knew Iris was. Sometimes I could taste the alcohol as it slid over her tongue and down her throat. Signey and Paige were in regular communication, and though they tried to keep Iris and me out of their work-related conversations, they slipped occasionally. Between that and social media, I knew I was right. Iris was drinking more than usual, which was already a lot. I tried not to pay attention, but it was easier said than done. I missed her like I'd miss my own heartbeat.

Getting high was my form of escapism, though it didn't help matters really. I was so stoned one night that I called her. She didn't answer, of course, so I sent a text message that said: *I'm just as high as you are drunk. Are we feeling better yet?* She didn't respond, as I knew she wouldn't. It was pathetic and petty, but I couldn't take it back. I didn't even bother to apologize.

One night, I was in a weed-induced fantasy about Iris, so focused, it felt as real as the floor I was lying on. After I slipped into bed, I swore I could feel her hands on me. I swore I could feel her breath on my neck. Even after the effects of the weed faded, I could still feel her. Within twenty-four hours, I got out of bed only a few times, for only a few minutes. I didn't know where I was, but I knew I was with her. The weed only amplified it. My body felt like a prison, a hell that kept me from her, so I'd get high to reach her. Though I was learning I didn't need it. I rode whatever it was for as long as I could.

When I came back down to earth, it took every ounce of willpower I had to keep myself from calling her, from reaching out in any form. I wanted to know if she felt it too, if she was wherever I was. But all I could do was check her Fodoary, and as expected, she had just posted. "Oh, Iris," I whispered. The photograph was of her staring into the vast desert landscape, and I was the photographer. The caption read: *far away. joshua tree national park. september 2014.*

I held on to those feelings—those feelings that we were always together—as best as I could, but reality was always ruining my life. We were apart physically, and it was hard to focus on anything else. The crushing breaths of her absence were far too heavy.

Signey was still in bed when I got up for work the next day, but the kitchen table was decorated with shiny star confetti and a gift bag. The balloon tied to the chair read: *Happy Birthday!*

Was it November 3 already? A month and a night since Iris broke up with me. I didn't even want to get out of bed, let alone celebrate my pathetic life.

I pulled a customized journal out of the gift bag. On the cover was a line from a poem I'd written two days before I met Iris. *Life and Magic are free to coexist.* I ran my fingers along it, feeling humbled and grateful and horrible all at the same time. Amid my slip into oblivion, I had forgotten all about Signey's birthday a few weeks earlier. It was days before I remembered. I was so wrapped up in my misery that I couldn't see the world around me. I was solely engulfed in everything that was Iris and me.

I checked my phone constantly at work, waiting for a call or a message or an email or a post on social media—anything from Iris, anything to know if she remembered it was my birthday. But all I got was the inkling in my soul that she was thinking of me.

Heartbroken that she hadn't reached out, I stopped at the store after work to pick myself up a birthday cake. It felt like it'd been a million years since Ryder had dropped mine into the bushes the year before. I stubbornly denied Grant's offer to take me out to dinner. Signey would be at work and I wanted to be alone. I wanted to wallow in pity, get stoned, devour some cake, and then cry myself to sleep.

I picked out a Neapolitan ice cream cake—the one that Iris and I would use to smooth things over—but put it back within seconds. The last time she had brought one over, it sat uneaten in my fridge until I found it a few days after we broke up. I threw it into the garbage after crying over it for half an hour. I settled on a red velvet cake instead.

I snagged a cheap bottle of wine and headed for the checkout.

I wondered if the cashier would wish me a happy birthday after checking my ID, but she just handed it back. I put it in my wallet and went to grab my debit card, but it wasn't there. I rummaged through my purse and all my pockets, but I couldn't find it. The only money I had was the collection of coins at the bottom of my purse. The lady at the cash register had little patience or sympathy for my misfortune, and the one in line behind me had even less.

I remembered that my debit card was on my desk and apologized. As I started to leave, I heard a man's voice from the other side of the annoyed customer behind me. "Here," he said as he reached forward, handing the cashier a twenty-dollar bill. "I got it."

I recognized his voice and felt a rush through my body. I knew who it was before I even turned to look. It was Charlie, Iris's stepdad. I was too thrown to deny his offer before the cashier handed him his change.

"Thank you, Charlie. You didn't have to do that," I said. I thought he wouldn't know how I knew his name, since he hadn't given it the day of the accident, but his smile said otherwise. I stepped to the side and waited as the cashier rang up the customer behind me, and then him.

"How you doing, kid?" Charlie asked as we walked toward the exit.

"I'm okay," I said. "How are you?"

"Oh, I'm alright, just picking up some things to make Iris dinner before I head back north tomorrow. Just got in this afternoon and then back already tomorrow. Not enough time in life sometimes." He gave me a sympathetic look as we stopped just outside the store.

I held my mouth shut tightly and nodded my head.

"I recognized you right away when she showed me your picture a couple of months back," he said. "She sent it, asking if I did."

"I didn't know she did that. I told her about the accident. I didn't realize who you were at the time though. She wasn't really talking to me then…Small world, right?"

"Something like that."

I hesitated for a second, wondering if I should, but asked, "How is she?"

"Oh…" He paused, trying to hide the visible concern that painted his face. "She's Iris. You know how she works…She's hiding how she is."

I nodded slowly.

"I know she's hurting though," he said. "I don't know much… much about you or how she feels…But I know whatever it is, she's feeling it deeply."

"Can you tell her…" I stopped myself and bit my lip. "Never mind." We sighed simultaneously. "Thanks again," I said, lifting my bag with the cake and wine.

"My pleasure. It's not a party for one, I hope."

I shrugged.

"Happy Birthday, Callahan."
"Thank you," I said, surprised.
"She was saying how it was."
"Oh…"
"I'll see you around, kid." He gave me an encouraging smile and nodded. Then he headed to his red pickup that I had rear-ended almost four months earlier.

I sat on my couch alone that night—drinking the wine straight out of the bottle, and eating the cake without bothering to cut a slice—amazed that of all days, I ran into Charlie on my birthday. Iris never reached out, but seeing him warmed me enough to feel okay anyway.

37

"Are you coming?" my mom asked as she tapped on my bedroom door at her house.

I stared blankly at the purple wall and moaned.

Eight years after I left for college and not much had changed in that bedroom. Childhood stuffed animals and school art projects still lined the shelves above my desk. The bookcase still held stacks of old magazines and yearbooks. And posters of Elliott Smith and Ani DiFranco still covered the wall above my old clunky television.

"Callahan! Come on! Cora and Rhett are waiting!" My mom's voice lacked the patience it had just moments earlier.

I moaned again. I rolled off my bed and opened my bedroom door just as my mom was about to knock again. I stared through her like her head was a jellyfish. "What's the point?" I asked.

"The point is, it's Christmas and your family wants to see you, but they won't all fit in your bedroom, so let's go."

"I don't care."

"Yes, you do."

Sure, of course I did, but Iris was supposed to be with me, so not much. It was just another Thursday as far as I was concerned. All the days were blending together anyway. Time was a blur.

"And maybe engage a little today," she continued as I brushed by her. We had spent Christmas Eve with her family, and I didn't utter more than three words the entire time. "Cal." She grabbed my arm and looked into my bloodshot eyes. "Did you have to get high?"

"Look who's talking."

My mom rarely smoked anymore and never got blazed out of her mind before visiting family on Christmas, so it was a cheap shot.

"Oh Jesus," she said.

"Yep. Happy Birthday, Jesus."

I stormed down the stairs.

I moped around my aunt and uncle's house until secluding myself in the sunroom. Nathan had asked if there was anything alive inside me. I told him that there wasn't, so he said that Grandma moved on after Grandpa's passing quicker than I was getting over my brief relationship. I was upset mainly because he was right. It felt like I'd been mourning Iris since the day I met her.

"How are you feeling?" Cora asked after she sat down in the wicker chair across from me.

"I'm dizzy," I said.

"Do you need some water?"

"I have some. Thanks." I pointed at the water sitting beside my empty wine glass.

"Half full or half empty?"

"I don't know. Half alive or half dead?" I replied before taking a sip of water. "I can't live like this anymore."

"So don't live like this anymore."

She made it sound so easy.

"I don't know what to do," I said. "I'm just so tired. I just want to call her. I just want to wish her a Merry Christmas. But she doesn't want me to."

"I don't think it's that she doesn't want you to."

"Then what is it?"

"I don't know, Cal. I don't know," she said and let out a sigh.

I pulled my lips back in a sorry smile and shook my head. "I scared her away. I kept talking about how we were soulmates and everything weird that happened between us." I let out a nervous laugh under my breath. "She didn't want to talk about it. I just thought we needed to put it out there, ya know."

"I know."

"But I guess that's where I went wrong. We didn't need to talk about it. We don't talk about the grass being green or the sky being blue. It just is. I should've just let us be."

"I think it was just too much, too fast, but that doesn't mean you shouldn't have talked about it. You two have something special, something so rare that most people can't even dream about. We don't talk about the grass being green because it's ordinary. You're not ordinary."

My mind flashed back to the night in Joshua Tree, and I laughed softly under my breath.

"What?" Cora asked.

"I told her that."

"That you're not ordinary?"

"That we're extraordinary."

Cora and I fell into silence. I turned my gaze to Billy, who was staring out the window. He seemed so content in his cage. I figured it was because he didn't know any different. His world was that house. Everything outside was an illusion.

"I don't think she broke up with you because you talked about it," Cora said. "She probably does need to be alone right now. You can't take that away from her...Give her time."

"Yeah..." I sighed and drank my glass of water. "It's just...I don't feel like I exist without her."

Cora stared at me until she couldn't bear to. She pressed her lips together and shut her eyes. A tear slipped out and rolled slowly down her cheek. I looked away and felt a lump in my throat. I tried to clear it, but it was stuck. Cora sighed softly and we allowed our eyes to meet again. *You exist, you exist, you exist,* I could feel her say.

TO BE HER GIRL

"I'm sorry," I said, barely above a whisper.
"What for?" she asked, not much louder.
I tried again to clear the lump in my throat.
Cora sighed again. "Do you remember what Grandma said when Grandpa died? She said, 'My heart is broken, but there's still air in my lungs.'"
One of Billy's white feathers floated across the room, and I thought of Dalfour Hickey.
Later that night, I called Iris, but she didn't answer. I left a sheepish voice message saying that I just wanted to say hello and hoped she was doing well. All I got back was a measly text message. *merry christmas callahan. hope all is well with you too*

A couple of days after Christmas, I headed down to Manhattan with Cora and Rhett. I could never sleep on airplanes, but I shut my eyes as soon as I sat down. I didn't feel like there was anything to see. I didn't even want to go to Manhattan, but I didn't want to be in Niagara Falls either. I didn't want to be anywhere.
"Are you okay?" I heard a woman's voice ask. The music was pouring through my headphones, and I paused it to catch the response. I didn't hear one for a few moments and wondered if I'd imagined the voice. When I heard crying, I opened my eyes.
"My father just died," the woman in front of Cora said. I could see her between seats and she looked younger than me. Parents aren't supposed to die until you're at least middle-aged. I thought about Iris being orphaned at only sixteen.
"I'm so sorry," the woman in front of me said. I knew from seeing her as we boarded that she was about forty or so. She had a strong presence that made me want to keep looking, but my desire to shut out the world was stronger. I imagined that she was the type of person who could make her captor cry by digging into his past, and then bake him cookies while waiting for the police to arrive. I wanted

her to comfort me too.

"Thanks," the other said through her sniffling. I watched the tears slide down her round cheeks, falling onto her jacket. They looked monstrous in size. "I hope you're able to hold your father close," she continued.

"He passed as well...Hard to believe it's been ten years now."

"I'm sorry...Does it get easier?"

There was a pause and I waited attentively.

"It gets different...I'm Iris, by the way."

A painful longing filled my body, as it always did when I heard that name. I could see Cora look my way out of the corner of my eye. She must have been listening too. I turned my music back on and turned up the volume. I didn't want to hear any more.

The flight attendants gave their lecture on safety, and I stared blankly at the informational packet tucked into the seat in front of me, wishing the woman sitting in it had a different name. I shivered, so I put up my hood and crossed my arms, holding them tightly against my body. I thought of Iris rubbing my bare arms in Amber's excessive air conditioning. I turned my head to the window and shut my eyes again. The world was so cold. I just wanted to curl up inside her.

On New Year's Eve, I sat cross-legged on the bed in the guest room, brushing the ashes off Cora's blanket with one hand and holding a joint with the other.

There was a knock at the door, and then Cora entered with my invitation. She stared at me for a moment too long before saying, "You know she doesn't want this for you."

"No, I don't actually because she won't talk to me," I said.

"Have you tried?"

"To talk to her?" I pulled back half of my mouth in a disbelieving smirk and shook my head.

TO BE HER GIRL

"Well, I don't want this for you," she said. "Please come with us."

I shook my head again. I didn't even want to be awake at midnight. Ringing in the new year without Iris felt like greeting the dawn without the sun. It just didn't make sense.

Jerry-Garcia ran by Cora and into the room. He jumped onto the bed and curled up at my feet.

"I'm fine," I said. "I'm not alone, see." I leaned forward and gave his belly a rub.

She sighed, wished me a happy new year, and then went out to live her life. I made no attempts to live my life outside my own head. I reached for the lighter and lit up the world between my fingers.

I drifted to sleep before midnight, despite the noise breaking through the window. New York City was counting down the clock to a new set of days without me.

I thought time was an illusion anyway, something placed on earth to keep us from experiencing everything all at once. I figured if I kept my eyes shut, I could manipulate it. I could be with Iris whenever I wanted. And so with eyes closed, I went back and I went forward, any time but when I was. I went to every memory and every fantasy of Iris that my mind could find. But whenever I opened my eyes, I was always when I didn't want to be. The illusion was something I couldn't break. Even when I felt her, she was still a ghost.

That night I dreamt Iris and I moved to New York City together, but I thought nothing of it at the time. It was just another fantasy.

38

After the new year, I felt an increased sense of urgency to reach Iris. I tried to brush it off as a long bout of post-holiday blues and my debilitating heartbreak, but by the start of February, I knew there was more to it.

I woke in a cold sweat at one a.m., consumed by fear and a torturous pain. My eyes shot wide open and I stared sharply at the wall. "She's with someone. Oh my God. She's sleeping with someone right now," I whispered.

The darkness remained silent. There wasn't so much as a passing car to disrupt my harrowing thoughts. I stayed as still as the air around me. I fell back asleep with my heart thumping like a giant stomping down a brick road.

Despite my intense grief stemming from Iris, she was where I went. She was always where I went. I dreamt we were hiking through the woods on a hill, making our way up to the top. I had stopped and was clinging to a tree. Iris was laughing and kicking through the leaves on the ground. There was snow on the branches and some messed in with the dirt, but it was no longer snowing. The hood on Iris's heavy winter coat was up anyway. It was white with fur trim and unlike anything I ever saw in her closet. "It's okay," she said. She encouraged me along with a smile so bright, it could have melted the snow. "We'll make it," she kept saying. "We're doing just fine." And when she put out her hand, I took it.

Later that day, I sat in the break room at work, not sure what to make of my middle of the night waking nightmare. I tried to focus on the dream instead. I checked Iris's Fodoary to see if she had posted anything new. She hadn't, so I closed the app. A few seconds later, I opened it again and refreshed her page. And there she was, in a new picture, wearing the exact same coat that she wore in my dream, hood up and all. And so I knew I'd been right. She was with someone.

The caption read: *winter in nashville. february 2015.*

"She went without me," I whispered to myself. I wiped the tears from my eyes and threw out the rest of my lunch. I felt too nauseous to eat. I carried on with work in a daze, speaking only when I needed to.

When I got home, I did my best detective work, made easy by modern technology and social media. I scrolled back to a picture that Ryder had posted in December. It was of a group of friends casually crammed together into a large restaurant booth, and I had felt a punch in the gut when I saw the man sitting beside Iris. I didn't want to think anything of it at the time, but it gnawed at me like a rodent gnawing on its cage.

It was Clate Wright, a sculptor from Nashville. He was tall with a beard and a bit rough around the edges—a man's man with large hands. I imagined they were always dirty and didn't want them anywhere near Iris. His physical appearance was the complete opposite of every person she had ever dated. Brooks and the others before him had been short and slender with baby faces. Clate was a tree trunk compared to their twig bodies.

And then there was me—a skinny woman.

My brain creaked and certainty rushed through my body, cracking my bones. I felt my blood boil and then stew in sadness. If she needed time to herself, who the hell was he?

I couldn't take the questions hammering away at my brain and called her. I wasn't the slightest bit surprised when it went straight to voicemail. Another email it was. I told her about my dream and asked why I'd been hurting so much since she'd been in Nashville. I tried not to be too blunt or mention Clate. I thought she might respond immediately, like she had the last time, but she didn't and I wanted to hate her.

Around midnight, I went for a walk. I wandered alone down Sunset Boulevard. There was something about a quiet night on a busy street that stirred me. I stopped in front of Jem's and watched a couple made out in the parking lot. It felt like I had a block of wood with sharp rusty nails sticking out of it, poking at my flesh, where my heart should have been. I hadn't been inside since the night Iris and I found our table covered with candles.

I continued my stroll and found myself outside Amber. I hadn't been there either. There was a *For Lease* sign hanging in the window. Amber, named for tree resin that preserves its inhabitants for eternity, was closed. It felt like a cheap analogy.

I wandered over to Echo Park Lake and watched the fountain reach for the sky. Flames consumed that wooden block inside my chest. I wanted to jump into the water and free it from its agony.

I heard the sound from my phone that indicated a new email. I knew it was from Iris. I pulled my phone from my pocket and read it. She didn't say much, other than wishing me well. She answered no questions directly, but said she was in Nashville working on a photography project. She ended the email with more well wishes, and I nearly threw my phone into the lake.

After I found out about Clate, the sharp pain would come and go, but the dull pain always lingered, like a bee sting that left behind a swollen lip. I tried to convince myself that I was wrong, that it was just work-related, but Signey put herself on the line and asked Paige point-blank. And then Paige put herself on the line and gave the answer I was afraid to hear. Iris and I were spinning a web and trapping

TO BE HER GIRL

people in it.

I tried to keep my thoughts away from Iris, but training my mind not to land on her whenever it wandered was like teaching a fish how to walk. I still talked to her every single day, hoping she'd feel my words, hoping telepathy was real. Sometimes I'd talk to her while looking at myself in the mirror, staring down my own eyes. I figured my reflection had to listen, didn't she?

On the first Sunday morning of March, I was sitting on the floor and leaning up against the wall when Signey walked into the living room. Bob Dylan spun on the record player, and I ate my breakfast like a child being forced to eat peas.

"What are you doing?" Signey asked, stopping right in front of me. "Are you eating eggs?"

I took a bite of my scrambled eggs. Just the smell of them made me nauseous. "Iris loves eggs," I said.

"Callahan...I know you miss her. I know. But it's been five months. And you don't like eggs."

"On Sundays we listen to Bob Dylan," I said, ignoring her concerns.

She sighed and made her way into the kitchen.

The next Sunday, I held *The Essential Bob Dylan* in my hands again. It was the only Bob Dylan album that I owned on vinyl. I put it back and played Patti Smith's *Horses* instead. I stepped over to the couch and sat down, slouching so much, my back hurt. It curved like a crescent moon.

"This isn't how it's supposed to be," I mumbled under my breath, tuning Patti out. I wondered how much longer I could stare at the wall. At what point would life require movement? I figured at least until the record stopped spinning. I'd have to get up and flip it to the other side. Music. I'd move for music. But until then...

My phone rang and a picture of Cora consumed its screen. It sat on top of *The Bell Jar*. Signey had put it on the coffee table for me, knowing it soothed me when my soul felt as gritty as sandpaper.

Signey had left the night before to visit St. Louis, her hometown. I asked her not to, but she threatened to reach out to Cora when I dropped her off at the airport. I wasn't talking or eating much, and she could barely look at me anymore. I feared I was sucking the life right out of her. I hadn't slept in four days and couldn't remember what the inside of my eyelids looked like, nor could I remember the last time I wrote.

I didn't answer the phone. Instead, I texted Iris. *You won't find it there...but you already know that.* She didn't respond, understandably so. I couldn't imagine what she'd say. I couldn't believe I'd said it. Who the hell did I think I was? Her one and only savior?

When the record stopped spinning, I headed into the kitchen instead of listening to the other side. Music couldn't save me any more than reading or writing could. I figured I was a lost cause.

I pulled a long knife from the wooden block that sat on the counter. I touched the cold steel to my arm and then slid it across my stomach. Drawing blood had never appealed to me. I stared the knife down before grazing it across my wrist. It barely even broke my skin. I tossed it into the sink and rubbed my scraped wrist.

I sat down on the floor, feeling like a pathetic heap of bones, and sulked in my heartbreak. I eyed the Peter Pan painting that hung above the stove. To die for what you live for, now there's the adventure, I thought. I sat a few minutes longer, but eventually I lifted my pathetic bones off the floor and headed into the bathroom. Dying on the kitchen floor didn't sound too adventurous.

I drew a bath and took off my clothes, leaving them in a pile on the floor. I cowered into the tub and felt the warm water rise around me. When it reached the drain below the faucet, I shut it off and slid my head below the surface. Come back, Iris, come back, I thought with every gasp above it. I submerged into the water, like I was baptizing myself, and begged Iris to appear before me again.

But she never did. It was only me in that tub.

As the winter faded to spring, I wasn't sure if I was even trying to regain my life, or if I was merely muddling through it. Everything felt messy, dreary, obsolete. Life was something I was too tired to chase.

Signey had quit Jem's and was working for Paige. But shortly after she returned from her visit to St. Louis, her mom was diagnosed with breast cancer. "I'm sorry," she said after she told me, "but I have to be there for her."

I nodded, unsure why she was apologizing to me. It was her mom with the cancer.

"I have to be there. I know she'll beat this, but I don't know how long it'll take."

I nodded again, realizing what she was saying. "She will beat this. I know that too," I said.

"I'm sorry…I just can't promise I can pay rent while I'm gone."

"It's okay. I understand."

"I'm so sorry. I'll help you find a new roommate."

"Don't worry about it. You've got enough to deal with right now."

"I'm sorry," she said again.

And then we both cried. I didn't know what was left of my heart to break.

I told Signey I'd handle it myself, but I had no plans to. I didn't want a new roommate, and I didn't want a new apartment. I was comfortable in my misery right where I was. But even with the short notice, I couldn't be mad about it because Signey was doing what she had to. I was just mad that her mom was sick. And I was mad about everything else too.

I envisioned myself living on Grant and Daniella's couch after I lost my apartment because I couldn't make rent on my own. I knew Grant would be there to catch me after my stubbornness doomed my life.

Then I thought about living in my car. Its cramped space would reflect how I felt. I thought I could quit my job and live on the road. If I could start getting published again, maybe it'd cover gas and my remaining bills. Only I still couldn't write anything worth reading.

Getting out of Los Angeles for a while sounded better every day. The possibility of running into Iris and Clate played in my mind like a broken record. The scenario was anxiety-inducing no matter how I imagined it. I considered calling Jared Stein and living in his garage. But what was for me up north, other than Iris's hometown?

Signey and I gave our notice on the first of April, and I still hadn't a clue where I was going. When I got home after work, I wandered around our apartment trying to soak in all its details before we dismembered it. I looked into Signey's bedroom and it was already half in boxes.

I went into my bedroom and pulled the box out from beneath my bed—the box full of the things that reminded me of Iris. I sat on the floor and sorted through it.

It had been six months since I'd seen her. Six months since I felt the softness of her skin. Six months since I ran my fingers through her hair. And it had been two weeks since I'd heard her voice anywhere outside my head. I had deleted the videos and voice messages off my phone, just not before storing them safely on my computer, an external hard drive, a flash drive, and my iCloud.

I took out the 45 of "I Got You Babe" and went into the living room to spin it on the record player. I sat against the wall and dropped my head. I had no idea where I'd be sitting a month from then. But I knew it wouldn't matter. I could always find a place to live, but I'd still feel homeless without Iris.

I shut my eyes and massaged my temples, trying to focus.

Well, I could sit here and cry, couldn't I? I thought. I could allow my spirit to be completely consumed by failure and loss. I could curl up in a ball and wait for nature's reaper to take its hold, rotting away to a crippled corpse. Or I could stand back up. Well, I could, couldn't I?

That was when I decided to go back to New York.

39

"Well," I said.

Signey stood in the doorway to our apartment. We had finished piling her things into her storage unit the night before. I still had a week left.

"Well," she said.

"Thanks for putting up with me."

Signey smiled and I could see that her eyes were watering. Like me, she had no set plan, no idea when she'd return to Los Angeles. Her mom's cancer was steadily progressing, and the battle seemed to steepen every day. Signey had already lost her aunt to the same disease four years earlier.

"Give your mom a hug for me," I said.

"I will."

"Drive safe. Let me know when you get there."

"And you do the same." Her eyes scanned our apartment one last time, then we hugged, unsure when we'd see each other again. "Love you, Cal," she said.

"Love you too."

I watched as she walked down the stairs and through the courtyard. When I couldn't see her anymore, I closed the door, sat on the floor against it, and cried.

I thought about letting Iris know that I was leaving town, but somehow found the strength not to. I apologized after my snarky text message, but she didn't say anything back. The last time she had spoken to me was the email almost three months earlier. I didn't figure me leaving town was something she'd be too concerned about.

I met Grant at Rowe's the night before I left Los Angeles. It was still hard to go anywhere I had gone with Iris, and I hesitated before opening the front door. Grant was sitting at our table and had already ordered my drink.

"Sorry I'm late," I said, sitting down across from him. I took a sip of my beer and opened the menu, even though I always ordered the same thing.

"No worries...For old times' sake," he said. "I can't believe you're leaving me. You better not be gone for too long."

"I won't be. I won't survive in Niagara Falls, and Cora and Rhett will only keep me for so long."

"When do you go there?"

"I don't know." I sipped my beer. "I don't have a time frame for anything. I'm officially unemployed and useless."

"You'll figure something out. You always do."

"I hope so. What will be, will be."

"What you will, will be." He took a swig of his beer.

The waitress stopped beside our table and looked at me. "Hey, long time, no see," she said. She was a bubbly yeasayer in her early twenties. Her parents owned the place, and she'd been our waitress for as long as we'd been going there. "How've you been? How's Iris?" She also had a keen eye for detail and remembered everything. It had been seven months.

"I don't know," I said. I looked at Grant, who had his elbow on the table and his fingers pressed firmly between his eyes.

"Oh…" She pressed her lips together.

TO BE HER GIRL

"I'll have the personal pizza with spinach and tomatoes," I said.

She nodded, scribbled on her notepad, then looked at Grant. "The usual for you too?"

"Yep. Eggplant Parmesan, please and thank you."

She scribbled on her notepad again and picked up our menus.

"Thanks," I said.

She gave me a sad smile and walked away.

"That was awkward," Grant said.

"Yeah, this is a perfect example of why I'm leaving."

"You can't let Iris push you out of your own life."

"That's not what I'm doing…Not what I'm trying to do anyway." I sipped my beer, contemplating.

Grant sighed. "Then why'd you stop going to concerts with me?"

"Because what would've happened if she was there? It'd be one thing for us to run into each other, but if she's working, it's just…I want to see her, but I wouldn't want to disrupt her at work."

"So you're disrupting your life instead."

"You're just upset I'm leaving."

"Aren't I allowed to be?"

"Well, yeah, I mean, I'd be mad if you weren't." I laughed lightly.

"I know you're doing what you feel is best. I understand. I'm just thinking…Why is it that you want to be with her so much? So much so that being without her almost killed you."

"What? Why do you want to be with Daniella? Because I'm in love with her. I'm allowed to want to be with her."

"I didn't say you weren't. I know how much you love her. I know that's the root of it all…It's just…this extreme…it's not healthy. It hasn't been since day one." His voice cracked and tears filled his eyes. "And I wish I would've said something sooner."

My heart sank deep into my stomach. "It wouldn't have mattered. Like you said, love is the root of everything. That's why it always comes back to her."

"But what about you? You're in pain more than you're in love."

I took another sip of my beer. "Let's not talk about it then."

After dinner, Grant followed me back to my place. "Well, this is sad," he said. His voice echoed through my almost empty apartment. He hadn't been there since he helped move my furniture a few days earlier. I had made my last stop at my storage unit that afternoon. All that was left was either coming to New York with me, going into the dumpster, or being tossed onto the curb. "Why don't we drag the couch out now and you can crash at my place tonight?" he asked. The couch was getting the curb treatment.

"Nah, that's okay. Manny, the dude next door, is gonna help me in the morning."

He nodded and looked around again.

"Ya know, you could crash here," I said, pointing at the couch already in its pull-out bed position. "It'd be just like last time."

He smiled and tousled his hair. "Daniella already joked that I would."

"I thought she might."

He jumped onto the mattress and the springs creaked. "Ah, man," he said, sprawled out on his back. "I can't believe you're tossing this couch."

"Hey, if you want it, it's all yours. There just wasn't any room."

My life in Los Angeles was crammed into a five by ten-foot cement box.

"Oh, I almost forgot," he said, sitting up. "I have that map for you."

He left to retrieve a map of the Sedona vortexes from his car. I sat on the pull-out and let myself cry until I heard his returning footsteps. I wiped the tears from my eyes as he came back inside.

"I've only been to the one by the airport, but I'm sure the others are just as good," he said, sitting down beside me.

"Thanks," I said, taking the map with my damp fingers.

"The energy is incredible. I'd try to explain it, but you just have to feel it for yourself. I promise you'll feel better...even if just for a minute."

"A minute would help."

I set the map down next to me and went to grab my lighter and a joint from the kitchen counter. When I came back into the living room, Grant was sitting with my guitar, playing a song he wrote at my grandparents' house with my grandpa's guitar.

"Is it falling through space? I cannot tell, maybe it's heaven, and we're already in hell, but if flowers are here, how could that be? Are you falling through space, just waiting for me?" he sang.

I sat beside him and closed my eyes, remembering how I felt when he wrote it. We had been sitting in the sunroom watching my grandma alone in her garden. It was after the barbecue she insisted we have the week after my grandpa's passing. I tried to fight the sob fighting its way up my throat as I watched her, but his song soothed me into submission.

A song about death was the last thing I wanted to hear, sitting beside Grant on that old pull-out, but he always took gloomy subjects and made them glow, like a lantern in a dark cave, or those plastic stars packed away in a box, and I surrendered again. I listened and smoked the joint with tears in my eyes, wondering what death was. A transformation? An escape? Would it bring me closer to Iris? I didn't know. I just knew I was tired.

"How many times do you think we've died?" I asked after he finished the song.

"One less time than we've been born," he said.

"Maybe we die a little every day."

"Sure, but maybe we're born a little too. Every breath is a new one."

The next morning, Grant woke me up at the crack of dawn. I may have stepped aside from any of my responsibilities, but he still had to go work.

"Promise me you'll take care of yourself. I'm going to need you back here in one piece," he said as we stood at the door.

I nodded slightly. I didn't want to make a promise I wasn't sure I could keep. We stared at each other for a few seconds before he hugged me so tight that I thought my heart might shoot out of my mouth.

"Well…" I said. "Thanks for holding me up when I was dead weight."

"You were never dead weight."

It sure felt like I was. My body was shrinking, but I'd never felt heavier.

I hugged Grant again and told him I loved him. And then he was gone too.

I stared at the couch for a few minutes after Manny helped me drag it to the curb. It was old, but I was sad to see it go. It felt symbolic to see it alone on the dried-up grass. I hoped somebody would scoop it up and give it new life. I gave it a nod and then abandoned it like I had everything else, like Iris had me.

40

With Los Angeles in my rear-view mirror, I hit the road around noon. I tried not to wonder when I'd be back or when I'd see Iris again. I tried not to think about my life in Los Angeles or my days in college. California needed to be invisible, if only for that time. The road was my new home.

"How do you feel about me leaving?" I asked Iris as I drove down the 15. "Can you feel the distance growing between us?"

Just as I finished talking to the air around me, Leah John's "How Would You Feel?" began to play. The first time I'd heard it was sitting beside Iris in her living room with Leah and Jamie. "How would you feel if you couldn't get me alone? How would you feel if I left on my own?" Leah sang.

"I asked you first," I said and changed it to a different song.

As the sun began to set that night, I saw a road sign for a restaurant called Cora's. I was in the middle of nowhere—empty desert for miles—and since the clock was of no importance, I took a detour. I wasn't paying much attention and drove past the turn. I only noticed it as I ran the stop sign. I pulled into a parking lot to turn around, but stopped to look at the sunset. It was a few seconds before I noticed what the sign standing right in front of it said. Encased in a red heart on top of a thirty-foot pole was *Iris's Diner*. "Of course," I said, laughing and shaking my head.

I texted Cora a picture and said, *I can't make this shit up*

The next morning, I spent an hour or so at the Grand Canyon. I didn't see the point in staying any longer. It all looked the same and it reminded me of Iris. Neither of us had ever been, and it was a place we talked about visiting together. I felt cheap being there without her. I cried and apologized for going without her.

I got to Sedona in the early afternoon. Driving into it felt like driving straight into a dream. Its picture-perfect boutiques illuminated against the red mountains behind them. I couldn't grasp that it was real. I already felt better.

I wandered for a while and ate lunch at a small cafe. I chose it because the logo was a green eye like the one on Iris's favorite mug. When I returned to my car, I took out the map of vortexes that Grant had given me and drove to the closest one. I tied Iris's bandana around my neck and hiked to the top of the rocky vortex near the airport. It was crowded and touristy, but I sat on the edge and blocked out the world.

I wasn't sure what to expect or what to believe. Could there truly be pockets of space that circulated greater energy? The world all seemed so distant to me. What did it matter where I was? But after soaking in the view, I closed my eyes and felt it rush through me. The air carried a healing force that engulfed me, and it was like I wasn't even human, but a light floating above the red rocks. I only knew I was human because I felt tears slip out from below my lids and dampen my cheeks. I asked if Iris and I would find our way back to each other, hoping there'd be a clear as day sign to follow, but I didn't need one. I trusted what I felt.

By the next day, I felt restless again. I screamed all the way through Texas. I screamed every word I wanted to say to Iris but couldn't. "How could you? How could you do this to us?" My voice cracked as I sped down the 40. The tears raced down my face just as fast.

TO BE HER GIRL

"Iris!" I screamed her name at the top of my lungs over and over again. "Iris! Where are you? Please, Iris! Iris!" My heavy sobs eventually fell to a soft whimper and I whispered her name softly. "Iris, I love you. I love you. I love you," I repeated. "Iris, please." Maybe she couldn't hear me, but that didn't mean she couldn't feel me. "Please." I begged all day; I just wasn't sure what for. I kept my hand on the passenger's seat, but she wasn't there.

As I drove into Nashville the next night, "I Got You Babe" was playing on the radio. I didn't know if Iris was in town or not, but I didn't feel that she was. I was just there to visit my friend, and like my stops at the Grand Canyon and Sedona, to see a place I never had before.

I stayed with Maggie Alonso, my roommate in college. She got a job in the music industry and moved to Nashville after graduation. We spoke sparingly in the years since, but had been close enough to fall back into our friendship whenever we did. When she reached out to me shortly before I left Los Angeles, I told her about my drive to New York, and she insisted I make a pit stop.

Maggie didn't know much of what I was going through. She didn't even know of Iris. The only picture of Iris that I had ever posted on social media didn't give her name. I had captioned it only with a heart, and I didn't know if Maggie even saw that. I thought a few days with her would be refreshing. I wasn't sure if it was a good idea, knowing Iris and Clate were bouncing around, but I figured if I was meant to see them, I would; if not, I wouldn't. Sometimes I had to let the wind decide how it swirled around me.

The problem was Maggie's constant blabbering about her cousin's wedding. The week before, she'd been in San Francisco to be a bridesmaid for it. All I heard for three days was *Iris's wedding this* and *Iris's wedding that*. It was like a hammer to my head. I didn't figure I could hang out with anyone who knew an Iris ever again. Weren't there any other names? I smiled and listened, not once mentioning my Iris.

On my last night in town, Maggie and I sat at a high top table at a bar. It was long and narrow, and far from any other tourists. "Oh my God," Maggie said.

"What?" I asked.

"Do you know who Leah John and Jamie Lear are? Because they just walked in. And if you don't know them, then I'm going to play her new album later because it's amazing and you'd love it."

I choked on my beer. I put down the bottle and nodded my head, then patted my chest, trying to compose myself. I turned around to see them standing at the bar and then looked back at Maggie. She tried to be coy as she took a picture of them with her phone. I considered hiding my face as they walked by, but I knew they'd see me eventually. The bar was too small not to.

Jamie kept walking, but Leah saw me as she passed our table. She stopped, tilted her head to the side, and said, "Hey."

Jamie stopped, turned around, and walked back. "Hey, how's it going?" he said in the same surprised tone that Leah had used.

"What's up?" I replied, letting out a soft laugh with my breath. I looked at Maggie's confused face and then back to them.

"What are you doing in Nashville?" Leah asked, smiling.

"I'm going to New York for a while, so I stopped on the way. This is my friend, Maggie."

"Hi," Maggie said.

"Hey," Leah replied. "Does Iris know?" she asked me.

"Does she care?"

Leah sighed. "She cares."

"Then why is she dating Clate Wright?" I asked.

Leah and Jamie glanced at each other. I knew they knew him.

"Exactly." I sighed. "I'm sorry."

"Don't be. It's a good question," Leah said.

"Jamie! Leah!" a man in what must have been a ten-gallon hat shouted from the back of the bar.

They both turned to look. "Hey, man!" Jamie shouted.

They looked back at me. "Well, I hope you enjoy the rest of your trip. It's good to see you," Leah said.

I nodded my head. I could feel the water welling up at the bottom of my eyes and hoped nobody could see it.

"I'm sorry," she said, acknowledging that she could. She stepped forward and pulled me in for a hug.

I nodded my head again and faked my smile. I raised my hand in a slight wave to Jamie just as he did the same. "Bye, guys," I said. "Nice seeing you."

I watched them walk to the back of the bar and then looked at Maggie, who stared at me with eyes as wide as the horizon.

"They're friends with my ex-girlfriend," I said. "And yeah, her name is Iris, so it's been fun listening to you talk about your cousin's wedding."

"I'm sorry," Maggie said. "Why didn't you tell me to shut up?"

"I don't know." I took a sip of my beer and noticed Leah walking toward our table.

She stopped by my chair and sighed heavily. "Listen," she said, "I've known Iris for a long time. And I know we don't see each other as often as we'd like, but I've never seen her look at anyone the way she looked at you. That's why I asked how y'all knew each other when we met. There was something in the air around you two. And I know how heartbroken she was after you broke up. But she is who she is, and sometimes all she does is shoot herself in the foot. And sometimes there's just no tellin' her nothin'. So just, ya know, just…"

I could see her searching for words. "Okay," I said. "Thanks."

Hold on, hold on, hold on, I could feel every ounce of my being tell me.

I lay on Maggie's couch later that night and checked Iris's Fodoary for the first time since Oklahoma. She was in California. I didn't know where Clate was and I tried not to care. I knew Iris was because she had posted a picture of a man at Venice Beach and noted it'd been taken that day. But it wasn't the date or the location of the photograph that struck me. It was the man in it. He wore a shiny white shirt and his yellow pants were brighter than the sun. His smile was so wide that I didn't know how she contained it within the photograph. In the caption, she called him a sparkly angel and thanked him for the feather. It was Dalfour Hickey.

I wrote a comment that said: *Remember the man I met in the desert...*
Why couldn't I ever let things be?

On the last night of my trip, I sat at an Ohio rest stop and played my guitar. After a few minutes, I stopped strumming to watch a group of twenty-somethings who looked like they were straight out of Jack Kerouac's *On the Road*, strange with wide eyes and ragged clothes. I half expected them to hop into the bed of the next pickup to stop—and I thought maybe I'd go with them. New York was approaching too fast, and I didn't want to get there yet. The road felt like freedom. I thought of Iris much more than I planned to, but she was my constant, and with every breath of life I took, I was reminded of her. I couldn't escape the air.

The most haggard of the bunch was likely the youngest. I figured he was barely out of his teens, but he looked like he'd been on the road for years. His hair was long and scraggly, and there were holes in his dingy t-shirt and the knees of his blue jeans. I tried to keep my face from expressing the displeasure of his stench as he approached me. He smelled like a cigarette at the bottom of an old bag of fast food.

"Hey, you got change for a twenty?" he asked, stopping in front of me.

"No, sorry, I don't have any cash."

I did.

"Ah, man, bummer. Ah, well. I guess I don't need any more vending machine crap anyway," he said. "You play?" He pointed at my guitar.

No, I'm just sitting here holding it, I thought.

"Not very well," I said.

"Ah, I'm sure you're fine. As long as you feel it, right?"

I thought maybe I felt things too much. "Yeah, I guess. You?"

He sat down beside me at the picnic table. "Nah, I used to play the drums though."

"Why'd you stop?"

"I sold my kit. I still beat on things though."

"Oh."

"Not people or animals or anything like that!" He put his hands up and laughed.

"Well, that's good."

He dropped his hands. "So what are you doing out here all alone?"

I tensed up and gripped my guitar. A stranger noting that I was alone wasn't comforting, no matter his friendly demeanor. "I'm driving across the country. California to New York."

"Ah, cool-cool. Yeah, we're exploring and whatnot." He pointed at his buddies sitting on the curb. "Things got lame back at home."

"Where's home?" I asked.

"Georgia," he said.

I could tell. His southern accent was pulsating off my eardrums.

"Maybe I'll make it to California one day," he continued. "West coast, best coast, right?"

"Right," I said. I felt bad for lying about the cash. But I didn't want to back-pedal because then he'd know I lied.

"Hey," a woman shouted at us. She looked about my age and like she was about to drive a Volkswagen van to Woodstock. She walked over and stopped in front of us. "Hey, you ready? Who's your friend?" she asked. Her accent was much subtler than his.

"Oh, hey, I didn't catch your name," he said to me.

"Iris," I said.

"Iris drove from California," he said. "This is Tara. I'm David."

"What brings you on the road, Iris?" Tara asked.

I hesitated but said, "A broken heart."

"Who broke your heart?" she asked.

"My girl…My ex-girlfriend."

"Did you thank her?"

I stared blankly.

"Iris...Didn't your mama ever teach you any manners?...You always thank the ones who break your heart. They're the ones who remind you that you deserve happiness...Think about it."

I nodded, not wanting to think about it.

"We're leaving," she said to David. "Nice to meet you, Iris."

"You too," I said.

She walked back to the others, who were already piling into an old minivan.

David watched them for a few moments, then directed his attention back to me. "We're not born thinking that we deserve to be miserable. It's the world that weighs us down growing up. If someone breaks your heart, they're stripping you down to your core, so you can remember...That's what she meant," he said.

I thought of the dream I had a year earlier. "We need to knock you down to your core...in order for you to build each other back up," the man deep in my subconscious had told me.

"That makes sense," I told David.

"Yeah...Hey, well, I better go," he said as he stood up. "Enjoy the road. I hope life treats you well."

"Why start now?" I laughed under my breath. "Thanks. You too."

"Why not?" He flashed a toothy grin and off he went.

I loaded my guitar back into my car and drove for a few more hours. I didn't have much farther to go, but I needed one more night of solitude. It was just me and the bugs using my windshield as an efficient form of suicide. I wondered if I crashed how long it'd be until someone found me. There wasn't so much as a deer anywhere near that pavement.

When I got to my last motel, I took a moment to gaze at the moon that had been chasing me. I wondered if Iris was looking at it too.

41

I sent my mom text messages throughout the morning—pictures of road signs and familiar scenery. She'd been a nervous wreck since I left Los Angeles the week before. I figured she'd be watching for me out the front window when I pulled into the driveway.

But the driveway was empty.

I hopped out of my car and went to unlock the front door. But my key didn't work. I took a step back to gaze at the white door. It was a few moments before I realized it was a new one.

I drove across the country, but nobody was home and the locks were changed. All I could do was laugh. I snagged the bottle of wine from my car that I'd been saving for that moment. I unscrewed the top, sat on the porch swing, and chugged.

My mom pulled into the driveway five minutes later. There was no rational way to be upset with her for not being there to welcome me, when she had been at the grocery store stocking up on my favorite foods.

"You drive too fast," she said, walking up the front steps.

"Actually I drove really slow," I said, still swinging on the wooden porch swing. "You just have poor time management."

We laughed and shook our heads.

She set down the bags of groceries. I stood up and we hugged with the bottle of wine still in my hand. I took a step back and offered it to her.

She shook her head no.

"It's good," I said.

"No thanks," she said. "Maybe later." She picked up the groceries and took them inside.

I followed her and put the wine on the coffee table. I scooped up Jack, my mom's cat, and sat down on the couch. It felt strange to be there. I was relieved and tired and anxious and excited. I had no idea what my life was anymore or what it would be. I had no clear path. I was going in blind.

I collapsed onto my bed after unloading my car. I rested my eyes for a few minutes before rummaging through my bag for the weed I had hidden. I rolled myself a joint, took a hit, and said, "Now what?" I left Los Angeles because I was lost and broken. But what I was supposed to do when I got to New York, I didn't know.

I sat on the floor and the rainbow-striped stuffed monkey dangling from my closet door knob stared at me. I'd won first place in a short story contest in seventh grade, and the prize was a gift certificate to a local bookstore. But instead of getting books or anything beneficial for my writing, I got the monkey. I figured it was taunting me all those years later because I hadn't accomplished much else since.

I combed through my desk drawers to find that old story and read it. It was a complete rip-off. What a fraud, I thought.

I read through old notebooks with pages that bled of story ideas, baby names, and poems that were crammed with grief. If they had been a cry for help, they weren't doing much good stuffed in that drawer. Reading them took me back to the early aughts when I thought the world would lay out my dreams because I had suffered enough. But what had I been suffering from? My best guess had come in the form of a poem about a tiny alien living in my brain, tugging at the nerves, and another in my heart, pulling its strings. It felt weird to read those depressing thoughts, knowing I had written them at such a young age, and it felt weird to know how little I had changed. I wondered if I'd be depressed forever.

In the last notebook, I found poetry about a mysterious love—an all-consuming, yet distant love.

I pulled a stack of old magazines from the bookcase and skimmed through a copy of *Rolling Stone* from 2006. I stopped when I came across a photo of Colin Dumont, then gasped loudly when I read *photo by Iris Humphrey*. My eyes jumped right to it as if they knew it was there. My heart felt like it was swallowing itself. It was broken and happy and beaming with pride all at the same time. Iris hadn't just been a mystery person living in my poetry; she was actually there.

Around three in the morning, I crawled out of bed, unable to sleep despite my exhausting trip. There was something in an old notebook that clung to me like a baby to its mother. It was an idea for a story about a girl who meets a boy when they're thirteen. They bond for the summer at camp, but when the season ends, they go their separate ways. As an adult, she still remembers his piercing eyes and bright smile. And above all, she never forgets how he made her feel. She knew there was a reason she still couldn't shake him, so she sets out to find him.

I grabbed another notebook from my bag and scribbled down new thoughts. I changed the boy to a girl and started to write a novel. That monkey could stare all it wanted, but I was going to accomplish something beyond a library contest.

―――

My mom stared at me as I stirred my soup that afternoon. I hadn't had an appetite in months. "Eat something. You can't starve heartbreak," she said. "You can't let her kill you."

I rolled my eyes. "I'm not letting her kill me," I said. Though I couldn't deny how dead I felt at times. Each day was different. "I still love her. I still believe in us. It's all I have."

"That's where you're wrong though. It's not all you have." She sighed softly under her breath. "Do you still want to marry her?"

"Of course I still want to marry her," I said, smiling. "Yeah, she smashed my heart into a billion pieces, but every piece still beats for her. Wherever she is, whoever she's with, whatever she's doing, I love her."

"That's unconditional love," she said casually.

"I guess so," I said, watching Jack lick his paws. "And ya know, it's not even about marriage. That's just one of the few traditions that I actually want a piece of. I want to spend my life with her. I want to learn with her and grow with her. I want to see her smile and hear her laugh. And I want to be there for her when she can't. I want to hold her hand when she's scared and sit beside her when she's sick. I want her to know that she'll always have somebody who wants for her and loves her more than anything else in this world. I just want…" I sighed.

"I know…"

"I just want her to be happy."

"What if she's happy with that Clate guy?"

"Must you use his name?"

"Sorry."

"Then I want her with him," I said. "But I still think he's temporary."

"Maybe he is."

"I'm crazy though, right?…She left me without a hope in the world, but I believe anyway. I love her anyway."

"They call it crazy in love for a reason."

I laughed and shook my head. "I guess so," I said before finishing my soup.

A little while later, I went to The Pond where the family picked my brain about my trip. We sat in my aunt and uncle's living room, and my cousin's chihuahua jumped into my lap. I pet her and mentioned that I had to go see Molly, my dad and Rebecca's corgi.

"She's outside somewhere, probably playing in the—" Rebecca said before coming to a sudden stop.

"You can say it," I said.

TO BE HER GIRL

"Irises."

I bit my lip and allowed myself a second to get lost in her. Iris was a lot like the flowers, flowy and kind of all over the place, but in the most beautiful way. They weren't in bloom yet, but Molly always seemed to love them. I thought she had good taste.

"So a semi ran me off the road," I said.

The next few days were rougher than I expected. I would cry at the drop of a hat, without cause or warning. I was trying to enjoy my free time, trying to conjure up ideas for my novel, but I couldn't focus. When my mom asked me to help with the dishes, I got all tongue-tied and burst into tears. I made a beeline to my bedroom and shut the door behind me. I slid down the wall, sat on the floor, and clutched my knees to my chest. "These aren't my tears," I said to myself. "Something is wrong with her."

I could only imagine it had to do with Clate. My gut was telling me that it was over between them, and I hoped she would finally take the time to herself that she needed.

And then it was her birthday.

I went to the Falls, hoping it'd help me let go. I thought there must be some sort of magic in the mist. It was what my grandpa had always said. And I needed magic. But it only made me miss her more. Beauty always did that.

My dad called as I was leaving. "Hello," I answered.

"Hey, do you want to go the Falls tonight for the fireworks?" he asked. It was Victoria Day in Canada.

"Well, actually I'm..." I said. "Actually, ya know what, yeah." I knew if I didn't keep busy, I'd have my own falls drowning my face. Or even worse, I'd call her.

We cooked out and then went to a park near the Falls. Everything felt fine at first, but why I thought seeing fireworks on Iris's birthday was a good idea was beyond me. A few minutes into the show, I texted her.

Happy Birthday, Iris. I'm watching fireworks right now and I'd say they made me think of you, but we both know I always am already. I hope you're having a great day. I miss you and I love you forever.

I wondered if she would have replied had I not said the L-word. At times, I envied her ability to shut me out. And I wondered which was worse: to fall so completely into something you couldn't have, or to run away from something you could.

As we left the park, I ran into a group of classmates from high school, which was always the last thing I wanted to do. We made small talk, pretending that we cared, and I did my best to hide how utterly disappointing I thought my life had been since I'd seen them last. It only made me more depressed, and I spent the rest of the week in hiding. I didn't want to be seen around town. I didn't want to be recognized. I had to get out. I had to get to Manhattan, where I could be just another face in the oblivious crowd.

42

"Callahan! Hey! You're skinny as a rail!" Rhett shouted as Cora and I walked into the apartment. My already slim frame was down twenty pounds since my time with Iris.

Jerry-Garcia came running toward me, and I knelt down to pet him. "Nice to see you too," I said to Rhett. I stood back up and he gently gave me a hug, worried that he'd break me in two.

"Sorry, I was just teasing," he said. "If I thought you were too skinny in a super unhealthy way, I wouldn't have said it like that."

"It's okay. I know. I lost weight. It just happened quickly and without me noticing, so it probably wasn't very healthy."

"Well, I'm sure Cora will make sure you eat well."

I smiled at Cora. I'd been counting on that.

"So what are your plans for the summer?" Rhett asked.

"Well, first she's going to get a job," Cora answered for me. It was her idea that I spend the summer in the city. Finding a job was her only stipulation.

I went into my new bedroom to settle down and settle in. I was still antsy about being so far away from Iris. I had fantasies about running into her and everything falling back into place, like in all those romantic comedies I'd seen a million times. I lay on my bed with Jerry-Garcia, and Cora tapped on my shut bedroom door.

"Yeah?" I said.

She entered with a newspaper in her hand. "How are you feeling?" she asked.

I sat up and she sat down, nudging Jerry-Garcia to scooch over.

"I'm good," I said. I thought if I could convince enough people, then maybe I could convince myself, and then maybe I actually could be. But she looked at me like she didn't believe me. "I miss her and that will never change as long as we're apart. The only way to deal with it is to live through it, so here I am."

"Well, one step at a time. It's all you can do."

"Thanks for letting me stay here."

She smiled and tossed me the want ads.

After a few days of unsuccessful job hunting and uninspired writing, I went to Mason's for dinner. I missed California and he was a little piece of it. I was feeling nostalgic, even for the bad times, because perhaps, looking back, they weren't so bad. It was always the present that stung me.

"No big Memorial Day party for you?" I asked when he greeted me at the door. "That's not the Mason I know." I smiled and set my drenched umbrella against the wall.

"Not in this rain," he said with a smile. "It's good to see you, Cal."

"You too," I said.

We hugged and I followed him into the kitchen. I set a bottle of wine on the table. It was already set up and had a vase of daffodils in the center.

"Nice flowers," I said.

"They're my roommates."

"Oh, are they here?"

"No, but they probably will be soon. You still eat meat, right?" he asked, pointing at the steak on the counter.

"I do. Sounds good." I took off my coat and hung it over the back of the dining chair. I joined Mason at the counter to help him finish cooking our meal.

He glanced at me beside him without words and smiled. I smiled back, feeling utterly normal.

"Hey, you've had that shirt since college," he said, pointing at my old Beatles t-shirt that said *LET IT BE* across the front. His smile was so warm, I could feel it.

"Actually I've had it since middle school. My dad got it for me for my thirteenth birthday." My laugh faded as I thought of my old Grateful Dead tee that Iris kept. It had been a gift from my dad the same year. I held on to things for entirely too long.

Mason and I talked mostly about college over dinner, and I wasn't sure whether I wanted to hit life's fast-forward button or its rewind. The clock on the wall ticked away, reminding me that I didn't have access to the remote.

His roommates walked into the kitchen moments after we finished cleaning up. I was surprised to hear Irish accents come out of their mouths. I spoke a little about my uncle before snagging the wine and joining Mason in his bedroom. I'd already downed two glasses. My weight loss made it feel like four.

"You wanna watch a movie or something?" he asked.

I placed the wine on his nightstand and sat down on his bed. The same blue Mexican blanket that he had on his bed in college covered it. I rubbed my hands over the coarse fabric. I had lost my virginity on top of that blanket. "Whatever you wanna do," I said.

"How about this?" he asked, clicking on his computer's mouse. "When You Were Young" by The Killers poured through the speakers.

"Ah, the old playlist," I said.

His face lit up and he sat on his bed beside me. "You remember."

"Of course I do."

The past lingered through the air as we embraced a few moments of silence.

"So…" he said. "Why are you really here?"

"In your bedroom?"

He smirked. "In New York."

"I told you…I needed a break from L.A. I was sick of my job, ya know. Plus my roommate moved."

He pressed his lips together and raised his eyebrows, nodding his head slowly.

"A breakup," I finally said.

"Oh…I'm sorry…It was that bad?"

I nodded my head.

"Wait…How long were you together?" he asked.

I knew he was thinking about the previous summer when we made out on his couch.

"Six weeks," I said.

"Oh."

"I know. It sounds pathetic, but it'd been a long time coming. I knew the moment I laid eyes on her that she was my future. I just didn't know what it meant at the time. So after it ended so quickly, I—"

"*Her?*" he interrupted.

I unwillingly held my breath, then blew the air out through my mouth. "Yeah…Don't worry, I wasn't hiding behind you or anything. I guess you just never know who you're going to fall in love with."

"What happened?" he asked.

"She ran away." I played with my fingers, wishing I hadn't brought Iris up.

"I thought that was your job," he said.

A loud clap of thunder startled us both. I stayed silent, hoping he'd laugh after his jab, but he didn't.

"And you just let her go?" he asked.

"Well, I willingly returned her apartment key."

"Six weeks and you already had a key?" He combed his fingers through his hair, tempting me to do the same.

"After two weeks." I laughed under my breath and picked up my wine glass.

"Wow, that was quick."

"Yeah…" I slid back and turned to rest against the pillows. There must have been at least a half dozen of them. I slipped my feet under the blanket at the foot of the bed. I didn't want to talk about Iris, which was a rare feat.

He sighed. "Well, aside from leaving the state, how you dealin'?"

I drank my wine as I watched the lightning's reflection in the mirror. I never answered that question. I was in his bed, wasn't I?

We silently listened to the rolling thunder and the music coming through the computer speakers. Eventually he stood up and asked if I wanted a glass of water. I nodded and he headed into the kitchen. Part of me wanted to sneak out through the window and never come back, but I just drank the rest of my wine instead.

He returned with two glasses of water and set them on his nightstand next to the empty wine glass. I sat up and swung my legs over the edge of his bed. He sat down next to me and ran his fingers through his hair again.

"I thought I was holding you back," I said.

"What?" he asked.

"You were happy and I was sad. I didn't want you to be sad too, ya know. You wanted to go out and do things, and I just wanted to sulk. I was afraid I'd rub off on you."

"Being with you made me happy."

"But did it?" I asked. "Did it actually?"

"Yes."

"Are you sure it wasn't in spite of me?"

"Why do you find it so hard to believe that I wanted to be with you? I loved you, Cal."

"I loved you too. I guess it just wasn't in the way that was meant to last."

"Maybe not," he said. "But we had fun while it did though, didn't we?"

"We did." I placed my hand on his chest and kissed his pouty lips.

It didn't matter how drunk I was. I wanted to kiss him. I wanted to be with him. I was tired and worn out and I wanted somebody to hold me. And if it couldn't be Iris, I wanted it to be him.

I woke up early the next morning to the thunderstorm still raging outside, and still in Mason's bed.

"I'm sorry, I shouldn't have stayed," I said, noticing he was awake too. I sat up and stared out the window.

"I wanted you to," he said. "But I'm sorry if you're still hurting over this girl. Maybe I helped though…if only for a little while."

"It's hard to move on from the one who saved you," I mumbled.

"How'd she save you?" he asked after a long silence.

I felt him sit up beside me, tugging the blanket a little, but I wasn't listening. The birds perched outside his bedroom window distracted me. I felt inspired by their calmness in the chaos.

"What?" I asked, redirecting my attention his way.

"How'd she save you?" he repeated.

"By showing me that only I could save myself." My eyes returned to the empty window, and the now absent birds reminded me of their freedom.

After the rain subsided, Mason walked with me to the subway. I had a sinking feeling of regret in my stomach. I cared for him and I loved him still. But he wasn't Iris.

Cora was in the kitchen when I got back to the apartment. "Didn't expect you to be back from Long Island," I said while hanging my coat on the rack.

"Rhett had to go into work. Some sort of design catastrophe," she said while rinsing dishes in the sink. "Didn't expect you to not be in bed."

"Oh, how's his family?" I asked, ignoring the latter remark.

"Good…Wait. You were wearing that shirt yesterday. Where were you?" she asked and turned off the water.

"Having sex with Mason."

"Oh," she said as she raised her eyebrows. "You didn't say her name again, did you?"

I laughed and shook my head. "No. I kept my mouth shut."

"How was it?"

I shrugged and went into my bedroom. It wasn't fair to compare sex with Mason to sex with Iris, given the dramatic difference of its nature, but it was like drinking from a muddy puddle when I had already tasted the holy water.

After a lot of wandering around my first week in the city, I didn't do much of anything the second. Cora grunted at the sight of me sitting on her couch with my computer when she walked in the front door one late afternoon. "You haven't moved," she said.

"You're home from work early," I said, trying to deflect.

"Why don't you go hang out with Mason or something? Get off the couch."

"Well, he's at work and I'm not in the mood to go to a museum. I don't think I should see him again anyway."

"Why?"

"Because I'm pretty sure he wants to date again and sleeping with him was stupid…I think maybe I just needed one last time with him…to let go, I guess…and to realize that I don't ever want to be with anybody but her. Even if I can't have her."

"Cal, you have to live your life. You can't just sit around waiting for her. And you can't do it on my couch."

"You told me to come here."

"I also told you to get a job."

"I'm looking, Cora." I turned my computer around to show her that I was in fact looking. "Just because you're not charging me rent doesn't mean I don't have other bills to pay."

My college education wasn't benefiting me much in my job hunt, but I was still in student loan debt up to my eyeballs. I was also still making payments on my car that was sitting unused in my mom's garage.

"Okay, well, how's the writing coming along then?" she asked, sitting down beside me.

"It's not," I muttered.

"Why not?"

"Have you ever written a book?" I asked sternly.

She sighed.

"I didn't think so," I said. "You stick to saving the environment and I'll stick to what I'm supposed to do."

Whatever that is, I thought.

"Okay," she said.

"There's open interviews at this restaurant on Third. If I leave now, I can still make it."

"Oh, I worked on Third in college."

"Oh, you mean when you abandoned me." I closed my computer and placed it on the coffee table. I tilted my head and raised my eyebrows.

"What?" Cora asked, bewildered and smirking.

"You were gone for the worst years…High school," I said, only slightly kidding.

"Oh, please." She waved her hand in the air. "You hated me when you were in high school. I always tried to call you, but you never wanted to talk."

"Yeah, well, you could've texted or something."

"What? In 2002? It took like ten minutes to type 'What's up?'"

We laughed at the horrors of our first cell phones.

"At least I didn't move all the way to California for college," she said.

"You moved to Manhattan the year after 9/11."

"Touché." She nodded her head and pursed her lips. "What's

this about?"

"I don't knoooooww," I whined as I stood up. "I never know."

"Go get a job."

"Yeah, okay."

I headed to the restaurant on Third and after scoping it out, I left. There was no way I could be a hostess at a restaurant that played elevator music all day. I'd lose my mind. Whatever I had left of it anyway. Only I couldn't go home because Cora would know that I ditched the interview, so I walked over to Washington Square Park instead. I sat down next to a guy playing a song on his purple ukulele. I felt it rush through me and I knew it reminded me of Iris. I just couldn't place my finger on what it was.

He strummed and sang, "I remember your words like the palm of my hand, and the feel of your skin slipping through me like sand, I wasn't ready to catch you, but I long for your kiss, it was you who once told me that freedom doesn't have to sleep with loneliness."

Eventually it dawned on me. It was "The Moment I Came Alive" by Colin Dumont.

When he finished, I pulled a dollar bill from my bag and tossed it into the ukulele case sitting at his feet. I walked away and settled onto a bench beneath the trees. I pushed Iris to the back of my mind and watched the people as they moved around me. I relished being back in a big city. It was a lot easier to hide.

When I got home, Cora and Rhett were sitting on the couch watching the news. I sat in the chair to join them.

"How was the interview?" Cora asked.

I shrugged. "Meh."

"How was the rest of your day outside of this clearly exciting job interview?" Rhett asked.

"Meh."

After a few minutes of quietly watching the television, Rhett picked up his glass of water, took a sip, and then placed it back on the coffee table.

"Why can't you ever use the coaster? It's right there," Cora said.

She picked up the glass and placed it on one of their tile coasters.

"Jesus Christ, Cora, it doesn't even fucking matter," I said, glaring at her.

"Um, what?" she asked.

"It's just a fucking table."

"Yeah and it's a nice one, and I would like to keep it that way."

"Whatever."

"What on earth is your problem?"

Rhett sat quietly as Cora and I bickered back and forth. I wasn't sure why I handled it the way I did, but I knew why I was upset. I missed Iris not using the coaster. I missed her leaving her dishes everywhere but the kitchen sink. I missed her cracking her knuckles at three a.m. I missed everything. I thought Cora should be grateful just to sit beside Rhett—coaster or no coaster.

I went into my bedroom and put Colin's album on. I curled up on my bed, wondering where Iris was and what she was doing. It'd been a week since I last checked her social media. It was a hard habit to break and I wanted to know what she was up to, what incredible photographs she'd taken that week.

I pulled up her Fodoary and noticed the most recent shot had been taken in New York City. I scrolled to the next and it was too, as was the next and the next. My heart pounded hard against the inside of my chest. I looked through Felicity's recent pictures and saw one of Iris sitting on a couch. She had her bare feet on the coffee table, and there was a glass next to a coaster. The caption read: *New Roommate*.

43

I got a part-time job at a record store in Midtown. It wasn't far from The Massey Gallery and I ran into Ryder before work one day. "I saw that you were in town and I've been meaning to get a hold of you," he said. "Let's grab drinks later."

"Just tell me where," I said. I didn't really want to, but I figured it was better than drinking alone.

"The Renée Pub."

I squinted at the name. "I'm off at seven."

"See you then."

I walked to the pub after work, which was conveniently located next to the subway entrance. I made note of it, just in case I needed to make a quick escape. Ryder was the reason I knew Iris, and I wasn't sure if I could handle it.

I walked inside and right to the bar. I moved the metal barstool and it made a loud squeal against the floor. A man, who sat a few stools over, looked at me in disgust. I sat down while he blabbed obnoxiously on his Bluetooth. I ignored him and ordered the lightest beer on the menu, which was a Guinness Blonde.

As I took my first sip of alcohol, Adele's "Rolling in the Deep" started to play on the stereo. I spit the beer back into the bottle. Some of it spilled over and out. I had Guinness all over my hand. The man a few stools over looked at me in disgust again. The song just wasn't laughable anymore. With Iris, I dove into the deep end, but still hit the rocks on the bottom. I was just grateful "Someone Like You" wasn't playing.

I wiped off my hand and the bottle. I listened to Adele and chugged my beer.

"Hey-hey-hey," Ryder said, sitting down beside me. "So how've you been?" He waved the bartender over. "You want another?" he asked me.

I shook my head no. I still had half a bottle.

"Same as hers, please. Thanks," he said.

"I'm fine," I said. "How are you?"

"I have three sisters," he said, giving me a concerned look. "I know that fine never means fine." The bartender placed his beer in front of him, and Ryder handed him his card. "Thanks," he said. "Tab it."

"Well, I've been better. But I'm okay," I said.

He nodded and took a sip of his beer. "So I heard you and Iris were a thing."

I stiffened my posture and clenched my jaw.

"And honestly, I wasn't surprised," he continued. "Not really anyway...What happened there?"

I sighed. "Well..." I paused, wondering if I should explain the whole bizarre story. "We ran into each other at Jem's one night and ended up going back to her place and talking all night."

"Oh, so you word-banged. That's the ultimate first date."

"What?" I laughed.

"Ya know, when you just talk for hours and hours with someone you connect deeply with."

"Oh...Yeah, we did that a lot...For six weeks anyway." I sipped my beer.

"Did you hear she moved to town too? Funny, huh?"

"Oh," I said, then sipped my beer again. I tried to act surprised, as to not admit to internet stalking my ex-girlfriend, but with a hint of melancholy to show that I didn't want to talk about her. Even though I did. Nine times out of ten, I did.

"Felicity has a showing at the gallery this weekend," he said. "You should swing by."

"I don't think that's a good idea."

"Oh, was it that bad of an ending?"

I sighed. I wanted to tell him that it wasn't over, but I kept my lips sealed.

"I'm sorry, I shouldn't have brought her up," he said.

"You know Clate Wright…right?" I asked.

"Yeah, he's a good guy," he said nonchalantly.

I nodded slightly.

Realization of why I asked lit up his face, and he shook his head. "Well, no, I mean, he's not that great, kind of stubborn and aloof."

"I liked your first response better."

He sighed. "Honestly, I don't know him very well. He's a great artist though. Good with his hands."

"Okay, I didn't need those details."

"I didn't mean…Sorry," he said, laughing. "You know that's over, right?"

Relief filled my body. "Yeah, I thought so. Have you talked to her recently?"

"Yeah, last night actually. She seems to be doing alright. She was pretty drunk. But we all were. She seemed better than the last time I saw her anyway." He took a sip of his beer.

"When was that?"

"December. It was the night she met—" he said before cutting himself off.

I raised my eyebrows.

"Sorry," he said. "I'm not sure why I was gonna say that." He made a fist with his hand and covered his mouth.

"So she met him on a night when she was really, what, depressed?" I asked.

He removed his hand from his mouth. "I guess."

"And he just like, what, swooped in and saved the day?"

"I don't know…Maybe she just needed somebody to lean on."
"I think she did a little more than that." I drank more.
"Yeah, I'm sorry."
"Yeah, me too."
"People need people."
"I suppose so."
We both took a sip of our beer. Whatever Iris needed Clate for, I hoped she got it.
"Did you already know we were together?" I asked. "In December."
"Yeah," he said, "I knew while you were still dating. I was with Felicity when I saw that you posted a picture of her on Fodoary. So Felicity told me. I liked the picture too." He smiled.
"Oh, yeah." I nodded and smiled lightly, remembering that he had, and realizing I had missed his smile.
"Yeah, I meant to get ahold of you actually, but then I found out it was over so I didn't want to bother you. And I didn't say anything to Iris about it in December."
"Did you ask about me last night?"
"I did," he said. "I wondered if she knew you were in town."
"Did she? Does she?"
He nodded his head yes.
"What'd she say?"
He shrugged. "Not much."
"She changed the subject, didn't she?"
"Yeah, to something about a constellation. Astronomy talk."
I smiled and shook my head. "She didn't change the subject," I said. I laughed under my breath.
"What?"
"The constellation." I laughed under my breath again. "Iris and I…we can't escape the stars."

―――――

My phone buzzed as I was walking to the subway after work the next day. I stopped to check it, and like usual, I hoped it was Iris. But it wasn't. It was a long text message from Rebecca.

So your dad and I were talking to the old grump across the street the other day. He rambled on about the supreme court's ruling on same-sex marriage and how terrible he thought it was.

My heart sank. Same-sex marriage had just become legal across the United States, but it seemed some people were still quick to denounce my love, to deem it unworthy of holy matrimony.

Your dad said, "Excuse me, but what is so terrible about it?" as calmly as he could. And the old grump went on about how he had a nephew who was gay and how he still loved him, no matter how "wrong" it was, but he just didn't want that lifestyle being forced upon him. And so I said, "Being gay is not a lifestyle. It's love." To which your dad added, "Nobody is trying to make you gay." Well, the old grump started rambling about the bible and so your dad and I looked at each other and then walked away. We weren't in the mood to hear him brand his bigotry as religion. For a history teacher, he's sure on the wrong side of it. Anyway, I thought you'd like to see the new addition to the flagpole.

And then she sent me a picture of a gay pride flag flying high on the pole. The rainbow waved proudly against the blue sky with the old grump's house in the background.

I placed my hand over my beaming smile, and just as I was about to reply, I felt someone bump into me as they walked by. I dropped my hand and lifted my head to apologize. She turned to do the same, but we both caught our words before they fell. We stared for a few seconds before I nodded my head just a little. *Yeah, it's me*, I thought, reading her eyes. I wondered if I should say anything, since we'd never met, but Felicity spoke up first.

"Hi…" Her voice rose like she was asking a question.

"Hi…I'm Callahan."

"I thought so," Felicity said.

We stood in silence for a few awkward moments as I gathered the courage to ask about Iris. "How is she?"

"She's good."

"I was with Ryder Massey last night and he said that she was living here now."

"Yeah, for now anyway."

"Same here…For now anyway," I said, knowing she already knew. "I've been staying with my sister and brother-in-law since May."

She nodded.

"It seems everything with me and her always happens at the same time," I said.

She nodded again. "I'm sorry, but I'm actually running late for a meeting."

"Oh, okay. Well, it was nice to meet you…Thanks for being there for her."

She gave me a faint smile and walked away.

Then I covered my mouth with my hand again.

A few days later, I had the courage, or lack thereof, to reach out to Iris.

July 2, 2015
Dear Iris,

It was New Year's that I dreamt we moved to New York City together…and here we are. I imagine you've heard by now that I ran into both Ryder and Felicity recently. My heart races knowing how close we are. It's been much too long and I feel weak in your absence. My body aches for your touch, though sometimes, my toes just curl at the thought of it…

Anyway, I'm not really sure why I'm reaching out. I guess I just want you to remember that I'm still here and always will be. There's no changing that. Time can't steal who we are.

It was my grandma who used to say, "You can't be mad at time. It's like being mad at the earth." Still, it often feels meaningless without you. Though I swear there are nights when I can feel your fingers graze across the small of my back, no matter how far away they are, and I hope the charade of space and time has brought you my touch as well.

I miss you.
Love,
Callahan

TO BE HER GIRL

It went unanswered and I wanted to take it back. Every time I reached out, it felt like I was resetting the clock.

As the summer spun by, it got harder to push Iris into the back of my mind. When I was sick or tired, it was still her voice that I heard in my head, instructing me one step at a time and calming me down. Whether she was telling me to take a sip of water or to crawl into bed, she still took care of me when she was nowhere to be found. I heard her in my head so often that sometimes I swore she even answered the questions I asked aloud, like complete conversations that had me stuck in a trance, knowing she wasn't there physically, but talking to her like she was. Sometimes the telepathy even kicked up a notch, and it was as if we were making love with a world between us, like a cosmic orgasm that left me breathless.

One night, bitter and annoyed, I tried to fight her voice inside my head. "I just want to say hi," she kept saying.

"No. No. No," I whispered while lying in bed. "You're not real. You're not here."

"I just want to say hi." Her voice was playful and determined. "I just want to say hi." She laughed and I sighed heavily. I was tired of feeling crazy.

A minute of her silence passed, and I grabbed my phone and scrolled through Fodoary. I wasn't even looking at the pictures; I was just trying to distract myself. But a few pictures in, one caught my eye. It was of the stump of a tree, taken from above, with what appeared to be three lines carved into it. That's weird, I thought. And then like a bolt of lightning, I realized it wasn't simply three lines carved into that tree. It was the word *Hi*.

I heard Iris laugh in my head again. And without even closing my eyes, I could see her smile. Even in my mind, she was as vivid as art. She wasn't the one who posted the picture, but she always got her message across somehow. Her soul would reach out, even when her mind couldn't bear to.

I put my phone on my nightstand while smiling and shaking my head. "Okay," I said. "I hear you." I closed my eyes and lay still, laughing at the insanity of my existence.

———

I always wondered if Iris would reach out "for real" or if we'd run into each other, or if maybe I'd bump into Felicity again. I saw Ryder occasionally, but at the end of August, he moved back to Los Angeles to work at the gallery on Melrose. His sister wanted to spend some time in Manhattan, so they swapped positions and apartments.

On his last day in town, I lay on my bed, hiding from the sunshine of the mid-afternoon, and he texted me. *Hey, having some people over tonight. You should swing by.*

Hey, I replied. *I'd love to see you before you leave…but I have to ask…will Iris be there?*

She said she would be

I sighed, wondering what to do. *Does she know you're inviting me?*

I didn't tell her, but she knows we're friends

I waited a few minutes before replying. *I don't think she'd come if she knew I was. She'll probably leave if I do…I don't want to cause any problems …I'm sorry…maybe I shouldn't come…*

That sucks but I get it. See you next time I'm in town?

Absolutely. Have fun tonight and give LA a hug for me tomorrow!

I will

I tossed my phone to my side and curled up in a ball. No more than thirty seconds later, I shot up and opened my closet door. I rummaged through my clothes before stopping suddenly. I groaned, then moved somberly to the couch and told Cora about the invitation and my indecisiveness.

"I wasn't gonna go, but then I was, and now, I don't know…I should go. I gotta go…Right? What am I doing? I'm so stupid. I could see her tonight." I groaned and clenched my fits in the air. I pounded them into my thighs. "What the fuck is wrong with me?"

Cora stared at me and sighed.

"You don't think I should go, do you?"

She shook her head no with sadness seeping through her big brown eyes.

"I'm so tired of chasing her." I exhaled a loud groan. "If she wanted to talk to me, she'd talk to me. I get that. But I want to see her so bad, so there's a part of me that just doesn't care."

"Cal, that's normal, but—"

"But I can't go back to the way things were. I know. I have to let it be. I have to leave her alone. Like I should've done in the first place." I paused and exhaled intensely. The adrenaline rushing through me was escalating. "But then, I don't know, if I hadn't, would we still have gotten together? I guess I'll never know."

"Why didn't you just let it be? In the first place."

"Because I was scared. I didn't understand. How did I know what I knew? Why did I feel what I felt?" I inhaled, trying to catch my breath, then blew the air out, slow and steady. "I thought I was crazy, and I was seeking validation from her that I wasn't."

Cora nodded her head with the slightest motion.

"But she wouldn't give it," I said.

"It wasn't her job to."

"But then she did, when we got together…And then she broke my heart again." I leaned back on the couch and stared at the ceiling for a few extended moments.

"So why are you reaching out to her again?" Cora asked.

"I'm not. I haven't in almost two months."

She nodded silently again, which annoyed me.

"Because I need her," I said, sitting back up.

"No, you only think you need her."

I stared at Cora, soaking up her words without wanting to. I exhaled loudly through my nose as I looked down. I shook my head, then looked back at Cora. "How do you have a normal relationship?" I asked. "What sort of gene did you get that I didn't? Is it because you got more time with Mom and Dad when they were together? You got more of the good times than I did. Ya know, before Dad was drunk all the time and Mom cried all night."

"I haven't forgotten about the bad times. I just choose not to focus on them."

I rested my head on the back of the couch and stared at the ceiling again.

I fell asleep early that night and dreamt of Iris wearing white overalls over a dark blue tank top. The next morning, I saw pictures from Ryder's get-together where Iris was wearing white overalls over a dark blue tank top.

"She came to me last night…in my dream," I told Cora later that day.

"What happened?" she asked, tossing shirts into her small suitcase. We were going to Niagara Falls the next morning.

"Nothing. She was just standing there, watching me…But the outfit she wore in my dream was exactly what she wearing last night while I was dreaming…I'd never seen that outfit before."

"Okay, so tell me again why we're paying psychics when you already are one."

44

"Callahan. Callahan. Callahan," I said, sitting across from a woman who I thought might offer me a little peace of mind. I looked outside through the window behind her. A wren landed on a post in her garden.

It was my first visit to Lily Dale, the mecca of mediums tucked between the hills and small lakes of Western New York. As soon as I stepped foot onto the grounds, I noticed how the air felt both light and heavy, simultaneously. It was like I was in the eye of a hurricane. It was calm, but something was brewing all around me. It felt a lot like being around Iris.

Cora and I went to Niagara Falls for our mom's birthday, and Lily Dale was where she wanted to go. We each had our own individual readings with different mediums, and it wasn't long before mine, a forty-something woman with a bob haircut and violet eyes, won me over. After tapping into me and describing the colors of my aura, confirming the yellows and oranges that Grant had once told me, she mentioned a woman who loved gardening—a woman who was proud of me. I wondered if my grandma was working overtime with Cora's and my mom's readings as well.

I hoped she'd mention Iris. That was the reason I was there. Iris and my mess of a life. But the longer I sat there, the more I wondered how she wasn't picking up on that, on Iris, the most important aspect of my life.

"Do you travel a lot?" she asked.

I sighed internally. Couldn't she tell I was buried beneath a broken heart? What did travel have to do with Iris?

"Not really," I said. "I did drive from California in May though. And then I moved down to Manhattan."

"I'm seeing constant. Constant moving…You don't move around for work or anything?"

"I stand behind a cash register most of the day," I said, wondering what she was talking about.

"What about before? No frequent traveling?"

"My friend and I used to drive around a lot, but no, not really."

She scrunched her face as if it'd better help her understand what she felt.

I wondered if my writing would afford me to travel soon, but just as I was about to ask, I thought of Iris and how she was always somewhere new with her camera, how she used to tour with musicians, and how she would travel just because she could.

"Could you be picking up on someone I think about a lot?… Someone I love?" I asked, relieved that I finally had the opportunity to bring up Iris.

"Possibly," she said. "Say their name three times."

"Iris. Iris. Iris."

She closed her eyes for a few moments and then opened them. She grabbed her pencil and scribbled, *very intense*, onto her yellow paper. She nabbed that quickly.

"Iris is tired," she said after a deep breath, almost apologetically.

She described Iris to a T and continued to scribble words onto her yellow paper as she spoke.

Match. Connected. Missing. Longing. Age factor. Fear. Spiritual. Home. Soulmates.

And *fuchsias*.

Along with my yellows and oranges, she saw fuchsia in my aura, and she saw it in Iris's too. Other than claiming it to be rare, she didn't say much about it, and I didn't ask. But I'd learn it was associated with love and purity, emotional tension and burning passion, strongheartedness and the preparation for a change—a change for the better.

After the conversation veered away from Iris, she asked where I was from.

"Niagara Falls," I said.

"Would you believe I've never been?" she said. "How far away is it?"

"Seventy-seven miles."

She laughed at my assured response.

"At least from my mom's house," I continued. "That's what the GPS said. I remember because that's the year Iris was born." I sighed behind sealed lips. "It always comes back to her."

"But you've been trying to take a step back lately, haven't you?" she asked with certainty.

"I have to."

"You have to. It's the only way to her," she said, reiterating the knowledge I'd been burying beneath my desperation.

"It's hard to let go," I said. "I told her I'd never give up."

"Letting go and giving up are not the same thing. Letting go is to release resistance. Giving up is to lose hope. Give her time. Give yourself time. You're both in a whirlwind right now, but there is a plan. You have to trust the process." She stood, signaling that my time was up. "You're fine," she assured me before engulfing me in a firm hug.

I left the medium's house and walked down the narrow road to the park. I waited in the shade of a tree where Cora, my mom, and I agreed to meet after our readings. There was a slight breeze, and I watched a small white feather struggle to escape from the blades of grass it was stuck between.

A few minutes later, Cora walked up and sat beside me. She tucked her wavy brown hair behind her ears as the wind blew through it.

"How'd it go?" I asked.

"Grandpa wants me to work less," she said.

"Well, then how would you afford our nice apartment?"

She rolled her eyes and laughed. We never talked about how wealthy Rhett's family was. Growing up, our mom would joke about us marrying rich. Cora would stomp her feet and say that she could support herself. And she could. But she still married rich.

"What's he want from you?" she asked.

"I don't know, but Grandma's proud of me."

"What for?"

"I don't know."

Cora laughed and shook her head. "You're better than you realize."

"Thanks," I said. "We talked mostly about Iris though."

"I figured." She sighed. "What'd she say?"

"Nothing I didn't already know, but she tapped into her through me. And I think she actually confused her for me at first. I wish I could tell Iris that, but I can't…Even though we once shared a head with two faces."

"What?" Cora laughed.

"Oh, Mom was talking about Zeus earlier. The myth is that there were humans who had four arms, four legs, and one head with two faces. Zeus split them apart because they were too powerful. And so they were destined to spend lifetimes searching for their other half."

"Oh, yeah, I remember that story. And actually there's a good lesson there." The white feather blew onto her foot and she brushed it off.

"What's that?" I asked.

"Zeus split the humans into two equals, not one superior and one lesser. Maybe you need to see yourself in the way that you see Iris."

"Maybe."

"And you're already whole, Cal. She doesn't complete you any more than Rhett completes me."

"Maybe," I said again. "But I need her like water. She nourishes me. She makes me stronger. She makes me better."

"Okay, but maybe she needs to figure herself out first. Otherwise she'll just drown you."

I sighed. "If you haven't figured yourself out, don't even bother trying to figure out somebody else."

"Grandma?"

I shook my head no. "Dad. After Iris broke up with me."

"He's right," Cora said, "and he would never tell you that Rebecca completes him. She compliments him, just like Rhett compliments me and Iris compliments you. She's the yin to your yang, the land to your sky, the mirror to your vision. She's your partner, not your keeper."

"It feels like she is though," I said.

"That's because you give her all your energy. And you have since the day you met her. You use her as a distraction."

"I love her."

"I'm not saying you don't. But what have you done for you, for Callahan, for my baby sister? You've been depressed for your entire life and that's no way to live."

"Iris said that happiness comes in moments."

"Stop making everything about her!" she shouted.

I pressed my lips together tightly. If Cora yelled, she meant it.

"You have to focus on you," she said, returning to her calm tone. "I miss you…you before her."

"Are you saying she made me worse?" I asked defensively.

"I'm saying you have an unhealthy level of attachment to her. You're addicted to her. And I miss you being you. I miss Callahan. Maybe the two of you truly are connected deeper than any of us could ever understand, but you're still Callahan and you have to be Callahan…Not just Callahan and Iris, but Callahan, Callahan, Callahan."

I leaned against the trunk of the tree. I closed my eyes as another breeze crept through. I opened them when I felt a tickle on my cheek. I reached for my face and realized it was the feather. It floated away and I closed my eyes again. "I wonder what's taking Mom so long," I said.

"She's coming," Cora said.

I opened my eyes to see her walking our way, looking equal parts mystified and at ease. Her smile was contagious.

"What's got you so excited?" Cora asked.

"She said there was a baby coming," my mom said.

Cora and I glanced at each other.

"Don't look at me," I said to my mom.

She laughed. "How'd it go?"

"She told me I was intense," I said.

"You are intense," Cora agreed.

"Thanks."

"What'd you say?" my mom asked.

"I'm sorry."

"Oh," she said, laughing.

What was I supposed to say when a woman who communicated with the beyond for a living thought that *I* was intense?

45

On Iris's thirty-ninth birthday, I hopped on my bike and peddled through the evening's light rain, wondering where she was and what she was doing. I wondered if she missed me and if she wanted me back. But mostly, I wondered how she was. I wondered—I *hoped* she was healing like I was.

It'd been almost a year since I reached out to her last—that email after my run-in with Felicity, and before the medium expressed that taking a step back was the only way forward. But while biking around Manhattan's lower east side for an hour, I felt that maybe it was okay to reach out again.

May 18, 2016
Dear Iris,
　I'm not sure how to begin this letter. "Hi. How are you?" just doesn't seem to convey what I want to say or know, but Hi. How are you?
　I heard you were back in Los Angeles. Signey says that she sees you sometimes and told me about Paige and Kate's new store. (It was nice of them to take Signey and her mom out for dinner last week. She got another clean bill of health just today.) I saw the photographs you took for the latest collection. You haven't lost your touch, not that I believed you ever could. I admit I couldn't for a while, but I do still keep an eye on your work from time to time. I hope you know that I am endlessly proud of you.

As far as me, well, I'm still in New York. Cora and Rhett have graciously welcomed me, even though I've stayed much longer than anticipated. I've been working at a record store, and recently I started interviewing musicians and writing articles for the store's website. I've also been writing a novel. I'm in revise! revise! revise! mode and hope to have a publisher soon. I try to trust that it will find its way to the light of day when the time is right, though it's not always easy. When I was talking to Grant about it the other day, about my occasional impatience and recurring doubts, he said, "Don't measure your success by the weight of others. Your worthiness is your own." He was right, like usual. We put expectations on ourselves based on those around us. But I can't compare my life to anything but my own past. And so I'm proud of myself. But the truth is, I'm not sure I could have made it this far without you.

After we ended whatever we were, I wasn't sure how to move forward. It felt like my life was being torn to pieces, and at times, I didn't care to glue them back together. Last August, I spoke with a medium who told me I was in "The Dark Night of the Soul," which became evident as I continued to feel lost and drained throughout the fall. It felt like a giant was shaking me, causing my insides to drop to the ground, and then gouging out whatever remained with a spoon. There were times I wasn't sure if I'd make it. The sky and my own heartbeat seemed so far away.

I was full of anxiety and dealing with an onslaught of physical aches that left me weak. Sometimes it felt like my heart was pounding in my chest like a gavel, and like my brain was trying to escape my skull. I was always in tears or on the verge of them. I was tired in every way that a person could be tired.

It's funny, isn't it? How being reborn feels a lot like death.

It's still hard to believe how much I've grown since I met you, and since I saw you last, but especially over the past few months. You'd be glad to know how much I enjoy cooking now. Cora even says that I'm good at it. Though my dishes are all vegetarian these days. I made a few friends at the record store and we hang out just enough to keep me sane. And while it feels weird to describe myself as sober, I haven't smoked or had a drink in months. I guess I just needed to focus. I ride my bike and/or run nearly every day, and yoga is now a daily routine. (Mostly.) It's still hard to calm my mind, but I meditate often too. I'm probably the healthiest I've ever been. Though sleep still eludes me every now and then. One

TO BE HER GIRL

step at a time, I guess.

My grandma always said, "The flower doesn't complain when it rains; it only grows," and I think for a long time I was too comfortable living in the rain, in the sadness of it, rather than embracing what it had to offer after it subsided.

I accepted that whatever hole I felt inside me, I was trying to fill with you. Only it wasn't working because you were already there. You've always been a part of me, Iris. I'll always believe that. But I'm still me. And so I did something that I should have done years ago. I started talking to a therapist and taking antidepressants again, as well as anti-anxiety meds. They help. But the true change came when I realized that I was only trying to get better for you. I needed to get better for me too.

The night we met I said, "Thank you," and I mean that now more than ever. Through all the ups and downs, it was our love that carried me through, and for that I will always be grateful. You have shown me the truth of unconditional love, and no matter how this life plays out, I will always carry you with me. I love you, Iris, with all my heart and all my soul; for loving you is everything there is, and everything there ever will be.

Happy Birthday, Iris.

I miss you.

Love,
 Callahan

It was hard to cram a year of my life into a letter. I left out the two crushes I had—the boy from the record store with the shaggy hair, and the girl with the seafoam green eyes and a sleeve tattoo. Nothing came of either, though they both reminded me I was still alive. They just weren't Iris. Nobody could ever be Iris. She was the only person I ever looked at and saw forever looking back at me. People could shout about other fish in the sea until they were blue in the face; I just wasn't interested.

I had also forgotten to tell her that I forgave her. I forgave her for ignoring me and then leaving me. I forgave her for hurting me. And I forgave myself. For what I did to her, and for everything else.

The next afternoon, Iris posted a picture on Fodoary of a small mosaic box that sat in the center of her barnwood coffee table. It was made of glass and filled with dried-up flower petals.

rebuild. los angeles. may 2016.

I couldn't believe my eyes. I had thrown those shards of glass and old petals away, but there was no mistaking them. She saved them. I thought that was as good as it'd get, until I got an email later that night.

Dear Callahan,

I'm glad to hear you're doing well. I know I didn't show it, but I worried about you often. I still do. I guess I always will. I'm sorry for not responding when you tried to reach out. I thought it would be easier if I didn't. I'm sorry if I was wrong.

Congratulations on writing your novel. I am so proud of you and I hope I get to read it someday soon. I'm putting together a book of my photography right now. Both old shots and new. The photograph of the waves is on the cover.

Speaking of, I went to the beach recently. I couldn't seem to look at the photo anymore until I did. It almost felt like that small black and white shot was robbing me of the true memories of that place. I knew only those waves and those jagged rocks. I knew only the sadness of losing my mom. I had to change that. I had to go back. I had to feel the sand between my toes and smell the ocean as it carried me through time. I swore I heard my mom laugh as the waves nearly knocked me over. It was freeing and healing. I thought of you and of the night we met, and I wondered where you were. I wondered if you were thinking of me.

When I moved to New York, I needed a change. I wasn't sure where to go until Felicity offered to let me stay with her. I didn't know you were living there until after she did. I almost called you after she ran into you. I try not to wonder what would have happened if I did, or if I had responded to your email. It felt like I was running away, and it only makes sense that I was still running toward you.

I do still love you, Callahan. I always will.

I read through my mom's journals the other night and gave pause to something she wrote. "Life is very strange. Don't ask too many questions…but ask them all." I think I get it. It's like: be observant, but not demanding. I guess we're not meant to know everything, but it helps to live with eyes open.

Like you, I started talking to a therapist. I've also spent the past few months regaining my focus and finding the path I had buried under bad habits and alcohol. I drowned myself more than I should have, but at times, I thought it was the only way to ensure that every breath didn't hurt.

Beyond that, I am doing well. Charlie took me out to dinner for my birthday, and your letter was a great way to cap off the night. And in this moment, writing to you, I feel happy.

You rise, I rise. I rise, you rise.

I miss you too.

Love,
  Iris

Tears soaked my face as I read her words. I thought about replying or giving her a call, but for once, I let it be.

46

I sat on the edge of my bed as the light broke through my bedroom window. The sun was rising after another night of failed sleep. I could hear Cora and Rhett getting ready for work, and the pitter-patter of Jerry-Garcia's feet outside my door. I got up and grabbed my guitar. I could only stare at the ceiling for so long, and there weren't nearly as many tiles to count in that small bedroom. I sat down on the edge of my bed and strummed. Like writing, it was therapy shooting through my fingers.

I had spent most of the night wondering if I made a mistake three weeks earlier, if I missed an opportunity by not responding to Iris's email. It was June 8, three years to the day since we met, and I couldn't stop the memories from consuming me as they rushed through my veins.

I played the guitar for a while and then went into the kitchen for breakfast. I ate a blueberry muffin and then fell asleep on the couch. I didn't wake up until the afternoon and felt groggy when I did. I couldn't remember anything from my dream, only Iris's presence. I had asked her to meet me there. It was all I could do. It was only after I accepted that the separation was merely an illusion that I found any peace. If she wasn't at my side physically, I had to believe she was everywhere else.

I grabbed my phone and checked her Fodoary. I hadn't done

that since the day she emailed me. There was a new time-lapse video of the sunset into sunrise. She set it to Bob Dylan's "Tonight I'll Be Staying Here With You."

The tears fell from my eyes, painting my face like a canvas. "Liar," I said. "You didn't stay."

No matter the peace I had found, when reality sank in, my heart sank with it.

I got in the shower and stood like a defeated statue. My head was dropped, and my back hunched over. "I don't understand," I said. "I've been doing so well...but it still hurts. Without her, it'll always hurt. Why? If the separation is just an illusion...why does it hurt?" I sat down while the water poured all around me. I held my legs to my chest and looked all over my body. "Because I'm human," I said. "Arms...human. Toes...human. Skin...human. Cuts and bruises ...human. Heartbeat...human."

I accepted my tears and let them fall. Sometimes I had to give in. I had to be human. I couldn't deny the sadness I felt any more than I could deny loving Iris. And being without her only reinforced how much I did.

After stepping out of the shower, I rubbed the foggy mirror and stared deep at my own reflection. "You exist, Callahan Thomas," I said. A light laugh slipped out under my breath, as if I was only then acknowledging it, or just finally accepting it. I was alive. Heart-beating, lung-breathing, feet-walking. With or without Iris, I was alive.

Back in my bedroom, I sat at the desk with my computer. I watched every video and admired every photograph I had saved of Iris. My smile caught my tears as I combed through the memories. After I finished, I crawled into bed and closed my eyes. Iris once told me that we remember in photographs, and all I wanted to do was flip through the album.

After a while, the sadness that had been griping me all day faded, and I sat on the floor to meditate. I wanted to experience the opposite side of the wheel of emotions that we spin on earth. I closed my eyes and listened to my heartbeat, while the electricity surged through me. After a few minutes of stillness and calming breaths, I felt it wash over me—the bliss, the love, the oneness, Iris. I took a deep breath and exhaled slowly, feeling the air swirl through my lips. I opened my eyes and said, "I believe. I believe. I believe."

Shortly after I heard Cora and Rhett come home, I headed out of my seclusion and into the living room. "Hey," I said.

"Hey, have you had dinner?" Cora asked.

I shook my head no.

"We're going to the new place on Eleventh," she said. "You wanna come?"

"My treat," Rhett said.

"Yeah, sure," I said. "Thanks."

We walked to the new restaurant, and it reminded me of Rowe's. Cora and Rhett slid into the booth and I sat down across from them. I was looking over the menu when "Tonight I'll Be Staying Here With You" began to play. I laughed softly under my breath and closed my eyes, feeling Iris rush through me. I opened my eyes and saw Cora and Rhett smiling in confusion.

"On Sundays we listen to Bob Dylan," I said.

"It's Wednesday," Rhett said.

"I know." I laughed under my breath. "I know."

As we approached the apartment after dinner, I decided to keep walking. I headed to the waterfront and walked along the East River. A crow cawed and landed on the path beside me. She hopped along, but I stopped to soak in the moment. I leaned against the barricade and stared at Brooklyn on the other side. I thought about Mason and realized it'd been almost ten years since I met my first love, the primer to Iris's infinite paint.

My mind wandered and I thought about Travis and Michael, and Signey and Grant. I thought about Brooks and Clate, and Paige and Leah and Felicity. I thought about Dalfour Hickey, and I thought about Ryder. I wondered when I would have met Iris had I not known him, because somehow, at some point, it still would have happened.

My phone buzzed and I grabbed it from my back pocket. It was a text message from Grant. *Hey, hope you're doing well, Cal. Miss you.* It was a frequent message we sent to each other, but I knew he remembered what June 8 was.

You too, I replied. *And I am. I was just thinking about you actually. Couldn't have made it through the past decade without you, especially the last few years.*

Yes, you could have.

Maybe…but you sure as hell helped. Thanks for everything. And please remember it always works both ways…how are things with Daniella? They'd been going through a rough patch that Grant had tried to downplay because I wasn't there to see it. It was Signey who filled me in because she was worried about him.

Things are better, he replied. *Thanks*

That's good

We just had to sort some things out that we'd been avoiding.

Yeah, don't avoid things. What's inside will always come to surface. Even if you don't know it's there. Even if you try to fill it with something else…

We're all here to learn.

Yeah, but sometimes you don't even see the lesson until the test is over and done with.

After a few minutes, he replied, *Yesterday I was thinking about your grandma. The first time I met her, she told me that everybody I met could be a teacher, if I let them.*

I remember that…and she was right, I replied, standing there at the river, thinking of all the people who had come and gone from my life. *There are different kinds of soulmates and lovers, different people for different times, different teachers for different lessons…but there's only one who lives inside you. Iris will always be my greatest teacher.*

Maybe so, Grant replied.

If I hadn't met Iris, I'd still be miserable at that old job, I'd still be getting high or drunk every night to combat it, and I'd still be focused on how depressed I was, rather than trying to get better.

Maybe so, he texted again.

And I don't think I could've written my novel without loving her. Just like you said it would, it came to me when it was time
Your love was a story dying to be told.
Maybe so, I wrote.
Maybe so.

On my way back to the apartment, I stopped as I caught a glimpse of the moon. It was a perfect crescent peeking through the clouds, only slightly more visible than the hidden moon from three years earlier.

When my grandma would tell me to pay attention to the moon, I never understood why, but after my time with Iris, I began to. Sometimes the moon is new, sometimes full, sometimes hidden behind the clouds, sometimes lighting up the sky, but like Iris and Pyxis, always there. And as I stood there watching the clouds pass it by, I smiled, knowing our love would outlive even the moon.

Iris Humphrey was the last thing I expected when I least expected it, but she was the best damn thing that ever happened to me. In three years, not a day went by that I didn't find her, that I didn't crave her. She was both the calm in my breath and the adrenaline rushing through my veins. Every question and every answer led me to her. And it was her who led me to myself.

PART V

Perhaps to make peace with the unknown was the greatest gift I ever gave myself.

Somebody once told me they wanted a love that devoured them. And at first I thought, be careful what you ask for. But then I thought, yes, find that love. Find the one who drags a knife along your chest and exposes your heart, the one who cracks your bones and forces you to set them anew. Find the one who sets your soul on fire and burns through your core. It is only then you will know that you can rise from those ashes.

Between working on my novel's revisions that led to the eventual offer of publication, I wrote this memoir. I wrote because I didn't know what else to do. I didn't know where else to put her, to put us, so I did what I knew words could do. I put us in amber. But unlike the unexpected closing of the ice cream shop with that name, the writing of this afterword should have been expected by anyone paying attention. As the story goes, I couldn't find myself until I got lost in her. But as it turns out, we were both there all along.

As time passed, Iris and I kept our distance. She was never far from my thoughts; I just learned to live around them. I had to find my own joy outside of her. For as much as I wanted to be her girl, I had to first be my own. It wasn't easy, but sometimes you can't stand tall with another until you can stand tall in solitude. It was her who taught me that in her absence. And with every broken piece of my heart that I picked back up, I learned something new about myself.

And how weird it was, to wake up in a good mood, to be happy just because, to simply remember the blessing of my own heartbeat.

Cora caught a glimpse of my mindless grin one afternoon, not long after I finished writing the first four parts of this story. "Are you sure you don't want to stay in New York?" she asked, rubbing her pregnant belly.

"It's a done deal," I said, walking toward her on the couch. The record store was opening a new location with an adjacent music venue in Los Angeles, and I offered to relocate.

I sat down beside Cora and took a sip from my glass of water. "Plus you need my room for a nursery. I think it's safe to say it's time for me to go home," I said, placing the glass on a coaster in front of me.

She grabbed my hand and put it on her stomach. I smiled, feeling my niece move around inside. I kept my hand there until she stopped moving. I could already tell she'd be just as persistent as I was.

"Home is an awfully big word," Cora said. "Do you mean Los Angeles or…?"

"Yeah, but you know I really mean Iris. 'Home' was the first word she ever said to me. She'll always be my home."

"You're alright, Cal, with or without her. You know that, right?"

"Yeah." I took another sip of water. "I just wish we could try again."

Maybe I didn't need her, but I wanted her.

"Are you going to call her?" Cora asked.

"No."

I put the glass back on the coaster and leaned against the couch. I closed my eyes and thought of the word 'home' falling from Iris's lips that first night, and I fell in love with her, all over again. It had been two years since I'd seen her, but I still fell in love with her every single day. Sometimes it was a memory, like when she'd scoop peanut butter from the jar with her finger or something she said. Sometimes it was a photograph she'd taken or the sound of her voice. Then sometimes it was a song on the radio or a bird in the

TO BE HER GIRL

sky. But every day it was something. Every day I felt the rush, the butterflies, the bliss.

And every day, I still do.

After promising Cora that I'd visit as often as I could, I threw on my denim jacket and went for a walk. It was a cool fall day, the tenth of October, and I wandered around for almost an hour, soaking up the sun and the city that brought me back to life.

On my way back to the apartment, I strolled through Tompkins Square Park. I stopped to feel the cool rush of air as it swirled around me. I looked down just as a small fuchsia feather, from the boa of a nearby child, floated over my feet. For the better, I thought, for the better. I smiled and gripped my necklace. Dangling from the silver chain was a topaz, my own birthstone. I started to walk again, but when I heard a man's voice shout, "Eulaine!" I stopped and looked around. I'd never met anybody who shared my grandma's name.

I wasn't sure where the voice came from, but as I walked again, I felt those familiar waves grow in my stomach. I stopped and slowly turned around. I held my hand above my eyes, trying to get a better look, but the light was hiding her face. I couldn't see her, but I could feel her.

Some time passed before I could move. My pace was slow—one foot in front of the other, one breath at a time. I stopped a few feet in front of her and noticed the necklace resting upon her freckled chest. She touched the chain with her fingers, and I wondered if she caught me looking. The sun bounced off the small mariner's compass that I had given her two years earlier.

We both slid our sunglasses to the top of our heads and my eyes met hers. I felt my heart skip a beat or two before returning to its natural rhythm, as it again met its reason. Iris stepped forward, closing the distance between us, and gently touched her hand to my cheek. I smiled lightly and her mouth reflected mine. And like the blending horizon, I could feel everything collide. Time and space. Human and soul. Fate and free will. And finally I heard it, like the wind swirling through the trees, eternity was saying hello.

thank you

Mom and Keriann for being the brightest lights of my life; for your unwavering and unconditional love, support, and encouragement; for believing in me more than I ever believed in myself; and for being a part of Callahan's world from the beginning.

Grandma Jeanette, Josh, and my beautiful family and friends who have stood tirelessly by my side, lifted me up, and graced me with your love.

And Jenny.

ABOUT THE AUTHOR

Emily Cradduck tells raw and heartfelt stories about love, loss, and mental health. She lives in Los Angeles.

You can find her and her stories online here:

emilycradduck.com
emilycradduck.medium.com
twitter.com/craddux
instagram.com/craddux
facebook.com/toysofthesun

Made in the USA
Coppell, TX
24 June 2021

57847612R10198